EASYTIMES

DAVID W. ROBERTS

Published in Australia by Sid Harta Books & Print Pty Ltd,

ABN: 34632585293

23 Stirling Crescent, Glen Waverley, Victoria 3150 Australia

Telephone: +61 3 9560 9920, Facsimile: +61 3 9545 1742

E-mail: author@sidharta.com.au

First published in Australia 2020

This edition published 2020

Copyright © David W. Roberts 2020

Cover design, typesetting: WorkingType (www.workingtype.com.au)

Roberts, David W.

Easytimes

ISBN: 978-1-925707-20-5

pp414

ABOUT THE AUTHOR

David Roberts migrated as a qualified teacher from the United Kingdom. After seventeen years working as a teacher, deputy principal and principal in country New South Wales, he became a university academic. University appointments and consultancies enabled David to travel widely and broaden his horizons. Now retired, he lives with his wife in Adelaide.

This is his second novel.

*For all who have lived in, are living in,
or will live in a retirement village …*

G'day. My name's Francis Sempione, Frank to my mates. For thirty years I was the General Manager of Sempione Brothers, Building and Construction Works Pty Ltd, headquartered in Adelaide. We were three brothers at the start, but Giorgio died of mesothelioma a couple of years back; inhaled too much of that shocking asbestos stuff many years ago. My youngest brother, Antonio, is still about though, and decided to retire from the building industry at the same time as I called it quits.

Our biggest project by far was the building, from scratch, of no less than eight retirement villages for Mr Crocombe, millionaire developer and financier. From the outset, Mr Crocombe wanted his retirement villages to be easily recognisable as an entity to the public, so he stipulated that each village should have the word "easy" incorporated into its name. Over almost twenty years, Sempione Brothers proudly constructed the following eight retirement villages: Easycome,

Easygo, Easyplace, Easyhills, Easystay, Easylife, Easyhomes and lastly, Easytimes.

The same firm of architects were employed for all the retirement villages and it was fascinating to see how there were subtle improvements in the design of the units, facilities and overall layout from one village to the next. By the time we commenced work on the eighth, and final village, I think we had achieved a very high standard in all respects. Naturally, Mr Crocombe, as a capitalist, was in it to make money, but to his credit, he was genuinely concerned to make his retirement villages attractive, comfortable and safe for the elderly folk who were to spend some of their twilight years there.

Having been so heavily involved in the creation of all eight "Easy" retirement villages, I naturally took a keen interest in their progress and some of the characters who chose to reside there. I was frequently invited to major events such as openings, ten-year celebrations, fetes, fairs, significant birthdays and major concerts. Everyone seemed to know me, Frank Sempione, the master-builder of the "Easy" villages. Occasionally, somebody would complain about a bit of shoddy work, or a design fault, but overall, I was well received, and the work of our company praised.

During the twenty years of construction work, a plethora of interesting things happened; sometimes before even a brick was laid. At one site, for example, we discovered a midden which we duly reported to the authorities. The location was left untouched and elders from the Kaurna Nation came to inspect it. It remains today, as a respected location on the edge of one of the villages.

A gruesome discovery was made when we were land clearing at another site. A badly decomposed human body was unearthed, that of a young female. The police and forensics are yet to identify the unfortunate soul, although they have their suspicions. By a strange quirk of fate, Unit 13 was erected immediately above this ghastly find, however, it is a well-kept secret.

Over time, I have come to know a number of the characters who have taken up residence in one or other of the villages. Some have colourful pasts, a few are famous, and others are simply amazing personalities. Of course, stories of their exploits get bandied about, and no doubt become more and more exaggerated with each telling. Having a quiet beer with some of the residents gives me the chance to hear their stories. Sometimes my brother, Antonio, joins me as we enjoy the company of the "not-so-youngs" and listen to them yarning away.

One evening, quite late, Antonio and I were driving home after an evening with friends at the Easytimes Retirement Village. Antonio, being a teetotaller, was at the wheel. We were discussing an extraordinary series of events that concerned several of the people we knew well in that village. It was Antonio who first came up with the idea that we should write a book about the strange happenings there. I laughed at the idea initially, but slowly came around to his way of thinking.

Most people dismiss retirement villages as being the refuge of the aged, the "has-beens", pleasant old folk incapable of doing very much anymore. The occupants are perceived as being "past it" as far as fresh romance or crime is concerned.

Retirement doesn't just refer to giving up work, it also means abandoning longings for new romantic attachments, and previous criminal activities are certainly long forgotten, never to be repeated.

However, from the retirement village of Easytimes comes this story of passionate romances and a series of bizarre criminal activities leading to a horrendous climax. Don't be fooled, retirement villages, like anywhere else, are places where things can, and do happen. The pace of life might be slower, but events can be just as dramatic.

As you get to know the characters in this story, you may be lulled into a sense of genteel security. Easytimes seems to be a place for happily and contented retirees who are all about craft groups and afternoon teas, gentle exercise, playing bowls and doing friendly things for their neighbours. But you might be surprised!

I have, of course, changed the names of the places and the participants, to avoid possible detection.

Francis Sempione

CHAPTER 1

'Well this is it,' Snoddy announced, guiding the car slowly around a row of witch's hats that occupied too much space in the entry drive.

Mary peered dubiously through her passenger's window at a dozen apartments in various stages of completion. 'Are you sure this is the place, Snoddy?'

The overweight Snoddy swivelled his cumbersome head around as far as it would go, to glance briefly at his wife. For months they had been discussing selling their family home and moving into what everybody referred to as a "Retirement Village". 'Certainly is,' Snoddy confirmed.

Mary appeared anything but impressed by such a messy, seemingly chaotic, building site. Timber frames were strewn about randomly, cement mixers were whirring and half-naked brickies yelling at each other above the noise of blaring car radios. When Mary stared disapprovingly at one of the nearest brickies, he gave her the finger with a particularly menacing thrust of his hand. She blushed, looked quickly away, bit her lip, but remained silent.

Mr and Mrs Snodgrass had seldom agreed on anything, from the very first time they had gone out together, almost fifty years ago. The disagreements had started when Mary told James that Snodgrass was a ridiculous surname. 'Why don't you do one of those legal name changes? No sensible person is called Snodgrass,' she had protested.

Little did Mary know, at the time, that James Snodgrass had, throughout his younger years, defended the name Snodgrass valiantly in the school playground against all comers. From kindergarten onwards, he had endured sniggers and taunts about his funny sounding name. His Dad told him to always stick up for himself and for the family name, Snodgrass. 'Don't take it son, thump 'em.' And thump 'em he did.

James' little kindergarten companions quickly learnt that James Snodgrass was not to be trifled with. He preferred to be called "Snoddy" but try teasing him about his full name and you would regret it. James also found it necessary to reinforce this simple concept when he first attended primary school and again at high school. Because James was a very large lad, blessed with both speed and agility, he never found it necessary to repeat the lessons. So, Snoddy he became, and Snoddy he remained.

At the pimply age of fifteen, James met an equally pimply Mary, in Mrs Pullinger's 10G high school class. For the first time in his life, Snoddy felt a strange and inexplicable attraction for a member of the other sex. He soon found himself jostling for a desk near Mary so he could look at her, and, if she ever stopped chatting to all her girlfriends, occasionally saying something to her. Mary smelt nice too. Each morning Snoddy looked forward to the alluring whiffs of Mary's perfume. She had an adorable smile and Snoddy longed to be the main recipient. Sadly, Mary's smiles were almost always directed elsewhere. Occasionally, other girls would make eyes at Snoddy, but he never responded. It was Mary, and only Mary, that interested him.

Snoddy was happiest on the rugby ground where he played right lock forward for the under-sixteen school rugby team. His bulk and speed made him a highly valued team member, and because of his sporting skills, he became a popular lad. He was never happier than when he ended a game caked in mud from head to foot, or sporting a black eye, or some other impressive injury.

The next year, Snoddy and Mary found themselves together again, but now in Mr Ainslie's year eleven class. The pimples were still there and the perfume too, but Snoddy's need to get to know Mary better was intensifying. He didn't know how to make the first move though. At night he would toss and turn, planning what he would say to Mary next day, and where and when. He even prepared little speeches in his head which he would practise until almost word perfect. Snoddy was also aware that Mary's birthday was fast approaching. Perhaps he dared to give her a present? But how could he do that without everyone seeing? Sadly, for fear of the embarrassment, Snoddy ended up doing nothing.

Year twelve, the last year at high school, and again Mary

and Snoddy shared the same home classroom. If Snoddy didn't pluck up the courage to approach this beautiful and desirable girl soon, it might be too late. Once school finished at the end of the year and they had graduated, who knows where they would end up? Very likely they would go in separate directions and Snoddy would be left alone and distraught without Mary to pine over. As it turned out, fortune took a hand.

It was a Saturday afternoon in late July. Snoddy had heaved and sweated his way around the rugby ground for eighty minutes, and now, delightfully smothered in mud, with his boots hanging around his neck, he was cycling home. Snoddy was particularly pleased with himself because he had scored a try under the posts, which was easily converted, so that his team had narrowly won the match. As he turned a corner, close to home, he saw a girl on her bike swerve alarmingly to avoid a car that suddenly pulled out in front of her. The girl, and her bike, ended up in an ungainly tangle on the ground in the middle of the road while the offending car continued on its way, apparently unaware of the accident it had created.

Snoddy did what any decent young lad would do; he stopped to help. The girl was lying there obviously distressed, angry and crying. She wore a sports uniform of some kind which exposed her legs to full view. As Snoddy lifted the bike up to release the unfortunate lass, he was staggered to discover that the owner of these delightful legs was none other than his longed-for Mary.

'Come on,' he said gently, 'we have to get you and your bike off this road.'

Mary, who was still groaning and whimpering, accepted

the muddy hand offered to her, and in some pain, raised herself up into an upright position. With the help of this muddy, good Samaritan, she hobbled over to the side of the road, where her rescuer sat her down on the kerb and quickly trotted back to retrieve the damaged bike. Mary began to inspect the various injuries to her anatomy. One elbow had a nasty graze and the side of her leg was also red and sore. Her wrist was painful too. The muddy rescuer plonked himself down next to her on the kerb and inquired how she was. It was only then that Mary began to wonder about the identity of her rescuer. She stole a quick glance at the large and very dirty young man looking anxiously at her.

'Snoddy, it's you!'

Snoddy smiled, shyly. 'You've got some nasty cuts and bruises Mary, and your bike is busted. My house is just down the road. How about you come back to my place and we can patch you up? Mum will be home and you can ring for your parents to come and pick you up.'

'Oh Snoddy, that's so kind of you. Did you see that idiot drive out in front of me?'

Snoddy still couldn't believe his luck. Whoever had driven their car out in front of Mary was his friend for life. Mary stood up gingerly and started limping painfully. Seeing this, Snoddy parked her damaged bike up against the fence and helped her onto his bike. Carefully he pushed her along, side-saddle, all the time admiring her deliciously long legs. Mary, perhaps surprisingly, found she needed to lean on him for better balance. Snoddy deliberately took his time, so he could savour her close presence for as long as possible, and was quite heartbroken when they arrived at his front gate and he reluctantly helped her off his bike.

These recollections of her first meaningful encounter with her husband-to-be, Snoddy, were far from Mary's mind today, however, as they drove slowly towards the only structure in the retirement village that appeared to have been completed. A large sign was affixed to the side of the building:

EASYTIMES RETIREMENT VILLAGE
Two and three-bedroom units available now
Inquire within, or ring, 08 8392 2809

They pulled into the visitors' car park and Snoddy began the tedious, slow process of extricating his substantial bulk through the car door. There was no doubt in his mind they were making cars smaller these days. And the distance down to the ground was getting farther as well. Perhaps Mary was right, when she told him that what he really needed was a truck. Long gone were the times when he was a force to be reckoned with on the rugby ground moving easily and speedily all over the pitch. The sad decline in his physical capabilities was not unexpected, he mused, now that he had just turned seventy.

Mary, on the other hand, was slight of build and spritely. At 69 she was determined to remain passably fit and despaired that Snoddy had allowed himself to become obese. She ate carefully, much to Snoddy's annoyance, who, from time to time, felt it necessary to sneak away to a fast food outlet for an extra boost of greasy fat and sugar. Mary walked the dog every day, at least once, and attended Scottish dancing lessons on Wednesday evenings. She was not averse to a few laps of the Olympic pool when friends invited her along. A good diet and an active life meant she still had a healthy libido, not that her sexual desires were ever satisfied these days, as Snoddy had lost interest many years ago. Mary longed for some warm intimacy and even dreamed of having secret affairs with some of the raunchy men she came across when enjoying her various physical activities.

Mary and Snoddy's relationship intrigued their long-time friends. The couple appeared to disagree about everything of any importance, and yet, there remained a strong thread of love that bound them together. Despite their countless differences, they muddled through, and somehow, the marriage survived. Recently, however, Snoddy had decided he wanted to live in a retirement village, but Mary, who dearly loved her home and garden, had no intention of moving. It was with considerable reluctance that she had agreed to even come to see Easytimes Retirement Village.

'Snoddy, I don't know why you want to sell up and come and live with a village full of dithery old people, who spend all their time sitting around complaining about their aches and pains. If you live with a bunch of oldies you will age prematurely yourself. What you need to do, Snoddy, is lose a ton of weight and get active again. I'm far too young in spirit to go into one of these awful retirement places.'

Snoddy had heard it all before. Mary had always been feisty and called a spade a spade. Nevertheless, he knew he was ready to move on. He unashamedly admitted that he no longer could be bothered to handle the jobs that needed to be done about the house. He had abandoned his vegetable garden, which had been highly productive at its zenith, and no longer did the pruning or small paint and carpentry jobs around the place. He was far too heavy and cumbersome to climb ladders to clean out gutters and had totally lost interest in keeping the fence at the back of the garden in good order. James Snodgrass reasoned that if they sold up, they could move into a retirement village and he would no longer be pestered by Mary to do *anything*. He had worked hard all his life, so now he was entitled to put his feet up and pay others to do everything.

Having finally extracted himself from the car, Snoddy lumbered slowly towards the entrance of the building that called itself, "Sales and Reception". Mary glanced back over her shoulder at the young man who had given her the finger so vigorously only a moment ago and quietly marvelled at his firm, tanned physique. He was shovelling sand into the cement mixer and the combination of sweat, rippling muscles and tattoos excited her momentarily.

'Good morning, Mr and Mrs Snodgrass. How wonderful to meet you. My name is Robert Tinson and I'm the sales manager here at beautiful Easytimes. Please, do come in.'

Mary had an in-built dislike of all salespeople. She couldn't stand the endless drivel they went on with, and the forced enthusiasm they all exuded. *Looks like we are in for a gobful here*, she thought, and it was all she could do to hold her tongue. Snoddy, on the other hand, liked a salesman who was confident, enthusiastic and prepared to do anything to please. He immediately felt he could do business with this Robert bloke. Not surprisingly, Mary and Snoddy had reacted differently to the sales manager.

'Isn't this a fabulous site for a retirement village?' gushed the sales manager, looking expectantly at the Snodgrasses for affirmation. Snoddy managed to raise a positive grunt and a nod of his head, but Mary remained unmoved. Unperturbed, Robert Tinson prattled on, 'If I may say so, you are extremely clever to come to this particular new retirement village because there are huge advantages if you get in early.' Snoddy interpreted these comments as meaning that he could get in quickly and no longer have to worry about maintenance, whereas Mary thought only about the dust, mud, noise and disruption of building work going on month after month all around her.

'If you get in early you can pick the unit you want, the colour of the carpet and even the plants you would like us to put in your garden. Isn't that just great? The first occupants will get all these benefits. And, of course, in a few months' time, the prices will start to increase. So, if you purchase now, you will save yourselves a heap of money.'

This made sense to James Snodgrass, who was able to muster another of his approving grunts. Mary remained unconvinced. 'But Mr Tinsel, the building works are going to be under way for a year or two at least. We would have to put up with all the noise, the dust, the smell and trucks coming and going constantly.'

'Actually, my name is Tinson, not Tinsel, but please call me Robert,' the sales manager replied. 'I do take your point Mrs Snodgrass, but, be assured, we will do everything we can to lessen the impact of any noise and dust. We are getting heaps of interest from the public, you know, and it would be so sad if you delayed and then discovered that we have completely sold out.'

Mary sniffed, disbelievingly. 'How many units have you actually sold, Mr Tinson?'

The sales manager was reluctant to give Mary a definitive figure. Truth be known, he had only a handful of deposits to date, and the plan was for Easytimes Retirement Village to eventually have no less than 250 units. It was early days of course, but to have to admit that perhaps three, or four units looked to have been definitely sold was not a good sales pitch.

'Oh, Mrs Snodgrass, the interest is enormous. I have shown dozens through already and I'm finding it difficult to keep up with it all. This is such a delightful bush-setting, I know the units will be snapped up before you can say "Robinson Crusoe".' Mary vaguely recalled reading about a character called Robinson Crusoe in her youth. Wasn't he the fella that was shipwrecked on a desert island somewhere? This place looked a bit like a desert island, she thought, with all the trees felled and bulldozed into massive piles around the edge leaving a waste land in the centre where the village was to be built. She gave another of her disapproving sniffs.

As was so often the case, her husband appeared to be impervious to her feelings, and was displaying an embarrassing amount of interest in the village and listening intently to Mr Tinson's verbal diarrhoea. In fact, Snoddy was now clearing his throat; a sure indication he was going to say something.

'Robert, are you able to show us some floorplans please?'

Mary glared at her husband, who studiously ignored her. Snoddy, she feared, was being sucked in by this idiot of a sales manager.

'Of course, Mr Snodgrass. Please follow me next door where I have all the unit designs beautifully displayed on the wall. I know you will be most impressed. These designs are the very latest in styling and come complete with a host of special safety features for the elderly. You will love them, I know.'

Snoddy was relieved to find that the chair he was sitting on had substantial arm rests so that with a decent heave he was back up on his two feet. 'After you my dear,' he said, rather too sweetly. With yet another sniff, Mary followed Mr Tinson out of the room into what appeared to be another office. Pinned to a large notice board were eight floor plans. Every floor plan had an exotic sounding name attached to it. She had registered "Royale", "Mediterranean", "Hacienda" and "Roma" before Mr Tinson interrupted her viewing with his next verbal barrage.

'Now, Mr and Mrs Snodgrass, it is most important that we select a unit design that satisfies *your* needs. What do you have in mind with regard to the number of bedrooms you would like?'

And so, it went on …

Half an hour later, Mary was at last able to persuade Snoddy that she needed to get home, and they must take their leave of the loquacious Mr Tinson. Snoddy and Robert, Mary had observed, seemed to have hit it off rather well and were enjoying a far too "matey" chit-chat. Snoddy came away clutching a folder containing photocopies of the eight different unit designs and a leaflet entitled, "An Introduction to Easytimes: Your Wonderful Future!" *Fat chance of that*, thought Mary, as she did her best to bundle her husband out of the building and guide him towards the car. Snoddy, however, was way past the stage where he could be bundled anywhere. Waddling was a better way to describe his slow means of locomotion.

As they negotiated their way out round the witch's hats, Mary stole another naughty look in the direction of the lusty young man who had rudely caught her attention earlier. There he was again. This time he flashed her a cheeky smile and waved. Mary pretended not to have noticed but was reminded of the times, perhaps thirty years ago, when Snoddy still presented as a strapping, fit and virile husband. How she missed those special times of love and passion.

The entrance gates were still only half built. Another car was approaching the gates as they were leaving and, with a sudden surge of interest, Mary exclaimed, 'Good heavens, this looks like the Fishers. Surely they're not considering coming to Easytimes?' Snoddy stopped the car and wound down the window. Sure enough, it was their friends of many years, Mike and Penny Fisher, who likewise pulled up at the gates.

'Hi Penny, what are you doing here?' yelled Mary, before either of the two men had time to open their mouths.

'We're thinking of moving here!' Penny shouted back.

'Well, how about that. We are in a bit of a hurry right now, Penny. Would you like to meet us for a coffee tomorrow at The Cornishman and we can exchange opinions? Ten-thirty okay?'

'We'll be there!' shouted Penny. 'Cheers for now.'

'Cheers.'

The two men, who had not yet uttered a word, were urged to get moving by their respective wives. Snoddy was quietly pleased to have had this encounter though, because if the Fishers were thinking of making a similar move, it might encourage Mary to be a little less negative about purchasing a unit at Easytimes Retirement Village. Perhaps, Snoddy thought, he would get his way after all.

CHAPTER 2

The Cornishman was located along a small lane coming off the main street and a tingling bell welcomed patrons as they entered. The proprietors actually hailed from Cornwall and had, unashamedly, decorated their cafe with all things British. Coloured posters adorned the walls depicting famous landmarks from the mother-country; Buckingham Palace, Windsor Castle, Stonehenge, together with several enticing photographs of Cornish coves and harbours. If the cafe wasn't too noisy, customers could listen to recordings of traditional English music and songs of the sea playing in the background. The tables were covered with Union Jack tablecloths and the chairs boasted red, white or blue cushions. In the centre of each table, sat some kind of British emblem; a bulldog, a miniature Big Ben, which chimed every quarter of an hour, a bright red London bus and even one of those weird looking London taxis. Quaint but fun, thought Mary. Snoddy considered all this Pommie stuff a bit stupid. For the life of him, he couldn't see why England, Australia's arch enemy in almost all sporting pursuits, had to be celebrated like this.

Mary quickly gravitated towards the table with the stern looking British bulldog, sat down and grabbed a menu. Snoddy followed, brushing aside several empty chairs on his way to the table his wife had selected. He could never understand why these places had so many chairs and tables packed in so tightly together. Finally, after almost tripping over a lady's black handbag, strategically placed so as to do maximum damage to any unsuspecting customer, he reached his destination in the far corner of the cafe, somewhat out of breath.

'Isn't it quaint? It reminds me of our time in England. Do hurry up and sit down, Snoddy.'

Snoddy was wrestling valiantly with a chair, the legs of which refused to disentangle themselves from the neighbouring chair. Finally, with a sigh of relief, he was able to isolate his chair and lower his sizeable girth reasonably accurately onto a bright red cushion. The chair groaned but held. The lady, whose handbag he had trodden on, was still glaring at him. For a brief moment he contemplated sending her a rude sign, but just in time noticed that Mary was watching him.

They had arrived a few minutes early, so Mary felt obliged to make polite conversation with her husband to fill in the time.

'Isn't it wonderful that Penny and Mike are thinking of coming to Easytimes, dear?'

For once, Snoddy found himself in agreement with his wife, and permitted a positive kind of a grunt to pass his lips. 'I'm so looking forward to hearing what they think of Easytimes as a retirement village. With Mike's background in real estate, his advice will be particularly valuable, don't you think Snoddy?'

Snoddy's mind was elsewhere. The menu he was studying offered a tantalising selection of desserts and he was deeply engrossed in an important decision. So far, he had narrowed it down to a chocolate eclair, a slice of tiramisu, or perhaps even a serving of death by chocolate. His ruminations were, however, rudely and abruptly interrupted.

'Snoddy, if you're thinking of ordering a dessert, you can forget it. With your weight problem, you don't need any more sugar. No desserts for you, and that's final!'

One of the disadvantages of being married to the same woman for almost fifty years was that Mary always seemed to know precisely what he was thinking. He hadn't mentioned anything about having desserts, but Mary knew what he was craving and had swiftly put an end to it. He lowered the menu and peered across at Mary. She had her "I'm not open to negotiating" look on her face, and he knew it was useless to argue. The most he could look forward to was a pot of tea. Snoddy was just getting reconciled to his miserable morning tea prospects, when he received a hearty smack on the shoulder.

'Here they are, Penny. Gobbling up their tucker before we even arrive. Typical!'

Mike had bounced in from a side entrance and surprised the Snodgrasses with a left flanking attack. If opposites attract, then Mike and Snoddy were always destined to be great mates.

Mike was shortish, slim and boisterous. Despite being in his late sixties, he oozed energy and was irrepressible. Mike was one of a rare-breed who always seemed on a high, and nobody could recall seeing him ever downcast or despondent. With such a positive outlook on life, he was well-liked by everyone and great fun to have at parties. As the manager of a real estate business, he had always stayed clear of politics, and in his retirement had steadfastly remained apolitical.

Penelope, or Penny, as she was known, was a bit of a greenie. Not the watermelon type, who appears green on the outside but is a rabid red, communist inside. Nevertheless, she had given a lot of thought to where she stood in the scheme of things, and was a strong supporter of renewable energy, increased refugee settlement and serious action on climate change. Sadly, Penny was "anti" many more things than she supported; coal, uranium, gas, oil, exploration for minerals, off-shore drilling, fracking, live animal exports, nuclear-waste dumps, even spending money on the armed forces, and the list went on and on. Fortunately, for Penny's friends, she did not try to ram all her ideas down their throats, but raised her views whenever it was timely, and then, always in a considerate and polite manner. Penny's softer, well-reasoned approach to changing people's thinking, may well have won over more converts than the more ardent activists and radicals.

Penny was a retired primary schoolteacher and had only been married to Mike for twenty years or so. Both she and Mike had endured first marriage breakdowns, but, between them, had successfully raised three youngsters resulting from their earlier liaisons. A few months ago, Penny had commenced dialysis for end-stage kidney disease (ESKD), and the difficulties and challenges that went with fronting up for dialysis three times a week, had convinced them both that they now needed to move into a retirement village. Easytimes was conveniently located only two kilometres from Penny's satellite dialysis centre.

'Lovely to see you, Penny and Mike,' exclaimed Mary, jumping to her feet and lavishly dispensing hugs and kisses. 'Fancy meeting you at Easytimes. We are dying to hear what you thought of the place?'

There was a flurry of activity as the newcomers commandeered chairs from nearby vacant tables and seated themselves on red, white or blue cushions. 'Hey, whatever happened to green cushions?' Penny inquired.

'All the green cushions have been sent away to be recycled to provide renewable energy,' quipped Mike, never lost for a quick response.

'Before we order, tell us what you thought of Easytimes?' Mary persisted.

Mike responded first. 'Well, I have been checking out their regulations and conditions, and, compared to other places we have looked at, this one is pretty good.' Snoddy was particularly pleased to hear this, as it was further proof that Easytimes was offering a good deal, and Mike's expert opinion, as a real estate agent, was likely to help sway Mary's thinking positively.

Unbeknown to Snoddy, however, Mary had another reason for being excited at this glowing report from Mike. For several years now, Mary had had a secret crush on Mike. Although she still loved Snoddy, in a passive sort of way, she longed for more from their relationship. Sometimes she wondered whether her yearning for sex at her age was abnormal, but recently, she had read an article in the Readers Digest that reported that having fulfilling sexual relationships was not uncommon, between fit couples, well into their eighties. She really enjoyed Mike's lively company, and on lonely nights was occasionally given to dreaming of being in bed with him. Then her conscience would jump up and down and tell her she should not have such naughty thoughts, as they would be deeply hurtful to both her husband and Penny. But, she reasoned, as a compromise, it would be exciting to have Mike living nearby in the same village. It would provide a kind of closeness, although not the real thing.

'And what about you, Penny? What did you think of Easytimes?'

'It's a bit hard to say when the place is in such a mess still, but the maps and unit designs looked good. If Mike thinks it's a good set-up, I'm all in favour. It's really handy for my dialysis centre too, and will save me about three hours of travelling every week.'

'So, have you two signed up already?' Snoddy inquired, hopefully.

'Next week probably,' Mike replied. 'What about you folk? Are you going to move in?' Mike looked from Mary to Snoddy, and back again.

'Snoddy is keen,' said Mary, 'But I'm not so sure. I think I need to sleep on it before deciding.'

Again, Snoddy's spirits lifted. Mary had certainly come

around to giving the matter serious consideration after being totally against the idea initially.

'Time to order,' announced Mary, picking up the menu again. 'Anybody having a Cornish pasty? They do terrific ones here with a handle on them.'

Ten minutes later, their orders were delivered to their table by an attractive lass, dressed in a traditional Cornish milkmaid's costume. Mike attacked his full English breakfast with much gusto; the two ladies, rather more demurely, loitered over their carrot cake; whilst the unfortunate, deprived Snoddy, looked on enviously as he sipped Earl Grey tea.

The lively conversation revolved around Easytimes and what it would be like to live there. Mike had brought along a map of the planned development site showing the location of all 250 units and facilities. They started selecting their preferred units. Both couples, it seemed, had decided definitely on three-bedroom apartments with double garages attached.

At one point, one of Mike's slippery mushrooms shot off his plate and skidded across his map to end up on top of the planned swimming pool site.

'Wow, a swimming mushroom,' laughed Mike.

'The first one to dive in the new pool,' giggled Mary, eying Mike off admiringly.

'Excuse me for interrupting, but I couldn't help overhearing your conversation,' came a sweet, but clipped voice, from over Snoddy's substantial right shoulder. All heads turned, Snoddy's with considerable difficulty, to see the owner of these dulcet tones. Standing behind Snoddy was a beautifully dressed woman with immaculate hair and a stylish Amani handbag. 'I do hope you will forgive me, but I believe I heard you speaking about the Easytimes Retirement Village which I visited this morning, with a view to purchasing an apartment there.'

'Well, how about that!' Mike exclaimed, with some difficulty, as he had just loaded a substantial quantity of baked beans into his mouth. 'Pull up a chair, darling, and join us.'

The others were somewhat taken aback by Mike's overly familiar response that had clearly embarrassed this stylish woman. Calling a complete stranger "darling" was hardly polite. Penny resolved to have words with her husband later.

The last of the baked beans, having now been properly dispensed with, allowed Mike to jump up, grab a spare chair from the nearest table, and plonk it down next to him, 'Here you are,' he said effusively, with a wave of his arm.

The stranger smiled shyly at Mike and accepted the proffered chair. Four pairs of eyes scanned their unexpected visitor intensely. They noticed that she was not only smartly dressed but her manner of bearing was lady-like too. Penny and Mary were particularly impressed with the high quality of her apparel and the discrete, but tasteful, jewellery. They felt depressingly dowdy in comparison. The men, on the other hand, recognised a stunningly attractive woman, slim, smart, and oozing with the "X" factor. They speculated the woman to be from English aristocracy, and, in true Aussie style, began thinking how they might, "bring her down a peg or two". The visitor felt obliged to explain her intrusion further.

'My name is Rosemary Tattersall. I am recently widowed,

and retired, and I'm looking for somewhere new and different to start a new life. Easytimes looks promising to me. I want to move away from the suburb where I have so many happy, but now sad, memories.' With another shy smile, she looked around the foursome who proceeded to introduce themselves.

'It's so nice to meet you. I hope I can remember all your names.' Another sweet smile.

Surprisingly, it was Snoddy who spoke next. 'So, Rosemary, do you think Easytimes is the sort of place you are looking for?'

'I think it might be, Noddy.'

This unfortunate slip of the tongue sent the foursome into a fit of giggles, which took a moment or two to subside. It was Mary who came to Snoddy's rescue.

'It's Snoddy, short for Snodgrass, actually,' she beamed at the hapless Rosemary.

'Oh Snoddy, I do apologise,' Rosemary coloured prettily under her make-up. There was an awkward silence, disturbed only by Mike, who was still chasing the very last of his baked beans around his plate, but with little success.

'Another Earl Grey tea?' It was the Cornish wench back again, looking expectantly around the five faces for a response.

'Oh, that's for me, thank you so much.' Rosemary's posh English accent was unmistakeable.

'How long have you been out here, Rosemary?' asked Mike, performing the last rites on his breakfast which required a vigorous scrape across the entire surface of his plate with a scrunched-up piece of toast, which was then thrown, unceremoniously, into his mouth. Penny cringed, and made another mental note to speak to her husband, when they got home, about such uncouth behaviour when in public.

Rosemary seemed unperturbed, 'Just over four years.'

'Only four bloody years!' exclaimed Mike.

Penny glared at her husband. Poor table-manners was one thing, but swearing was quite another. What was wrong with Michael? Were his mushrooms off? She had heard shocking stories of fungi being eaten by people who thought they were consuming mushrooms, only to find out later, they had eaten some weird, toxic toadstools. Perhaps she had better get Mike away before he started using the "f" word? But Mike wasn't finished yet.

'Jesus Christ, Rosemary, you're only a new chum, then?' Rosemary hesitated a moment, puzzled at being addressed as a "chum"; a word that was reserved only for males back in the UK. After four years "down under" she was still occasionally encountering strange "lingo" for the first time.

'Yes, I suppose I am.' Again, the sweet, shy smile.

'Sorry folks, we have to go,' Mary chimed in. 'How about we all meet here again in two weeks if we are still starters for Easytimes Retirement Village? That includes you too Rosemary.'

Mary's suggestion was greeted by acclamation all round. As they gathered up their belongings, Mary looked across at Mike, hoping to catch his eye and flash a smile, but was disappointed to see him fussing like an old chook around Rosemary with whom he was obviously smitten. This undue attention to the English beauty had not been missed by Penny either, who added it to her burgeoning list of things to speak to her husband about.

Snoddy, with his bulk, managed to steer a safe path back through the chairs and remembered not to trip over the elderly lady's handbag this time.

With a few last waves and farewells, three vehicles left The Cornishman and headed for their respective destinations. Rosemary, elated at finding some potential new friends; Mary and Snoddy returning to their humdrum life; while Penny spent the whole journey back home haranguing her husband about his wicked ways.

CHAPTER 3

Arthur Stokes was relishing his early morning run through the leafy suburbs of Adelaide. Some regarded him as a fitness freak, because, at the age of 65, he still ran or swam every day, irrespective of the weather conditions. Today he had decided to take a diversion and run out to see the new retirement village everyone was talking about. He pounded along Fortescue Street, adjusting his sweatband as he went, and in a couple of minutes found himself at the formidable main entrance to Easytimes Retirement Village. Although the gates were still under construction, there was sufficient brickwork in place to convince visitors that the entrance would be a grand edifice when completed. Access was easy, so Arthur ran on through the gates to view the progress.

The workmen were starting to arrive in their trucks, utes and dusty Holdens, but work had not yet begun. Arthur ran around the new streets with their curbs and drainage virtually completed and then on to the dirt road surfaces rolled compactly and ready for sealing. He noted the spaciousness of the layout from the surveyors' pegs and the natural beauty of the setting. The bulldozers had finished clearing the area, leaving native bush surrounding the village on three sides. Completing his circuit, Arthur returned to the street where all the building was happening. Two or three units were already at lock-up stage and the painters and decorators were present there with all their paraphernalia. It was pleasing to see that no two units were the same. Variety in design, roof and garage door colours and solar panel settings ensured the future occupants would have some sense that their new home was unique. Arthur was impressed.

Tomorrow would be the second anniversary of the passing of his wife. Sophia had been everything to Arthur. For years she had battled breast cancer, and on several occasions, they believed they had beaten the insidious disease, only for it to return in some new guise. Sophia had fought valiantly and remained positive throughout her cruel journey. Everyone who knew Sophia was inspired by her example. Nature had dealt her an unfair hand, yet she had never given up, become bitter or sought sympathy. She remained a loving, generous person, to the very end. Indeed, she had felt blessed that she had cuddled her first grandchild only a few days before she died at the premature age of 58.

Arthur had found it incredibly painful to accept the loss of his beautiful wife. The only way he managed to deal with the constant gnawing grief was by intensifying his work and play ethic. As a social worker he took on additional cases, in excess of a normal workload, so that he was working long hours and even at weekends. He increased his running until he was completing half marathons on a regular basis. This combination of long-distance running and working overtime meant that when he needed sleep, he literally collapsed into his bed in an exhausted state, and consequently, slept reasonably soundly. His friends worried about him, fearing a complete breakdown, since he had never really allowed himself time to grieve. Only Arthur knew that he cried for hours when pounding the streets alone.

After two years, the dark gloom was slowly lifting, and Arthur's thoughts were starting to move from the past, with his beloved Sophia, to a vague and unknown future. Living alone in a large house, with so many memories, provided no enjoyment. His three children were long married and living elsewhere, and the second grandchild was expected in a week or two. Retirement was beckoning too. He needed to start afresh. He liked the area where he lived, and had many friends nearby, so a retirement village such as Easytimes might be the answer. Arthur resolved to arrange his work commitments so he could take time off next Monday to visit the sales manager at Easytimes.

* * *

Monday morning promised to rapidly become another forty degree plus day. The sun blazed out of a cloudless sky and Arthur was pleased he had chosen to swim laps in the Olympic pool instead of running. The Bureau of Meteorology was warning of extreme fire danger across much of the state with freshening northerlies during the afternoon. Arthur lowered the outside blinds to help keep the house dark and cool and set off for Easytimes in his car with time to spare. He was due to meet the sales manager, Robert Tinson, at 9.30am.

As he turned into Fortescue Street, he felt the car lurch suddenly and had to battle hard to correct the steering that appeared to have developed a mind of its own, causing the car to swerve all over the place. He pulled up on the side of the road. 'Bugger! A puncture!'

Arthur climbed out of the air-conditioned comfort of his vehicle and inspected the offending wheel. It was a blow-out puncture for sure, and a large tack of some description could be seen firmly ensconced in the tyre. Arthur had many talents, but mechanical skills was not one of them. The offending tyre was on the hot side of the car, where the sun was beating down relentlessly, and made the body work too hot to touch. It was such a long time since Arthur had had to deal with a puncture, that he struggled to recall the series of steps he needed to take. He could remember where the spare wheel was housed, but where would he find the jack? And where the heck was the spanner? The jack he managed to unearth reasonably quickly, but there was no sign of the spanner.

With beads of sweat breaking out all over him, Arthur was forced to rummage around in the passenger's glove compartment to locate the manual which he hoped would tell him where to look for the spanner. After a few minutes searching through the manual, and letting fly a succession of expletives, he eventually found what he was looking for. He returned to the boot and, yes, there was the spanner, exactly where it was supposed to be. Next, Arthur dragged out the spare wheel, and in doing so, successfully managed to get grease and dirt stains all over his clean and neatly ironed shirt. Trying to loosen the four wheel-nuts elicited another round of sweat and expletives; some stupid idiot had tightened up the nuts unreasonably tightly. Now he needed yet another gadget that was used to raise the jack. Arthur had forgotten he needed this extra implement and had not sighted it whilst rooting about in the boot. So, it was back to the car's manual again to find out where the gadget might be lurking. This proved an even more challenging task, because he didn't know the name of the gadget he was looking for. He searched the manual's index under "J" for "jack elevator," "jack handle" and "jack-lever" without success. Eventually, he found what he was looking for listed under "W" as a "wheel-nut wrench".

As a result of this succession of mechanical incompetency, Arthur finally rocked up at the sales manager's office half an hour late, and in no mood to exchange pleasantries. He parked the car out in the scorching sun, and didn't need to sniff under his armpits to know that his BO index was on the extreme scale. Grumpy, still flushed from his exertions, he wiped away the last of the perspiration from his brow, and hurried towards the sales manager's office. At least it was a bloke he was meeting. In his dirty, smelly state, he would be ashamed to be meeting a woman. A sexist thought, he realised, but then he was from that older generation for whom the way you dressed actually mattered.

As Arthur turned the doorknob, he noticed the amount of dirt and grime on his hand. Had he looked in a mirror, he would have been aghast to see grimy streaks of dirt across his brow as well. So it was, with grease paint in full view, that he unexpectedly came face-to-face with a startlingly attractive woman, whose demeanour exuded both class and sophistication. Tall and slim, the lady greeted him with a twinkle in her eyes and a lovely smile.

'How do you do? You must be Arthur Stokes? I think you might perhaps be a wee bit late for your appointment?'

Now, Arthur realised that he had been labouring outside in the hot sun for forty minutes, and that he certainly wasn't in his best form, but he was sure that the sales manager he was due to meet was a man called Robert Tinson. Yet here was this stunningly attractive woman who knew his name and that he was late for his appointment. Presumably then, this woman had replaced Robert Tinson at short notice, or perhaps, worked as the sales manager on Mondays.

'I do apologise for being late, I had a puncture', he stammered. 'As you can see, I have been grovelling about on the ground trying to fix it. Could you possibly get me a glass of water, please? This was a clean shirt this morning ...' Arthur stopped mid-sentence, realising he was babbling on stupidly, and feeling acutely embarrassed at his scruffy, grubby appearance.

The gorgeous woman was still smiling sweetly at him and seemed to be almost relishing his discomfort.

'I'm so sorry you have had car problems, Arthur. I understand you are here to find out more about Easytimes?'

'Yes, I am. Look, would you mind awfully, but I really do need that drink of water, please?'

group of potential Easytimes buyers meeting regularly at a cafe called The Cornishman for coffee and a chat. Robert Tinson had picked up this snippet of information from none other than Ms Tattersall, who had told him she had stumbled across the group recently. The sales manager divulged this news to Arthur with another wink and a knowing look. Arthur had to admit, that the possible presence of Ms Tattersall, did make the get-together more appealing. He decided to arrange things at work so he could attend the next coffee morning at The Cornishman.

CHAPTER 4

James Snodgrass was glued to the television set. The Wallabies were playing the All Blacks and twenty minutes into the game, to everyone's amazement, the score was 6-3 in Australia's favour. For many years the All Blacks had reigned supreme in the world of Rugby Union; "the game they play in heaven".

'Tackle him, tackle him, tackle him,' Snoddy yelled, as the big New Zealand winger headed for Australia's try-line.

'Oh, do be quiet Snoddy. I can't hear myself think.'

'Got him!' shouted Snoddy, punching his fists in the air and quite oblivious to Mary's pleas, 'And tackled him into touch as well! Great work guys!'

Mary knew how to quieten her husband down. She rammed her foot down on the pedal of her elderly Brother sewing machine and concentrated hard on the bit of stitching sitting in front of her. For some reason, that remained a mystery to both of them, whenever the sewing machine fired up, it set off scores of lines of static shooting horizontally across the television's screen so that watching was impossible.

'Mary, turn that bloody thing off!'

'On one condition Snoddy …' Mary responded, easing her foot off the pedal.

'What's that?' snarled Snoddy.

'As soon as the rugby ends, you promise to finish cleaning up that branch that fell in the back yard last night and then run the mower over the lawn.'

Snoddy realised with a sigh that he had been outmanoeuvred. Watching the rugby internationals was one of his favourite pastimes; a time for him to briefly re-live his own exploits on the rugby field. It always amazed him how his rugby watching time seemed to always coincide with Mary's need to use that wretched sewing machine. Inevitably, Mary would only agree to switch off her machine after she had extracted a promise from him to do something that needed doing about the house. Little did Snoddy realise that the sewing machine trick was a clever ploy by Mary to get him to actually get off his bum and do something. Unbeknown to Snoddy, the same bit of stitching had now remained on the sewing machine for several rugby seasons.

Four hours later, Snoddy and Mary were about to start tea. It had not been a rewarding afternoon for Snoddy. The All Blacks were all over the Wallabies in the second half with the final score being 21-6. Grumpily, Snoddy had then lumbered out into the backyard to do the jobs Mary had assigned to him. Physical work and Snoddy simply did not mix anymore. At seventy years of age, Snoddy felt he had done his bit and he should be allowed to vegetate peacefully in his own comfortable armchair. He was past doing any hard yakka nowadays. Surely the United Nations had created policies by now about the rights of the elderly? The right to a comfortable sedentary life, with no physical exertion had to be at the top of such a list. Mary, he ruminated, was quite possibly contravening the rights of the elderly by shoving him out the back door to clean up branches and mow lawns. He would Google it.

As a result of his outdoor work, Snoddy had two splinters in his hand and a sore back that he was sure was worsening by the minute. He also felt exhausted and wondered whether he would manage to stay awake throughout the meal. He looked disdainfully at the large bowl of pumpkin soup sitting in front of him with a miserable sprig of tired-looking parsley floating about, but concluded that his head flopping down into this steamy mix might be a rather messy business and could land him in even more trouble with the wife. With an effort, he fumbled for his soup spoon and took a tentative slurp.

'I'm too old for this caper, Mary.'

'Oh, stuff and nonsense, Snoddy. It does you good to get outside and do a bit of work. Pass the pepper please.'

'I could have a stroke, or a heart attack.'

'You're far more likely to have a stroke or a heart attack from sitting about on your backside all day, Snoddy. A sedentary life is the new killer, you know.'

Snoddy didn't know, and certainly felt disinclined to agree with his wife's views.

'I get so tired doing any gardening these days. Now, if we move into Easytimes, I'd be spared all this work. They do everything for you there. No lawn mowing, no cleaning up, no painting. They will even change a lightbulb for you if necessary.'

Mary wiped her mouth with her napkin and gave one of her rebellious sniffs. She was hardly in a good mood herself. It was a Saturday evening, and once again she was resigned to spending the whole evening stuck at home with only Snoddy for company. They hardly ever went out on Saturday evenings anymore. Snoddy showed no inclination to take her out to the movies or for a meal. She had given up suggesting they might see this or that film, which had been well reviewed or had been recommended to her by a friend. Whenever she hinted at a restaurant, Snoddy always had an answer ready: 'It's too far away.' 'The food's awful there.' 'I don't like Indian, it's far too spicy and greasy.' So Mary felt trapped. Only a few years ago they would never have stayed home on a Saturday night. An evening with friends down the pub, off to the footy, or occasionally they splashed out and went to the theatre or a concert. Usually, the stimulus of a couple of drinks and a fun night out led to some fulfilling sex afterwards.

Mary collected up their two soup-bowls and dished out a less than appetising looking plate of scrambled eggs on cold toast. Snoddy regarded the meal that had been plonked down before him with little enthusiasm and was about to remark that they always had the same thing on Saturday nights when something told him that Mary perhaps was not in the mood to tolerate any more complaints. As Snoddy slowly consumed his uninviting scrambled eggs, a plan began to materialise in his head. By the time he had the last mouthful, nicely balanced on his fork, he had decided his plan was a potential winner.

'Mary, would you like to go out somewhere next Saturday evening?'

Mary stared at her husband quite taken aback by the question. For a moment she was lost for words. Snoddy's invitation had "come out of left field" as one of her friends was prone to saying.

'It might be a pleasant change?' her husband added.

'I haven't got anything to wear.'

Now this statement always puzzled Snoddy. There were rows and rows of Mary's dresses and coats and other items hanging up in the wardrobe.

'I'm sure you'll find something,' Snoddy assured her.

'This is all very sudden, Snoddy. Where were you thinking of going?'

'Your choice entirely, my dear.'

'Crikey, Snoddy! What's got into you suddenly?'

Snoddy shrugged his considerable shoulders and attempted a rare smile. 'Just thought it would be nice, that's all.'

Mary smelt a rat, a particularly large one. Was Snoddy finally getting sick and tired of pumpkin soup, followed by scrambled eggs every Saturday night, or was he up to something more sinister? Cautiously, she decided to play along with Snoddy's surprise invitation.

'How about that new Indian restaurant that opened up a few weeks ago?' Mary thought she detected a grimace come across Snoddy's face for a brief moment, before he responded.

'Okay, will you book it?'

* * *

Next Saturday came around all too quickly and a table for two was booked for 7.00pm at The Taj Mahal. Surprisingly, Snoddy had not changed his mind or invented some feeble excuse for not going. They showered, dressed and drove the short way down to the bright lights of the restaurant. Snoddy went through his usual procedure of huffing and puffing as he dragged his legs out of the driver's seat, and was at last standing upright on terra firma.

'Come on,' exhorted Mary, 'Let's get stuck into some good old Indian tucker.'

Snoddy waddled along as fast as he could and a moment later they were inside the restaurant waiting to be shown to their seats.

'Ah, Mr and Mrs Snotgas,' beamed a smart young Indian man.

'No, the name is Snodgrass, thank you,' Mary corrected him, firmly.

They were shown to a table in a corner, reserved no doubt for romantic couples. Surrounded by intimate lighting, the young man quickly returned and lit a candle in the middle of their table, at the same time flashing them a knowing smile. He left two menus.

Snoddy was relieved to see that everything on the menu was written in both Hindustani and English. However, he was more interested in the list of wines. Here he was pleasantly surprised to discover the extensive range of local wines available, together with many new listings that he had never heard of before. He searched for a red wine he was familiar with. An Indian lass with bright red lipstick, long painted fingernails and a colourful sari was at his side in no time. 'Would you like to order drinks, sir?'

'Oh, yes, thank you. We'll have a bottle of Jacob's Creek Cabernet Sauvignon please.' At least this was one wine Snoddy remembered enjoying some years ago.

'Snoddy, are you sure we can get through a whole bottle?'

'Absolutely. Why not?'

'Well it's years since we drank a whole bottle together. And you can only have two glasses if you plan to drive us home.'

They sat sheepishly, unaccustomed to being in such close proximity for so long with nothing to do. They both tried to make polite conversation, but it all seemed so artificial. It was a relief when the wine finally arrived together with the samosas they had ordered for their entree. The wine helped ease the tension somewhat, and they were both finishing their second glasses before they began to relax. It was time for Snoddy to move on to stage two of his master plan.

'Mary, I rang our good friends Mike and Penny yesterday. They have decided definitely to move into Easytimes. It would be great to be there with them. Perhaps we could go out with them on Saturday nights like we always used to do?'

Mary did not answer immediately. She had suspected all along that this sudden and surprising dinner date was a trap that Snoddy had been planning. Take her out, get her slightly tipsy, and then when her guard is down, ask her to agree to go into Easytimes. Well, she was not going to fall for the oldest trick in the book. She looked defiantly into her husband's hopeful, pleading eyes.

'Mr Snotgas, I am awake to your tricks. You are going to

have to do a lot more than just take me out for dinner once in a blue moon, to persuade me to say "yes" to going into Easytimes!'

45

CHAPTER 5

Mike and Penny Fisher were having a rough morning. Penny was seated at the breakfast table with a cup of steaming herbal tea, whilst Mike was roaming about like an expectant father. As Mike traipsed into the kitchen on his third circuit around the house, Penny could endure it no more.

'Mike, what *are* you doing?'

'Lost my bloody car keys!'

'Oh Mike, not again. Why can't you just put your keys in the bowl in the hall where all the other keys are kept?'

'I usually do. I'm supposed to be at the Golf Club by nine. I might have to borrow your car, Penny.'

'No way, I have to go for my dialysis, and it starts at ten.'

Mike left the room again, uttering a string of expletives as he went. He had looked in all the usual places; trouser pockets, dining room table, where he had sat watching TV last night and all around the computer in the study. 'Shit, where the hell can they be?'

Penny was standing in the doorway, holding her cup of herbal tea, as Mike commenced a fourth circuit.

'Have you looked where you left them last time?'

'I don't know. Where was that?'

'In your car.'

Without another word, an agitated Mike headed for the door that led directly into the garage.

A moment later, Mike was back, looking distinctly sheepish.

'Did you find them?'

'Yup.' An embarrassed Mike was deliberately avoiding looking at his wife. He knew only too well what she was thinking. At least she was decent enough not to say, 'Told you so ...'

'What's the matter now, dear?'

'Now I can't find my bloody cap!'

'Probably because it's sitting on your head,' Penny observed simply.

Mike raised a hand to his head. Penny was right, as usual. He moved round the table to give her a parting peck on the cheek as she asked, 'Have you got your sticks? Have you got your balls?'

'No need to be rude, Penny.'

With a shake of her head, Penny sat back down to enjoy the last of her herbal tea, as her husband's car could be heard scrunching its way down their drive.

* * *

That her husband still had his balls, Penny knew only too well.

Mike was very active on the sexual front and wanted to make love at least once a week and quite often twice. She realised that frequently she disappointed him in bed. End stage kidney disease (ESKD) was a libido killer. The doctors, renal nurses and nephrologists were great, and took the time to explain the likely symptoms and nasty side-effects to expect from being on dialysis. Like everyone else on dialysis, she experienced fatigue and soreness around her fistula. Sometimes she felt unwell. Severe leg cramps were a constant problem, frequently hitting her hard in the middle of the night. None of the medicos, however, had mentioned the lowering of her libido. Nowadays it was far more difficult for her to get sexually aroused and she found, increasingly, that she just submitted to Mike's needs. She never refused his advances, but at times it was little more than lying on her back and thinking of old mother England. How she wished she could be more sexually responsive again for the man she loved so much.

It was time to go for dialysis. Penny changed into warmer clothes. Lying inert for four hours or more in a dialysis chair, having your warm blood removed, filtered of the toxins that build up in the body when the kidneys don't function properly, and then having her own blood returned, cleansed but colder, meant that as the hours of dialysis proceeded, her temperature gradually dropped. Penny had a lovely electric blanket, a wool Binet and fur-lined boots to wear, all of which she kept handy in her locker at the Dialysis Satellite Centre that she had been attending for nearly four years now. Even in the heat of summer, she needed to don this additional apparel to stay warm.

Unlike Mike, Penny had no problem finding her keys and began the half-hour drive to her dialysis satellite centre, a journey she had embarked on, three days a week, every week, for four years. She was all too aware that it was these amazing dialysis machines that were keeping her alive. Only last week, one of the elderly patients at her centre, who had been on dialysis for ten years, had decided she did not wish to continue any more. Inevitably, being on dialysis meant one's health slowly declined until many patients reached a point where they were no longer prepared to fight on. Death followed a few weeks after declining treatment. Refusing dialysis was, in reality, a form of voluntary euthanasia.

Penny had hoped, by now, to have been offered a kidney transplant, but a compatible kidney had not eventuated. Mike had offered one of his kidneys, but the surgeons were not prepared to take the risk, as he was being treated for hypertension. Live donors were the best for kidney transplants, but it was major surgery to donate a kidney, and, as with any surgery, there was always an element of risk. So Penny was to go on waiting and hoping, waiting and hoping. Perhaps a suitable kidney from a deceased person would one day become available?

Five hours later, Penny, tired and irritable, arrived back at the house. Her wonderful husband had prepared a salad, which he retrieved from the fridge and had ready for her as she came in from the garage.

'Hi gorgeous. How did you go?'

'My fluids were okay, but I had a new nurse today, and she was hopeless at sticking the needle in. After three failures she had to get Lucy, one of the most experienced renal nurses to come and do it. So, I ended up with four puncture wounds today.'

Mike gave Penny a big cuddle, making sure he avoided her sore arm, and sat her down in front of the salad. 'Now what would you like to drink?'

'The usual please. I am so lucky to have you as my unofficial carer, Mike. A couple of the ladies at the satellite centre have nobody to look after them at home. I can't imagine coming home to an empty house when you have just spent several miserable hours on dialysis, feeling lousy, and then having to prepare something to eat. You may lose your bloody keys, and your cap, Mike, but you are always here for me. If only I could get a transplant, life would be so, so much better.'

Mike poured a glass of water for Penny. He knew that alcohol, although not banned, was frowned upon for those on dialysis. It was all to do with retaining the correct fluid balance. Only a limited amount of total fluids could be consumed each day. 'I know you are not feeling the best Penny, but we really do need to decide soon whether or not we will make the move to Easytimes.'

'For me, there are two huge positives in moving there, Mike. The village is located very close to where I go to dialyse and where my nephrologist has his practice. Secondly, I get tired very quickly these days. This house is getting too much for me. A smaller apartment would be so much easier to manage. But what about you Mike? How do *you* feel about making this move?'

Mike had correctly second-guessed Penny's views and had

been mulling the matter over himself for a couple of weeks now. He understood Penny's thinking, but was most reluctant to leave a house into which he had invested so much time and energy. During the last fifteen years, since they bought the place, he had erected a substantial workshop, completely landscaped the garden, installed thirty solar panels and developed a quality water storage and reticulation system. Penny, a strong environmentalist, had worked alongside him, all the way, ensuring that everything they had completed together was environmentally friendly. They had planted for sustainability, using natives, and minimal watering. Artificial lawns had been spurned, since they were a plastic product, and, wherever possible, they had used natural materials for the rockeries. They were proud of their efforts and were now reaping the benefit of being surrounded by beautiful trees.

Mike was a positive fellow and able to see the advantages around any issue and to downplay any perceived disadvantages. When confronted with a challenging decision, Mike had the commendable ability to make the best of the situation. And so it was that he accepted they must move to Easytimes for Penny's sake. All the hard work they had done about the house would surely translate into valuable assets and have substantially increased the value of their property. Mike leant over and gently kissed his wife.

'I'm more than happy to go to Easytimes. Tomorrow I will put our house on the market and arrange for the payment of a deposit for Easytimes.'

* * *

Paying the deposit was easily done, but the whole process of selling the house was far more complex. Following the recommendation of some friends, Mike engaged the services of a local real estate agency. The company promised to send someone around at 3.00pm the very next day to undertake what they described as "a preliminary review" of the property. This was enough, however, to put both Mike and Penny into panic mode. To put it bluntly, the house was in a mess! Mike was torn between cleaning out the shed that had accumulated fifteen years of junk, or doing a complete blitz in his study, where old papers, files, boxes, books and bits of defunct technology lay scattered about as if hit by a cyclone. There was also a large wooden desk, but it too had become a dumping ground for more rubbish, and was never sufficiently cleared to be useful. It was much easier these days to use a laptop that could be taken anywhere. There was insufficient time to attack both the shed and the office, so in the end Mike determined to fix the study and to put a padlock on the shed. He reasoned that he could always tell the real estate agent that he had lost the key so they couldn't inspect the shed.

The shed and study were essentially recognised as male domains by the Fishers. Therefore, their upkeep clearly fell to Mike. Penny was equally aware there were parts of the house considered to be hers. A spare bedroom had become Penny's craft room. Here she had accumulated the where-with-all for a string of different crafts that Penny had fallen for, but then lost interest in, over the years. There were boxes full of bark to be used for bark paintings, materials for making soft toys, equipment for string art and several other boxes that had been there so long that Penny had no idea anymore what they contained. She had always meant to get stuck into cleaning out her craft room, but her kidney disease had drained her of the energy she needed. So, the room remained in a state of near chaos. Penny decided to be perfectly honest with the agent and tell him or her that she was unwell and needed help to tidy the room up. It was the truth and the agent would just have to accept it.

3.00pm the next day came around quickly. Penny had spent the morning on dialysis, and was home, but feeling delicate. Mike had worked late last evening and had done an amazing job in his study. Piles of discarded papers, cardboard boxes and old files were now stacked outside, ready to be loaded onto a trailer, if Mike could get his mate to lend him his. Mike had even managed to run a duster over what remained in his study and to get the vacuum cleaner into operation. Cleaning was one of Mike's pet hates. To Mike's mind, cleaning was quite simply the process of moving dirt from one place to another.

The antique grandfather clock in the hall was just starting to chime the hour when the doorbell rang. Mike was nowhere about, so Penny opened the front door. On the doorstep stood a man in his forties, almost completely bald, clean-shaven and wearing spectacles with lenses so thick that they made his eyes appear to shrink to the size of peas. He wore a rather tired-looking suit, a modest blue tie and well-polished black shoes. He gave Penny a cheesy smile and held out a flabby hand.

'Afternoon.'

'Good afternoon,' Penny smiled, and grasped the flabby, lifeless hand.

'Stephen,' the man offered, still with his cheesy smile, but withdrawing his hand.

'Ah, you must be from the real estate agency, here to do a preliminary assessment? I'm Penny Fisher.'

'Indeed.'

'Where would you like to start?'

'Upstairs.'

The little man, she observed, seemed capable of using only one word at a time. She smiled and ushered him into the hallway. Stephen wiped his feet thoroughly on the welcome mat, as if terrified of bringing another speck of dirt into a spotless house. With another cheesy smile, he removed a pen from his top pocket with a flourish, tucked his clipboard under his arm and looked expectantly at Penny. Penny had already mentally dubbed Stephen "Mono-man" and wondered, vaguely, whether Stephen could actually speak in sentences. They had just reached the foot of the stairs when Mike came charging around the corner.

'Oh, Mike, this is Mono-man, I mean Stephen. He's here to check the house over for us.' Penny felt acutely embarrassed at her unintended rudeness, and sincerely hoped Stephen hadn't noticed her gaffe. 'This is my husband, Mike.'

The dead-fish hand was extended again and the cheesy smile appeared once more.

'Mike,' Stephen acknowledged, with a little nod.

'Would you like one of us to accompany you as you walk around the house?'

'Please,' Mono-man replied.

Mike and Penny looked at each other inquiringly. Which of them would accept the thrilling task of escorting Mono-man around the house? The job did not exactly offer a bundle of laughs, or any meaningful conversation. Realising Penny was still tired from dialysis, Mike offered to be the escort, and the two men ascended the stairs. Penny retired to the lounge and gratefully left the two men to it.

Mike traipsed along behind Stephen like a lamb following its mother. Stephen seemed to have lost his tongue entirely now that he was "on task". They went into all four bedrooms with Mike making the necessary excuses for Penny's spare room chaos, where the two of them could barely fit. Stephen inspected the bathrooms carefully, all the while writing furiously on his clipboard, and finally they trooped off downstairs.

As they entered the lounge, where Penny was still sitting, thumbing through a magazine and already starting to feel dispossessed, Stephen finally felt compelled to speak. 'Mrs Fisher,' This two-word extravaganza was accompanied by yet another polite nod and the cheesy smile.

'Mrs Fisher,' mimicked Mike, as he followed meekly behind Mono-man and offered an even cheesier smile and a grossly exaggerated nod to his wife.

Penny broke into a bout of giggles at her husband's lampooning.

The grand tour of the downstairs continued, until Stephen opened up again with another request, 'Outside?'

They duly left the house and trudged about the garden,

front and back, as Mono-man's pen continued to flow across the pages. Finally, they reached Mike's padlocked shed, which he had thought to pretend was inaccessible as a result of him losing the keys. Mono-man headed straight for the shed door where he stopped, turned to Mike questioningly, with his hand held out and demanded, 'Key?'

Mike gave up. To feign the loss of the key would only result in Mono-man returning later, so he thought he might as well get it over with now. Mumbling a few flimsy excuses, Mike fished the shed key from his trouser pocket and opened up. He had forgotten what a dreadful mess the place was in. Mono-man needed only one quick look.

'Indeed,' he uttered, ominously.

In the circumstances, Mike felt he had got off rather lightly. Mono-man could have been forgiven if he had said something far less flattering, such as, "shocking" or "disgraceful" or "chaotic". Mike locked up quietly and gloomily followed Mono-man back to the house.

They entered through the back door, to find Penny in the kitchen, armed with a pot of tea and some biscuits, pleasantly arranged on a china plate. 'Stephen, would you like to join us for a cup of tea?'

To their surprise, the chance of a cup of tea seemed to transform Mono-man. He readily sat himself down, ordered his tea with milk, together with four spoonfuls of sugar and beamed at them.

Now, Penny and Mike never touched sugar, so Stephen's request for four spoonfuls of the stuff put Penny into a minor tizzy. Did she *have* any sugar? If she did, where the heck was it? She started to root about in the food cupboard, desperately looking for a container at the back of one of the shelves that might say "SUGAR". With a sigh of relief, she discovered a jar, covered with a layer of dust, but announcing itself as "White Sugar". Surreptitiously, she wiped it clean and conveyed the container to the table, hopefully before Mono-man's tea was getting cold.

Mono-man did not appear overly perturbed about the delay in producing some sugar and used the waiting time productively to help himself to several biscuits. There was to be yet another minor hitch, however, because Penny had forgotten that a teaspoon is needed to transfer the sugar from the container to the cup and to then do the requisite stirring. Once this problem was overcome, Stephen felt disposed to open up about the results of his "preliminary review". No longer "Mono-man", Stephen proceeded to outline a long list of things to be done before he would recommend the house as being "sale-ready". The list was sufficiently lengthy to require a second cup of tea for Stephen, who was now obliged to turn the long-lost sugar container on its side in order to scrape out another four meagre spoonfuls of sugar. Penny realised that if a third cup was requested she was in serious trouble.

Eventually came the decision as to when Stephen was to return to check that everything had been completed to his satisfaction and the house could be officially declared "sale-ready". The officious little man made it abundantly clear that failure to meet his high expectations might mean his company would decline to put the house on the market. A date for the reassessment was finally agreed on, and another two biscuits consumed, before Mono-man was at last on his way.

Mike and Penny had accepted a two-week stay of execution. That very evening, Mike arranged to have a large skip delivered to their house and rang his mate to borrow his trailer, while Penny offered her cleaner another whole day's extra employment to sort out her craft room, together with the possibility of even more hours to spring clean the entire house. Finally, Penny wrote two items at the top of her next shopping list; sugar and biscuits.

CHAPTER 6

The day for the next gathering at The Cornishman soon arrived. The original two couples, Snoddy and Mary, and Penny and Mike, were to be joined by two others, intent on moving into Easytimes; the classy Rosemary Tattersall and the athletic Arthur Stocks.

Rosemary was the first to arrive, and she procured a table in the corner of the café, beneath a large Cornish lobster-pot affixed to the wall. In the centre of the table stood a small tin model of what she presumed to be a Dartmoor pony. She sat down, parked her bag on a second chair and her umbrella on a third, to show that she had taken possession of the whole table and its six seats. The surface of the table was crumb-strewn and a large blob of strawberry jam sat suggestively immediately behind the Dartmoor pony's backside. Rosemary discretely moved the pony to a new position and caught the eye of the young waitress to come and clean up.

Rosemary had arrived early, and while she waited for

the others to show up, fell to reminiscing about her dear departed husband, the love of her life. Like so many English couples, they had frequently gone driving and hiking at weekends and found cosy little cafes to enjoy tea and scones, or roasted chestnuts near a roaring fire followed perhaps by an exotic looking cake. How she wished he was with her now. The Cornishman bravely attempted to re-create an English cafe, but, try as it did, it couldn't quite make it. Rosemary's husband had died in a shocking multiple car pile-up on the M3. She still missed him desperately, but just recently had reached a stage in her grieving when she felt ready to try to move on. She remained a most attractive looking woman and at the age of 62 could still turn heads. Indeed, a couple of men had already shown interest in having a relationship. But she was not ready yet. A week or two ago though, she had taken an instant liking to this man called Arthur who she had met at Easytimes. He was expected to join them in the cafe shortly, and rather surprisingly, in anticipation, she had found herself taking extra care to dress well and in how she applied her make-up. Most significantly, she had removed her wedding ring for the first time since she had married.

'Good morning.' Rosemary looked up to find a much cleaner, and less flustered, Arthur standing in front of her.

'Oh, hello Arthur. No punctures today then?'

Arthur laughed pleasantly, and sat down opposite Rosemary, so she had a moment to study him more closely. Slightly taller than she, he was tanned, slim and athletic looking. She estimated Arthur to be about her age and found his slightly creased face friendly and attractive. The hair was thinning and greyish but tidy. He was dressed in smart casuals as he had to return to his duties as a social worker afterwards. What she particularly liked about his countenance was that it exuded warmth and generosity. Some men's faces were like that, you just knew by looking at them that they were decent, honest human beings. Arthur's blue eyes were fixed on hers and she felt a slight tingle all over.

Arthur's blue eyes were actually busily absorbing more information about Rosemary. Beautifully dressed, she radiated an air of calm sophistication. Arthur knew nothing about women's fashions but somehow he recognised good taste when he encountered it. There was nothing vulgar about Rosemary's apparel, well-fitting without being tarty, just a hint of cleavage and yet he could tell she was well-endowed. She was so different to many women these days who found it necessary to reveal as much of their boobs as possible. But it was Rosemary's face that interested Arthur most. Despite her age, the face was still delightfully proportioned and the make-up had been applied sparingly and skilfully, a bit of eye-shadow, lipstick and perhaps rouge. Rosemary still retained a lovely soft, pale English skin. Arthur was pleased to note that her fingernails were painted, but there was no sign of weird multi-coloured stick-on fingernails that set his teeth on edge. He had assumed Rosemary was single when they had first met out at Easytimes, and this was now confirmed by no ring appearing on either hand.

This brief moment of mutual admiration was rudely interrupted by the noisy arrival of Mike and Penny.

'G'day folks,' thundered Mike, 'How are we today, then?'

Rosemary and Arthur jumped to their feet as if they had been yelled at by a sergeant-major and turned to look at the instigator of this hearty welcome. Rosemary instantly remembered Mike as the man who had insisted on calling her "darling" when she had politely asked if she could join them, having overheard their conversation about Easytimes. She tolerated these blustery sorts of males, but seldom found them particularly profound, or attractive. She regarded them as usually superficial, full of talk, but not much more. Penny, she had much more time for.

Rosemary introduced Arthur.

'So, have you signed on the dotted line yet?' Mike asked, looking at Rosemary.

'Not yet, I'm still considering all my options,' Rosemary replied, resuming her seat.

'What about you, Arthur?'

'I'm the same. I have a couple of other places to check out still.'

'Well, it's the early bird that gets the worm. We've signed up. The manager gave us a bottle of Brown Brothers Tawny Port as a sign-up gift. It's a nice little drop.'

Arthur and Rosemary were in the process of congratulating Mike and Penny, when there was an almighty crashing sound near the entrance of the café. Tables and chairs went tumbling in all directions, fortunately with nobody on them, before a figure began slowly to emerge from under one of the tablecloths that had also fallen to the ground. There was an eerie silence as everyone in the cafe swivelled around to see what the commotion was all about. As they watched, the tablecloth continued to wriggle like some kind of giant amoeba, at the same time letting out a cacophony of strange grunts, groans and expletives. Finally, a head came into view. It was Snoddy's.

The appearance of Snoddy's head was the signal for a frantic flurry of activity. Snoddy's wife, Mary, let out a scream, the café's proprietor came charging out to see what had happened, and the waitress started apologising profusely to the elderly lady into whose lap she had spilt a serving of toasted sandwiches. Apart from the old lady dealing with the unexpected arrival of toasted sandwiches, everyone else jumped to their feet to see better, or moved in the direction of the commotion to see what they could do to assist.

As the rest of Snoddy's more than substantial torso appeared, he was surrounded by willing hands who pulled, pushed and heaved until he was vertical. Snoddy was then bombarded by a spate of searching questions, 'Are you okay?', 'What do you do for an encore?', 'Any bones broken?' Snoddy shook himself, moved his outer limbs about to see if they still functioned, and finding everything still moved, gave a general grunt of appreciation.

'Where there's pain there's life,' mumbled Snoddy, debating which part of his anatomy was most in need of his closer attention. Mary was quickly by his side, offering sympathy and taking his hand to lead him over to the table where the others were settling down again. For several more minutes Snoddy enjoyed all the attention that was being heaped upon him, until the little Cornish apron-clad waitress breezed up to the table to take their orders. As a result of Snoddy's dramatic and unrehearsed entry, nobody had yet concentrated on what to order. The waitress was asked to return in five whilst they all embarked on a serious examination of the menu.

You can learn much about a person's lifestyle, and their underpinning philosophy by observing their eating habits. Snoddy got in first when the waitress reappeared, and without any hesitation demanded a full English breakfast "with the lot". This being a Cornish establishment, a full English breakfast even included cockles and muscles as an optional extra. Snoddy saw no reason why such delicacies should escape his attention, and nodded his agreement. Mary rolled her eyes and shook her head in disbelief but kept her silence. Mindful of her figure, she ordered modestly, toasted cheese and tomato on ryebread.

Penny, forever watchful to maintain her correct fluid balance for dialysis, requested only a pot of herbal tea. Her husband, Mike, torn between Snoddy's tempting feast, and Penny's critical eye, opted for a middle of the road Cornish pasty with mushy peas. Arthur and Rosemary, both conscious of the need to maintain a reasonably healthy diet, ordered a pot of green tea and a plate with two spoons so they could share a piece of carrot cake, without extra cream.

Mike was the instigator of most of the topics of conversation that ranged broadly across selling houses, real estate agents, removalists, contractual arrangements with Easytimes and possible dates for moving in. Everyone chipped in with comments, except Snoddy, who was too busy communicating with his full English breakfast with its optional extras, to offer any meaningful contributions. He was just happy that nothing seemed to be broken after his fall and that the conversation was all positive with regard to purchasing units at Easytimes.

Rosemary and Arthur enjoyed the closeness of sharing their carrot cake and both privately wondered whether they might share more than just carrot cake one day in the future.

Penny, despite her pallid, grey face, so typical of those with renal disease, was championing her green credentials. 'One thing I will not accept is artificial grass lawns' she announced, 'they are made from plastic and the oceans are chock-a-block already with mountains of the stuff and killing our marine life at an alarming rate. Scientists think that before long there will be more plastic in the world's oceans than fish!' She was supported by her friend Mary, although it had never occurred to Mary, before Penny's statement that artificial lawns might be made of plastic.

'And, I'm sure those artificial lawns are all made in China too,' Mary added, knowingly, realising that blaming China was always a sure way to seal an argument. Everyone around the table concurred, and Mike assured them he would check out with the manager whether artificial lawn was being proposed and report back at the next meeting of the group.

Soon it was time to leave. Mary escorted Snoddy closely this time, ensuring he had a clear and wide passage through to the exit. Mike and Penny held hands as they thanked the young lass who had served them. Rosemary and Arthur hung back, reluctant to part company. Arthur had toyed with the idea of asking Rosemary out for a date, but then thought better of it, and merely asked for her contact details, in case they wished to exchange news and views about transitioning to Easytimes.

CHAPTER 7

The dreaded day arrived when Mono-man was due back for his next inspection of Mike and Penny's home to determine whether it was sale-ready. It was a Saturday morning and the Fishers were trying to relax over breakfast. Mono-man was expected at 9.00am. Penny's cleaning lady had worked miracles in the spare bedroom and it now resembled a normal room again, complete with clean curtains, a single bed and furnishings. The whole house had been spring-cleaned and smelt like some kind of flowery perfume. Penny could not abide the use of any cleaning chemicals apart from a couple of environmentally friendly products that she had finally given the tick of approval to, after a thorough Google search. Mike's study had also been subjected to an intensive spring clean, so much so, that he no longer felt it was his "pad". Nothing was out of place, but he now felt nervous whenever he entered the study, in case he disturbed the orderly arrangement of any furnishings. The room might look tidy and professional, he reflected, but now he could never find things.

As the signature tune for the ABC's nine o'clock news bulletin filled the kitchen, there was a ring at the front door. Penny and Mike looked glumly at each other. They had resolved that Mono-man's visit was a necessary hurdle along the path to moving to Easytimes and that they would be sweet and kindly towards the officious little man. Mike swivelled himself off the breakfast stool and headed for the front door. He swung the door open and was surprised to find no Mono-man standing there with his clipboard tucked under his arm. Instead, an attractive young lady stood on his doorstep, smilingly generously at him. Mike always recognised a good-looking sort when he saw one, and this young lass certainly didn't disappoint.

'Hello, I'm Jenny Cosgrove. I've been asked to do an inspection of your house and to apologise for Stephen who cannot come today because he is unwell.'

'Oh, I'm so glad to hear that,' Mike blurted out, and then realised what an unfortunate statement he had just made. 'What I mean is, I'm glad you are here, and I'm sorry that Mono ... um, Stephen, is unwell.'

Jenny looked at him with a somewhat puzzled expression, but quickly recovered her composure. 'Stephen gave me his notes from his first visit, so I know what to look for.'

'Rather a long list I believe?'

'Yes, but I have seen longer ones.'

Heartened by this revelation, Mike ushered Jenny Cosgrove indoors and enjoyed the waft of some exotic perfume as she floated past. 'Perhaps you would like to meet my wife first? She is in the kitchen.'

'Thank you. I always find kitchens are an excellent place to start. They are the most family-friendly rooms.'

'Would you like a coffee or tea before you start?'

'A glass of wine would be more like it,' Jenny laughed.

Penny was delighted to hear the news of Stephen's replacement and immediately offered to escort Jenny around the house. Although she trusted Mike, she somehow didn't like the idea of her husband showing such an attractive young woman through their bedrooms and bathrooms. She realised she was, perhaps, a bit old-fashioned in her thinking. Mike could show Jenny around the garden and the shed.

The tour of both the house and garden went smoothly and Jenny was pleased with all the work Penny and Mike had done. She didn't stay for a cuppa but assured them that the house was now sale-ready and she would be happy to list their home for sale within twenty-four hours. She left them a brochure that explained the sales process, the costs, and how they could enhance the house whenever potential buyers came visiting. It was the usual things; leave every light on, have vases of flowers strategically displayed, play well-known classical music softly in the background and even spray a pleasant aroma around the rooms. Above all, create the feeling of a warm, happy home. Jenny promised to give them a ring well before any clients were due to arrive, and stressed the importance of Mike and Penny being completely off the property whenever there was to be a viewing.

* * *

The process of selling the property seemed straightforward enough. Look after the house inside and out, and leave everything else to the agent. What proved a nightmare, however, was the "down-sizing". Somehow Mike and Penny had to rid themselves of masses of furniture, ornaments, paintings, tools of every description, unnecessary equipment and the accumulated clutter from twenty years of married life. The unit at Easytimes was probably less than half the size of their current home. They knew where to start though; invite the kids to put claims in for the things in the house they would like. So they contacted the three offspring from their first marriages, now in their late thirties, early forties, to come and do just that.

First to arrive was the feisty daughter from Penny's earlier marriage, Rebecca. Rebecca had had a number of torrid affairs but had never tied the knot with any of her suitors. She was a geologist and her field work had taken her all over the world, working with different mining companies on mostly short-term contracts. Mike often joked that she was as unstable as the rocks she studied, with their faults, slippages and volcanic eruptions. Currently, she was living with a palaeontologist, who insisted on filling up their small apartment with dozens of rocks, full of fossils. Apparently, when he was short of space, he even put rocks on their bed, and Rebecca had reported that on a few occasions, they had arrived home very late at night, desperately tired, and had had to sleep with rocks still strewn about all over their bed. Opening her eyes, first thing in the morning, to be greeted by a large rock, containing trilobites, or be confronted by a lump of smoky grey quartz, did not appeal. It hadn't done much for their sex lives either.

Rebecca flitted through the house at a great rate of knots, pausing only occasionally to look at some item a second time.

'Thanks Mum, but no thanks.'

'What do you mean by that?' Penny asked.

'I don't want any of it. All the furniture is "old hat" and your taste in art is appalling.'

'I beg your pardon?'

'Sorry Mum, but there is nothing here, except a couple of saucepans, that I would ever use.'

'Rebecca, you must be joking. Out of the whole of this house, there is *nothing* you want, except a couple of saucepans?'

'That's right Mum. Have you tried the Salvos? I believe they take old stuff?'

'Old stuff! Mike and I spent thousands and thousands of dollars buying our furniture and carefully selecting paintings at art shows. And what about the electrical goods? Surely you could use a nearly new fridge, or the Miele washing machine, or the Miele clothes dryer?'

'We've got all that sort of stuff, Mum. Anyway, that fridge is far too big for our small kitchen.'

'Oh dear, I'm so disappointed.'

Rebecca realised that she had been a bit too abrupt with her well-meaning mother, and softened.

'Alright, I'll take that small photo of Cradle Mountain hanging in the hallway. We might have a space for it somewhere.'

And so, it was, that Rebecca came and went, taking with

her just two saucepans and a small framed photograph of Cradle Mountain in Tasmania.

It was a very different scenario when Mike's twin boys, Tom and Geoff, turned up together three days later. Both had been married a few years and had recently started their own families. Money was tight, and like most young couples, they wanted everything instantly, if not earlier. Mike was constantly amazed, and concerned, at the attitude towards money that many of the younger generation displayed. When he married the first time, they could afford little. The first place they lived in contained an old double bed that creaked alarmingly, a metal table and two chairs. They also had a sofa with the stuffing coming out, an old rug on the floor, a kitchen stove and a small fridge. That was it! Curtains were out of the question, and an old sheet with a tear in it, hung over the window in their bedroom to offer some privacy. But they made do. They had to. That's the way it was in those days. Gradually, they acquired more items of furniture, but painstakingly slowly, and only when they could afford it. Lay-bys were virtually unheard of, but boy, were they proud when they had saved up enough money to buy a decent bed, and the installation of cheap curtains had made them feel like millionaires.

Young people today, Mike reflected, seemed unfazed by the size of their debts. If they wanted something, they bought it. It was as simple as that. Both his boys had high mortgages. If they wanted a large item, they just re-negotiated their mortgage. Tom had done this to build his garage, and Geoff did the same in order to install a swimming pool in the backyard at an exorbitant price. So, when the two boys rocked up, Mike expected that they would be more than happy to load up the trailers with heaps of their gear.

Well, Mike was right, but what he had not anticipated was that Tom and Geoff would essentially want the same things. Whereas Rebecca had scorned almost everything in their house, the boys fought tooth and nail over virtually every item. Fortunately, Penny was at dialysis when they arrived and was spared the nastiness. Mike found himself trying to be arbitrator, referee, judge, negotiator and peace-maker all at the same time. He thought he had been quite professional by supplying his two boys with a clipboard and pen on arrival, so they could list the items they wanted, as they wandered through the house. At the end of the afternoon they returned their clipboards with extensive lists, some items crossed out, complete with none-too-complimentary comments attached to them, and both still snarling at each other.

When Tom and Geoff had left, Mike poured himself a large gin and tonic and collapsed into his favourite armchair. He felt disgusted at the way his boys had behaved. Where was the appreciation for what he and Penny were donating? Did they have any idea how much of their savings had gone into purchasing everything brand new in the first place? And what about the emotional attachment that develops towards certain items? Several of their landscapes, for instance, depicted scenes he and Penny had become very attached to over the years from holidaying there. It was hard not to perceive his sons as greedy, insensitive and ungrateful.

Mike was recharging his glass as Penny arrived home. She was always feeling flat and tired after dialysis and slumped down exhausted on the sofa. A gin and tonic might buck her up, but it was not permitted. Feeling guilty, he emptied his half-consumed second glass of gin and tonic down the kitchen sink, and suggested water or tea for Penny. Looking at her sitting quietly on the sofa with so little vitality, depressed him. How much longer did she have to suffer? Would she ever receive a transplant kidney? The organisation, Donate Life, he knew, was doing a wonderful job encouraging Australians to register with them as being willing to donate their organs after death. But despite their efforts, after four long years, Penny was still waiting. Some, he had heard, waited seven years!

Recently, Mike had read that some twenty countries had adopted a new policy with regard to transplants known as "opt-out". This law guaranteed that, after death, the seventy human organs suitable for transplanting automatically became available to those needing transplants, unless the family wished to specifically "opt-out". Australia, and most of the world's nations, however, remained with an "opt-in" policy. Under an "opt-in" policy, individuals had to be pro-active and register to say that they wanted their organs made available when they were deceased. Mike felt certain that Penny would have had a better chance of a new kidney if Australia was to adopt an "opt-out" approach. So strongly did he feel about this matter that he had spoken to his local member of parliament on a couple of occasions.

Fortified by a cup of Earl Grey tea and two chocolate biscuits, Penny felt strong enough to question Mike about the visit from his two boys. She was not surprised to hear about all the disagreements and merely remarked, 'We will still need a few of the items on their lists when we move to Easytimes. You had better ring them up and tell them.'

Next day, Tom and Geoff turned up separately with ropes, spiders and trailers and ferried their pickings back to their respective homes under the watchful eye of Penny. She wanted to be sure that nothing disappeared that would be needed at Easytimes. She was pleased the twins had turned up at different times so no more arguments erupted.

Now, it was time to prepare for their move to Easytimes.

CHAPTER 8

Robert Tinson, sales manager at Easytimes, was peering at his computer as he slowly scrolled through the list of clients he had seen over the last few months. The summary statement indicated he had interviewed no less than 176 prospective purchasers and this had translated into 36 apartments sold. No one had moved in yet, but all 36 clients had paid their deposits, selected their apartments from the master plan, and signed contracts. The Board of Directors should be pleased with his progress, he mused, and better still, his job looked safe for another year or two since there were still 214 apartments to sell.

These pleasant thoughts were rudely interrupted by an almighty crash of thunder. The lights flickered and Robert was relieved his computer was equipped with a surge control device to protect it in such circumstances. The heavens opened and the rain tumbled down. April, in Adelaide, is the month when the weather systems usually changed from hot and dry to cool and wet. Most people welcomed the more unpredictable autumn weather.

Glancing at his diary, Robert noticed that his next customers should have arrived ten minutes ago. Having performed his introductory spiel 176 times already, there was no trace of nervousness in his delivery anymore. In fact, he wondered if he wasn't a bit too energetic, too dominating, at times. Perhaps he should pull his horns in a tad and adopt a more considered and mature approach?

His office door suddenly flew open and a hefty woman stood on the doorstep swearing at him.

'Bugger this weather. Turn the bloody tap off will yer.'

Before Robert could say anything, the intruder shook a large umbrella, in and out, several times in quick succession, folded it up and then looked about for somewhere to put it. 'Don't you have one of those bloody umbrella things?'

The woman, and her umbrella, dripped and oozed all over his lino floor, creating a series of little puddles. Springing into action, Robert disappeared under his desk to fish out a metal waste-paper basket that he thought might suffice as a temporary wet umbrella receptacle. Scurrying across the room to place the said item in the corner of the office, he felt his legs slide from under him, and, like a neophyte ice skater, he crashed inelegantly to the floor. Robert was unsure which part of his anatomy hurt most. It seemed to be a close contest between his right elbow, his backside and his left shoulder. His metal waste-paper basket had skidded across the floor offloading a trail of rubbish on its way and smashed into his water-dispenser. When Robert looked up, the large woman, who had caused all his problems, was standing over him with a wicked grin on her face.

'Well, it's a bloody long time since I've had a man throw himself at me like that.' The substantial lady chortled.

Robert began the painful task of checking he was still, more or less, whole. His shoulder hurt most. He must have wrenched it somehow, but then it pained his elbow when he tried to caress the aching shoulder. 'I'm sorry,' he muttered, as he scrambled up into a vertical position.

'Bloody rain held us up. Coming down cats and dogs it is. Couldn't see more than twenty metres ahead. You 'orright?'

Robert walked gingerly back to his desk. 'I'll get the mop,' and he limped painfully out of the office.

When he returned, he was surprised to find no less than three soaked individuals now standing in his doorway in various stages of divesting themselves of sopping umbrellas and items of wet clothing. The puddles on the floor were now in danger of coalescing into a small lake as Robert began his mopping.

'You'll never get all the bloody water up with that thing. Go and get a bucket or something.'

Robert didn't know who this formidable woman was, but he obediently retreated to find the bucket that he should have brought in when he collected the mop. He knew when he was beaten.

It was nearly ten minutes before the floor was wiped up, three umbrellas were happily dripping into his waste-paper basket and Robert had resumed his seat, although not his confidence. Three people now sat on chairs in a row looking expectantly at him.

'I 'ope you run this retirement joint better than you run yer bloody office,' the large lady opined.

'I do apologise. Today is the first really wet day for months. Now, my name is Robert Tinson. Before we start, can I get you a cup of tea or coffee?'

Again, the large lady acted as spokesperson, 'No thanks mate, we're bloody late as it is, and I've got to get 'em both to the quack. So, cut out the bullshit and tell us what yer got.'

Robert glanced at the elderly couple sitting quietly on either side of this formidable spokesperson.

'Now, this must be Mr and Mrs Nettleton?' He smiled meekly.

'Course it bloody is. And I'm their eldest, Jayne.'

Robert wondered how such a silent, demure couple could possibly have produced such a monster of a daughter, twice their size and so aggressive. Were the senior Nettletons to be permitted to say anything?

Before he had a chance to open his mouth again, Jayne announced in her booming voice, 'They're both getting too bloody old and decrepit to live in a big place, so I've told 'em they gotta move to a place like this. They can't do much. Dad's got arthritis and Mum's all stooped over with bloody osteo. Best thing for 'em is to get in 'ere with all the other old cronies. I'm far too busy to look after 'em at my 'ome.'

Robert had heard similar scenarios many times before, although not quite so explicitly. Jayne was clearly not for trifling with, but he was deeply concerned that neither Mr or Mrs Nettleton had yet uttered a word between them. What did *they* really think? Were they being harassed by their bossy daughter to do something they were fundamentally against? Bullying of parents, by offspring, was not uncommon these days, and Robert was fearful that this was what he was witnessing. He was keen to sign-up more customers, but not if they were unwilling.

'Mr Nettleton, are you wanting to move into a retirement village like Easytimes?'

Mr Nettleton was a neat little man, clean-shaven, tidily dressed in a tweed jacket with a hanky protruding from his breast pocket. The hanky matched his tie, thus making him quite a dapper dresser. With a curt nod and the faintest of smiles, Mr Nettleton replied, 'Aye, we be ready.'

Robert recognised a Scottish accent, but he was unsure what part of Scotland Mr Nettleton hailed from. Turning to Mrs Nettleton he asked the same question. Mrs Nettleton was a plumper version of her husband, also neatly clad in tweed, wearing glasses and a modest dab of lipstick. She rubbed her hands together nervously but agreed they were both happy to move.

'There, I told yer. They're both nearly bloody eighty you know,' Jayne added, as if to settle any lingering doubts. 'Should've moved in bloody years ago.'

Robert sensed that his usual leisurely sales pitch that took around half an hour to complete, followed by a ten-minute whiz around the village and another fifteen minutes inspecting a display apartment, was a lost cause. He would have to be more flexible this time, especially as Jayne was already gathering herself together, as if to leave.

'It looks as though you are in a hurry to get to your doctor's appointment and we have hardly covered anything yet. Would you be able to come back and see me again when you have a bit more time?'

'No bloody chance of that,' Jayne trumpeted. 'They don't bloody well drive anymore. I 'ave to bring 'em in, and I'm working all week. What do yer think Mum and Dad? Wanna move 'ere?'

Everything was moving far too quickly for Robert. He might be a bit of a gung-ho salesman, but he realised that there were a number of critical matters of a contractual nature that must be fully discussed first, and he would never try to sell an apartment sight unseen. Suddenly, Jayne jumped to her feet and declared, 'Time to go, or we'll miss the bloody doc.'

Robert had a brainwave, 'How about I come and visit you in your home, Mr and Mrs Nettleton? I can chat to you in a leisurely way and explain everything about the village and then bring you back here to have a good look around. What do you think?'

'Bloody good idea,' Jayne retorted.

And so, it was settled, and arrangements were made for Robert to visit the Nettletons on the next Wednesday afternoon.

* * *

It was not far to the Nettleton's place in Old Noarlunga. Robert was on time as he pulled up in their driveway amongst shady deciduous trees just starting to turn to their autumnal colours. He was no expert on deciduous trees, but appreciated that the specimens around him must be very old and much loved. The garden looked in need of a good work over, something the elderly couple were probably no longer able to provide. Three stone steps led up to the front door where Robert pulled on a brass bell cord. He was looking forward to having some quality time with the Nettletons, without the over-bearing presence of their daughter, Jayne.

It was the stooped Mrs Nettleton who quietly opened the door, 'Please come in Mr Tinson.'

'Please call me Robert.'

'Very well. My name is Anne, and my husband is Jock.'

Ten minutes later, Robert was enjoying an afternoon tea of freshly baked scones with lashings of home-made strawberry jam and proper Devonshire cream. Also, on his little side-table was a steaming cup of English breakfast tea. Complete with a well ironed napkin across his knees, he was ready to begin.

Jock's arthritis had prevented him standing up to greet Robert, but now with a devilish twinkle in his eye he declared, 'And there's a wee drop of the good stuff when you've had yer tea.'

Robert was halfway through his sales pitch, when Anne excused herself for a moment, and returned with a rich fruitcake laced with generous amounts of whisky, which she proceeded to dispense. This, thought Robert, was the most enjoyable sales experience he had had for months.

An hour later, after he had answered all their questions, shown them the eight kinds of apartments available, he suggested they might like to accompany him in the car so he could show them around Easytimes.

The Nettletons turned out to be a delightful couple and so different when not in the company of their overbearing daughter. Jayne, it transpired, was their only child, adopted when she was nearly three. The Nettletons were at a loss to know where her colourful language had come from, but were used to it by now, and hardly noticed it anymore, unless she slipped further and started using the "F" word. Jayne, they said, wasn't terribly bright, but her heart was in the right place and she meant well.

Robert drove them around the village and allowed them plenty of time to inspect the display apartment which was fully furnished and made to look as "homely" as possible. They were impressed, and by the end of the afternoon when Robert took them home he felt certain that he had his 37th customers lined up.

As Robert pulled out of the Nettleton's driveway, he reflected on this delightful couple and what he had ascertained; they were quiet and humble, yet they had achieved so much. Jock had been a professional musician, who began his career as a violinist with the BBC Scottish Symphony Orchestra and then spent his working life moving around the world playing with several other renowned orchestras. At the age of sixty, he had accepted a contract as first violinist with the Adelaide Symphony where he stayed until his retirement at the age of seventy. He still had an enviable reputation as a dedicated teacher with many grateful pupils scattered all over the globe. Jock had even tried his hand at composing, and the ABC's Classic Music Station occasionally played a few of his better-known works.

Anne Nettleton was just as impressive. She had met Jock in Edinburgh, where she was completing a PhD in English literature. They had fallen madly in love, and she was quite happy to follow Jock around the world, as he moved from one musical challenge to the next. With her PhD she never had any problems finding work with universities as a tutor or lecturer. Anne had written a couple of books in her field, published widely in international journals, and was a long-time supporter of Amnesty International. Their only disappointment had been their failure to have their own children. Despite all the help and advice from the experts, it just didn't happen, so they had adopted a three-year old orphaned child who had lived next door when they were residing in London.

Robert felt well pleased with his visit. He had also remembered to tell the Nettletons about the next gathering of the group he now referred to as "The Friends of Easytimes" who met at The Cornishman on Tuesdays. He was sure that these regular gatherings of potential "Easytimers" was a positive event for all who attended. Robert hoped the Nettletons would make the effort to put in an appearance and had even offered to drive them there if necessary.

CHAPTER 9

It was a beautiful sun-filled Sunday morning and Arthur had just finished a ten-kilometre run with the Hash Harriers, up one side of the River Torrens, across the footbridge, and back down the other side. He felt good. The slight pain he had been experiencing in his right knee recently had subsided, and he was enjoying the company of his fellow runners. His time had improved too.

The Hash Harriers were a funny lot. Most of the members rocked up on Sundays, ran their hearts out, and then undid most of the good work by retiring to a pub and carousing all afternoon. The die-hards justified their behaviour by arguing they were merely rehydrating after sweating so much. Arthur seldom joined them at the pub as he was not a big drinker. Nevertheless, he envied them, because many of the joggers were married couples, or courting couples, and he knew they would have fun together as a group. Being single, he felt less inclined to participate.

As he climbed on his bike to cycle home, he couldn't help thinking about Rosemary. Two women were clammering for his attention nowadays. His dear wife, who had so sadly left him more than two years ago, and now, increasingly, the beguiling Rosemary. His emotions were confused, and seesawed between feelings of grief for Sophia, and a longing to know Rosemary better. He still experienced pangs of guilt that he had even allowed one minute of his time to be devoted to thinking about Rosemary. And yet, Sophia had urged him not to stay lonely if he ever found the right partner. Could it be that Rosemary and he might become an item? Was it too early, since Sophia's passing, to contemplate such a thing?

As he entered the end of his street, something told him he must act. The thought of coming home to an empty house yet again, and for the rest of the weekend, was just too much. He resolved, there and then, to ring Rosemary and invite her to join him for a coffee at a cafe around 3.00pm. As soon as he had made up his mind, he felt a surge of excitement and anticipation race through him. Sophia surely wouldn't mind, for he was only doing her bidding, in a low-key sort of way. Just inviting someone to join him for a coffee was perfectly harmless. He found Rosemary's number on his mobile and called.

'Hello, Rosemary here.'

'Oh, hi, this is Arthur. I'm feeling a bit lonely and wondered whether you would like to join me for a coffee this 'arvo?' There, he had done it. It felt almost like forty years back in time, when he used to have to summon up all his courage to invite a new girlfriend out for a first date.

'That sounds nice, Arthur. Where were you thinking of going?'

Panic! He hadn't thought of anywhere. How stupid could he be? He had been so consumed with the business of inviting her out, that he hadn't given a thought to where they might meet. There were half a dozen places he frequented from time to time, but he had not considered which ones were quiet enough that you could have a decent conversation, or were reasonably close to where Rosemary lived. His mind was racing. He couldn't even think of the names of the places he usually visited. Rosemary was still waiting for him to reply.

'Arthur, are you still there?'

'Yes, yes, I'm here. Have you got a favourite place near you?'

'Oh yes, there's a place in the main street called, "The Copper Kettle". It serves all sorts of naughty stuff like eclairs, tiramisu, death by chocolate and the coffees are to die for.'

'Great, please give me the details and I'll meet you there about three.'

Arthur headed for the shower, but took his time to lather up and wash thoroughly. A thorough shave and a generous application of after-shave completed his ablutions. He dressed casually, had a snatch of lunch, checked all his emails and was in the car by half past two, ready, for what his GPS informed him, would be a half-hour trip.

* * *

Cruising down the main street, Arthur had no problem spotting The Copper Kettle. You couldn't miss it because, true to its name, it displayed a monstrous copper kettle that stuck out about two metres above the shoppers' heads. It might look like copper, but if it was the real thing, he was sure it would have been knocked off as soon as the cafe had opened. Parking was a hassle. Eventually he found a park that was a five-minute walk away, so he didn't fetch up at The Copper Kettle until nearly a quarter past. Not a good start!

As he entered, his heart was thumping more energetically than usual. He put it down to nerves. Looking around he recognised Rosemary waving from the back of the cafe. He manoeuvred his way around tables and chairs and reached her with an apology.

'Sorry, I'm late, couldn't find a park nearby.'

'Yes, I should have thought of that, Arthur. This place is barely a ten-minute walk from my home and, selfishly, I didn't think that you would be driving. This cafe is always popular at weekends. So, my turn to apologise.'

Robert was captivated. Was Rosemary really 62, as the sales manager had alleged? She looked stunning, dressed simply in a white blouse and well-fitting jeans. The blouse was open enough to be interesting, but not too revealing. He liked her clear, clipped English accent with its emphasis on the last syllables in words. She was smiling warmly at him and there was laughter in her eyes. Again, he noted her expert use of make-up. It was there, but barely noticeable. No rings, but a pretty green Maori pendant provided a bit of colour. He felt sure that Sophia would approve.

'Have you ordered?'

'No, I was waiting for you.'

'Let's go and see what's on offer.'

They spent five minutes drooling over the wide selection of "naughties" as Rosemary called them, and then resumed their seat armed with the table number 35 sign.

'Just my age,' joked Robert.

Rosemary looked at him carefully, with a Mona Lisa smile playing about her lips. 'Can I try and guess?' she asked playfully.

'If you want.'

'Well, I can tell you are really fit and strong. You have an attractive tan, a good mop of hair, which looks, shall we say, distinguished. You are still working full-time, so, I'm going to guess you are ...' Rosemary hesitated before declaring, cautiously, 'sixty?'

'I'll take that,' laughed Robert.

'Come on, tell me Robert. I want to know. How old are you really?' She put her hand softly on his arm.

'Okay, I'll tell you, if you promise to tell me yours?'

'Deal.'

'I turned 65 last month.'

'Well, you are very well preserved, Robert.'

'And you, how old are you, Rosemary?'

'A very young 62, but still a sad one.'

Their flirtatious exchange was interrupted by a young man appearing with their orders.

They spent at least an hour together and only parted company when the cafe closed. Their conversation had roamed across their respective backgrounds, life experiences and the pros and cons of moving into Easytimes. They found each other's company exciting and easy, with plenty of laughter along the way. As they left the cafe, they both knew, instinctively, that this was indeed a first date and there would be more to come.

* * *

As Rosemary strolled home, she felt a warmth and feeling of contentment she had not experienced since before the tragic and sudden death of her husband. The dreadful emptiness had lifted just a little, and at long last, life seemed almost worth living again. Everything appeared slightly brighter, sounds and colours more intense, the clouds in her mind starting to disperse; even time itself appeared to be passing quicker.

Rosemary realised she had been slightly flirtatious with Arthur, but interestingly, he had reciprocated. Deep down, through all her months of grieving, she had known that she was still capable of having a loving relationship with someone else. Despite feeling so miserable for so long, she had somehow managed to keep herself fit at the gym, and to dress attractively in the hope that someone might one day come along. She knew this was working for her, because she had noticed men looking at her, or wanting to engage in conversation. Then she remembered the two men at the gym, who, at different times, had asked her out but she had declined. Somehow, Arthur was different. She felt at ease with him, for they shared the same tragic loss of a loved one, and were both struggling to emerge from the doldrums. Rosemary knew she wanted to foster this new friendship.

As Rosemary went about her chores that evening, and prepared dinner, she found herself wondering, 'What would Arthur think of this?' This simple question kept popping up uninvited, but she found it necessary to try to answer each time. 'What would Arthur think of her apartment? Would he like the meal she was preparing? Would he approve of her choice of music?' and, 'What would he think of her taste in reading so openly displayed on her bookshelves?'

As Rosemary slipped into her nightdress that evening, the last question to pop up, before she went to sleep was, 'Would Arthur like me in this nightdress?' She slept amazingly well that night.

CHAPTER 10

It was an unusually warm day in early May for the next meet-up at The Cornishman. A blustery wind from the north-east was doing its best to dislodge the last of the autumn leaves and whirl them about the pavements. 'A northerly wind is a sure sign of a cool change,' Mike remarked, as he and Penny entered the little bit of Cornwall. The others were already seated and chatting like old friends. They had pulled two tables together and placed eight chairs around in a rough rectangular shape. Snoddy and Mary sat at one end with Arthur and Rosemary on either side of them.

'Greetings folks,' Mike declared, as he walked around the table to greet each in turn, followed, less demonstrably by Penny.

'What's with the extra two chairs?' he inquired.

'We have two newcomers coming,' announced Mary. 'Robert Tinson rang me yesterday to ask if it was okay for two more people to join us.'

'Do we know anything about them?' asked Arthur.

'Robert said that she is a doctor and he is a muso,' replied Mary, feeling quite important that she was the sole keeper of this information. 'And they are Scottish.'

The usual silly comments came from some around the table. 'Aye, better get them bagpipes out of the cupboard then ...' from Snoddy. Mary, rather daringly, wondered whether at last she would find out what the Scottish men actually wore under their kilts.

Mike was more interested in the Scottish national drink. 'We should be right then for a whisky whenever we want one,' he commented.

Next came a round of speculation about Loch Ness and its famous monster. Snoddy was a believer and did his best to convince the others that he had actually seen the monster when riding his motorbike along the side of the loch many years ago.

'Oh, nonsense Snoddy, you were probably half full of whisky at the time,' Mary retorted.

Snoddy was not to be dismissed so easily, however. 'Mary you weren't even there, and I had a witness.'

'Oh yes, and who was that then?'

'My girlfriend at the time. She was on the back of the bike.'

'I'm surprised there was room for her behind your big backside,' snapped Mary, starting to get wound up.

'I wasn't overweight in those days,' snarled Snoddy, glaring dangerously back at his wife.

Those sitting around the table were starting to feel uncomfortable; this looked like it was heading for a full-blown domestic. The situation was saved, however, when they became aware that they had been joined by an elderly couple, who were standing quietly behind the two empty seats. As always, Mike was first to react.

'G'day. You must be the folk from Scotland?' All eyes swivelled towards the newcomers and Snoddy and Mary's blood pressures started to slowly subside.

'Grab a seat and we'll introduce ourselves,' continued Mike, and he went around the group giving names and marital pairings only.

'Aye, it's good to meet you all,' ventured Jock, as he introduced his wife, Anne, and then himself.

Orders were placed and normal chatter resumed. There was considerable speculation as to exactly when the first apartments at Easytimes would be ready for occupancy. The consensus was that it would be sometime next month. Snoddy and Mary had definitely sold their home, Mike and Penny's place was "under contract" and both Rosemary and Arthur's places were now on the market. The likely occupants of at least four of the first ten apartments to become available at Easytimes were most likely sitting around this table together, already enjoying each other's company. Jock and Anne Nettleton were yet to select their real estate agent and whether they wanted it or not, for the next ten minutes received the combined wisdom of all present about the pros and cons of various agents. It probably left them more confused than before.

Rosemary and Arthur, the only singles present, had remained relatively quiet. As the conversations ebbed and flowed around them, they made occasional eye contact. It was only a couple of days since they had met up for a coffee at The Copper Kettle and memories of that occasion were still sweet. Arthur had decided to invite Rosemary out for dinner, somewhere romantic, where they could talk and learn more about each other over a pleasant meal with a bottle of wine.

The friendly chatter was suddenly and abruptly interrupted by a combination of gasps and groans. Everyone looked about to discover the sounds of agonising pain were coming from Snoddy, who was doubled-up, his hands across his chest and struggling for breath.

'Good God, he's having a heart attack,' Mary called out, as she jumped up from her chair and put her arms around her husband. 'Help him someone.'

Mary's plea for help received a sadly inadequate response. Apparently, nobody sitting around their table had any medical qualifications as a medical doctor, nurse, or even a paramedic. Snoddy was going red in the face, groaning pitifully and slowly slipping off his chair to the floor. With a thud he landed on the ground as everyone clambered to their feet aghast at the scene playing out in front of them. Mike yelled out, 'Is there a doctor or a nurse in here, please?' whilst several around the table fumbled desperately to find their mobiles and call an ambulance.

With the aid of willing hands, Snoddy was laid out on the floor and the chairs around him moved away to allow him some fresh air. Snoddy began jabbering incoherently, his head rolling from side to side, as he continued to struggle for air. Spittle started to froth from his mouth.

It was almost five minutes before the ambulance arrived. Nobody else in the cafe had come forward offering any medical assistance, so all they could do collectively was comfort Snoddy with fatuous comments such as, 'You'll be okay, Snoddy,' 'Don't worry, mate,' 'Just take it easy,' and, 'Keep calm.'

There was a bewildered, confused look in Snoddy's eyes as the paramedics stabilised him, wheeled him out of the building and placed him in the waiting ambulance. Mary travelled with him to the hospital. Penny and Mike, close friends over many years, split up. Penny drove their own car home while Mike took Mary and Snoddy's car to Flinders Medical Centre where Snoddy had already been rushed into emergency.

The remainder of the group, in a subdued mood, broke up and went their various ways. Arthur felt it was an inappropriate time to ask Rosemary to come on a romantic dinner date after the drama they had just witnessed. As they parted company, he told Rosemary he might give her a ring in a few days' time.

* * *

A few days later, Snoddy was discharged from hospital. Mary had endured a time of high stress, what with worrying over her husband's health, and lurking in the background feelings of guilt that she may have unintentionally contributed to Snoddy's heart attack by arguing with him so passionately, in public, about whether he had seen a Loch Ness monster

weight and the sex life you and your wife should be enjoying may well return. Okay, I've been tough on you both, but sometimes I need to be cruel to be kind. I want to see you both again in four weeks. How about 4.00pm on the 15th next month?'

Snoddy remained silent, in a shell-shocked heap, while Mary fumbled in her handbag for her tattered old diary, and was able to confirm that the time and date were suitable.

The delicate subject of sex, however, was to remain strictly taboo for the Snodgrasses for quite some time to come.

* * *

Anne and Jock Nettleton were disappointed about how things had worked out when they travelled to The Cornishman to meet future colleagues from Easytimes Retirement Village. The horrible scene with the obese man, Snoddy, collapsing shortly after they had been introduced had meant they had not had a chance to speak to anyone. They had gleaned no more information about Easytimes, which was a major reason for their visit.

That afternoon, the postal service delivered them an interesting letter from Robert Tinson. The letter was an invitation to all the couples and singles who had expressed an interest in moving to Easytimes and had paid their deposits. The letter went on to explain that it was advantageous for all future occupants of a retirement village to form a Residents' Committee. The purpose of such a committee was to represent the interests of all the residents in any discussions with management. It was, the letter explained, a legal requirement that this committee be formed prior to the opening of the village. Initially, there needed to be nine members, one of whom would need to be elected as the chair. A meeting to further outline the role of a Residents' Committee, and to elect the inaugural members, was to be held next Wednesday at the nearby bowling club. Afternoon tea would be provided. Future residents were urged to attend and an RSVP date had been included. Residents prepared to nominate to be on the inaugural committee would be asked to do so at the meeting and each would have an opportunity to speak in support of their nomination.

Jock had just poured out a Chivas Regal for Anne and himself when the front door flew open.

'Hi Mum, Hi Dad.'

The elderly couple exchanged glances. They had been looking forward to a quiet night at home, watching a couple of their favourite DVDs of "Yes Minister". It was not unusual, however for Jayne to come bowling in, totally unannounced, usually on her way home from work. Much as they loved their adopted daughter, there were times when they needed their peace and quiet. Jayne also had a nasty habit of deciding to stay for tea, which meant that Anne had to prepare extra food and try to "up the quality" of the meal.

Jayne bounced in, throwing her coat over the back of a chair, 'Longing to hear how your morning tea went at The Cornishman?'

'Sit down Jayne. Can I get you a whiskey?'

'You know I don't touch that bloody awful stuff, Dad. If you've got a decent beer, I'll knock it back.'

Jock knew his daughter enjoyed a bottle of Hahn and always kept a couple in the fridge for these sudden appearances. He felt his knees objecting strongly as he rose, painfully, and toddled off slowly to the kitchen, and returned a moment later with the beer but without a glass. Jayne ripped the cap off and took a big gulp, as if she needed it before being able to say anymore.

'The Tasmanians sure make a decent bloody beer,' she enthused. 'So, was it worth going?'

Jock creaked slowly back to his chair before answering. 'Yes and no,' and then went on to recall the incident with Snoddy and the chaotic and abrupt ending to the morning tea gathering.

'Cor blimey, that would have put a bloody dampener on things,' Jayne remarked.

Anne then chimed in and told Jane about the letter they had just received from the sales manager.

'Good God, they don't waste any bloody time, do they? Got any more coldies in the fridge, Dad?'

Jock was relieved to be saved another painful trip out to the kitchen, because Jayne, impatient as always, jumped up and went hunting for another Hahn herself.

Anne did the motherly thing when Jayne returned, and reminded her daughter that two drinks was quite sufficient when she was driving. She then went on to tell her daughter that the letter they had received from Easytimes was calling for nominations for the Residents' Committee.

'You'd better get onto that, Mum,' urged Jayne, as she swigged back another mouthful.

'Why dear?'

'To stop the bloody men taking all the positions. You know what they're like. You gotta have women on that committee, Mum.'

'Yes, I suppose so. I hadn't thought of it that way.'

'Put your bloody form in Mum and keep the bastards honest.'

At times, Anne worried about her daughter, in her fifties now and still single. There had been a couple of men in Jayne's life many years ago, but the relationships didn't last. Although Jayne had never disclosed it, Jock and Anne were nearly certain she was now a lesbian. She knocked about with a couple of other single women, and on a couple of occasions, had told her parents she had been out with them "on the piss". Jayne was a rough diamond.

'Got to go folks. Beth and I are off to a dykes' party tonight. Be good. Thanks for the beer, Dad.'

Jayne belched, none too discreetly, grabbed her coat, and departed with a bang of the front door.

CHAPTER 11

Mike and Penny were out looking at furniture for their new unit at Easytimes. Mike had spent an hour at the unit they were going to move into and had taken the dimensions they needed. They had been around all the large furniture outlets and had finally come to the conclusion that they would be better off to get rid of all their current furnishings and start completely afresh. This meant looking now for a specialist tradesman who could design and custom build whatever they wanted.

Penny was exhausted. Her energy levels were way down and she looked grey and gaunt. Mike felt so sorry for her. There was little he could do except shoulder more and more of the daily tasks of housework, shopping and gardening. The move to Easytimes would be a big help with only a small place to care for and Penny's dialysis centre virtually next door. Despite not feeling well, Penny bravely continued attending the medical check-ups that were required regularly, in order to remain on the nephrologist's active list of suitable kidney transplant recipients. She rarely complained.

They found a small cafe, proudly boasting the best coffees in Adelaide. Within a few minutes, they were safely ensconced in the corner with hot chocolates and a large piece of black forest cake and ice-cream for Mike. Penny's appetite had been gradually declining for years, another symptom of end stage kidney disease. Although it was warm in the cafe, Penny kept her coat on, for she felt cold much of the time, another typical symptom. Pulling her coat tightly around her, she passed her small pink meringue across to her husband, who scoffed it immediately with a grateful grin.

Diving into his back pocket, Mike yanked out an envelope from which he removed a letter.

'This letter came yesterday from the management at Easytimes. It's an invitation to nominate for a position on the Residents' Committee. I think I might nominate. What do you think?'

Penny asked him to read the letter to her, which he did, between slurps of his chocolate.

'No harm in it Mike. I'm sorry, but I don't think I'm up to taking on anything extra these days.'

'No problem, love. I can keep you posted on anything interesting that comes up on the Residents' Committee.'

'You have to be elected first, Mike. Don't count your chickens ...'

Mike laughed. They left shortly after, and Penny organised herself to spend the next four or five hours at dialysis.

* * *

Arthur had about five hundred metres more to run to finish the ten-kilometre circuit he completed almost every other day before breakfast. It was a pleasant way to finish, as the track wound its way through eucalypts and ended almost at his back door. He was on time for a quick shower and breakfast before leaving for work. The sun was struggling to rise above the horizon and there was a freshness in the air following last night's showers. Running recharged his batteries.

Suddenly, he felt his ankle turn and snap and he found himself rolling uncontrollably on the ground. He managed to break the impact of his fall to some extent with his hands and left shoulder as he slid to a stop on gravel.

'Oh shit! Augh, augh ...' He grabbed his right ankle, realising immediately he had done some serious damage. He stayed sitting on the ground, moaning with pain, wondering how he would get himself home. The palms of his hands were grazed and his left shoulder hurt, but it was his ankle that was screaming for attention. There was nobody about, so he would have to get up and do his best to struggle home under his own steam. In future he would take the advice of his running colleagues and carry his mobile with him. Slowly, and very gingerly, he got up and stood on his good leg. His right ankle was throbbing and when he tried to weight-bear on it, pain shot up the outside of his leg. Something was definitely torn or broken. He had managed to struggle a few paces, with intense pain, when there was a yell from behind, 'Wait on mate, I'll give you a hand.'

In a moment, a burly young man drew level with Arthur and asked him where he was headed.

'My back door. It's just around the corner. If you can give me the loan of a shoulder, I think I can hop all the way.'

'No problem, mate. Anybody at your place who can help you? You probably need to get to emergency and have it scanned.' Arthur chose not to answer.

They made their way slowly along the track, with Arthur trying not to reveal the amount of pain he was suffering. His rescuer insisted on delivering him safely into his house and sat him down while he found Arthur's mobile. With a cheerful 'Look after yourself,' the young man was gone, closing the back door behind him.

Arthur knew he needed to get to emergency. He couldn't remember if he had ambulance cover, so he scrapped that idea as a means of transport. All his friends would be at work, or travelling there by now. A taxi perhaps? It would be much better though if he could find someone to stay with him while he went through triage and waited for medical attention. Could he possibly ring Rosemary and ask her to take him? Did he know her well enough to ask such a favour? Was he pushing his luck too far? Would she still be in bed at seven-thirty?

He reached for his mobile, went to "contacts" and clicked her number.

'Hello, Rosemary here.' Despite the pain throbbing and pulsing through his leg, it was a joy to hear her voice.

'Hi Rosemary, it's Arthur here. I hope I haven't rung you too early?'

'No, it's fine Arthur. You just caught me. I'm off to my gym in a moment.'

Arthur hesitated. He had hoped she was just sitting about at home, doing nothing in particular, but now he felt awkward asking her to sacrifice her gym session just for him.

'Arthur, are you still there?'

'Yes, yes, I am.'

Something in the way Arthur responded, made Rosemary wonder if there was something wrong. She had always been perceptive; something her late husband had marvelled at.

'Is everything okay, Arthur? Aren't you usually going to work by now?'

'Yes, usually, but I have a bit of a problem.' All sorts of possible "problems" flashed through Rosemary's mind. She waited for him to elaborate, but he seemed reluctant to explain further.

'Is there anything I can do to help?'

'Possibly, but I feel embarrassed to ask you, especially if this is your time to workout at the gym.'

'Well, if you tell me what the problem is, it might help,' she replied with a hint of impatience creeping in.

'I've hurt my ankle, quite badly, and need to go to emergency. I can't drive. Could you possibly take me up to emergency at the Flinders Medical Centre, please?'

'Oh Arthur, I'm so sorry. Of course, I can. Give me your address and I'll come around straight away.'

Fifteen minutes later Arthur's doorbell rang. Using an umbrella as a walking stick, he hobbled to the door. He had put on a tracksuit, removed his shoe from his swollen ankle, and grabbed a couple of apples, in anticipation of a long wait at the hospital. Opening the door, he was relieved to see the somewhat concerned face of Rosemary looking up at him. She was still clad in her gym gear, black tights and joggers with a loose jumper. Again, he was struck by what an attractive woman she was, quite exceptional for someone in her early sixties.

When Rosemary discovered Arthur drove a Toyota Prius, she politely, but firmly, refused to drive it, and offered to take him in her more conventional car instead. En route to the hospital, Arthur detailed what had happened that morning and thanked her sincerely for coming to his aid. On arrival at the Emergency Department she dropped him off at the entrance while she drove off to park. Rosemary promised to come back and sit with him while he waited to be seen.

Arthur couldn't remember when he had last had to go to emergency, however the routine seemed much the same. He hobbled, with his trusty umbrella, over to the bespectacled lady, sitting behind what looked like a bulletproof glass, to register. He was able to answer the barrage of questions she fired at him with her practised professionalism and then was finally told to take a seat. With a sigh of relief, he slumped down onto a vacant chair with a spare seat next to it that he hoped Rosemary might occupy, for a short time, at least.

Rosemary arrived a couple of minutes later bearing two coffees and a sausage roll each. Arthur had missed breakfast entirely because he had been too busy ringing his boss and several clients cancelling the day's arrangements. These refreshments were most welcome.

The next three hours were bittersweet. Arthur was putting up with a lot of pain and the wait seemed interminable. Every time he thought he might be at the top of the queue of patients to be seen he was trumped by another more urgent case. Twice he had suggested to Rosemary that she should leave him, but she had insisted on staying, so she could drive him back home. In truth, Rosemary relished this opportunity to get to know Arthur a little better, and taking him home might also give her the chance to look his bachelor's pad over. She could tell a lot about a man by inspecting his digs. Arthur, of course, thoroughly enjoyed having Rosemary for company and savoured her attentiveness.

Finally, near midday, Arthur was called. 'Mr Stokes ...' Rosemary realised with a shock that this was the first time she had heard Arthur's family name. For a fleeting moment she wondered whether she would like to be called Mrs Rosemary Stokes, but just as quickly dismissed such a premature thought. She trailed along behind the hobbling Arthur.

A young doctor soon pulled back the curtain and introduced himself. There was a moment of embarrassment when he addressed Rosemary as Mrs Stokes. Rosemary corrected him.

It transpired after x-rays that a small chip of bone had been torn off the ankle bone and the treatment was a galumphing moon boot to be worn for six weeks. Strong painkillers were prescribed to be taken until the injury settled down. The doctor recommended Arthur stay away from work for a week and use crutches to get about. He could start to weight-bear gently at the end of the week. Arthur returned to the waiting room to get measured up for his crutches and have a crash course on how to use them. Meanwhile, Rosemary sought out the cafeteria run by the volunteers to buy some lunch.

It was mid-afternoon when Rosemary finally parked her car as close as possible to Arthur's front door. A natural athlete, Arthur had already got the hang of using crutches. She offered to come in to help with anything he needed doing, but he politely declined. Arthur assured her that he could manage everything. Rosemary was quietly disappointed, as she had been so looking forward to checking Arthur's place out.

'Rosemary, you have been wonderfully kind today. I'd like to invite you out for dinner as a way of saying thank you. How about next Saturday? I'll book us a table, but I will have to ask you to pick me up please.'

'Arthur, it's been a pleasure to help you and a chance to get to know each other better. I'd love to go out to dinner with you. Just give me a ring to confirm things.'

Arthur was sorely tempted to give her a kiss, just a quick peck on the cheek, but something told him not to be too hasty. Instead, he thanked her again, and waved one of his crutches in the air as she drove off.

His ankle was starting to ache again. The painkillers must be wearing off. But who cares, he thought, a sore ankle was a small price to pay, if it helped him to start a lasting relationship with the gorgeous Rosemary.

CHAPTER 12

The much anticipated dinner date had to be cancelled. Rosemary came down with a twenty-four-hour gastric bug on the Saturday morning. They agreed to postpone the outing until the following Saturday.

Arthur, meanwhile, had made good progress. The swelling had all but disappeared, there was little pain and he had started to gingerly weight-bear. A work colleague volunteered to collect him for work each morning and brought him home in the evenings. He still carried his crutches about, just in case, but hoped to ditch them completely before he met up with Rosemary come next Saturday.

No meet-up at The Cornishman was planned for this week because the inaugural meeting of residents moving into Easytimes was to take place at 2pm on Wednesday. Sales manager, Robert Tinson, emailed everyone two days before, to remind them of the importance of attending and attached an agenda. The meeting was to be held in the Lime Room at the Bowling Club, only half a kilometre away from the entrance to Easytimes.

Robert Tinson had been at the Bowling Club since midday making sure that everything was in order. This was an important meeting for him too. It was his job to chair the event and ensure that the Easytimes Residents' Committee was properly instigated. The occasion had added significance for Robert because his boss would be present. Robert felt that so far, he was in the boss's good books, as sales had been going well. He had also heard that interviews were to be held shortly to appoint the on-site manager for Easytimes. This would be a permanent, full-time position, whereas his current position, as sales manager, would finish once he had successfully sold most of the 250 units. In a way, he felt he was doing himself out of a job. The more effective he was as a sales manager, the quicker his current position would be terminated. Today, however, was a chance for him to demonstrate to his boss just how well he could run a meeting of the residents, and show he possessed the organisational skills to make an excellent on-site manager. It was important to excel.

Robert was expecting around forty residents to turn up. Just in case even more arrived, he had put out fifty chairs in tidy rows with a table out the front with three chairs. One of these chairs was for the boss, the second for the secretary he had employed to record the proceedings, and the third one, in the middle, was his. Three trestle tables, with paper tablecloths, were arranged along one side of the room on which two urns were quietly coming to the boil. Fifty china cups and saucers were in place, and he had double- checked that an assortment of teas and coffees were available. Eight neat plates of finger-food goodies were scattered across the other two tables along with a pile of paper plates. The secretary had been entrusted to select these goodies and prepare them all. Finally, Robert had double-checked that the projector was working, so he could present the powerpoint presentation that the boss had supplied. Last night he had practised his presentation several times and had even managed to incorporate a couple of jokes he felt would go down well with the oldies. He was all set, nervous, but ready for action.

Some elderly folk get stressed about the possibility of coming late to functions and are prone to arriving at least half an hour early. They like to get the best seats, where they can see well, and have their hearing aids properly adjusted in readiness. Others come early because they enjoy a good natter. Robert had anticipated both groups of early-birds, and had the urn bubbling away ready for use, and himself at the door to welcome everyone personally. He had even checked through his list of residents to try and recall faces and names. All in all, he felt well prepared.

Robert stayed at his "meet and greet" post, whilst generously distributing smiles and handshakes, and laughing with perhaps rather too much gusto, at comments he assumed were meant to be humorous, until his boss hurried in just a few minutes before the allotted starting time.

Robert had never really warmed to his boss. Mr Crocombe had built no less than eight retirement villages in and around Adelaide. Easytimes, he had assured Robert, would be his last village, but hopefully the best. Well over six-foot tall, Mr

Crocombe had, what you might call, "presence". He loomed over most people from his superior height, and when he spoke to you, fixed his piercing eyes on yours, until you were inclined to look away. Robert always felt that Mr Crocombe's penetrating stare was a kind of controlling behaviour, because very few people felt disposed to stare back. Today, Mr Crocombe looked more impressive than ever, in his pin-striped suit, bright red tie, with matching fob pocket, gold cufflinks and impeccably smart, shiny, black shoes.

'Good afternoon, Robert.' The acknowledgement was accompanied by a curt nod.

'Welcome, Mr Crocombe.'

'Expecting many?'

'Around forty I hope, Mr Crocombe.'

'I want to make a few opening remarks, please.'

'Of course. May I show you to your seat? We are almost ready to start.'

"Yes, let's get the show under way.'

Robert escorted Mr Crocombe to his chair, and used the microphone to ask everyone to please be seated.

The shapely young secretary, Robert had engaged from the Secretarial Agency, appeared from nowhere, and he introduced her to Mr Crocombe. She smiled sweetly at the big man, who seemed to take an unnecessarily long time to shake her hand and make her welcome.

'Ladies and Gentlemen, may I have your attention please?'

There was a high-pitched whistling sound as a grey-haired gentleman in the front row fumbled with his hearing aid. 'Ah, that's better,' he announced to all and sundry.

'I think you all know who I am. My name is Robert Tinson, and I'm the sales manager here at Easytimes. Looking around this audience, I believe I have met almost all of you, and some of you, several times. Welcome to this very historic occasion, the inaugural meeting of the future residents of Easytimes Retirement Village.' A ripple of applause ensued, and a few "yahoos" from a couple of the men present.

'There are two other people with me here; Ms Scarlett, who is an expert minute-taker, and the General Manager, and owner of the company responsible for establishing Easytimes for you, Mr Crocombe. Mr Crocombe, and his company, as you may well know, have completed no less than eight retirement villages already. With all this experience, I think you can be sure they have got the formula right.' Mr Crocombe would like to address you. Please welcome him in the usual way.'

Robert's opening remarks and introduction were warmly applauded, and Mr Crocombe rose and moved to the microphone.

Mr Crocombe spoke, for several minutes, about how, twenty years ago, he had had a vision; a vision to provide high quality retirement accommodation to thousands of ageing South Australians (a few of the more cynical men were overheard later during afternoon tea, agreeing that Mr Crocombe had indeed had a vision; a vision to become a multi-millionaire!). Mr Crocombe went on to tell his audience how he had travelled the world looking at international design models, before coming up with his own unique style.

'My arse ... he was having a round-the-world holiday with his missus on the money he had already fleeced from his tenants,' the chief cynic was heard to say at the back of the room as he stuffed another piece of fruitcake in his mouth.

Having delivered his soliloquy, Mr Crocombe smiled broadly, apologised profusely that he was unable to stay for afternoon tea, as he was flying to Brisbane, and wished everyone a long and rewarding stay at Easytimes. With a special extra smile for Ms Scarlett, he left the room to a half-hearted round of applause. Little chats broke out around the room until Robert called everyone to order.

'Ladies and gentlemen ...'

Robert began his talk by explaining why a Residents' Committee was so important, what its function would be, and that, at least in the interim, it could adopt the constitution of the last retirement village to have been completed. His short talk seemed to have gone over well, although Robert was most disappointed the boss had not stayed to hear how successful it had been. The powerpoint presentation worked without a hitch, and he had even managed to master using the laser pointer.

'Now, ladies and gentlemen, you may like to ask some questions before we move on to the election of the committee members? If you have a question, please stand and give us your name.'

Now, with any sizeable group of retirees you must expect a healthy smattering of cynics, but a less attractive character is the "smart-arse". There always seem to be one or two of them in any large group. The Easytimes residents were not to be spared. The "smart-arse" is usually male, pompous, egotistical and loves the sound of their own voice. Whenever they attend a public meeting, they are possessed by a sudden urge to be seen and noticed. Question times, they find, are simply irresistible. They are driven by some inner force to always ask a question. Whether or not the question is relevant, doesn't seem to worry the "smart-arse". Strangely, they seem impervious to criticism and carry on regardless.

A tall, thin man jumped to his feet. Ruddy-faced, with snowy white hair, he spoke with a Welsh accent.

'Mr Chairman, my name is Pete Johnson. My wife and I intend to move into your village in the next six months.' Pete's wife was looking at the floor with a practised look of resignation. She never knew what her husband was going to say, she just knew that he would always, without exception, ask at least one question and probably more. It was deeply embarrassing. Often, he would want to ask a late question when she knew all around her were picking up their bags and preparing to leave. Pete surprised her this time, though.

'Mr Chairman,' Pete paused for effect, 'In this day of equality between the sexes, should we not be guaranteeing that at least four men and four women are elected onto the nine-man Residents' Committee?'

'Nine-person not nine-man, mate,' a woman shouted from the back somewhere.

Pete turned around to face the voice, 'I'll see you afterwards Tessa.' There were a few sniggers around the room.

'Good question, Pete. There is nothing in the constitution about the gender make-up of the committee, but that would certainly be something to keep in mind if you need to have a vote.'

Another tall, upright man, with a moustache and military bearing rose to his feet. 'Mr Chairman, may I respond to that question please?'

'Yes, of course, Major Rogers.'

The major turned to look at his audience. He was a wiry, handsome fellow with intense blue eyes. Rosemary had visions of him, galloping across deserts, yelling and waving a sword like Lawrence of Arabia.

'The Australian army has for many years enlisted women. And they have made a fine contribution. However, we never appointed or promoted anyone solely because of their gender. It's quality that matters, not your sex.'

Three women and a man immediately jumped to their feet. Robert could sense a full-on argument breaking out and quickly moved to diffuse the situation. Reflecting on the incident later, he was proud how he had handled a potentially sticky situation.

'Ladies and Gentlemen, this is neither the time, nor the place, to debate such matters. I'd like to move to the next item on the agenda, which is the opportunity for each person who has nominated to be on the Residents' Committee to speak for a maximum of two minutes. We have received eleven nominations for nine places, so after everyone has spoken, we will hand out a voting slip and a pencil to everyone, together with the names of the eleven nominees, so you can make your choices.'

First to be called was Mike Fisher. Confident as always, Mike strode up to the microphone and gave a cheery welcome. His talk, together with a couple of jokes, went down well. He argued that his background, a career in real estate, would be valuable for the Residents' Committee, especially during the building phase. Instantly likeable, Mike received warm applause. Mary, sitting in the front row, still had the hots for Mike, and was observed to be giving him rather more generous acclaim than was perhaps appropriate.

Next to be called was Arthur, who took a moment or two to clump his way to the mic with his moon boot all too apparent. Rosemary had joked with him before the meeting that he was sure to win the sympathy votes. Arthur's talk was carefully prepared and well delivered. A career in social work had immediate appeal for many in the audience, and there were plenty of nodding heads when he had finished.

Third up, was the man from Wales who had already asked a question, Pete Johnson. True to form, Pete's talk was all about him and his exploits. As a bridge engineer, he tried to convince his audience that he had had a hand in the erection, or maintenance, of all of the state's main bridges. Pete was finally shamed into stopping, after Robert had rung the "two-minute" bell three times, and Pete had managed to squeeze out almost five minutes. His applause was lukewarm.

At last a lady was called to the microphone as the fourth nominee. Claire Bury told her audience that she was a retired infants' schoolteacher and had spent no less than thirty-three years at St Anne's Catholic School. Claire offered to start a Bible study group at Easytimes that would be open to everyone irrespective of their religious affiliations. Claire presented as a genuinely concerned Christian, but Bible study classes had little appeal to the lapsed Catholics and large number of atheists in the audience. Polite applause was Claire's reward.

Number five on the list was Major Rogers, who strode smartly out to the mic and raised it as high as it would go. He began formally, 'Good afternoon, ladies and gentlemen,' and followed this up with a brief expose of his military service. Interesting as it was, to hear about his various overseas postings, most people in the hall could find little from the major's career that would be helpful on a Residents' Committee.

Most in the hall were relieved to see that the sixth candidate was another woman. Mary Snodgrass moved to the mic, blushing and looking distinctly nervous. She was so nervous, in fact, that she forgot to lower the mic which was sitting a few inches up above her head. Once this was rectified, she mumbled through her talk by reading some notes she had scribbled onto a scrap of paper in her shaking hand. Few heard what she had to say but she received a few claps. Mary couldn't get back to the safety of her seat quickly enough.

Number seven had to be called for three times. It was Jock Nettleton, who had hardly heard a word of what anyone else had said all afternoon, because he had forgotten to bring his hearing aid with him. Jock's Scottish accent was sufficiently broad that many could not fully understand what he was talking about. But he came over as a lovely old eccentric, one of those characters that everyone warms to. When he mentioned he was a professional musician and would like to get some music going in the village, he won a lot of support.

The eighth person to be summoned was Rosemary Tattersall. Arthur couldn't keep his eyes off her as she rose and glided with almost stately poise to the front of the room, ignoring the mic. She was beautifully dressed and spoke with a clear "Queen's English" tone. Rosemary had been a model, and an air hostess serving with the British Overseas Airways Corporation (BOAC), the predecessor to British Airways. She received a mixed reaction when she offered to organise fashion shows in the village. Some felt she was "stuck-up" and "snobby", others were full of admiration.

Next on their feet was a lady of more than ample proportions, who bustled out to the mic with a generous smile. This was Betty Wise, chef extraordinaire, who, for many years had managed a bakery and had had a career that always revolved around the delights of gastronomy. 'Vote for me,' she said, 'And you will be well fed at all our functions.' Betty knew she was on a winner. 'Where's your apron?' someone called out.

Betty was followed by an even larger resident, Snoddy. He lumbered, with some difficulty, out the front, and gave a surprisingly humorous description of his time as a public servant and an obedient husband to Mary. Humour, they say, is the best medicine, and Snoddy's talk was well received.

Last of the eleven nominees to speak, was a small grey lady with a severe stoop who announced into the mic, that had to be held for her, that she was Henrietta Ostromoff from the USSR. Most of the audience were aware that the USSR, as a political entity, had ceased to exist after the tearing down of the Berlin wall in 1989. Henrietta's talk was almost impossible to comprehend as she rambled. Many in the audience felt sorry for her, and concluded she probably suffered early stage dementia.

Robert rose to his feet and thanked the eleven speakers and extolled their collective talents. Ms Scarlett then walked around the seated audience handing out pencils and voting slips, at the same time making sure that whenever she bent over a decent cleavage was visible, although the men present were too old and doddery to interest her.

Ten minutes later, the voting slips were collected up again by the cleavage-showing Ms Scarlett, and she and Robert counted the votes. Robert then called the meeting to order.

'Ladies and gentlemen, Ms Scarlett and I have counted, and re-counted the votes for membership of the Easytimes Retirement Village Residents' Committee. I will announce the nine successful nominees, but not necessarily in the order of the number of votes received. The following have been elected:

Claire Bury

Betty Wise

Major Rogers

Jock Nettleton

James Snodgrass

Rosemary Tattersall

Mike Fisher

Arthur Stocks and

Mary Snodgrass

'Thank you to the nominees, and to all of you, for your attendance. The members of the newly formed committee might like to get together straight away to decide when and where to hold their first official meeting. Please enjoy the delicious afternoon tea, very kindly prepared by Ms Scarlett.'

CHAPTER 13

Major Rogers immediately assumed full control. 'All the members of the committee over here, please.' Grudgingly, he had added the word "please" to his command. Having been used to his orders being followed, post-haste, in the army, he still found civilians a troublesome lot. They were reluctant to be led, moved far too slowly and did not accord him the respect to which he was normally accustomed. Nobody called him "sir" anymore which was bad enough, but at times he sensed low level disobedience, something he would never have tolerated when in the service. He felt like putting the more rebellious of the civilians on fatigues.

The eight other members of the committee slowly made their way over to the nine chairs the Major had quickly arranged in a circle next to the bar. They had wanted to sample the tasty finger-foods and pour themselves a tea or a coffee first. Jock's prostate was playing up, and he needed to visit the plumbing every couple of hours. Betty, the foodie, as a matter of professional interest, needed to collect one of everything on offer so she could make her own gastronomic comparisons and evaluations. Rosemary and Arthur linked up around the snack food, and then wandered over together to the Major's circle, holding their cups of coffee. Rosemary whispered, 'Arthur, I have made my first decision as a member of this committee. We can't possibly have this bossy Major Rogers as the chair of the committee. If he gets the job, I'm off.'

'Yep, me too ...'

'Thank you, ladies and gentlemen. Shall we get under way then?' the Major announced; it was a rhetorical question. 'Now, first up, we need to decide who will be the chair of this committee and then select a minute secretary.'

Mike responded quickly. 'Correct Major, but to conduct the election fairly, we need someone who is *not* a member of this committee to officiate.' Major Rogers looked annoyed, but realised Mike was right. The Major had hoped to assume the position of chair, without dissent, and perhaps even without an election being necessary.

'Accordingly, I have asked Robert Tinson to officiate for us,' Mike continued. As if on cue, Robert arrived on the edge of the circle. 'Over to you, Robert.'

Robert cleared his throat and glanced around the nine faces looking at him expectantly. 'I suggest we start with the appointment of the chairperson and then the secretary. So, I call for nominations for the position of Chair of the Residents' Committee.' Two hands went up; Major Rogers and Mike Fisher.

'Very well, we will need a show of hands please. Those who prefer Major Rogers, please raise your hand.'

One hand went up; the Major's.

'Those who prefer Mike Fisher, raise your hand.'

Seven hands were raised. Mike and the Major abstained.

The same procedure was to be adopted for the position of secretary, but nobody wanted the job.

'It has to be one of the ladies,' Major Rogers declared.

'Rubbish! That's a sexist remark!' It was Betty who had responded, and with some difficulty, as she had just deposited a particularly tasty looking strawberry jam tart in her mouth, one of the last morsels still on offer. There were murmurs of agreement from several committee members and the Major looked almost embarrassed.

Robert tried again, 'If nobody is prepared to be minute secretary, may I suggest you just take it in turns?'

'I'll do it,' Claire Bury offered.

Claire immediately became the hero of the group and received a little clap and several pleasant comments. Nobody liked being secretary!

Robert thanked them all and discreetly retired. Betty moved on to the penultimate cake on her plate, a small brandy snap, and Arthur risked a quick wink to Rosemary, who saw it, and coloured slightly. Mike took over, and quickly demonstrated that he was not new to the rigours of running a meeting.

The Major remained grumpy for the rest of the afternoon; clearly, he was unhappy about not getting his own way. However, by the end of an hour, the committee had in place a plan for a grand opening at Easytimes to be held on a Saturday in three months. By this date the first 60 units would be occupied and many other units spoken for. The grand opening would also be an opportunity for the committee members to promote their various skills and encourage other residents to get involved in future village initiatives.

Mike promised to organise a welcome BBQ at the newly completed Village Hall, Betty agreed to delight everyone with a selection of her favourite desserts and Rosemary would invite a dress and clothing company to put on a fashion display. Jock Nettleton agreed to provide live background music during the function, and, much to everyone's surprise, the Major offered to accompany Jock as a baritone. The two men agreed to start rehearsing next week. Arthur was given the job of establishing the village bar, stocking it, and serving the drinks on the day. This was a daunting task for Arthur, who was only an occasional drinker at most, and had absolutely no bar experience. Claire Bury, who thought she had volunteered only to be a minute secretary, now found her role expanded to become a full secretary and overall organiser of the event. Mary promised to help with promotion, while Snoddy was excused any responsibility for the time being, as a result of his recent heart attack.

The members of the Easytimes Residents' Committee wound up their inaugural meeting feeling elated and excited about the future. Even the Major seemed reasonably pleased as he and Jock exchanged musical ideas on their way out.

CHAPTER 14

Mary was driving. Snoddy, making a slow recovery, was not permitted to drive until cleared by the heart specialists. They had gone so far as to warn him that he may never be allowed to take the wheel again. Understandably, Snoddy was feeling grumpy, and was giving vent to his feelings by being an unpleasant passenger. He criticised everything Mary did. 'Apply the brakes earlier', 'You didn't indicate correctly at that roundabout. You should be in the left-hand lane'. Mary regretted now, that she had ever suggested they go for a drive, because they had been getting restless, and on each other's nerves, just mooching about indoors. A change of scene might, she had thought, brighten Snoddy up.

They were well clear of the traffic now and winding their way along a country road in the Adelaide Hills. 'You are hopeless at cornering,' protested Snoddy. Mary had had enough. It was time she taught her husband a lesson. In a fit of anger, she rammed her foot down on the accelerator and headed straight towards the next bend at an ever-increasing speed. As the car accelerated, she knew, with an uncanny sense of satisfaction, there was no hope of avoiding crashing into the guardrail immediately ahead. The speed limit sign they flashed past indicated the corner should be negotiated at a maximum of thirty kilometres an hour. The car's speedometer showed seventy. This was it. Snoddy was screaming and trying to grab the steering wheel. A split second later the car rammed the guardrail at over eighty kilometres an hour. Unable to withstand the force of the impact, the entire section of guardrail crumpled and the car catapulted into the air, where it began an eerie, slow-motion somersault. For several agonising seconds the car remained airborne, rotating slowly, before finally smashing down onto the canopy of a dense plantation of eucalyptus trees hundreds of metres below. There it bounced sickeningly, then fell, then bounced and fell again, as it smashed its way through branches until coming to rest at a weird angle, upside down, only a few metres above the ground.

Terrified and shaking, Mary opened her eyes. Unbelievably, insanely, she was still alive. There was no pain anywhere but her body felt numb. There was no sign of Snoddy. He must have been thrown out. The thick vegetation all around her was still and silent as if in deep shock. Gradually, she realised she was hanging, head down, through the gap where her driver's door had been. As she came to focus better, she saw that she was suspended above a cleared walking trail and there was a man standing on the trail looking up at her. It was Mike Fisher, the man she had secretly longed to have an affair with. As she stared at him, his face changed from surprise to recognition. Bizarrely, he smiled and blew her a kiss. Then she lost consciousness.

A bright light came on and somebody was speaking to her. 'Are you okay, Mary? You were screaming.' It was Snoddy's voice, but it couldn't be, because he was dead. Mary's foggy head slowly began to clear. She discovered she was hanging over the side of her bed with her head almost touching the floor. Somehow the bedclothes were wrapped around her from the waist down and had prevented her falling out of bed completely. The light was on, and a larger-than-life Snoddy was standing at the door in his aircraft pyjamas, looking down at her. Waves of relief washed over Mary as she realised she had experienced a horrific nightmare. 'Yes … sorry Snoddy, it was just a nasty dream. Go back to bed. I'm okay thanks.'

For several years now, Snoddy and Mary had not slept together in the same bed. They both felt a little ashamed about this, but Snoddy's snoring had intensified over the years as his waistline had expanded. There seemed to be a direct correlation between Snoddy's weight and the number of decibels his snoring attained. Since, sadly, there was no sexual activity anymore, separate beds meant both managed to have a reasonably good night's sleep.

Tonight, however, further sleep evaded Mary. Her dream had frightened her badly. Unlike other nightmares, this one was not floating quietly away into the misty world of forgetfulness. It had seemed shockingly real and she kept re-living the experience over and over again. Normally, she could easily dismiss a horrible dream and within a few minutes be blissfully back asleep. But not this time.

As Mary lay on her back, she pondered whether there was something in the notion that dreams could be interpreted, that they really did have meaning and could provide an insight into the future. She had heard that there were psychologists, or were they psychotherapists, who were interested in a person's dreams. When she had attended Sunday School, so many, many years back, she had heard about dreams in the Bible stories. She had vague recollections about a man called Joseph who had dreamt about seven years of plenty followed by seven years of drought and pestilence. Joseph had been able to correctly interpret his dream and consequently advise the Pharaoh to store grain during the good times so as to be ready for the bad times to come.

So, she mused, what did her dream mean? Was she, and Snoddy, to end their lives in a gruesome car accident? Or, and she rather liked this version, was Mike Fisher secretly in love with her? Was that what blowing a kiss had really meant? Perhaps Snoddy was going to die and she would be free to marry Mike? But what about poor Penny and her battles with kidney disease? Where did Penny fit into her dream? As this smorgasbord of ideas floated vaguely around in Mary's mind, she gradually came to the conclusion that they were inherently unhealthy and unhelpful thoughts. It was totally selfish of her to even think of Snoddy being killed, or that Mike would be remotely interested in her. Sleep crept over her eventually, and when she woke a few hours later, the nightmare had, thankfully, passed her by.

Mary checked the time, dressed, and went to the kitchen to prepare some breakfast. Getting breakfast for Snoddy was much easier these days; no more cooking up sausages, fried eggs, bacon and tomato, followed by toast, with lashings of full cream, butter and marmalade. Snoddy's heart attack had scared the wits out of him, and now, reluctantly, he had reformed his eating habits. Into his cereal bowl she deposited a couple of spoonfuls of oat bran, high fibre bran, two Weet-Bix and a generous portion of natural muesli. On top of this she placed cut strawberries and seedless grapes.

'Only one week to go,' announced Snoddy brightly, as he clumped into the kitchen, wearing clothes that were beginning to hang off him like seaweed as his frame shrank.

'Until what, dear?'

'Until we move into Easytimes, of course,' Snoddy beamed.

'Ah yes, dear,' Mary replied, far less enthusiastically.

CHAPTER 15

Dr Anne Nettleton and her husband, Jock, were sitting at the kitchen table each concentrating intensely on bi-coloured plastic boxes sitting in front of them, divided into fourteen equal compartments. It was time for the weekly tablet dispensing ritual that lasted around half an hour. Talking was forbidden, as the elderly couple popped out their tablets from their silver paper wrappers and placed them carefully and methodically into the correct cubicles for AM and PM each day of the week. Jock was the more fumbling of the two. Try as he would, he couldn't help the occasional tablet skidding across the table, or jumping annoyingly onto the floor. Any errant tablet, with a mind of its own, would endure a gentle admonition from Jock, 'Aye, yer wee bugger, come back here.' Anne was defter with her fingers and seldom had such mishaps.

It was almost predictable. Whenever the Nettletons were intensely pre-occupied, the door would fly open to reveal their adopted daughter, Jayne.

'Hi folks!'

This sudden intrusion caused Jock to jump, thereby dropping his container of hypertension tablets on the floor, where they spread out happily all over the carpet and under his feet. Anne dealt with the matter better, but still lost one of her fish-oil tablets which was later discovered on the floor as a small oily patch, having been inadvertently trodden on.

'Jayne, dear, couldn't you give us just a bit of a warning before you come charging in like that?'

'Sorry, Mum. What's the news then?'

'Not much dear. When you get to our age, you are happy there is no news.'

'How did the meeting up at Easytimes go?'

'Well, we both attended and your father has been elected onto the Residents' Committee.'

'Can't keep a good man down, eh Dad?' Jayne landed a playful punch on her father's shoulder, which, much to Jock's consternation, sent his container of blood pressure pills flying across the kitchen table yet again.

'Jayne, please calm down,' admonished Jock, 'We have a visitor coming here in a few minutes.'

'Oh my God, don't tell me the police have finally caught up with you, Dad?'

Jock ignored his daughter's attempt at humour. 'Our visitor's name is Major Rogers. He and I will be rehearsing a few numbers.'

'That's even worse. The bloody Salvos are after all your money, then. Don't let them hard-sell you, Dad. They're always down the pub rattling their bloody cans for more dough.'

'Thanks for your advice Jayne, however, Major Rogers is ex-Australian army. Nothing to do with the Salvos. I'm not sure whether you and the Major will get along, so you might like to make yourself scarce.' This was about as strong a statement as Jock ever made to his feisty daughter, and he hoped it might achieve the desired effect.

'A real live bloody major, wow! Never met one of 'em before. Should be fun to hang around.'

At that precise moment, the doorbell rang. 'I'll get it,' and Jayne bounded off down the short hallway.

'Morning, Major,' she declared in a hearty voice, eyeing him off as if she was assessing the qualities of a prize bull.

The Major was hardly expecting this full-frontal attack, but composed himself hastily, 'I understand this is the home of Jock Nettleton?'

'Aye, aye, sir,' and Jayne snapped to attention with what she thought was a passable salute. Unfortunately, she had used the incorrect arm, a detail the Major noted with some disgust.

Who on earth is this idiot of a woman?

The awkward silence was rescued by Jock, who emerged from behind his daughter's substantial form to greet the Major in a more respectable manner, 'Ah, Major, it's good to see you. Please come in. This in my daughter, Jayne.'

Major Rogers gave the slightest of curt nods to acknowledge the rude woman and declined to shake her extended hand. Removing his trilby hat, he followed Jock into the nether regions of the Nettleton's abode, there to reacquaint himself with Dr Anne Nettleton.

'Well, I'll leave you buggers to it.' Jayne grabbed her bag, and without further ado, departed. She would have liked to have stayed, especially as she was sure the Major would be fun to stir up.

With Jayne safely out of the way, normal life resumed for the Nettletons. Anne produced tea, coffee, cake and biscuits, which she placed on the dining-room table at the opposite end to the weekly tablet routine, that had yet to be finalised. A few of Jock's blood pressure tablets still remained on the loose, scattered about the floor.

Half an hour later, the polite small talk gave way to more serious business. Anne retired to her office to work on a paper she hoped would be accepted for publication in the *Times Literary Supplement* in the United Kingdom. Jock and the Major, moved to the piano in the corner of the room. Although Jock had been a professional violinist all his working life, he had also kept up a high level of skill with the piano. Generally speaking, it was easier to accompany vocalists on a piano.

The two men spent a happy hour pouring through music, and trying to settle on half a dozen songs from the world of opera and popular musicals, that might appeal to the residents of Easytimes for the grand opening. Jock then suggested the Major might actually like to use his vocal cords while he would accompany him on the piano. Much to Jock's relief, the Major did, indeed, have a well-modulated, easy to listen to, voice. Sharing musical experiences is an excellent way to break down barriers, and by the end of their session, the two men felt far more comfortable with each other and arranged a time to rehearse again next week. Jock hoped they had managed to select a time that would not be disrupted by another of Jayne's unannounced blow-ins.

CHAPTER 16

True to his word, Mike was anxious to fill Penny in on what had transpired at the inaugural meeting of the Easytimes Residents' Committee. Penny had returned late from dialysis just after six o'clock, cold and ashen-faced. Mike longed to give her a stiff whisky, or a tot of rum, anything to perk her up and give her a bit of colour. Instead, he sat Penny down in the lounge room, turned up the heater, and gave her a hot chocolate with a more than generous sprinkling of chocolate powder across the top. He waited until Penny seemed to have revived somewhat, before broaching the topic of the Residents' Committee.

'Are you ready to curtsey?'

'Curtsey? What for?'

'To me. I'm the foundation chair of the Easytimes Residents' Committee. I expect a curtsey every time you see me, as a mark of respect.'

Penny responded with a noise that sounded more like

a fart than anything else and laughed. 'That's great Mike. Congratulations, or should I say, commiserations?'

'Congratulations, I hope. I had to beat a certain Major Rogers to get the top job, though.'

'Oh, I've not heard of him before. What's he like?'

'Typical army officer, expects everyone to jump to his every command. I feel a bit sorry for the poor old bugger in a way, because he is so out of synch with civilian life. He upset the women by telling them that one of them had to be the secretary. He still thinks that doing anything secretarial is women's work only. And then, when I beat him for the job as chair, he got really grumpy.'

'So, who else is on your committee, Mr Chairman, and he who must be curtseyed to at all times?'

'Well, you know some of them. The committee is limited to nine people at this stage, but I understand that this can be increased to twelve once the village fills up. There's me and the Major, and then there's Rosemary and Arthur who you met at The Cornishman. I suspect there may be something going on between those two.'

'Yes, I agree. I have a nose for romance and you could tell that there was a bit of chemistry during that last meet-up. Who else is on the committee?'

'And good old Mary and Snoddy are on the committee too, which is great.'

'Oh, I'm so pleased. Snoddy must be feeling stronger.'

'Three others you probably won't know. There's a large, jolly woman called Betty Wise. She's going to be brilliant because she just lives for food. Apparently she ran her own bakery and has worked in the food industry for many years. She's a genuine foodie, and, it seems, is never happier than when she is catering for functions. Then there's an elderly gentleman from Scotland called Jock Nettleton. Seems a lovely guy. He has played in top orchestras around the world as a violinist. So he should be an asset. Lastly, there is a woman called Claire Bury. I'm not too sure about her. She was a schoolie in the Catholic system and strikes me as being awfully religious. At least she volunteered to be the minute secretary for our meetings. So the jury is out on her. On the whole, if they all gel, we could have a great little committee.'

'I'm so pleased for you Mike. I just wish I was feeling better and could do more to help.'

'Roll on that kidney that's out there somewhere for you, Penny. Once you get the transplant, you'll be a new woman.'

* * *

It was Sunday morning, and Claire Bury emerged from under her toasty warm blankets to the sound of the wind tugging angrily at everything in its path. The birch tree, just outside her bedroom window, was groaning and an empty flowerpot, or some other item, could be heard rolling along the ground. Concerned that the item careering about in the wind might be the pot plant containing daffodil bulbs the Ladies Church Aid had given her, Claire hurriedly stuck her feet into her slippers and raced outside, dressed only in her nightie. Yes, the pot was gone. It must have been blown across the lawn over to the fence she shared with her next-door neighbour.

A strong northerly was blowing, usually a sign that another cold, southerly wind-change was imminent. Nobody seemed to be about, so Claire decided to risk running across the lawn to rescue her precious pot, with its yet-to-be-seen daffodil bulbs. The wind swept around her, revealing every contour of her body in a most indelicate way. What would her church friends think if they saw her like this, half-naked, running about in her front yard? A flurry of heavy rain drops fell as she located the pot, as she had predicted, up against the wooden fence. She could see it was broken but she might be able to fix it. Hopefully that lecherous man, Sam, her next-door neighbour, wasn't about. She knelt down to pick up the pot, and a couple of the pieces that had broken off, when, to her horror, she heard Sam's voice.

'Morning Claire, a bit blowy, eh?'

Instinctively, she looked up to find Sam leering down at her from over the fence. By raising her head to look at him, she had afforded him a full and complete eyeful of her generous breasts. Shocked to the core, she grabbed the pot and its bits, and, without a word, turned and ran back clumsily to her front door. Sam giggled delightedly at the sight of Claire's bottom wobbling from side to side as she frantically disappeared around a bush.

Arriving at her front door, and now safely out of sight, Claire plonked the pot down and ran in. What an awful experience! She had always felt uncomfortable about Sam, who, she felt, regarded her as some sort of sexual object. She did her utmost to avoid him. Whenever they met, always unintentionally on her part, Sam made some sort of sleazy, suggestive comment or winked evilly at her. She rarely did any gardening on Sam's side of her house, just in case he popped up over the fence like he had just done. Sam was living on his own, which, Claire felt, made him even more dangerous. Roll on next week, when she could move into Easytimes.

Claire was a virgin. Raised by devout Christian parents, she had been over-protected, and, as the only child, spoilt. During her twenties and thirties, when she was most likely to get married, she had devoted much of her time to looking after her ailing parents. In these younger adult years, she had been plain, but not unattractive. She could count on one hand the men who had ever shown an interest in her. There was one man, however, on the teaching staff where she was working, who had taken her out a few times and she became very fond of him. But one evening, when he had brought her home, and they were sitting in his car, he had started to slip his hand up her dress. Pre-marital sex was, she knew, a sin, so she slapped him hard and left the car. That was the end of that!

Now, in her early sixties, and retired, Claire was lonely. Her whole life revolved around the church. She helped at Sunday School, was an elder for eight members of the congregation, read the lessons once a month and was an untiring worker for the Ladies Church Aid. Her social circle was almost entirely made up of members of her church. Claire had resolved, however, to try to widen her horizons when she went to Easytimes. Hence, her willingness to nominate for the Residents' Committee, which, to her surprise, she was now serving on, as the secretary. Having been a teacher all her working life, she had developed sound organisational skills, and just quietly, was rather looking forward to assisting with the planning for the grand opening in a few weeks.

The other members of the Residents' Committee seemed an interesting bunch, although she doubted whether any of them were church-goers. Naturally shy and reserved, Claire had not had more than a few words with any of them, but hoped she could find some new friends among the 400 or so people who would eventually be taking up residence at Easytimes. Of course, she would shun the men, and particularly any single men.

*　*　*

Betty Wise was thumbing through her recipe book, *Quick and Easy: Japanese Cooking for Everyone*. Friends were coming around for tea tomorrow, who had been on holidays to Japan, so it just had to be something Japanese on the menu. She had narrowed the main course down to either Tori no saka mushi (steamed chicken sake) or Tori no kara age (fried chicken with ginger) when her train of thought was interrupted by the ringtone of her mobile.

'Hello.'

'Oh hi, Mike Fisher here.'

Who the hell is Mike Fisher? I know the name, but I can't place him.

'Is it convenient to have a quick chat?'

'Yes, of course.' Betty didn't know whether to try to sound friendly, as though she had known this Mike Fisher for years, or to be ultra-careful. Perhaps Mike Fisher was some tiresome salesperson, who wanted to flog something, and she might have to terminate him quick time. So, she had used a neutral, cautious tone.

'I've had a bright idea about Easytimes, but want to sound you out first.'

At last a clue. This guy must have been at the Easytimes meeting. Oh crikey, now I remember, he's the bloody President, or whatever they call it.

Mike continued, 'Some of the retirement villages have introduced a Friday Happy Hour for the residents. Do you think this might work at Easytimes?'

Gathering her thoughts together quickly, Betty could guess what was coming next. She was going to be asked to be chief cook and bottle-washer for hundreds of hungry residents every Friday evening for the rest of her life. She kept silent.

'Are you still there, Betty?'

'Yes, I'm here.'

'Well, what do you think?'

'I think it is much too early to set anything up like this. The main hall and kitchen facilities will not be ready for at least another couple of months, so let's wait until then.'

'Okay, so you are not against the idea? You see, you would be just the person to be the chef- extraordinaire.'

Bingo! Betty had seen it coming, and she wasn't about to roll over and accept such a huge responsibility without considerable thought and a good chat to her husband, Gordon, first. Much as she adored cooking; providing meals en masse every week, was a very different proposition.

'Thank you for thinking of me Mike. I'm flattered. Let's talk about the idea again in a couple of months.'

'Okay, sounds good. Thanks for hearing me out. Catch you later.'

'Bye ...'

Betty decided the fried chicken with ginger would be the more delectable dish for tomorrow night's visitors.

* * *

A couple of days later, Betty and her husband, Gordon, were stacking their dishwasher. They had feasted on lamb, eggplant and okra casserole, with a pleasing bottle of McLaren Vale red, followed by a guava and banana fruit salad; authentic flavours of the South Pacific. From years of experience, Betty and Gordon knew that exotic meals, like the one they had just shared, resulted in them both feeling randy. Good food, wine and sex were a heady mix. Gordon's hands were already wandering over his wife's body and they knew not to wait any longer. They prolonged their pleasures by showering together, ensuring that the soap went everywhere. Drying each other down with fluffy new towels was the final tantalising foreplay, before they lovingly ravished each other.

Lying together, naked and fulfilled, Betty raised the matter of their imminent move to Easytimes.

'I had a call from Robert Tinson today, to say we are free to move in as of next Wednesday. We will need to book a removalist.'

'I'll get on to my mate at U-Move and see if he can get us a truck for later next week sometime.'

'Gordon, you have just shown me you are quite a manly fellow in bed still, but moving heavy furniture around at your age is not a good idea. And you have problems with your back. Let's play it safe, and get someone else to do all the heavy work for us?'

'Okay, you might have to host a few more major functions to pay for the move, though. These removalists are bloody expensive you know.'

'That's no problem. I have definite bookings for several weekend functions coming up and I make around $500 each time. I'll pay for it in no time.'

'Alright, I'll get a few quotes tomorrow.'

'Talking about functions, I had a call from Mike Fisher a couple of days ago.'

'Who the hell is he?'

'He's the chair of the Residents' Committee that I was elected onto at Easytimes.'

'Yup, I remember the guy now. Seemed a decent enough bloke.'

'He's as keen as mustard. He's asked me to run Happy Hour on Fridays at Easytimes.'

'That's a bit premature, isn't it? The facilities block isn't even built yet.'

'That's what I said. It's a big ask, and I certainly don't want to take it on while I'm making good money every weekend running functions. I've got two weddings coming up, a diamond wedding anniversary, and I'm catering for a couple of award ceremonies too.'

Gordon snuggled into his wife, starting to feel sleepy.

'Don't worry about doing volunteer work at Easytimes until you run out of catering contracts.'

Betty concurred. This fellow, Mike Fisher, might be a bit too pushy, and she was not for pushing.

CHAPTER 17

Arthur was scheduled to have his moon boot removed on Thursday, next week. It couldn't happen quickly enough. Not being able to drive was hugely frustrating and he felt himself starting to go flabby through lack of exercise. Friends and colleagues had rallied around to help with getting to work, shopping and any other matters requiring him to travel. Rosemary had been an absolute gem also. They met for dinner regularly now on Saturday evenings with Rosemary picking him up and then dropping him back home afterwards.

Their relationship was deepening, however they were content to let things progress gently and slowly. Both had been in beautiful, long-term and loving relationships before and forming a new relationship now, too quickly, would seem disrespectful to their previous partners. Make haste slowly, was the maxim. They had now reached the point where they could reminisce about their previous spouses honestly and openly. At first it had been difficult, and at times they were moved to tears. Discussing their earlier partners had become a part of the healing process and it was always done respectfully.

Each Saturday they arranged to visit a restaurant they hadn't been to before. This Saturday, it was to be "Mount Fuji", a Japanese Restaurant. They lingered outside for several minutes, discussing the colourful photographs displaying the wide range of Japanese dishes available within. Rosemary had visited Japan a few times years ago, when working for BOAC, so had a rudimentary appreciation of what to expect. They entered to the delicate sound of Japanese music and were greeted by a young Japanese woman wearing a stunning kimono, who bowed politely, smiled sweetly and inquired whether they had a reservation.

'Yes, please, it is in my name, Rosemary Tattersall.'

'Thank you. Please follow me.'

Gracefully, the waitress led them to a table in the corner with sets of chopsticks for two and a single crimson orchid in the centre. Smiling once more, the young lass pulled out their chairs, welcomed them to the "Mount Fuji", bowed again, and glided away. Across one wall was a giant mural depicting Mount Fuji with its snow-capped summit arising spectacularly from the coastal plain. A bullet train was flashing by. Other walls displayed pictures of famous Japanese temples surrounded by pink blossom trees, Samurai warriors and Geisha girls. The soft lighting, quiet music and décor combined to give the restaurant a delightful ambience.

Visiting a Japanese restaurant prompted Rosemary to talk about her experiences in Tokyo and Osaka many years ago.

'One of the challenges we young air hostesses had,

was staying away from the over-zealous men. It was not uncommon to be propositioned by Japanese men during the flight into Japan. It was a very patriarchal society in those days and the men thought they had every right to seduce us. I have to admit that a few of the girls did weaken, and instead of coming back to the hotel where we were accommodated, they elected to stay out all night. As you can imagine, they were total wrecks next day when we had to fly out.'

'What happened to them?'

'We did our best to cover for them, but if they were bleary eyed, and smelling of sake, the chief steward usually worked it out quick smart. I was a goodie-goodie, so it never happened to me, but they were usually given a strict warning and advised that if it happened again, they would be put on a formal disciplinary charge. That could mean being dismissed from BOAC.'

'Did that ever happen, someone losing their job?'

'Oh yes. One girl, Suzie, couldn't help herself. She was fired. I remember her telling me that she would have had to leave anyway because one of her Japanese suitors had made her pregnant. In those days, you were sent on your way if you ever fell pregnant, or couldn't keep up your glamorous appearance. It was all rather unfair, because the airlines wanted you to look beautiful as part of the promotion of the airline, but if you ever started any kind of a relationship with a passenger, you were out.'

'What about the male stewards? How did they get on?'

'Most of them were gay, I reckon, but they got the boot too, if they misbehaved.'

When the menu arrived, they spent a considerable time discussing what to order. A typical Japanese meal comprises soup, three main dishes, something raw, something fried and something grilled, served with rice and pickles. They decided not to risk miso soup (an acquired taste) and ordered sumashi-jiru, a clear soup. This was followed by rice with mushrooms, tofu with vegetables, teriyaki fish and pork curry. They were both out of practice using chopsticks, which meant that eating occupied longer than usual, and they both managed to decorate the tablecloth around their plates with more than an ample splattering of food. But it was fun, and tasty, and they vowed to return again another Saturday.

Rosemary and Arthur's conversations ranged across many topics; transitioning into Easytimes in the next week or so, Arthur's ankle, Rosemary's fitness routines, the Residents' Committee, the grand opening and their particular roles in that event. Being single, they had downsized already, and were not burdened with masses of furniture that must be either disposed of or stored.

The quiet ambience and subdued lighting, together with the Japanese wine, created a romantic mood that they both sensed. Rosemary positively glowed, and Arthur found himself wondering whether he dared to ask her into his apartment when she drove him home. She looked so attractive and he felt a yearning to touch her. Rosemary had been attracted to Arthur from the very first time she had met him, with his debacle over changing a wheel, but her fondness had continued to grow stronger every time they met. Recently, she had found herself wondering what Arthur was up to during the day or night. He was good looking and fit and they shared so much in common. His birthday was coming up soon and she had all but decided to buy him some clothing. They had been out together quite a few times now, and she pondered what she should do, if Arthur invited her into his apartment tonight. Was it too early still? She had to admit that she longed to be kissed and embraced by Arthur. Perhaps he was not ready though to make any intimate moves yet.

The evening had to end; it was Arthur's turn to pay the bill. He helped her drape her stole over her shoulders and she felt the warmth of his fingers as he did so. They thanked their gracious hosts, and walked into the cool of the evening, with Arthur galumphing along expertly now. They were quiet on the short drive back to Arthur's apartment, still savouring the pleasant time they had shared, but also anxious about what might happen next. The traffic was light and it was around ten o'clock when Rosemary parked the car outside Arthur's place.

'Thanks for another great night out, Rosemary.'

'No problem, any time, Arthur.'

'Your turn to pick next Saturday's night out.'

'Perhaps, somewhere where we can go dancing?'

'I'd love that, but my boot only comes off on Thursday, and I'll still be very weak and awkward.'

'Of course, Arthur, it was selfish of me to think of it.'

'Perhaps we can dance the night away the week after?'

'I'd like that.'

There was an awkward pause. *Is he going to invite me in? Should I accept?*

Should I be bold and ask Rosemary in? Am I being too hasty?
Arthur had his hand on the door handle. He looked longingly
at Rosemary. 'Good night, thanks again for a lovely time.'

'Good night, Arthur.'

Rosemary released the handbrake and moved slowly off.
She felt a deep sense of disappointment. She might not have
accepted an invitation from Arthur but he had not even
asked! Arthur was not happy either. Was he being stupidly
cautious? He had so wanted to invite Rosemary to come in
and have a coffee and perhaps a port. Was he gutless? He
went to bed angry and frustrated.

CHAPTER 18

Transition week arrived towards the end of August and the first thirty units were expected to be occupied by week's end. The weather, however, was not cooperating. The Bureau of Meteorology's seven day forecast mentioned rain all week with maximum temperatures struggling to reach fifteen degrees. A series of embedded cold fronts were passing over Adelaide making it cold, wet and windy. Inclement weather is the last thing you want when moving house.

Nevertheless, Robert Tinson was particularly excited about the coming week. It was his job to welcome everybody, hand over the keys to the apartments and the lanyards, with security entry cards attached, needed to open the gates to the village. Management had been magnanimous and donated a bottle of Clare Valley wine to the first thirty residents. Robert had these gifts lined up on a table, together with personalised welcoming cards. The main entrance gate was to be left open all week so that the fleet of removalist vans could freely come and go.

But Robert's greatest thrill was that he had just been appointed to be the first full-time manager at Easytimes with January 1st as the starting date. Sales of units had recently topped one hundred, and he had around forty more clients, with whom he was currently dealing and deliberating. An additional thirty units were expected to be available by late September and the handsome Facilities Centre was now almost completed. The finishing touches, and testing of the twenty-metre swimming pool and sauna, were scheduled to be finalised by next week.

Despite the miserable weather, the thirty brand new apartments stood proudly, ready to welcome their first occupants. There was a pleasing variation in architectural styles and the landscaping of the gardens had been carefully and professionally undertaken. Each unit included a lawn (front and back) and around thirty native plants in place. Eight solar panels were attached to every roof and a rainwater tank was discretely placed along the side of each unit. Gleaming new red and yellow topped garbage bins stood at the ready near each clothesline. All was in readiness.

Robert had done his best to limit the number of sales appointments during this week because he anticipated a variety of questions and concerns being raised by the newcomers. 'How do we work this oven? Are the phones connected? How do we secure the windows? Are the fire alarms functioning?' In many cases, he expected he would have to walk over to the unit in question to deal with problems, and actually demonstrate what needed to be done.

It was, indeed, a frenetic week. Construction workers and

tradies were there most of the time trying to get the next thirty units completed by the promised date. The removalist vans came and went constantly. Many of the newcomers had asked younger members of their families to help them get settled in, or had invited friends to come and view their new homes, so there were visitors' cars buzzing about everywhere. Between showers, some of the newcomers ventured out with their dogs to explore possible new walks. Many visited the Facilities Centre to have a sticky-beak at the billiards room, library, kitchen, swimming pool and main hall. The village was alive and Robert loved it.

Moving house inevitably has its downsides. By the end of the week, several backs were sore, knees and arms aching and tempers frayed. Inevitably, a few items had been damaged in transit and the relevant insurance companies could expect to be kept busy. Mud had been walked into units in a few cases with the tiresome rain persisting. Most annoying, were the items of furniture that had been brought over unnecessarily, or, in some cases, the sudden realisation that a piece of furniture had been disposed of that really was needed after all. Notwithstanding all these concerns, by late Friday evening, almost thirty units were occupied and their exhausted occupants looking forward to relaxing over the weekend.

The weekend, of course, was the ideal opportunity to meet the new neighbours. The weather cleared and the sun shone brightly on Easytimes. Impromptu barbecues were set up, and those that could find food, drinks and implements, shared with those who were yet to get themselves organised.

New friendships were launched, although, in a few cases, people met others who they decided not to mix with in future. Barbecues are great levellers, where almost any topic is fair game; much was learnt that first weekend about the near neighbours.

And so, the first folk into Easytimes Retirement Village began to settle in and create their own new lifestyles.

* * *

Mary and Snoddy felt particularly privileged because they had moved into number one at Easytimes. Snoddy, to everyone's amazement, remained on the strict diet his nutritionist had stipulated. He groaned and grumbled incessantly, which irritated Mary no end. She knew he was feeling better because they were back to disagreeing about just about everything. Deciding which items of furniture were to go to Easytimes, and which should be disposed of, had been a nightmare. Snoddy had so far lost twelve kilograms and his clothes were hanging off him like tree-vines. Mary still pined for Mike.

Mike and Penny Fisher had been in the village less than two weeks, when they received a phone call just after midnight from their nephrologist with the thrilling news that, at long last, he had a kidney for Penny from a 59-year-old deceased person. Could they get to the Royal Adelaide Hospital (RAH) by 6.00am tomorrow morning? Understandably, they had virtually no sleep that night, as they had to rise at 4.30am to arrive at the hospital in time. A kidney transplant was major surgery and Penny remained in hospital for the standard five days. The following month, immediately after surgery, was an enormously challenging one. Every day, weekends included, Mike and Penny had to be at the RAH by 7.00am for testing, assessment and adjustments to Penny's medications. During this month, Penny was ingesting around thirty-five tablets a day!

There was no way Mike could carry out his duties as chair of the Residents' Committee whilst Penny was dealing with her transplant issues. The committee met only once in his absence and made one decision; the grand opening would be delayed for at least another three months. Major Rogers had offered to take over as chair but was met by solid resistance from everyone present. A tentative new date was set for late-November, when the weather would be much warmer, and as many as another sixty units would be occupied.

Arthur Stokes had to delay his move into Easytimes by a week. Still working long hours as a social worker, he simply had insufficient time to sort everything out. He had finally dispensed with his moon boot, but it had left him with a seriously weakened set of muscles around the injury and the physiotherapist's exercises were taking longer than he had wished to get him back to a stage where he could exercise properly. Walking was all he could manage at this stage, although he was gradually lengthening his daily walks.

Rosemary was delighted with her new apartment. She had been able to procure a unit in a corner of Easytimes, surrounded by the high stone wall that encircled the village, and giving her a far larger garden than most other units. Being an enthusiastic gardener, she relished the opportunities.

Arthur's slower than expected recovery, meant they had not yet been out dancing and, sadly, she contracted a nasty bout of influenza that meant they had missed two of their Saturday night dinners. Arthur's unit was number 10 and was situated in the street directly behind Rosemary's, but she did not see much of him as he often worked late.

Anne and Jock Nettleton had moved successfully, but the whole business had totally exhausted them. Jock celebrated his 80th birthday on the day they moved and decided he was getting far too old for this sort of caper. Jayne had been coming around constantly and insisting that, this or that, had to be moved to a better position. Well intentioned as she was, she only complicated matters, and Jock finally snapped and told her they needed rest and not to come back till next week. Eventually, he pulled out his violin and played for a couple of hours, which had the effect of calming their nerves.

Major Rogers, and his meek, mild wife, Jillian, occupied number two. Everything was ship-shape and orderly in no time and he was out on the golf course the very next day, leaving his wife to sort out what he referred to as the 'smalls'. By this, he meant where everything went in the cupboards. The Major had supervised where the main furniture was to go, but left it to "the other ranks" to follow-up with the detail. All part of the delegation of duties. He still felt rather peeved that the Residents' Committee had not jumped at the opportunity to make him chair. A surly, ungrateful lot. He would have had the grand opening up and running in no time.

Claire Bury was comfortably settled in, next door to the Nettletons. She liked the elderly couple, but found Jayne far too boisterous and loud for her liking. As a good neighbourly act, Claire had taken around some lemon meringue pie she had been given at church on Sunday that was too much for her to consume on her own. Jayne, though, had been quite rude to her. 'Thanks love, put the pie in the bloody fridge will yer.' Hardly a polite way to appreciate her little act of charity. Sometimes she heard a string of expletives coming from next-door, emanating, no doubt, from the foul-mouthed Jayne. On another evening, Claire thought she heard classical music playing.

Betty and Gordon Wise had deliberately selected the unit closest to the spanking new Facilities Centre. Betty had her eye on the industrial kitchen that had been extremely well fitted out. Not only did it boast Miele ovens, refrigerators and a massive industrial-sized dishwasher, but it had been supplied with excellent quality crockery, cutlery and cooking utensils. Betty now pictured herself there as the first chef to produce Friday's Happy Hour meals. She would set the standard impossibly high. Their unit also reflected Betty's passion for producing culinary delights, because they had paid extra to have their kitchen enlarged. Gordon, as always, was happy to go along with his wife's gastronomic extravagancies. After all, he was the major benefactor of the delectable dishes she produced.

The peaceful, contented lifestyle, being experienced by the new residents at Easytimes Retirement Village, was, however, about to be challenged in a most unexpected way.

CHAPTER 19

Winter gradually made way for Spring. Outside the retirement village, the established suburban gardens had already displayed their annual offerings of snowdrops and daffodils, followed by hyacinths, tulips and now, the later blooming wattles, blue pacifics and native frangipanis were ablaze. New growth was everywhere, encouraged by the warming sun and the longer, halcyon days. Many residents in Easytimes were to be seen out planting in their gardens. It was warm enough to hang washing outside, instead of indoors in driers, or draped about clothes horses.

As usual, the yellow-clad postman, Fred, whizzed around the village on his motorbike, dropping mail into a few letterboxes late in the afternoon. The village planners had seriously debated whether to supply the units with letterboxes, because the volume of hand-delivered mail was dropping rapidly everywhere. So many people now relied on text messaging, mobile phones, emails, social media and the internet for their communications. Fred, on the other hand, was desperately hoping that snail-mail would still need to be delivered for a couple more years yet, to get him through to retirement. He now had ninety retirement units to deliver to, and next month, it was increasing to a hundred and twenty. He felt he was on a winner at the steadily expanding Easytimes Retirement Village.

The roar of Fred's two-stroke motorbike was usually enough to wake up the elderly residents who were enjoying grandma or grandpa afternoon naps. A few minutes later, they would come shuffling out, each with their own letterbox key, in the hope that some long-lost friend or a relative had dropped them a line in the old-fashioned form of a letter. Usually, they were disappointed, but hope always leapt up like a meerkat, every time the postman droned by. This Monday was no exception.

Now, the daily shuffle of the elderly residents out to their letterboxes needed to be timed correctly. If their timing was spot on, they reached the letterbox precisely at the same time as one, two or even three of their close neighbours did, and so, they were guaranteed a short chat about this, that, or the other. A few of the lonelier residents really welcomed this daily opportunity to say "hello" to somebody. There was the usual comforting chatter about only receiving bills in the mail these days, or "nobody loves me anymore", or, they might engage in a deep and meaningful exchange about the day's weather. Residents could be sure that somebody would declare that it was hotter/colder/wetter/drier than usual for this time of year. Agreement having been reached, the neighbours would turn about and shuffle slowly back to the safety of their abodes.

But this day it was different. Everyone in the village, without exception, found a black leaflet in their letterbox and it contained a disturbing message. The wording was frightening ...

This is a message from ISIS
Our women and children in Syria must be returned to
Australia immediately
ISIS calls for the support of everyone in Easytimes
Help us get our families home
Failure to help us will have serious consequences!

The letterboxes for units one to four belonged to the Snodgrasses, Major Rogers and his wife, Jillian, the Nettletons and Claire Bury, an eclectic mix. Fred was heard to pass by shortly after four-thirty, and a moment or two later a representative of each of these four apartments sallied forth, each armed with their small letterbox key. Today, it was an all-female team that assembled at the letterbox, because the Major was playing golf, Jock was working on one of Mozart's violin concerti, and Snoddy was enjoying an extended afternoon nap.

The first of the foursome to discover the black leaflet was Claire, who, on reading the message, crossed herself and offered out loud a brief, spontaneous prayer. The other three ladies looked at her with surprise and sympathy, for, they thought, she must have received some awful news in her mail from someone close. Claire then covered her mouth in shock and passed her black leaflet to Mary, who was standing closest.

'Good God!' exclaimed Mary, forgetting that Claire, with her strong Christian roots, had already just been in touch upstairs. 'How awful!' and Mary passed the leaflet on to Jillian. On reading the ISIS message, Jillian looked as though she might faint and leant on the brick letterboxes for support. Anne Nettleton, seeing the drastic reactions from the other three ladies, wondered for a moment whether she should even bother to look at this sinister leaflet. *It must be graphic pornography of the worst kind*, she surmised. The leaflet fell to the ground and, hesitatingly, Anne picked it up, turned it over and read the short text. 'How disgraceful,' she exclaimed, 'Have we all received one?'

There was a flurry of activity as the three remaining letterboxes were unlocked, and hands dived inside to retrieve whatever lay within. Indeed, they had all received the same leaflet. Anne was the first to think how they might respond to the situation.

'Fred has probably just delivered these. Let's catch him before he leaves the village and ask him where he got them from. There are no postage stamps on the leaflets, so they shouldn't be coming through the mail system, anyway.'

In unison, the four concerned ladies hastened towards the main gates. Being from units one to four, they lived close by and easily had time to take up positions in readiness to forestall the hapless Fred before he departed the village. A few minutes later the postman appeared, travelling faster now that his deliveries were done, and headed their way. The ladies began gesticulating wildly to wave the poor man down. Now, Fred had been a postie for nearly all his working life and had seen a thing or two during that time, but having four elderly dames waving their arms about like windmills and yelling for him to stop made him distinctly nervous. Puzzled and defensive, he pulled up to see all four ladies angrily waving small black leaflets at him. Before he had time to speak, he realised they were upset about these leaflets that they had, presumably, just found in their letterboxes.

Fred glanced at one and was quick to deny any knowledge of the black leaflets. He had never seen them before and was suitably shocked when he read the short message. He assured the agitated ladies that he was the only postie that ever came to the village and he had not missed a single day since the village had opened. He was at a loss to explain how they had landed in their letterboxes. The ladies relented, realised Fred was not the guilty party, apologised, and let him continue on his way.

'If Fred didn't bring these, then who did?' demanded Jillian.

Mary and Anne were both occupied on their phones. Other friends across the village had just discovered they had received the mysterious black leaflets too, and were checking around to see if their friends had also found them. Shortly, it became apparent, that all sixty residents had been included in the sinister leaflet drop.

'So, what now?' inquired Mary.

'Well, somebody, either inside the village, or outside, has left them here,' offered Anne. 'It's a malicious, nasty thing to do.'

'How could this person get in here?' queried Claire.

'Easily done,' responded Jillian. 'My husband reckons the walls are a piece of cake for anyone to climb over if they are half fit. He said he could still get over them himself, if he really wanted to.'

'So much for a secure, gated community then,' Mary added.

'Quite so,' said Anne, 'And there is nothing to stop someone waltzing in through the gates either, whenever one of our cars drives through. The gates stay open for about twenty seconds every time. Half the Australian Army could enter in that time.'

'I think we have to talk to the manager about this and also report it to the police,' Claire suggested.

There was general agreement about both suggestions, but the manager had already left work for the day, so that would have to wait until tomorrow morning.

'I'm on the Residents' Committee,' declared Mary. 'I'll ring around and see if we can have an emergency meeting to discuss what action we should take.'

Her three colleagues felt this was a good move. After all, this was why they had a Residents' Committee; it was there to act on behalf of the residents.

Small clusters of residents had assembled around the letterboxes elsewhere in the village, and were deeply disturbed to find these threatening black leaflets, and did not disperse back to their homes as quickly as normal. Reactions varied from those that laughed it off as a stupid prank, to those who were clearly terrified and wanted to call in the police immediately.

* * *

It is often said that great minds think alike. It might be hyperbole, to describe the minds of the members of the Residents' Committee as "great", but on this occasion they did concur that they must meet as soon as possible. By 6.00pm the nine members had arrived in the small meeting room in the new facilities block. As they walked, or drove to the venue, they reflected on their unexpected heightened responsibilities. In putting their names forward to be on the inaugural Residents' Committee, most had anticipated their duties to be almost entirely socially oriented, and certainly not dealing with an alarming event such as this.

Everyone was present. Mike was looking tired, as the constant daily travelling to the RAH with the recently transplanted Penny, had taken its toll. He was able to open the meeting on time, however, and to report that Penny was doing well, a positive way to begin proceedings. The Major was in a jolly mood, having had a couple too many drinks at the nineteenth hole, after a most successful round of golf. Jillian had had to pick him up as he was over the legal limit. Rosemary and Arthur sat together quietly enjoying each other's presence. Claire was feeling quite important and excited that she was on a committee that was about to determine what action should be taken over such an unexpected incident. Jock was there, pensive as usual, but exuding his warm personality. Snoddy and Mary were bickering over something or other. Last, but by no means least, was Betty Wise, who, true to form, had pulled over a table on which she had draped a tablecloth. Onto the tablecloth she unloaded a plate of hot sausage rolls and small pies, together with sauces, paper napkins and plates.

'Food feeds the brain,' she declared, wiping her hands on the colourful apron still affixed to her ample frame.

'Good evening everybody and welcome to this rather sudden, and somewhat distressing, extraordinary meeting. Thank you for making the effort, and a special thanks to Betty for supplying some eats. Three facts are already clear. First, everybody in the village received one of these leaflets; second, they were not delivered by Fred, our postman. The third fact may have escaped you; but today is the eleventh of September, which, in the US is referred to as 9/11. On this day in 2001, the world changed with the collapse of the Twin Towers and the attack on the White House.'

'Bloody Taliban, or was it Al-Qaida?' interjected the Major.

'In view of the message we have all received, it is my belief, the timing is not just a coincidence. Whoever deposited these leaflets, planned it carefully and, we would have to think, is an ISIS supporter. Let me stop there, and ask for your views please?'

'Makes sense. No doubt, some stupid little radicalised Muslim,' the Major agreed.

'I think we have to be careful about making hasty assumptions,' Arthur ventured. 'There is no disputing the three facts Mike has mentioned, but after that, everything is pretty much guess work. We could spend all evening making assumptions, but it won't get us anywhere. I think we should limit our discussions to what we, as a committee, should do, on behalf of the village residents.'

There was agreement around the group for Arthur's wise comment.

Claire piped up, 'I think we have to do two things; tell the police straight away and tell Robert Tinson in the morning.'

Again, there was consensus. Mike asked for a formal motion which was duly passed without dissent. 'As chair, I'm happy to contact the police as soon as we finish this meeting, but I will be taking Penny to the RAH early in the morning, and can never be sure what time we will return. Perhaps somebody else could go and talk to Robert Tinson in my place, please?'

'I'm happy to do that,' offered Rosemary.

'Thank you, Rosemary. Now, what else can we do, as a committee, that will be helpful for our residents?'

Betty was back on her feet, taking around the plate that still had some tasty morsels. 'I think we should send a note to all sixty units to tell them that we have met, and what we have decided to do.'

Again, there was agreement.

Jock spoke for the first time, 'If you read the message, it is clearly asking us for our help to get these Australian women and children out of the ISIS camps. There is also a threat in the last line. I don't think this is a one-off event. We can expect something more to happen, unless we show support, in some positive way, for these ISIS refugees.'

'Good God man, you're not suggesting we bring these bloody traitors back here to try and murder us all, are you?' the Major protested. Several people started speaking at the same time.

'Hold on, Major, I don't think that is quite what Jock was meaning.' Mike had raised his voice in order to restore order. 'The point Jock is making is that this may not be an isolated incident. If we don't do something to speak up for these people in Syria, we will probably get another leaflet that might be even more objectionable.'

'Surely this whole question is a matter for the Federal Government. There is nothing much we oldies can do,' Snoddy commented.

'This whole refugee thing is a highly divisive issue,' stated Rosemary. 'We won't all agree. For my part, I think the children should come home because they are innocent. They were forced to go to Syria or have been born there. But if we bring the kids back then the mothers have to come too.'

'Some of those mothers are just as radicalised as their bloody men-folk,' asserted the Major. 'What's more, some of the kids are also radicalised. What about that kid holding up a decapitated head, dripping with blood?'

'Okay, that's enough, thank you.' Mike resumed control of the meeting. 'Let's not argue about whether or not to bring the women and children home, let's concentrate instead, on what more we can do, as a committee.'

'Well, I have a suggestion,' said Arthur. 'It's easy to climb our walls or walk in through the gates. How about we ask management to install closed circuit television cameras and then put up signs to warn people to that effect?'

Again, there was agreement for this practical suggestion. Rosemary was asked to put this idea to the manager when she met him, and the committee would write to him, formally, as well.

Jock brought the meeting back to consider the actual

content of the leaflets again. 'Sorry, to bring you back to this, but there is a clear message. Simply, it is, "Help us, or else".' Jock looked around the group for support. 'As a group, we are not addressing the message itself. If we do nothing, we will be targeted again.'

'But how can we respond when we don't even know who is sending the leaflets in the first place?' asked Betty, with another sausage roll poised for demolition.

Nobody could answer Betty's question, but one more line of action did emerge. The feeling around the room was that the perpetrator was, most likely, one or more radicalised Muslim male youths from the local district. Jock was given the task of escorting Mike to visit the Imam at the nearest mosque situated about ten kilometres away. Hopefully, the Imam would know which of his flock was radicalised or heading that way.

Another conundrum remained. Why was Easytimes Retirement Village being targeted? Nowhere else, apparently, had been threatened. There must be some valid reason. Nobody, however, could come up with an acceptable motive. So, the second meeting of the Residents' Committee broke up with the members still concerned, and only feeling partially satisfied, with what they had achieved.

CHAPTER 20

Mike let himself back into his unit just after 7.00pm. Penny was watching the seven o'clock ABC News broadcast and told him that a quiche was awaiting him in the fridge. He gave his wife a kiss and told her he must contact the police before eating, which he proceeded to do.

The sergeant on duty at the Noarlunga Police Station took his call and listened attentively.

'I suggest you collect as many of these leaflets as you can and bring them down to the station tonight. Then, I'll give them to forensics first thing in the morning to check for DNA and fingerprints and anything else. Can you do that? The matter will also probably be reported to ASIO as a potential terrorist threat. You can expect your retirement place to be swarming with special officers over the next few days.'

Mike agreed to the sergeant's request, and promptly phoned Arthur and the Major to help. Arthur was asked to collect from units one to twenty, the Major from twenty-one to forty and Mike would handle forty-one to sixty himself. Next, he grabbed his quiche and shoved it in the microwave. Fifteen minutes later Mike left the unit and set off around his units. He received a variety of responses. No reply from a handful, who must have been away, out for the night, or perhaps, too frightened to open the door after dark. In the end, he collected thirteen leaflets from his twenty units. When he returned to his apartment, the Major and Arthur were already there. Between the three of them, they had gathered forty-five. Interestingly, the occupants of three units had refused to hand their leaflets over, insisting on retaining them as unique souvenirs. By 9.00pm the forty-five threatening leaflets were safely in the hands of the police.

* * *

Next morning, Spring was very much in the air. As Rosemary left her unit around seven, she was greeted by invigoratingly fresh air and the first rays of warm sunshine. A chorus of pigeons, blackbirds and the occasional wattle bird were celebrating the day with considerable relish. Far away in the gum trees a kookaburra was in full voice. Rosemary was dressed in her pink tracksuit and new running shoes. She didn't normally wear a cap, but it was the time of year when the magpies could be aggressive.

Waiting for her was Arthur, also clad in tracksuit and running shoes. Since moving into Easytimes they had teamed up to exercise together at 7.00am most mornings. Arthur did a few warm-up exercises with Rosemary and then let her go off on her own. His ankle was improving slowly, but running was still too much strain on the weakened muscles. So Rosemary ran for half an hour, or thereabouts, while Arthur walked. Somehow, they seemed able to manage their exercise routines so that they always met up briefly at the end. Indeed, Rosemary had been toying with the idea of asking Arthur to come to her unit, and share a cooked breakfast next weekend, when he didn't have to rush off to work.

Arthur's ankle was rather sore on this particular morning, so he cut his walk short and was sitting on one of the substantial brick letterboxes when Rosemary rounded the corner and ran towards him. She had a commendable running action, and looked relaxed and comfortable, as she neared him. He stood up, smiling, and felt a strong urge to take her in his arms, to hold her close and feel her shapely breasts moving up and down against him as she regained her breath. But he didn't. Rosemary pulled up, put her hands on her hips, and flashed him one of her dazzling smiles. 'Same again tomorrow, Arthur?'

'No problem, I'll be here. You might be able to tell me how the manager, Robert Tinson, reacted to the news about the leaflets.'

'Love to. Have a great day at work,' and with that, she disappeared back to her unit.

* * *

Robert Tinson's official starting time was 8.00am but he seldom made it by then. With three kids to get off to school and unpredictable traffic, it was usually closer to 8.15am by the time he checked in. Today was no exception. He had barely made his first cup of coffee for the day, when there was a knock on his door. 'Come in.'

It was Rosemary Tattersall, the best-looking sort in the village. Robert was mid-forties but was not averse to admiring a good-looking woman in her early sixties. He hoped his wife would have such good looks when she reached a similar age. Rosemary, he knew, was also blessed with impeccable manners, an engaging personality, style and was smart.

'Good morning, Rosemary, to what do I owe this honour?'

'Have you a few minutes to spare? Mike Fisher, chair of the Residents' Committee, has asked me to come and speak with you?'

'Yes, of course, grab a pew.'

Rosemary made herself comfortable on one of the two chairs that sat in front of the manager's desk, looked up, and flashed one of her disarming smiles. Over the next five minutes she relayed the happenings of the previous afternoon, when residents had discovered their unwelcome leaflets, the resulting emergency meeting of the Residents' Committee, and, finally, the actions the committee had subsequently taken. Robert heard her out, shaking his head a few times, before speaking.

'You guys have done well as a committee. Thanks for filling me in on the details. I hope nobody is seriously traumatised by what's happened?'

'Well, it's hard to answer that. I suspect that some residents had a disturbed night, worrying about the leaflets, and what may still happen.'

'Yes, indeed. Rosemary, do you have one of these leaflets you can show me please?'

'Yes, I kept mine.' Rosemary unhitched her classy shoulder bag and passed her leaflet across the desk to Robert, who read it a couple of times.

'It's nasty. If news about this gets out, it will make it more difficult for me to sell the remaining units. Hopefully, we can keep it out of the papers and avoid any journos getting wind of it.' No sooner had Robert expressed these concerns, than his phone rang making them both jump.

'May I speak to the manager, please?'

'Speaking.'

'My name is Chief Inspector Guy Brooks. I understand that the residents in your retirement village received unsavoury leaflets in their letter boxes yesterday?'

'Yes, that appears to be the case.'

'What do you mean, "appears to be"?'

'Sorry, Inspector. They all got one.'

'Thank you. For the time being, we are treating this as a terrorist related incident, so it is regarded as a potentially serious crime. However, we don't want to be overly alarmist, so I'm requesting that you do not go to the media about any of this.'

'Suits me Inspector. I'm going to find selling the remainder of the units here more difficult if people think they will be threatened, or in some danger if they live here.'

'Quite so. Keep everything as low key as possible, but be assured we are following this up. In about half an hour, I and a colleague will be coming to your office to interview you, and anyone else, who may be a person of interest. Kindly make the time available. We will be plain-clothed and travelling in an unmarked police car. Any questions?'

'No, no, no questions thank you.'

The call ended. Rosemary, sitting demurely, had heard every word but waited for Robert to speak first.

'Rosemary, can you think of anyone in the village who should be interviewed? Did anyone claim to have seen anything, for example?'

'No, the drop must have been done in the middle of the night when everyone was fast asleep.'

'What about the guy who drops off the newspapers early in the morning? Did he see anyone?'

'I have no idea. The police might want to ask him, though.'

'I need to cancel a couple of my appointments so I can meet up with these police. Rosemary, thank you for telling me everything. Please congratulate the Residents' Committee, when next you meet, for their quick, decisive action.'

'No problem,' smiled Rosemary, getting up to leave, 'I hope the interview is useful. If the police want to take further action of any kind, please let the Residents' Committee know.'

'Certainly,' replied the manager, 'I'll contact Mike, as the chair, if I need to.'

It was closer to three quarters of an hour before the plain-clothed police pulled up outside Robert's office. Robert had washed out a couple of extra mugs and dug up a packet of biscuits in case they were needed.

Three people filed into his office, only one of whom was wearing a police uniform.

'Good morning,' the eldest of the three smiled, and introduced his two colleagues. The young man in the police uniform was immediately despatched to do a circuit of the village wall, inside and out, to see if there were any signs of someone entering the village by climbing over the wall.

'Be back here in an hour,' the older man barked, who, as expected, turned out to be Chief Inspector Guy Brooks. Inspector Brooks and his offsider, a female officer, occupied the two vacant seats. The offers of tea/coffee and biscuits were all politely declined as they got straight down to business.

Robert repeated everything he had gleaned from Rosemary and reinforced his desire to keep this whole affair quiet for fear of losing potential new clients. The police were sympathetic, and confirmed it was in their interest also, to keep a cap on things. The Inspector disclosed that they were going to follow-up three lines of inquiry. First, they wanted to get a list of all the tradespeople who had been working in the village during the last couple of months. Most of these were employed by the one construction company that specialised in erecting retirement villages. Amongst their employees there might be a person, or persons, of interest. Secondly, they planned to send a police person, with an Arabic Muslim background, to speak with the Imam at the nearby mosque, and thirdly, they were going to check out all the printing companies in the district to ascertain where the mysterious leaflets had been produced.

Inspector Brooks saw no value in calling all the residents together at this stage, although they might, he said, call a meeting if, and when, they uncovered the perpetrator, or perpetrators, of this anti-social act. With half an hour still to spare before the young policeman was due back, they took a detailed map of the village that Robert supplied, and went out to get a feel of the lay-out of the place. Robert didn't see the police again as they drove off without coming back into his office.

Around midday he rang Mike Fisher to update him and outline the three lines of inquiry Inspector Brooks was pursuing. Mike had just returned with Penny, for what they hoped was their penultimate early morning visit to the RAH, and was grateful to Robert.

After talking to Penny, the Fishers agreed to hold a BBQ at their place for lunch on Sunday and to invite all the members of the Residents' Committee and their partners. The Fishers would provide the eats, but the visitors must bring their own drinks and a dessert if they wished. Mike and Penny sensed that such an informal event would help to bring the committee together, as an effective working group, and allow new friendships and ideas to blossom.

CHAPTER 21

Penny was feeling stronger every day and could do more than she had been able to do for many months when she assisted with the BBQ arrangements on Sunday. Lifting heavy items or moving furniture about were definitely still on her forbidden list, but at last she felt more motivated to do things and less fatigued. Every day she still swallowed a colourful cocktail of immune-suppressant tablets morning and night numbering thirty-five in total. As things settled down, this number would eventually reduce to about fifteen each day for the rest of her life. Transplants were still relatively uncommon, so she had become famous in the village as "that transplant lady".

It was another glorious day, weather-wise, the forecast was for sunshine, with a northerly zephyr and a maximum of twenty-three degrees. The back of the Fisher's unit was set up with chairs and a trestle table, laid out with all the items required for the BBQ, and three eskys, complete with ice.

Visitors could have a choice of sitting in the sun or shade. Mike and Penny grabbed a few minutes to sit down and survey their backyard before the first of their visitors arrived. A couple of rainbow lorikeets, oblivious to the two humans watching on, splashed vigorously about in the stone bird-bath Mike had recently installed. An occasional cabbage white butterfly fluttered by, and a less-than-welcome European wasp hovered around the lids of the tomato and barbecue sauce bottles, trying to make up its mind which was the tastier.

First to arrive was the elderly couple, Anne and Jock Nettleton. Jock was armed with a bottle of Drummond Whisky, a boutique whisky from the Orkneys, particularly favoured by Jock, because the Drummonds were distant relatives. Anne was petite, with snowy white hair and a weathered face that demanded to be captured by a decent portrait artist. She wore a pair of glasses, precariously balanced on the tip of her nose, seemingly ready to jump ship at any moment. Both Jock and Anne spoke with delightfully quiet, mellow, Scottish accents. 'My apologies for not bringing any desserts dear, but I hope you'll enjoy these instead?' Wrapped in butcher's paper, Penny discovered two handsome frozen kippers that she quickly stored away in her freezer. The Fishers were particularly partial to top of the range, Scottish kippers.

Just as Penny returned, there was a loud knock on the door. Standing there, straight as a dye, was the Major, with Jillian peeping at them from behind her formidable spouse. 'Greetings and salutations,' bellowed the Major and Mike thought he saw the Major click his heels as if coming to attention. Nobody had yet discovered the Major's first name, nor had anybody had the courage to ask, so he remained, "the Major". The Major was to be seen every morning leaving his unit at precisely seven hundred hours with his bulldog obediently at heel. The ladies in the village pitied Jillian, who seemed little more than a female batman to her army officer, and so went out of their way to invite her to anything happening. Jillian, perhaps not surprisingly, remained a quiet and rather timid soul. She had, however, turned up today with a tin of lamingtons, and the Major, with a slab of beer.

Next to turn up was Arthur Stokes, walking almost normally now, and replete with a bottle of wine from *The Seven Hills Winery* in the Clare Valley. Always an unassuming, cheerful fellow, Arthur was well liked by everyone. It was well known by the younger, single ladies in the village, that he was a bachelor and a social worker, which was a bit like a psychologist they thought, and so they had wondered whether they might be able to book a private session with him. Arthur, however, had eyes for only one woman in the village. Now that he was extending his daily exercise routines, he was looking fitter and more handsome than ever.

Close on Arthur's heels were Snoddy and Mary. Mary was all of a flutter when it was Mike that came to the door to welcome them. Snoddy's impotence had showed no signs of easing yet, and they were both beginning to think that the nutritionist had been talking a load of codswallop, when she had tried to convince them that a change in Snoddy's lifestyle was going to radically fire-up events in the bedroom. So, Mary still dreamed of nights of passion with Mike, who she had admired for many long years. To her credit, Mary was not in bad shape for her years, but hardly ravishing. She did impress Mike though, with her offering of a selection of delectable Haigh's chocolates. They also brought a bottle of non-alcoholic apple cider, as Snoddy was banned from drinking any alcohol, and Mary didn't have the heart to differ, although she thought she might sneak a quick drink or two during the afternoon when Snoddy wasn't looking.

Claire Bury arrived, looking very prim and proper, in a tweedy outfit. Claire didn't really approve of make-up, but today she had relaxed a little and there was a thin line of lipstick to be seen. Penny noticed Claire had a pleasant enough figure, but she never flaunted it. It was a pity that Claire had led such a sheltered life, dedicated to teaching her infant pupils and looking no further. Not surprisingly, Claire's drink of choice was a bottle of lemonade, but she had brought along a plate of homemade shortbreads that would be most welcome.

A couple of minutes later Betty and Gordon Wise fronted up, bearing an assortment of goodies. Betty had been busy in her kitchen and had created a generous sized pavlova, topped with strawberries, and accompanied by a container of her homemade strawberry ice-cream. Everything about Betty was larger than life, from her raucous laughter, to her buxom figure, and overly generous nature. Nothing was ever too much for Betty. She just loved to make the world a better place and was never happier than when churning out delicious repasts for friends and family. Gordon led a contented life, extremely well-fed, and frequently summoned to the kitchen as sampler-in-chief. The size of his stomach was testimony to his gastronomic duties.

Last to arrive was Rosemary, armed with a couple of excuses for her lateness. She flashed her film-star smile around the others, already assembled, and deposited another bottle of white wine into one of the eskys, at the same time placing a colourful, and healthy, fruit salad on the table with cream to accompany it. It didn't seem to matter what Rosemary wore. Somehow, she always looked stunning. Today she had an attractive yellow T-shirt, well-fitting slacks and cute earrings to match. She also had a small posy of flowers for her hostess. Seeing Arthur at the BBQ, she headed in his direction, a move that surprised nobody present. Tongues had already begun wagging around the village, that the first wedding of Easytimes residents might be in the offing. As they approached each other, the ladies watched intently for any signs of intimacy, but they were disappointed.

'Folks, may I have your attention for a moment please?' requested Mike, with a glass of wine in one hand and a BBQ fork in the other. 'Penny and I would like to welcome you all and thank you for coming. It's great that we have everyone here. We wanted you to join us for two reasons. First to help us celebrate Penny's successful kidney transplant, which happened over six weeks ago. As you can see, she is looking amazing. Unfortunately, though, she is feeling well enough to argue with me again now.' Laughter all round. 'Thank you also for your various gifts and yummy desserts. It was pleasing that nobody gave us a tin of kidney beans.' More laughter. 'The second reason for asking you here is to foster greater friendship, and hopefully cohesion between us all, as we assume the responsibilities of the foundation Residents' Committee. We have interesting days ahead, and, I believe, we have a first-class committee, and I look forward to working closely with you for the next twelve months. Hopefully, the unpleasant business with the leaflets was a one-off and will die a natural death. So, eat up, drink up, and enjoy each other's company. The snags, onions and steaks are just about ready.'

A ripple of applause circled the group and sporadic conversations broke out. Glasses were filled and pre-lunch nibbles enjoyed. Mike had performed well on the BBQ, and soon the group quietened down, as they tucked into the food on offer. Conscious of the environmental issues, Mike and Penny had provided real plates and cutlery that could go through the dishwasher. An urn was on the boil on a separate table for tea and coffee with proper china mugs. All this did not go unnoticed by the greener members of the group. A large container of Aqium, antibacterial hand sanitiser, sat in a prominent position at the end of the table, with a large sign, that read, "PLEASE USE ME BEFORE YOU TOUCH ANY FOOD". This was an initiative of Penny's, for she knew just how susceptible she was to any infection. Most of the group obliged.

As the warm afternoon progressed and the alcohol flowed freely, the group relaxed into party mode, and became less inhibited. Mary had latched onto her heartthrob, Mike, and they were chatting about when they were both at high school together. Arthur and Rosemary were talking but were being annoyed by the presence of the Major, who was leering rudely at Rosemary's breasts. The remaining ladies were talking tennis, something they all shared an interest in, leaving Gordon and Jock discussing classical music. Jock had not expected to find another kindred spirit in the village, apart from the Major, but it transpired that Gordon had played cello for many years and had reached grade seven. He still playedl with an amateur group at charity concerts.

Somehow, inevitably perhaps, the matter of the threatening leaflets was raised. Within a few minutes the discrete conversations ceased and the partygoers became quiet as they listened in on the main discourse. Fuelled by a few drinks, the discussion was lively. Snoddy, who had not been consuming any alcohol, was speaking.

'Whoever dropped those pamphlets around the village was malicious. They were intended to alarm and frighten the residents, and it sure worked. I reckon we may lose a few residents over this. Old folk who have come here for a bit of peace and quiet won't tolerate it.'

'Oh, nonsense Snoddy. How would you know what residents think? You sit at home all day on your big fat arse and barely ever leave the unit.' Mary was strident in her criticism, as she unashamedly attacked her husband in front of the others.'

'Have you been on the turps, Mary?' challenged Snoddy, 'I thought you promised not to drink alcohol today.'

'With respect, Mary, I think Snoddy may be right. I found the leaflets scary, and if it happens again, I'll think very carefully whether I want to stay here,' Claire added. Heads swivelled to look at her.

'Oh Claire, don't be such a coward. Running away, when something a little bit unpleasant happens, is the last thing you should do. It's tantamount to giving in to the idiot or idiots who did this. They win and you lose.' This comment came from Betty Wise, sitting behind a large portion of her own pavlova, and waving a warning spoon at Claire.

Poor Claire blushed deeply like a chastised child in one of her own infant classes.

Arthur, always a peacemaker, threw in his two pennies' worth. 'Claire, I can fully understand how you feel, and I'm sure there are others like you in the village, but we must never allow this sort of nasty act to control our lives in any way.'

'Here, here,' echoed the Major. 'What I want to know is, what are the authorities doing about all this?'

This was the cue for Rosemary, who reiterated the three actions the police were taking.

'Thanks Rosemary, but it's about bloody time we had some feedback from the police. It happened over a week ago and we've heard sweet nothing,' added Gordon.

'Perhaps, as chair of this committee, you should get onto Robert Tinson first thing tomorrow morning, Mike?' suggested Penny.

There was a chorus of agreement, and Mike consented.

It was clear to everyone present, that they were still haunted by the leaflet drop and its sinister message. Although few were prepared to admit it, there was a sense of unease when they meticulously locked up their units each night.

Around five o'clock, the party started to break up. The last of the drinks were downed, thanks were given and farewells made. Arthur, Rosemary and Claire stayed back to assist with the clean-up and washed up a substantial pile of dishes that would not fit in the dishwasher.

The three visitors left together just as it started to get dark. Rosemary and Arthur escorted Claire safely back to her unit before Rosemary invited Arthur to come to her unit for a light evening meal. They had both enjoyed a few more drinks than usual and were in a light-hearted mood.

'That Major is a real pervert,' Rosemary exclaimed, as she unlocked the front door, 'Did you see what he was doing?'

'I did,' replied Arthur. 'And, in full view of his wife.'

'I tell you Arthur, I was about to slap him one across the face, good and hard.'

'That would have livened up proceedings.'

'I loved my husband to look at me, particularly if I was nude, but that was because we loved each other and respected each other. It's my body, and I decide who looks at it. The Major's behaviour was gross.'

'We were the same. My wife and I relished the beauty of the human form. I guess we were both blessed with bodies that were beautiful and I suppose we revered them in a way.'

'Did you find that nakedness always led to intimacy, Arthur?'

Arthur was unsure how to reply to Rosemary, and quite where this conversation was heading. Of course, nudity often led to sexual activity. Men, he believed, were highly susceptible to the visual. Why else did women wear provocative clothes? This discussion was starting to arouse him. Was Rosemary doing this intentionally? Was this some sort of intellectual sexual stimulation? Deep down, he knew he longed to see Rosemary naked, and, if he did ... his mobile phone rang.

'Blast! I'm on call tonight. I have to take it, sorry.'

The magic moment was lost. It was like a broken spell. Rosemary hesitated, annoyed, waiting for Arthur to take the call and tell her whether he had to go. If she was going to continue in this relationship, she would have to get used to these kinds of intrusions. Things were just beginning to get interesting too.

'Rosemary, I'm so sorry I have to go. One of my clients has tried to commit suicide. I need to get there ASAP.'

'What about your meal?'

'I'll grab something on the way. Thanks for inviting me for tea. I would have loved to continue our conversation.'

'So would I.'

Rosemary walked towards Arthur with a sweet smile of disappointment. Almost instinctively, Arthur grabbed her hands and gave her a quick peck on the cheek.

'See you soon,' and he hurried out.

CHAPTER 22

Next morning, Mike Fisher rang the manager, to arrange a time when they could meet. Robert Tinson had a spare half hour from 11.00 to 11.30am.

Mike outlined the concerns of the Residents' Committee at their unofficial "meeting" yesterday that no more had been heard from the police, or the management of Easytimes, concerning the leaflet drop. It was, he emphasised, important that the residents should feel that some definite action had been taken. Hearing nothing only increased their fears. Mike even mentioned that a few residents were contemplating leaving, if nothing was done. This last point focused Robert's mind brilliantly. He had spent many hard months selling the abundant attributes of this village over its rivals, and would be devastated if residents now started leaving.

Following Mike's call, Robert spent ten minutes of his precious lunch break on the phone to the police, and finally convinced Chief Inspector Brooks, the officer in charge of the case, that he must front-up and speak to the residents. It was agreed that he would present a short update on Wednesday next week at 2.00pm.

Later that afternoon, Robert Tinson rang the General Manager, Mr Crocombe, to appraise him of the extraordinary meeting next week, and ran off 120 invitations to deliver to the residents. 120 units were now almost filled. Many of the new residents had moved in post-leaflet drop, and were so excited about their new abodes, they did not appear particularly concerned about an event they had not personally experienced. Another thirty units were due to be completed by the end of October, and, so far, Robert had not detected a decline in interest. His engagement diary remained full.

Robert's mood of optimism came crashing down, however, the very next day. The local rag had somehow got wind of the leaflet drop, and had gone to town with a story splashed across its front page.

ELDERLY RESIDENTS TERRIFIED BY ISIS PLOT

On Monday, August 16th, the elderly residents at the still to be completed Easytimes Retirement Village discovered a horrifying item in their letterboxes. The previous night, a person, or persons unknown, illegally entered the gated community, and left a black leaflet in everyone's letterbox. The leaflet contained a threatening message, which read:

<u>This is a message from ISIS</u>
Our women and children in Syria must be returned to Australia immediately.

ISIS calls for the support of everyone in Easytimes.

Help us get our families home.

Failure to help us will have serious consequences.

It is believed that many of the residents, who have only recently sold their homes and moved into what is, supposedly, a quiet and peaceful place of retirement, are considering leaving. When completed, Easytimes plans to have 250 units occupied, but it is now understood that the management is considering reducing the number of units in light of this unfortunate event. To quote one of the residents, 'Nobody will want to come and live here, if we are going to be targeted by ISIS.'

The unfortunate matter was reported to the police, at the time, and the police are understood to be carrying out investigations. When this paper contacted the police, they were unable to provide any further details.

We also contacted the Mayor, Angelina Davenport, for comment. She said she was 'disgusted' but surmised that it was 'Just a hoax, conducted by a young person, with a sick sense of humour.'

The residents at Easytimes have elected a Residents' Committee, which is trying to get to the bottom of this mystery.

It is to be hoped that an arrest will be forthcoming soon, allowing the residents at Easytimes to once again enjoy their retirement. After all, for them, it is supposed to be, 'Easytimes'.

This front-page article stirred up a hornet's nest. It is said that newspapers are in decline, that they are 'old technology', and nobody reads them anymore. Maybe so, but this article was read by many locals and quickly reappeared on a number of electronic media outlets. Reactions were varied. For the good folk in Easytimes, most of whom still received a daily paper, it set tongues a-wagging again. There was nothing in the article they didn't know already, however, and they were comforted somewhat by the announcement from the Residents' Committee that there was to be a police report to the residents next week.

Robert Tinson was particularly put out by this adverse publicity. It was now even more likely that the flow of potential new residents would dry up. He looked at his list of interviews for the day and noted that two had already cancelled. The phone rang. It was Mr Crocombe, General Manager and owner of the eight retirement villages, collectively known as "Crocombe Holdings".

'What the hell's going on at Easytimes, Robert?'

'Good Morning, Mr Crocombe. I assume you are referring to the newspaper article that appeared today?'

'I didn't ring you to talk about fluffy bed-socks! Of course, I am. Why wasn't I told about this?'

'I did report the matter to your office, but they must have decided not to worry you about it. I believe you were overseas on holidays at the time?'

'Well, they didn't tell me, and they bloody well should have done. Right, we have to go into damage control. Today, I will contact the paper and warn them that any more tripe like that article and I will be suing them for damages to my business. I will also get my marketing people to counter this negative stuff with a blitz on advertising for all my Crocombe Retirement villages. Is there anything else I should know?'

'Only that Chief Inspector Guy Brooks is in charge of

the case and will be coming to the village at 2.00pm next Wednesday to report to the residents on police progress in identifying who was behind this.'

'Thank you, I'll ring him and get him to pull his finger out. He will need to put more people on the case. I want results, and I want them pronto. If there is anything else that comes up, I want to know immediately. You got that? Ring my private secretary. If any silly young journalist wants to talk to you, get them to contact my marketing manager. Is that clear? On no account are you to speak to them.'

'Certainly, Mr Crocombe.' There was no answer. The General Manager had already moved on.

* * *

By the end of the day, the repercussions from the newspaper article had reverberated around a far larger audience. ABC South Australia and Broken Hill Radio mentioned it in their news bulletins, the local state politician rang Robert, to see if there was anything he could do to help, and Channel Nine wanted to know if they could come out and "do a story". Robert was relieved that he had been instructed to pass everything on to the marketing manager. Channel Nine never turned up.

Friday evening marked an historic "first" at Easytimes. Betty and Gordon Wise had toiled hard most of the day to provide a meal for Friday Night's Happy Hour. Everyone in the village had been invited, and no less than 122 had paid their $15 a head to attend. The bar would be opened and run by volunteers. Other volunteers had been rostered to set up, and lay the tables, to serve the meals, collect the dirty dishes and put them through the industrial-sized dishwasher. Betty and Gordon had enjoyed a lifetime in catering, so this was not a particularly challenging venture for them. They had stuck to a traditional menu they thought would be popular with almost everybody; roast beef and Yorkshire pudding with green peas, roast potato, and buttered baby carrots. Dessert was fruit salad and ice-cream.

There was an exciting feeling of bonhomie as the residents queued up to have their names checked off at the entrance and then found their seats. Tables of twelve could be booked, and Mike and Penny had booked a table for the members of the Residents' Committee, together with their spouses. By six o'clock everybody was seated. Mike and Penny sat near the microphone, as he had asked to say a few words before the meal. Penny was looking quite radiant. Clearly the kidney transplant was starting to improve her lifestyle and she looked far less tired and grey. Opposite them sat their old friends, Snoddy and Mary, arguing with each other as usual, about ridiculously insignificant matters. Mary looked quite charming, although Snoddy probably never even noticed, and if he did, failed to compliment her.

In the centre of the table were the Scottish couple, Jock and Anne Nettleton, sitting opposite Arthur and Rosemary. Jock was sporting a kilt and sporran and Anne complemented him with a matching scarf and skirt. Rosemary was her usual elegant self, beautifully dressed without being overly pretentious. Arthur looked athletic in a brand-new rugby top. Next along the table was the Major, one of only two or three men in the whole room, to wear a tie and jacket, with his unfortunate, downtrodden wife, Jillian, who really didn't look as though she was looking forward to the evening. Finally, perched at the very end of the table, was Claire Bury, wearing a plain and unattractive suit. So, everybody was present, with the exception of the hard-working chefs, Betty and Gordon, still slaving away out in the kitchen.

The Master of Ceremonies for the night was none other than the Welsh "smart-arse", Pete Johnson, who had missed out on being elected onto the Residents' Committee. It didn't take long for everyone in the village to work him out. He was a bore, full of his own importance and totally insensitive to the views of others around him. You could be quite rude to Pete Johnson, and he wouldn't even realise. Tall and gangly, he now strutted up to the microphone, which he yanked upwards to be closer to his mouth. He spoke for a moment or two, gesticulating wildly, before realising he had forgotten to switch the microphone on. Suddenly his voice boomed out across the hall.

'Ladies and gentlemen,' Pete sounded like the ringmaster at a circus, announcing the opening act.

'Ladies and gentlemen, may I have your attention please?' The room slowly came to order, as the diners with hearing aids became aware that someone was addressing them.

'My name is Pete Johnson, and I'm your host for the evening.'

This was greeted by several caustic comments from some of the men at the back of the hall when they realised who it was.

Pete continued, unperturbed. The calls of derision, he wrongly interpreted as being indicators of his popularity.'

'Welcome to the inaudible Happy Hour at Easytimes.'

Several voices yelled out together, 'It's not "inaudible" Pete, we can hear you!' and, 'It's "inaugural", you twit!'

Still undeterred, Pete soldiered on, unaware of his unfortunate malapropism. 'There's lots of yummy food coming up, but before we eat, our first chair of the Residents' Committee, would like to have a word. Please welcome, Mike Fisher.'

There was polite applause around the room, punctuated by a few blokes yelling out positive calls such as, 'Good on yer, mate,' 'Give it to us, Mike' and 'On yer Mike.' Mary, thrilled to see the man she idolised about to speak, let out a generous 'yahoo' much to the surprise of her table colleagues and Snoddy, in particular. Snoddy glared at her and filed the outburst away for a possible altercation with his wife during the main course.

'Great to see so many of you here tonight, on such a very special occasion. I hope you enjoy yourselves and take the opportunity to get to know more about your fellow residents. Many of you have yet to meet the other members of the Residents' Committee, so let me introduce them to you now.'

One by one, the committee members were called upon to stand and acknowledge the applause.

'I don't want to dampen your enthusiasm for the night, but I feel I should say a couple of things about the leaflets that were dropped into our letterboxes recently.' The room hushed further and Mike had everyone's attention. Even the workers in the kitchen stopped to listen.

'As you know, the matter is in the hands of the police, and Chief Inspector Brooks will be coming to this hall at 2.00pm next Wednesday to give us an update. I'm sure you will all want to hear what he has to say. Unfortunately, we have had some negative press. I don't need to tell you how harmful such publicity is for us. If people start thinking that Easytimes is not a good place to retire, then the value of our units will collapse. I'm sure nobody wants to see their life savings going down the drain. So, what can we all do?'

'Shoot the bugger who did it!' came from the side of the hall, somewhere. Mike ignored the interjection and continued.

'I admit it was a very unpleasant experience, and we are quite right to be angry, however, the way we all react to this, is most important. The worst thing anyone here can do is to up and leave their unit. This is not only cowardly but plays into the hands of whoever did this. They will think they are winning.'

'Hear, hear,' came from a few.

'I implore you, therefore, to stand together, support each other, and don't even think of leaving. What you say to your friends, and anyone outside this village, must never be negative. Speak about all the positives of living in this village, the wonderful facilities, the excellent friendships, the many activities we share together. Hopefully this business will blow over soon, and we can all get on with enjoying ourselves. Enough from me; enjoy the meal, enjoy the night.'

Mike's final comments were met with applause.

The first Happy Hour was considered a great success. The meal, even though mass produced, was appreciated by everyone, and Betty and Gordon's efforts were rewarded with a bottle of champagne at the end of the evening. Once the volunteers in the bar got their act together, drinks flowed smoothly, and MC, Pete Johnson, was successfully kept away from the microphone for most of the evening. Nobody enjoyed the corny jokes he tried to inflict on the crowd.

The behaviour around the Residents' Committee table was predictable. Mary spent most of her energy trying to engage Mike in conversation; it seemed ages since she had enjoyed such a lengthy time with the man of her desires. Penny, feeling a bit more herself by now, noticed Mary's unrelenting attention to her husband. At least, it was a change from Mary's incessant bitching with Snoddy. Snoddy, sulked most of the meal, and especially, when his wife ruled out any chance of ice-cream with his fruit salad. Rosemary and Arthur were absorbed in their own discussions much of the evening but spoke to others at the table just enough not to be thought rude. The Major and Jock spent much of the evening sharing musical experiences and planning a concert item for the unsuspecting villagers in the future. Anne, Jillian and Claire made up a threesome at the end of the table, where Anne discovered that the other two ladies were avid readers and she could share some of her past as a Professor of English Literature.

Before the end of the evening, Betty and Gordon escaped from the kitchen and joined the table. Betty never came empty-handed; she plonked down a plate of home-made dark chocolates in the middle of the table for all to enjoy, together with a wicked warning that dark chocolate was an aphrodisiac.

It was not late when all who had participated in the inaugural

Happy Hour returned to their respective units. A few had driven, but the majority were happy to enjoy the pleasant evening and walk. Anne and Jock put on the kettle for a nightcap drink and chatted about what had transpired during the evening. Anne was thinking of starting a Book Club for residents and knew that both Jillian and Claire would probably join. Jock was full of the ideas that he and the Major had been throwing about and was keen to try some kind of an evening concert with the Major and himself as leading acts. They were sure there was other talent in the village who might be persuaded to also perform, if they had sufficient time to rehearse.

The bell rang, not once, not twice, but four times. Anne and Jock looked at each other. 'Probably Jayne?' suggested Jock.

'A bit late, its half past nine. Be careful Jock, just in case.'

'I'll make sure the chain is on before I let anyone in.' Jock assured his wife and padded off slowly to the front door. It was indeed their only daughter, Jayne.

'Hi Dad. Just been out with the girls and was passing by, so I thought I'd drop in and cheer you up.'

'I don't think we need any cheering up, Jayne. We are quite happy, thank you.'

'What, with all this shit flying about?' Jayne strode into the lounge and greeted her mother, 'You must be worried Mum, with all the crap in the papers?'

'Not particularly, dear.'

'Well you should be worried. The value of these units will plummet. Nobody will want to come here. They'll think it's spooked by bloody ISIS cranks.'

'I think you are exaggerating, Jayne,' Jock responded.

'No way. Everyone has been talking about it. My friends are saying it should be renamed bloody "Uneasytimes".'

Both Anne and Jock smiled at the new name. This was typical of their daughter, going off like a cracker over some minor matter. She had always been excitable, and age had not mellowed her as yet.

'Can we get you something to eat or drink, dear?'

'No thanks, Mum. I just popped in to see if you are okay, with all the crappy publicity. How many people have left the bloody village? Do you know?'

'None, as far as we know,' replied Jock, curtly.

'That's not what the papers are saying, Dad.'

'Well, papers cannot always be trusted to get their facts correct. You should know that, Jayne.'

'Got to go folks. Did I tell you; I've got a new lover at home?'

'No dear?'

'Her name's Madeleine and she leaves all the others for bloody dead.'

The elderly couple were not quite sure how to respond to this last titbit of news, chucked to them as a child chucks a crust to the ducks.

'That's nice, dear,' was all Anne could muster.

In a flash Jayne was off again, anxious to get home to her Madeleine.

CHAPTER 23

2.00pm Wednesday couldn't come around fast enough. Every seat was taken ten minutes before the hour, and those that had left their run a little late, were obliged to stand at the back of the hall. Four chairs, a table, a microphone and four glasses of water were in place. The chairs were to be occupied by the General Manager, Mr Crocombe, the manager of Easytimes, Robert Tinson, Mike Fisher and Chief Inspector Guy Brooks as guest speaker. Journalists had been denied entry to the village, a potentially dangerous move, since secrecy only makes journalists more determined than ever to find out what is happening.

Many of the residents were in the hall for the very first time and had spent a few minutes before the meeting looking at the décor and furnishings. The village flagpole had been erected outside the main entrance to the hall and proudly flew a brand-new Australian flag. A small team of residents had been rostered on to be responsible for the raising and lowering of the national flag at sunrise and sunset every day of the week. The Major had been put in charge of this group and had trained them carefully to go through the appropriate procedures correctly.

The general feeling, expressed by the residents, was that the architects had done an excellent job with the hall. It was light and airy, well set up with a retractable screen, ceiling projection, and a top of the range sound system. Amazingly, even the chairs seemed comfortable.

The four men entered right on time, and moved straight to their seats, with the exception of Robert, who positioned himself behind the microphone. Tapping the microphone, to check it was working, he opened the meeting. First, the three men in the spotlight were introduced and then Robert took a few minutes to summarise the situation to date. At this juncture, he called upon the detective to provide his promised update.

Chief Inspector Guy Brooks was a large man (in all directions) and looked impressive and formidable in his full uniform. He took his time to reach the microphone, and once there, reached into his top inside pocket, to retrieve some papers. Placing these on the lectern, he then fumbled in a side pocket to produce a pair of reading glasses. Adjusting the microphone, he cleared his throat and looked out across his audience. Many years ago, at a police training course entitled *Handling the Public*, the participants had been instructed to take their time and scan their audience before speaking. It was all part of showing you were not nervous, and that you were in total control. If the truth be known, Brooks was distinctly nervous, for he had never before been called upon to address such a large crowd.

'Mr Crocombe, ladies and gentlemen. Can you hear me all right at the back?' Not waiting to ascertain what the answer was to his question; he began reading out his prepared speech anyway.

'About ten days ago, I was given the responsibility of investigating the mysterious letter-drop that occurred throughout your village. Today, I have returned to outline what progress has been made.

'We started by examining the leaflets themselves, and searching the walls surrounding your village, to see if we could find the access point of the perpetrator or perpetrators. The leaflets provided no assistance at all, as they had been handled by many people, and so we had multiple fingerprints all over them. We believe we discovered the entry point, however. A set of fresh footprints were located at the back of the village where building is still being carried out. We have made a thorough analysis of these footprints that may come in handy in future. We recommend that the village install video surveillance cameras, as soon as possible, to cover all access points, and that you advertise this fact to the public as a deterrent.

'The leaflets, we presume, were produced on someone's printer either at home or at work. We have checked around all the commercial printers and nobody has any record of such a request. When you think about it, it is hardly the kind of message you would give to a commercial printer.

'I have spoken, personally, with the local Imam in charge of the nearest mosque, located ten kilometres away. I don't think he was particularly pleased to see me, or to hear my story. I took with me a young policewoman who speaks Arabic. Eventually, he did cooperate, and told me that there was a handful of teenage boys in his congregation who he regarded as rebellious and angry. He refused to disclose their names but promised to talk to them individually about the matter. He has not contacted me again.

'As you know, I'm sure it is possible that one, or more, of these lads may have been radicalised and might feel moved to do something like this. So, I have also asked the Imam to provide me with a list of any people in his congregation who still have family stranded in Syria. That list should be emailed to me shortly.

'Finally, I received a list of all the men and women working currently on this village site and during the last three months. Most have been with the same construction company for a few years, and the foreman knows them well, and was happy to vouch for them. There are three young men, doing some of the less skilled jobs, who are on overseas work visas from Tuvalu, PNG and Timor Leste. All three are practising Christians, and so the boss felt they were most unlikely to be wanting to bring family home from Syria.

'So, for the time being, we have drawn a blank. But we will continue working on the case. The crime is still very much "active" so, please rest assured, we are monitoring the situation and are continuing with our inquiries. I'll stop there and invite any questions. If you have a question, please use one of the roving microphones.'

Mr Crocombe jumped to his feet and in his loud, booming voice announced, 'Thank you for your report, Inspector. I'm disappointed, however, that more progress has not been made. I will arrange forthwith, that video cameras be installed to cover all the exterior walls of the village.' This move was met by a ripple of applause.

Robert Tinson had, by now, reached the microphone and reiterated the Chief Inspector's invitation for questions. He was not surprised to see that the lanky, Pete Johnson, was first on his feet, and waving his arms about for the man with the roving microphone to bring it over to him. Audible groans could be heard. Robert marvelled at how quickly reputations were established in such communities.

'Mr Chairman, I have a question I would like answered, please. Is it true that many people who were coming here to live, have already changed their minds?'

'Thank you, Peter. I don't think the Inspector should be expected to have to answer that.'

'True, but *you* can, Mr Chairman,' demanded Pete Johnson.

'It is not strictly true, no. Only three or four couples have declined to join us at this point,' Robert responded. This answer resulted in a low buzz of conversation, until another question was asked, this time by Arthur.

'Chief Inspector, from your experience, do you think this leaflet drop is a one-off event, or do you think that the perpetrator is likely to continue harassing us?'

'That's a good question,' the policeman responded. 'It's always difficult to predict criminal behaviour. I am hopeful, however, that the amount of publicity and police interest in this case will have put the wind up the offender, or offenders, and they will not be stupid enough to re-offend. My prediction is that nothing more will happen, and that everything will quieten down. Hopefully, in twelve months, the matter will be almost totally forgotten.'

A couple more questions followed before Robert Tinson wrapped things up and thanked everyone for their attendance. The villagers, feeling slightly more optimistic, wended their ways home.

CHAPTER 24

A couple of days later, Betty and Gordon Wise were entertaining Mike and Penny at an evening barbecue at the back of their unit. The warm sun was setting, and the evening choruses of blackbirds, eastern spinebills and pigeons were competing with each other as they settled down for the night. A couple of mosquitoes made their presence known, by circling their targets, but cunningly staying just out of reach. Gradually, the colours faded from the small but vibrant garden plants around them. The back lawns were growing well now, and the sprinkler system was set to come on twice a week, for ten minutes, until the end of summer. The residents had been assured that this was sufficient watering, although many would sneak out when they thought nobody was looking and give the grass an extra drink.

The four retirees were enjoying each other's company, sitting around a table laden with culinary delights that had emanated from Betty's kitchen. As always, Betty had excelled, and a platter of several cheeses and biscuit choices, together with a selection of olives and dips, kept everyone happy. The boys were drinking beer, and the ladies were partaking of a glass of wine from McLaren Vale. Not surprisingly, the conversation turned to village gossip.

When a couple of hundred retired folk find themselves enclosed within the walls of a gated village, it is almost impossible to avoid the scuttlebutt flying about the place. The romance between Arthur and Rosemary was top of the list. There was much speculation as to whether they were actually sleeping together yet, and whether everyone would be invited to the nuptials, when it happened. It was hard to imagine a couple better suited to each other. Betty had already declared an interest in making their wedding cake.

Penny surprised the foursome with the news that she had twice observed the mousy Claire Bury, being picked up by a dark man in a green Toyota Yaris and being whisked off somewhere. Penny suspected it was a suitor, but the others laughed her theory down, claiming it was either a church friend, or the minister from her church. Nobody felt any malice towards Claire, it was just that she was so unworldly. She had spent her whole life stuck in schools, observed Mike.

Anne and Jock were already a popular couple in the village. Rumours had spread around the village that Jock had played his violin to both the Queen and the Pope. Others claimed that Jock had been a soloist at one of the famous Promenade Concerts in the Royal Albert Hall some years back. They all agreed he was a valuable asset to the village and that they must do their best to move him off all the classical stuff and get him playing some decent country music and a bit of jazz. Don't waste his talents. Anne, however, was a bit of an unknown still. That she had a PhD in English Literature was well known, but speculation was rife with regard to which particular field she had made her name. Some said it was children's literature, others said it was Scottish poetry, and a small break-away group was convinced her area of expertise was historical romance.

The Snodgrasses were always good for a laugh. Snoddy had, it was agreed, worked hard to lose weight, although he had been known to weaken occasionally and to grab a cream bun on his way out of a room, or steal a mouthful of crisps when he thought he was unobserved. That his girth had reduced was not denied, and he was often to be seen nowadays walking around the block on a regular basis. Snoddy and Mary, when out together, were a scream. They literally disagreed on everything. They would snap and grump at each other all day, as if it was perfectly normal behaviour, much to everyone's dismay until they knew the couple better. It was difficult to see how they had remained married for so long. 'It wouldn't be their sex life,' laughed Gordon, 'With a weight problem like his, he would never be able to get it up!' This comment brought a stern rebuke from Betty.

Next up for discussion on the rumour mill were the Major and his insipid wife, Jillian. It was now known that the Major did actually have names; he was, Major Charles Rogers, ex-British army, later seconded to the Australian forces. Pets were permitted in Easytimes Retirement Village and the Major was the proud owner of a British bulldog. There was nothing noteworthy about the animal, except that it had a bad reputation for leaving its excrement about the village after being walked around by the Major. You could hardly blame the dog, but you could blame the Major, and several residents had already complained to Robert Tinson, who, it seemed, had done nothing about it.

A couple of the Major's neighbours had reported hearing orders being bellowed inside his apartment, and now people were suggesting that poor Jillian was "inspected" at 0700 hours every morning for her dress and the tidiness of the house. Nobody had ever been invited inside the Major's unit, so it was presumed that military standards of order prevailed. A number of residents had tried to get Jillian away to give her a break, however she never confided in anyone about her mysterious life in unit 2. Shy and introverted, little was known about Jillian or how she occupied her day.

Next, the discussion moved to the recent visit of Chief Inspector Guy Brooks. Essentially, this was considered a non-event. The police seemed no closer to ascertaining who the culprit, or culprits, were. Apart from the decision that video surveillance cameras were to be installed along the perimeter wall, not much had eventuated from the senior detective's visit. Three weeks had now elapsed since the leaflet drop and the residents were starting to become hopeful that the whole nasty matter would just float away on the mists of time, and they could all get on with their lives as if nothing had ever happened.

*   *   *

While the BBQ guests at the home of Gordon and Betty

Wise were getting down to the serious business of devouring an eclectic range of cooked treats, a green Toyota Yaris waited patiently at the main entrance for Claire Bury to press the button on her phone that would open the gate. Seated inside was Moses Lobrida, a member of the same church Claire attended every Sunday. Moses, and his family, had arrived as refugees over twenty years ago from Ethiopia. Four years ago, Moses' wife had died suddenly from pneumonia and Moses' two children, having completed their degrees, had recently moved interstate leaving Moses a lonely man. Eventually, Moses had decided that he must take himself another wife. He had paid a good price for his first wife, Martha; in fact, no less than twenty-four head of cattle. He no longer owned cattle here in Australia and realised that matrimonial matters developed very differently. He had looked around the congregation of St Andrews and the only single lady in her low sixties was Claire Bury. She seemed pleasant enough, so he went out of his way to develop a friendship with her, with the notion, in the back of his mind, that if they got along well, he would ask her to marry him.

This was the third time Moses had come to the village to take Claire out, and Claire was wondering what his long-term intentions were. Long ago, she had abandoned the idea she was ever destined for marriage. Around the age of forty, she had accepted that she had been placed "on the shelf" by society, and she had better create a life for herself. Consequently, she had dedicated her life to her teaching career, going way beyond what the average teacher managed, as far as additional duties were concerned. Many hundreds of children had benefited from the quiet, loving environment she had created in her classrooms. But now, retired in her mid-sixties and set in her ways, it had taken her some time to appreciate that Moses might be "courting" her. The man seemed sincere, and she liked him as friendly company. He was black, but that didn't worry her. She knew some people married, or re-married, in their sixties, but did she really want to totally disrupt the comfortable lifestyle she now enjoyed, with just her cat for company?

With a sense of some trepidation, Claire pressed the button on her phone and admitted Moses. A couple of minutes later the bright green Yaris pulled up outside her unit and she quietly left, making sure she locked the front door. Moses, with a big smile, was holding the car door open for her.

'Thank you, Moses. A nice evening?'

'Yes, it is Claire.' Moses folded his large frame into the driver's seat, and they set off.

'Where are we going?'

'Somewhere special, Claire.'

'Oh, where is that then?'

'An Ethiopian restaurant.'

'Really, I didn't know there was one in Adelaide.'

'Oh yes, more than one actually. We are going to the closest one. I have ordered a table for two. We should get there in time.'

Claire, whose only trip overseas had been once to New Zealand, began to dread what was in store, and wondered whether she would cope with the exotic dishes likely to be on offer. More to the point, would her stomach cope with all those hot spices and strange tastes that it had never before experienced? Supposing she was horribly ill on the way home?

'Moses, do you think it's wise to take me to an Ethiopian restaurant when I have never before tasted Ethiopian food?'

'Oh, I think you'll be okay. I won't order anything too way out.' And he laughed. 'It's called *The Abyssinian*. That used to be Ethiopia's name many years ago.'

They lapsed into small talk until Moses pulled up near the restaurant and rushed around again to open the door for Claire. He had not done this door opening business before and Claire wondered why he had suddenly started tonight. Ominous, she thought?

The meal turned out to be much more palatable than she had expected, and she quite enjoyed some of the dishes. Entree was Yemiser Selatta (lentil salad); the main, Yatalkete (fresh vegetables with niter Kebbeh) and dessert, Yemarina Yewotet Dabo (honey bread). Claire even allowed herself a glass of wine, a rare concession for her. Moses had a couple of glasses of wine and assured her he would not drink any more as he was the driver. When they had finished the last of the dishes, Moses opened up.

'Claire, I want to speak to you about something personal.' He was looking directly at her now, and she felt embarrassed, and dropped her eyes to her empty plate. She had an awful feeling he might be about to hold her hands, so she kept them safely clasped on her lap. 'We are both single and lonely. We're not getting any younger. We might live for perhaps another twenty years. I think it would be good for both of us if we had a partner to care for. It would be company, and make life far more enjoyable. If one of us gets ill, the other can help. I don't want us to hurry into anything, but I wonder if you might think of marrying me one day?'

There was a long silence. Claire was gobsmacked, and for a moment, quite incapable of answering sensibly. Nobody had ever proposed to her before, in fact, she had only ever been invited out by one man and that was decades ago. Was Moses serious? Had the wine gone to his head? Did she hear correctly? Marriage was for people who are in love, whatever that meant. She did not "love" this man. He was nice enough, and she found his company pleasant, but marriage …? Moses was still looking at her, questioningly. Claire had a thousand thoughts scrambling about her head all at once.

'Well, Claire, what do you think?'

'Moses, I … I don't know what to think. It's very kind of you … but …marriage? Marriage is a big thing, it's a huge commitment. You hardly know me … I hardly know you, Moses. It's much too early to entertain such an idea.'

'I did say, "one day" Claire. I am quite happy to wait, to see if you like the idea.'

'Yes, thank you. I don't want to sound ungrateful, but this has come as a bit of a shock, Moses.'

'Of course. There is no hurry. Take your time. But think of all the advantages of having a partner for the rest of your life. The more you think about it, the more it makes good sense.'

'Yes, I'll give it some thought,' Claire answered, feebly.

Claire left *The Abyssinian* that evening in a daze. The journey back to Easytimes was a blur. She was aware of Moses making a few comments along the way, but nothing registered.

This was going to take some time to think through. What about their finances? Did Moses have any money? Was this a ploy for her to end up looking after Moses because he had very little money? Was he tricking her? What on earth would her friends and cousins think if she suddenly got married at her age? What would her cat think if a strange man came to live at her unit? And then, most horrifying of all ... what if Moses expected sex? She was a virgin. She didn't know the first thing about sex.

Claire didn't sleep well that night. She had far too much playing on her mind.

CHAPTER 25

Jillian was woken up before daylight by her husband demanding sex. Obediently, she pulled up her nightie and let him have what he wanted. Long gone were the times when she actually enjoyed intimacy with her husband. Years ago, he had been far more considerate and would make some attempt at foreplay, so she could at least feel aroused and savour the experience. Sadly, she could count on one hand, the number of times she had called out with the thrill of an orgasm during her entire married life. Charles couldn't seem to help himself, he had little patience for anything except his own selfish gratification. In a couple of minutes everything was all over, Charles pulled up his pyjamas and stomped out for his shower, leaving Jillian lying in bed feeling no better than a receptacle. Sometimes she wondered if she had grounds for rape, but always came back to the fact that Charles still suffered from post-traumatic stress disorder (PTSD).

Charles' last posting had been to Timor Leste over twenty

years ago. He had been forty-five at the time and was based in Dili, in charge of logistics, as he was considered too old for frontline active service. His was an office job, ensuring that supplies reached the Australian troops wherever they were stationed in the mountains that stretched, like a crocodile, along the centre of the island. Charles had never explained to her what had actually happened to him. All she knew was that he had been in a place where he was ambushed. Wounded in the leg, he had been evacuated to hospital in Darwin where he spent three weeks recovering. The leg healed well enough, but he was psychologically scarred and eventually came home, angry and disturbed. After several months putting up with Charles' anti-social and sometimes violent behaviour, they had sought help together, which was when the diagnosis of PTSD had been confirmed. With treatment, he had improved, but still had periods when he became depressed or behaved irrationally. Nightmares were fewer now, but still terrifying when they did occur.

Jillian and the Major had settled into an uneasy routine at Easytimes. She fulfilled the role of the obedient housewife, ensuring that meals were always on time, the unit was kept spick and span, and everything was in readiness should they be going shopping, or departing for appointments. Charles was happier if he was locked into a tight daily routine and could quickly become angry if things weren't right. Life for Jillian was far from happy, or fulfilling, but she coped by doing her best to anticipate Charles' needs and surrendering to his foibles. When not housekeeping, she occasionally went out with one of the women from the village, some of whom seemed to have sensed that all was not well in her household. Jillian never opened up to anyone about the pressures she was constantly under. She filled in any spare time watching television (always what Charles wanted to watch) or pursuing her lifelong hobby, philately.

Charles' routine days normally began at 0630 hours with a shower, followed by walking his British bulldog, Timor, for half an hour. He expected to sit down to his cooked breakfast at 0730 hours consisting of two poached eggs (soft) and three rashers of lean bacon (not overcooked). This was backed up by two cups of black coffee and two slices of wholemeal toast (not overdone), always served with proper butter and chunky marmalade. Woe betide Jillian, if anything was not up to standard. Similar, exacting routines prevailed throughout the day. If there was to be any variation to the daily grind, Jillian would have to negotiate this with Charles the day before so he could be mentally prepared.

The Army had retained Charles on the payroll for almost a year after the ambush in the hope that he would make a complete recovery. Eventually, the decision was made to discharge him on a full disability pension when he was only forty-six. Jillian had had to give up her job as a public servant to look after Charles. Recovery was painfully slow. The psychologist had explained to Jillian that he would never again be able to live a totally normal life; the demons would always be with him. At least now he saw his psychologist only once a week. Charles read extensively, mostly historical novels and military history, enjoyed classical music, and spent nearly two hours most afternoons working out at the gym.

Physically he was very fit and still presented as a fine figure of a man.

Moving into Easytimes had been a nightmare for Major Rogers and Jillian because it totally upset their daily routines. It had taken almost six months to settle Charles down until he was reasonably accustomed to his new environment. On the plus side was Charles' budding friendship with Jock Nettleton who shared his love of classical music, and the interest Charles was taking in the newly established Residents' Committee. Jillian was feeling quietly optimistic that the worst of the move was over and that the future might become more bearable.

*   *   *

To an extent, Arthur and Rosemary were becoming creatures of habit also, in that they met every morning, except Sundays, at 7.00am for a run together. Both found the half hour to an hour running every morning invigorating and helped charge up their batteries for the day ahead. They fell into easy conversation with few topics remaining taboo. It had been a wonderful way for each to learn more about the other and they felt close. Although the rumour-mongers about the village believed they were sleeping together, this was not the case. Having had such special relationships with their first spouses, neither wished to cheapen what was developing into a beautiful new romance. Marriage had never been mentioned between them, yet both sensed that this was what they hoped for. Rosemary, being a bit of a traditionalist, had decided, for the time being anyway, to wait for Arthur to make the first move.

It was a glorious early morning, the first day in November. The air was deliciously warm already and the sun was just appearing over the Adelaide hills. Bees were busily foraging on the few plants in the village that were in flower, and a willy wagtail cavorted about on Arthur's lawn as Rosemary approached. She was breaking in a new pair of running shoes and wearing red shorts that showed off her shapely tanned legs perfectly. Arthur appeared at his door and thanked his lucky stars he was about to go exercising with such a beautiful woman. He gave her a peck on the cheek and they set off, slowly at first, to warm up the muscles. Later, they would stretch out more, once they were warmed up.

To reach the main gate their route took them past the Facilities Block with the flagpole outside flying the Australian flag. The small group of village volunteers, responsible for raising and lowering the flag every day, had never missed a beat and the flag was always to be seen fluttering proudly from the masthead from before sunrise until after sunset.

They both noticed it at the same time. There was no Australian flag! Instead, a limp black flag was hanging from the top of the mast.

'What's that flag, Arthur?'

'I don't know, but it looks a bit like the ISIS flag.'

'Oh, Arthur that's terrible. Whatever it is, we've got to get it down straight away before anyone else sees it.'

'Agreed. Let's run around to the Major's place at unit two. He trains the volunteers who raise the flag, and will know exactly what to do, and how to do it correctly.'

They were at unit two a minute later and knocked loudly

on the Major's front door. Quite often they saw the Major returning from exercising his dog, Timor, at about this time in the morning, so they knew he was up and about. The door opened to reveal the Major, hanging onto Timor's collar as the bulldog strained desperately to get at the unwelcome visitors.

'Good morning Major. We need your help please. Someone has removed the Australian flag, and in its place put up what looks horribly like the black ISIS flag. We are not experts in lowering a flag, and so are here to ask you to please come and get it down before anyone else in the village sees it?'

'Good God! What a bloody cheek! Yes, of course. I'll come now.'

Manoeuvring Timor out of his way, the Major quickly closed the door and accompanied them to the flagpole. A slight breeze had picked up, so that the flag was now fluttering and clearly visible.

'That's ISIS for sure,' asserted the Major. 'It's a black standard, with the shahada and the seal of Muhammad in white,' he continued, as he unleashed the rope.

'What's the shahada?' asked Rosemary.

'It's an Islamic creed,' replied the Major, as he slowly lowered the offending flag. 'It says, "There is no God, but Allah".'

'This is really serious,' a worried looking Arthur declared. 'It's probably the same person who dropped the leaflets into everyone's letterboxes?'

'Could well be,' the Major agreed, as he held the flag out for them to inspect. Across the top was the shahada with the white seal beneath with more indecipherable writing on the seal as well. 'This flag is totally outlawed in many countries and it's against the law to display it on a flagpole in Australia. I'd like to get my hands on the bastard who did this.'

'So would we all. What do we do now?' asked Rosemary.

'Well, my main concern now is to find our Australian flag. Pete Johnson was on duty this morning and should have raised our flag about six o'clock this morning before daylight. I went out with Timor early, but it was still dark, and I didn't come this way. You guys finish your run, and I'll contact Pete to see whether he saw anything.'

'What will you do with the ISIS flag?' Arthur inquired.

'I'll keep it, of course, and then pass it over to the police.'

'Do you think we should look about to see if our flag has been dropped around here somewhere?' inquired Rosemary.

The newly planted bushes and grasses were too small to provide any effective hiding places, nevertheless Arthur and Rosemary did a circuit around the immediate area without sighting the flag. The Major was walking back to his unit by now, carrying the ISIS flag, so they turned back towards the main gate and set off on their somewhat truncated run.

'What was the point of raising that flag on our flagpole?' Rosemary asked.

'A reminder, I guess. As far as I know, nothing happened after the leaflet drop. Nobody went out campaigning to bring back the ISIS families stranded in Syria, or even contacted their politicians. So, perhaps whoever did the leaflet drop, now feels aggrieved that nothing has happened.'

'Yes, that makes sense, but we have also had our flag stolen. If they can find the flag, then they should discover who the criminals are?'

'To be honest, I don't think the police have a clue as to who the perpetrator is. Maybe there is something they can glean from the ISIS flag? It must have been acquired from somewhere. You can probably buy the flag online.'

'It all gives me the creeps. I'll give Mike a ring as soon as we get back. He may want to call the Residents' Committee together again. Oh, and I'll put Robert Tinson in the picture as well, because I know you have to get off to work.'

'That would be great, Rosemary, thanks.'

A few minutes later they were back in the village, sweating lightly, but feeling better for the activity.

Arthur showered and left for work and Rosemary followed through on her two phone calls.

CHAPTER 26

Things moved fast. Mike called a meeting of the Residents' Committee for 5.30pm, the Major took the offending ISIS flag down to the local police station to be handed to Chief Inspector Brooks, and Rosemary contacted Robert Tinson to report the whole flag raising business. Robert then contacted Mike Fisher to ask if he could attend the evening's meeting so that the residents and their manager could be "on the same page". On hearing about the ISIS flag incident, Chief Inspector Brooks hot-footed it up to Easytimes to interview the Major and Rosemary, bringing with him a junior constable to hunt for the missing Australian flag and any other evidence.

The story of the unwelcome ISIS flag, discovered atop the village masthead, circulated around the denizens of Easytimes Retirement Village all too quickly. There was much tut-tutting over cups of tea and coffee as friends shared the news. It was perhaps the audacity of the action that worried most folk. The six men responsible for raising and lowering the Australian flag on a daily basis were ordered by the Major to assemble at 0900 hours to conduct a thorough search of the grounds surrounding the flagpole. The search proved fruitless.

Robert Tinson contacted head office to report the matter. He asked to speak to Mr Crocombe directly, but was informed that Mr Crocombe was still overseas and he would need to talk to the CEO in Mr Crocombe's absence. This he did, although the facts of the case he could impart were few. The CEO promised to have a replacement flag delivered later in the day and asked that it be raised ASAP. The CEO stressed the need to keep the residents "calm" and to play down the incident. Above all, the media must be kept at bay, as any negative publicity could have deleterious ramifications for attracting residents to the village.

On time, the members of the Residents' Committee assembled again in the hall that evening. Penny had arrived early to put on the urn and lay out sufficient cups and saucers. Never without a welcome offering, Betty appeared, prior to the meeting, with a chocolate mud cake, paper plates, serviettes and spoons. Mike allowed everyone to collect cake and victuals before calling the group to order.

'Good evening everyone. Thank you for coming to this extraordinary meeting being held in rather trying circumstances. I have had a call from Chief Inspector Brooks asking if he could please join us for this meeting, as a non-voting observer. There was no time to contact you all individually, so I said to drive out here as I didn't anticipate any objections. I hope I'm right?' Mike scanned the faces of the eight people sitting in a rough circle around him. 'Okay ... there being no objections, we will welcome him. Arthur, would you mind grabbing an extra chair please?'

There was a knock on the door and the portly figure of Chief Inspector Guy Brooks appeared.

'Please join us Inspector. We are just starting.'

With a few welcoming smiles and comments, the Inspector found the vacant chair and parked his oversized posterior firmly in place. 'Good evening, everyone,' he beamed.

Mike began by asking Rosemary and Arthur to outline, in detail, what they had seen on their run. Between them they recounted the events. 'And Major, did you walk the dog this morning?'

'Indeed, I did.'

'Did you see anything, Major?'

'Not on my walk, no. It was still fairly dark, so a black flag in a black sky would have been almost impossible to see.'

The Inspector cleared his throat. 'Is it in order for me to ask questions?' Getting a clearance from Mike, Inspector Brooks continued. 'Major, at the start of your walk, did you pass the flagpole before or after the time the flag was supposed to be raised for the day?'

'Afterwards. Later I checked with Pete Johnson that he had raised the flag promptly at 0600 hours. It would have been about 0620 hours, when I and Timor passed the flag.'

'Timor?'

'That's my dog.'

'Ah ... I see, and what time did you come back from your walk?'

'About 0650 hours, Inspector.'

'Did you notice which flag was flying when you returned, Major?'

'No, on my way back I go a different way, so I don't go past the flag.'

'So, either flag could have been up there when you left and returned?'

'Yes, I suppose so.'

'Now, I understand that Rosemary and Arthur, you were the first to see this ISIS flag?'

'Correct,' replied Rosemary and Arthur, in unison.

'And what time was that?'

'About five past seven,' Rosemary responded.

'So, whoever did this did so between about five past six, after Pete Johnson had raised the Australian flag, and five past seven, when you two runners noticed the flag had been switched,' mused the Inspector out loud.

There was no dissent from the group, so Mike went on. 'Inspector, did you, or your police assistant, discover any evidence?'

'Sadly, no. Nor did we find the missing flag. Presumably, whoever did this, also decided to souvenir the Australian flag.'

'Or destroy it!' Claire interjected, angrily.

'Quite so,' the Inspector agreed.

'May I make a comment please?' It was the manager, Robert Tinson.

'Go ahead, Robert,' invited Mike.

'The management is quite frantic about this latest development. Put bluntly, this is terrible for business. We are already losing potential customers, and this latest outrage will only exacerbate things.'

'Not only are you likely to lose potential customers, but you could be losing residents who are already here,' Jock observed.

Heads swivelled towards the broad Scottish accent, inquiringly.

'Do you know of anybody going, Jock?' asked a worried looking Robert.

'Aye.'

'Who?'

'The wee lass, who lives behind us, told me this afternoon she's up and out of here,' asserted Jock. 'She's a widow, and a nervous sort of a lassie.'

'What's her name please, Jock?' Robert asked.

'Mrs Rusedski. She lived under the Russian thumb until 1989 and is terrified of this sort of behaviour.'

'I know another couple who say they are leaving.' Betty chimed in. 'Fred and Tracey Sinclair live near us, and are coming to see you tomorrow, Robert.'

Robert looked visibly distressed.

'Okay,' said Mike, 'Let's discuss what we can do to stop the rot. Some people will always overreact, but we do need to do something as a committee to counter these negative feelings. Suggestions please?'

'What about another well-written letter dropped into everyone's letterbox,' suggested Rosemary. 'The letter should try to allay peoples' fears and be up-beat about life in the village at the same time.'

This idea was welcomed, and Robert promised to draft

an appropriate epistle, and have it delivered to everyone later tomorrow.

Arthur spoke. 'I think it would be good for morale, if we could bring forward the first village concert, and get everybody involved and excited. This would help to distract the residents from these concerns and unite them in a common cause.' Again, there was support for this idea, and a new date was set for Saturday, two weeks away.

Robert Tinson spoke again. 'I am very concerned about the unsavoury publicity that will result from this incident. Is there anything more we can do to prevent this happening?'

The general consensus was that inevitably, these kinds of stories will leak out eventually and that it might be wise to invite a preferred journalist from the local paper to the village. This way, there was a better chance that the news bulletin would, at least, be accurate. Robert, seeing the sense in this argument, agreed to organise an interview with the press once he had cleared the matter with head office.

'Inspector ...' it was Mike again, 'Have you made any more progress with your three lines of inquiry?

The inspector appeared to wriggle uncomfortably in his chair; he had not expected this question and was ill-prepared.

'Err ... um ... well, yes ... and no. It would seem that the person, or persons, responsible for this flag incident are the ones who also did the leaflet drop some weeks back. We will work on that assumption, anyway. So we will continue checking the workforce still employed here in the village, and the young men the Imam identified as being "at risk" of radicalisation earlier. Now that we have an ISIS flag in our possession, we will try to determine where it has come from. There are several online sources, I understand, so this may not help us much. But, rest assured, we will continue to actively work on this case.'

There was little confidence, or enthusiasm, regarding the Inspector's comments. Clearly, the police had not had a breakthrough yet and were no closer to finding the offenders.

'Thank you, Inspector. If there is anything we can do to assist you in your inquiries, please get in touch.' Mike wrapped up, and Inspector Brooks, seeing there was nothing to be gained by staying, excused himself politely, and departed.

The next hour focused on more detailed planning for the upcoming concert. Everyone went away feeling more up-beat about the gala event to come and how as many residents as possible could be enticed to come and participate.

* * *

Robert Tinson managed to get clearance from HQ next morning to proceed with an interview with someone from the local rag. At midday, his internal phone rang; a female reporter was at the main gate asking permission to enter and speak with him. Pressing the gate entrance button, Robert wondered how he should handle the interview; low key, unstressed, was probably his best option.

Moments later a motorbike roared into the sheltered area outside his office, and a young woman alighted, removed her helmet and unstrapped a backpack. In an instant she was at his office door.

'Hi, I'm Jessica. Nice to meet you.' She held out her un-gloved hand.

Looking at this bright, attractive young woman made Robert feel quite ancient. Jessica would be only a few years older than his eldest daughter but was already a trained journalist and practising her trade. They spent half an hour going over the facts together, checking Jessica had the names spelt correctly and taking a couple of photographs of the flagpole at the centre of the drama. Robert did his best to play down the event and even suggested it might just be the work of a prankster. Then, with another shake of his hand, Jessica was off, assuring him that a short article would probably appear in the paper later that week if the editor liked what she wrote.

The paper must have been short of news, because, the very next day, Jessica's so called "low-key" article was splashed across the front page in monstrously large font together with a coloured photograph of the village's flagpole flying the black and white ISIS standard.

Village Targeted Again!

Our reporter, Jessica Wilson, was invited yesterday to the Easytimes Retirement Village to meet the manager, Robert Tinson, to discuss another sinister and frightening event that occurred there two days ago.

Sometime between 6.00am and 7.00am on Tuesday, November 1ˢᵗ, a person, or persons unknown, entered the village illegally and stole the Australian flag that flew proudly from the village's flagpole located outside the main office. Not satisfied with this malicious act, the perpetrator then had the audacity to raise the black and white ISIS flag (seen here pictured).

This abhorrent act was discovered by two of the fitter members of the village when they left for their daily run, shortly after 7.00am. Arthur Stokes and Rosemary Tattersall were, understandably, shocked and angry to see what had happened. They immediately reported the matter to Major Rogers who is in charge of seeing that the Australian flag is correctly raised and lowered every day. The area around the flagpole was thoroughly searched by police later on, but the Australian flag was not recovered.

Readers will remember that a few weeks ago all the residents in Easytimes Retirement Village received a chilling message in their letterboxes. The leaflets said:

<u>This is a message from ISIS</u>

Our women and children in Syria must be returned to Australia immediately.

ISIS calls for the support of everyone in Easytimes.

Help us get our families home.

Failure to help us will have serious consequences.

Easytimes Retirement Village will soon have 250 units available for retirees. The manager, Robert Tinson, reported that sales were going well, until the appearance of the leaflets, which frightened some of the new residents, and may have dissuaded potential new occupants from purchasing units in the village. It is believed that some current residents are seriously considering leaving the village, fed up with this continuing eerie business with ISIS.

The Police are investigating and are appealing to anyone

who can assist them with their inquiries to come forward. Chief Inspector Guy Brooks is in charge of the case.

This front-page article set tongues a-wagging inside the village and out. The photograph of the mast, displaying the ISIS flag, had, of course, been photoshopped but it was the re-printing of the original message that had appeared on the leaflets that captured the attention of many readers. Undoubtedly, the content of the message had been ignored. Nothing had happened to assist the return of the families stranded in refugee camps in Syria. If nothing had so far been done to help them, could the malicious harassment be expected to continue, and perhaps worsen in the weeks ahead? Another concern, discussed by many villagers, revolved around why the Easytimes village was still being singled out for this treatment? Nobody could yet offer a plausible answer.

CHAPTER 27

Snoddy and Mary were bickering over whose turn it was to choose what they would watch on television this evening. Their viewing interests had little in common. Snoddy was into sport and current affairs programmes, whilst Mary loved a juicy soapy, or well-acted drama. Normally, they just took it in turns to be the "TV program controller" and this system usually worked well. However, everything had been thrown out of routine, because they had had a surprise visit last night from their son and his wife. The arrival of the young fry had, of course, meant entertaining them, so the television had remained off all evening.

'Last night was your turn, Snoddy, so tonight it's mine.' insisted Mary.

'That's not fair, Mary. I didn't get to choose what I wanted to see last night, because we had family here, so I should be able to choose the programmes tonight.'

'Fiddlesticks! Have you forgotten that we agreed, years

ago, that if we missed a night, that was it? Bad luck! Neither of us could then claim the right to run the TV programming again the following night.'

'I don't remember agreeing to that, Mary.'

The argument looked destined to be going nowhere when they were interrupted by the ringing of the doorbell. Snoddy, who had by now lost some more of his unwanted kilograms, was able to rise from his armchair reasonably adroitly and lumber, still somewhat bear-like, to the front door. Swinging it open, he was surprised to find the Nettletons standing there, expectantly. Jock held a brown paper bag with what appeared to be a bottle of wine inside, and Anne was smiling over a large plate, covered with a cloth.

'Hello,' said Snoddy in a friendly voice.

'Hello,' replied the Nettletons, still smiling and looking hopeful.

'Would you like to come in?' asked Snoddy.

'Well, yes, that would be nice,' replied Jock.

Snoddy did his best to hold the door open and flatten his body up against the wall to provide sufficient space for the Nettletons to enter with their surprise gifts. He noticed Jock and Anne exchanging querying glances as they entered.

'Nice night?' suggested Snoddy as he closed the front door behind them and wondered why the Nettletons had turned up at their unit.

'A bit windy,' commented Anne, looking awkwardly at her husband.

At that moment, Mary breezed in, all smiles, and brushing aside the tiff that she and Snoddy had been busily engaged in just before this unexpected visit of their neighbours, invited the Nettletons to take a seat. Having made this offer, she realised, to her horror, that one of their armchairs was piled high with a week's worth of her bras, pants and stockings and the second armchair was brimming with all Snoddy's smalls and their towels, for at least the past week, or perhaps even longer.

Mary had meant to get everything sorted and put away before she and Snoddy sat down for their evening meal, but somehow had been distracted. Jock and Anne remained rooted to their spots, unsure quite what to do. There were two other vacant chairs in the room, each next to a small side table.

'Snoddy, would you please go and get the laundry basket and move all these things off the armchairs. I thought you were going to get it done earlier, dear.'

Snoddy glared at his wife. Putting away the clean clothes was *not* one of his allotted tasks, and here was Mary, inferring that it was a failure on *his* part, that their underwear and other garments were still draped about all over their armchairs. Temporarily outwitted, Snoddy, grudgingly, left the room to find the laundry basket.

This left Mary standing in the middle of her sitting room, resplendent in a dirty apron, and wondering why on earth the Nettletons had arrived at their door, armed with what looked like a bottle of wine and a plate of something.

'It's so nice to see you,' Mary smiled, lamely. 'To what do we owe this honour?'

'Well ... err ...' Jock stammered, 'We ... err ... we thought we were coming to have an evening meal with you tonight?'

Mary managed, with a supreme effort, to control her instinctively sharp tongue and to keep her mouth firmly closed, but she couldn't disguise the look of astonishment that flashed across her face.

'Oh, really?' she managed, at last.

Seeing Mary's obvious embarrassment, Anne now realised that something was definitely seriously amiss. Somebody must have got their dates mixed up. Either they had come over on the wrong night, or possibly the Snodgrasses had forgotten they had invited them over? The original invitation had come from Mary when she had consumed rather too many drinks at last Friday's Happy Hour. Was it possible that Mary was so drunk at the time that she could not later recall she had ever extended the invitation? What a ghastly mess, thought Anne.

Snoddy lumbered back into the room and without a word began heaving Mary's substantial pile of underwear into his laundry basket. Job done, he turned, and headed for their bedroom door, inadvertently dropping a couple of quite sexy looking black bras lying on the floor in his wake.

'Perhaps you have forgotten?' Anne suggested, gently. 'You had had a few drinks when you invited us,' she added nervously.

'Oh Gawd!' was all Mary could offer. Deep in the dark recesses of her brain, she thought that she had perhaps invited somebody around, but for the life of her she couldn't remember who it was, or when she had invited them, or, for that matter, what she had invited them for. While she was still trying desperately to get her synapses to connect, and provide some meaningful answers, Snoddy re-entered, gave a weak sheepish smile, and proceeded to throw all his underpants and singlets into the now empty laundry basket. Bending over was still a real challenge for Snoddy, so he made no attempt to pick up Mary's bras, still strewn about, as he exited again.

'I'm so sorry,' muttered Mary, still looking bemused. 'I think perhaps this *is* my fault. I may have had a couple of drinks and when I do that, I sometimes say silly things,' she smiled weakly and unconvincingly.

Jock came to her rescue. If the truth be known, the Nettletons had not been looking forward to spending a whole evening with the Snodgrasses, and now there was every chance the event could be totally aborted and the Nettletons could escape.

'Aye, it's easily done lassie. No problem. Maybe another time? But I do want to ask you both to come and sing in my choir. We are going to perform a few light classical opera choruses. Will you join us?'

Mary felt trapped. It was years since she had last sung in a choir, although she believed her voice was still passable. The least she could do to make amends to Jock and Anne for her stupid drunken invitation, was to agree to join.

Snoddy returned at this moment, unaware of what had been discussed in the last few minutes, whilst he had been knee deep in undies.

'What about you Snoddy? Are you in too?' asked Jock, hopefully.

'Oh, you don't want him, Jock; he's got a shocking voice. Sounds worse than a pregnant exhaust pipe. People will run away if they hear Snoddy trying to sing,' Mary interjected. She had already decided if she was to be dragged into Jock's choral activities, it would be without her husband tagging along and arguing all the time. 'When he sings in the shower, I worry that the light bulbs will shatter. He is so loud and so off-key,' Mary added.

'Well, people who sing in their showers usually make excellent choral contributions,' asserted Jock, much to Mary's surprise and considerable annoyance. 'It means they love singing.'

Poor Snoddy, was yet to contribute one word to these discussions, following his two demanding excursions to the bedroom with the Snodgrass's underwear. Now, he looked about him at the faces eagerly awaiting his response. 'What say you, Snoddy? Like to join us?'

'Well, actually, yes. I think that could be fun. As long as I don't have to stand for too long. I'll be okay if I can lose some more weight though.'

'Aye, you're a bonnie lad,' chorused Jock and Anne, while Mary gave a loud, disapproving sniff.

The Nettletons retreated gracefully a few minutes later from their dinner that wasn't. They left the Snodgrasses still carrying their bottle of unopened wine and Anne's sticky date pudding. Jock was, however, well pleased with the evening. They had avoided a difficult social outing and had gained two more members for his choir. Little did the unsuspecting new members of his choir realise, that he planned to hit them with several extracts from Handel's Messiah to sing at Christmas.

* * *

As Jock and Anne slowly wound their way home, lightning streaked across the sky and claps of thunder ricocheted all around. It was, perhaps, five hundred metres for them to walk back to their unit, but this was quite a challenge for Jock, whose arthritis did not respond well to such unstable atmospheric conditions. Anne had suggested before leaving that evening that they take the car, but Jock had been insistent that a short walk would not be too much for his ancient limbs. Now he was regretting that decision. A few large drops of rain splattered about them, as they did their best to keep moving as fast as Jock's complaining limbs would allow. They were ill-prepared however, having left their umbrellas at home.

They were only about halfway there with the storm intensifying. Flashes of lightning were all about, the wind pushing violently against them and the rain suddenly heavier and heavier.

'We have to find some shelter,' yelled Jock.

'What did you say?'

'Shelter, we must find some shelter,' he shouted back, as the wind blew spittle from his mouth across his face. 'This way ...' and he stumbled off the road towards the front porch of the nearest unit. Another crash of thunder shook the ground as Anne followed her husband towards the covered area. It was then that they both heard a terrifying yelp from an animal somewhere nearby.

'What was that?' shouted Anne, as she caught up with her husband. 'Did you hear it? It sounded like an animal. Do you think it was hit by lightning, Jock?'

'No idea,' responded Jock, 'but it sounded like the hound

of the Baskervilles.' Jock put his bottle of wine down on the ground, and shook himself, to remove some of the rainwater that had already penetrated his clothing. 'It certainly sounded like a dog to me.'

'Do you think, whatever it was ...' Another massive clap of thunder drowned out the rest of Anne's sentence.

'What did you say?'

'I think the animal we heard may have been hit by lightning, Jock. Should we go and see if we can help?'

'No way. We don't know where it was, and we could be hit ourselves trying to find it.'

The rain was pelting down even harder now and puddles were already coalescing into much larger ones. Suddenly, the streetlights flickered, flickered again and as if finally exhausted, went out. There was total darkness all around them now, punctuated only by the infrequent flashes of lightning. The temperature had dropped several degrees as they huddled together under the porch keeping out of the drenching rain. Conversation became impossible when the rain turned to hail and crashed violently and deafeningly all about them. It was five long minutes before the storm moved off.

Cold, wet and miserable, Anne and Jock felt for their unwanted gifts on the ground and, in complete darkness, headed out together, across the lawn, to find the road. Splashing through unseen puddles, with occasional flurries of rain still attacking them, they reached the hard road surface, turned right, and virtually felt their way, slowly, along the macadam surface.

'How will we know when we get back to our unit?' asked

Anne. 'We can't see anything. We should have brought a torch with us.'

They were saved by the lights of a car, coming along slowly behind them. The driver pulled up next to them.

'You folks okay?' It was Arthur Stokes with Rosemary Tattersall in the passenger seat.

'I think so,' replied Jock. 'Really glad you came along though, because we couldn't see a thing.'

'What number are you?'

'Unit 48,' Anne replied.

'Well my lights are shining onto number 46 at the moment, so you are the next one. Wait a second and I'll park so you can see your way to your front door.'

Jock and Anne thanked Arthur profusely. They had had enough. Jock fumbled for his key and they made it in safely. Shivering with cold, they hadn't even noticed there was another car parked in their driveway.

Once indoors, the elderly couple were surprised to see a glow of light in their kitchen. Then, to their horror, they saw the back of a person standing there. Whoever it was appeared to be busily engaged in some absorbing task. They stood and stared, not daring to move for fear of disturbing the intruder. It was then that the stranger turned around, and Jock and Anne realised with an enormous sense of relief, that the mysterious intruder was none other than their own adopted daughter, Jayne.

'Hi Mum, hi Dad, bloody awful storm. All the crappy lights went off as soon as I arrived. So I lit the two candles you keep for emergencies and I'm busy making myself some sandwiches. Where have you two been?'

Anne offered a brief explanation of their evening meal that wasn't, said they were horribly cold and wet, and had to go and shower and change. As she spoke, hey presto, the lights came back on. There was much relief all round. Anne and Jock disappeared, leaving their daughter with strict instructions to get them something hot to have for tea.

Half an hour later, the three of them were seated around the dining room table getting stuck into scrambled eggs on toast with a welcome glass of red wine. It was nearly nine o'clock, the storm had moved away completely, and Jock and Anne were starting to feel human again. Between mouthfuls, Jock outlined what had happened to them during the evening and how they had been caught in the storm.

Jayne was in a foul mood because she and her lesbian partner had had a massive argument. It had been brewing for a few days, Jayne said, and it blew up just before the storm hit. Jayne did not explain what it was about but had stomped out in a rage. 'Never going to live with that fucker again ever ... ever,' Jayne declared, with tears rolling down her cheeks. Jock filled her glass up with the last of the red wine (her third) and the elderly couple commiserated as best they could.

Jayne stayed the night and left for work at half past seven. Jock remained in bed, but Anne arose to give their daughter breakfast and moral support, as only a mother can do.

Having just rescued the Nettletons by providing the light for them to return safely to their unit, Arthur invited Rosemary back to his unit. Rosemary was at once comforted by this invitation, for she didn't look forward to going back to her lonely unit alone and without electricity, but she also felt slightly concerned. With the power off, she and Arthur would be obliged to have a candle-lit evening together, something she had always regarded as being highly sexually charged. Her husband had been a romantic soul, and they had frequently dispensed with electric lighting and dined alone by candlelight before making love. It was a delicious part of their foreplay and set just the right mood. She would slip into something seductive and allow the flickering candlelight to work its magic. They had several favourite CDs that also helped. It never failed.

And now this new man in her life, who she was falling in love with, was suggesting they should have a candle-lit evening together. She knew she wanted him, but they seemed to have tacitly agreed that sex before their possible marriage was not something they would indulge in. She was not sure though, that she could resist his advances should he make a move. So, it was with some trepidation, that she accepted his invitation and climbed out of the car. The light inside the car glowed for about ten seconds after they closed the doors, enough time for Arthur to take her hand and find the path that led to his front door.

Safely indoors, Arthur suggested she stay by the door while he felt his way around to the cupboard where the candles were stored. A few bumps and curses later, he arrived at his destination, and, grovelling around inside the cupboard, extricated a pair of tallish candles and a box of matches. With a little cheer he had them lit, and Rosemary moved into the room to admire the effect of the flickering light throwing strange, spooky shadows across the room. For an agonising moment she dreamt she was back home with her husband and hungry for a night of passionate lovemaking.

'What would you like to drink, Rosemary?'

Returning to the present, Rosemary could think of nothing interesting to request. 'Oh, whatever you are having, thanks, Arthur.'

'That doesn't help me,' replied Arthur, peering at her through the candlelight.

Earlier that evening, Rosemary had enjoyed two glasses of Rosé and she knew a third could seriously lower her resistance to any sexual advances, so she decided to play it safe. 'Just a coffee please.'

No sooner had she said it than the lights flickered back on, and the spell was broken. The candles were now superfluous, and, reluctantly, Arthur moved to snuff them out. He too, had felt the magic of the evening, romantic candles and the beautiful Rosemary.

They enjoyed a coffee together and around nine o'clock Rosemary said she must be going. She was involved in a lady's foursome teeing off at 7.30 in the morning, so needed to be up early. She apologised for not being able to join Arthur for his early morning run. It was raining again, so Arthur offered to drive Rosemary back the two hundred metres to her unit, which she gladly accepted.

As they drove along the quiet street that led to Rosemary's unit, with the rain still falling, their headlights picked out the figure of a man sitting on the side of the road. Arthur saw the figure first.

'Good God, who's this?' he exclaimed, sitting up and squinting to see better. 'There's someone just sitting there in the rain on the side of the road. Look.'

Rosemary, straining to see through the wet windscreen, could see the man now, hunched over, with an Akubra covering his head.

'Heck, poor bloke. Whoever it is must be soaked to the skin. Pull over Arthur. We must see if we can help. There must be something seriously wrong.'

Arthur parked opposite the reclining figure, who still hadn't moved. 'Oh God, I hope he's okay ...'

They jumped from the car and ran across the road, ignoring the rain. 'Are you all right?' yelled Arthur, above the sound of the hustling wind and driving rain, as he neared the figure. Whoever it was, failed to respond, and remained, head down, clutching at his knees with the Akubra affording little protection but sufficient to prevent them from seeing who it was.

'Please let us help you up and get you home out of this foul weather,' pleaded Rosemary, placing a hand on the stranger's shoulder.

'We have a car here, so we can drive you, if you wish,' offered Arthur, placing his hand on the other shoulder.

The stranger shook his head slowly but remained silent. Whoever this was must have been out here for some time, as he was soaked through and shivering. Arthur knelt down so he could see into the person's face and was shocked to find he was looking into the frightened eyes of Major Charles Rogers. The Major was the last person Arthur had expected to find squatting miserably on the side of the road. Normally, the Major exuded the utmost confidence and seemed to be so well grounded. True, the Major was regarded as a bit of an eccentric about the village, with his military bearing and somewhat autocratic ways, but he had been accepted. Many had seen the Major out walking his much-loved dog, Timor, in the afternoons, or perhaps early in the morning.

'Charles, we need to get you up and back to your unit. A hot shower, and perhaps a shot of gin should help. What do you say?' The Major gave a slight shake of his head but made no effort to move. 'Come on, let us help you up.' Still no response. 'Rosemary could you help by giving Charles a lift up on his right side and I'll give him a hand from here.'

Together they grabbed the Major under his armpits, and with a heave and the eventual partial cooperation of the Major, they raised him up into a standing position. Arthur kept an arm around his waist, as the Major seemed unbalanced, and likely to collapse, or fall over.

'Good on you, Major. How about we take you home in my car?'

The Major appeared dazed and started mumbling incoherently. His eyes were open, but not seeing. It was as if he was shell-shocked or perhaps groggy from excessive drinking. Arthur's strong arm was providing the support he needed to stay upright. Together, Rosemary and Arthur began to guide the tottering Major across the road to their car. There was no smell of beer or spirits, so it seemed unlikely he was intoxicated but something was seriously wrong.

'Do you think we should call an ambulance?' Rosemary asked.

'Well, let's get him home first and then we can decide. Jillian may be able to advise us too.' So they dragged, cajoled and supported the Major, splashing through puddles, until they reached the car. Rosemary swung the door open and with more encouragement and a bit of shoving they finally manipulated Charles into the front passenger seat as if he was a sack of potatoes. There he sat, looking exhausted, still mumbling.

A couple of minutes later, they pulled up outside the Major's unit, and Rosemary jumped out to alert Jillian, leaving the two men in the vehicle. The Major remained immobile, as if in shock and still shivering uncontrollably.

Rosemary had never been into Charles and Jillian's

unit, probably nobody else in the village had ever entered the building. Some of the villagers joked that it was a maximum-security area, guarded by Timor, the bulldog. She rapped loudly on the front door and a frightened looking Jillian opened it a couple of inches to see who was there. Recognising Rosemary, she clutched her hands across her chest and exclaimed, 'Oh Rosemary, I'm so glad you are here. Something terrible has happened.'

Instinctively, Rosemary opened her arms and Jillian fell into them sobbing. 'Oh, it's awful, Rosemary, it's awful.'

'Okay, now pull yourself together Jillian. What's awful? Tell me about it.'

'It's Timor. Somebody has murdered the dog and left an ISIS note. I don't know what to do. Charles found Timor when he left to take him out for his evening walk. Somebody has slit his throat, there's blood everywhere. When Charles found his dog, he went into a terrible rage and stormed out into the street and he hasn't come back. I don't know where he is.'

'Well, we have Charles with us. He's safe, but very cold and wet. We need to bring him in and get him showered and warmed up. We found him sitting beside the road. He seems very depressed.'

'Oh dear, of course he is. Charles really loved Timor. We have always had a dog, but this one was his all-time favourite. This one was special. He will be heartbroken.'

'Come out with me Jillian to help get Charles back indoors. He is very unsteady on his feet. We were wondering whether to call an ambulance but thought we should check with you first.'

'Yes, yes, of course.' Jillian did not wait to put on a coat, or change out of her slippers, and sploshed her way along the path behind Rosemary. Between the three of them they managed to coerce Charles out of the vehicle and back along the garden path. As he reached the front-door he suddenly became agitated, but lucid.

'Get your hands off me. I'm perfectly all right. Leave me alone. Clear off, the lot of you!' Charles appeared to have magically snapped out of his depressed state and to have regained his strength as he stood there, glaring defiantly, at the three people assembled around him. 'What the hell do you want? Get out of my house.'

'Charles, you might not remember, but Rosemary and I have just brought you home. We found you sitting by the side of the road in the pouring rain.'

'It's the dog. Somebody has murdered my bloody dog! Come and have a look. Timor's throat has been cut and whoever did it left another bloody ISIS message. Come with me. If you don't like blood and mess, then stay here.' The Major had taken charge again. He was back to his old self, snapping out orders, and expecting the lower ranks to jump to his every command.

Rosemary and Jillian stayed put and left the two men to go out to the back porch to view the grisly sight. The rain had eased somewhat, and most of the blood had washed away, leaving the soaked corpse of Timor, lying on its side. Stuck into the dog's flank was a meat skewer, holding down a piece of cardboard with a short typed notice attached.

'Don't touch anything,' instructed the Major, 'We have to get the police in on this.'

Arthur knelt down on the wet ground to read the note.

We asked for your help.
You have done NOTHING!
Let this be another warning.
ISIS

'Bloody idiots. They've got to be stopped. Fat lot the police have done to find out who is scaring the village out of its wits. I have half a mind to set up our own vigilante group to protect our interests. What do you think, Arthur?'

'I think you should get inside, have a shower and get warmed up before you catch a chill or something worse. But, before you do, put a call in to the police to come and see this for themselves.'

'You're right Arthur. Timor was my favourite dog, you know, and I've had plenty over the years.'

They turned from the distressing scene and headed back indoors. The Major appeared to have completely recovered his poise and authority and gave the local police station a call immediately. Meanwhile, the ladies retired to the kitchen, boiled the kettle and put out some biscuits on a plate. Both Rosemary and Arthur were soaking wet after their rescue efforts and appreciated something hot to drink.

'Police are on their way,' grunted the Major, as he trudged off for his shower.

The police were at the gate in under ten minutes and pulled up in the driveway a moment later. Chief Inspector Brooks and a young constable alighted. A nervous Jillian opened the door.

'What's been going on then?' demanded Brooks, glaring

down at the petite Jillian, who stood in the middle of the floor, head down and mumbling. Realising he had been a bit too full on, and that this lady was clearly distressed, Brooks eased off and tried a more empathetic approach. 'Sorry to hear you have been having some problems, Madam. We are here to help,' and he offered what he believed was a fulsome smile to try to ease the situation.

Jillian was clearly overcome. All her married life she had played second fiddle to her husband, who automatically took control of any awkward situations, and left her as the bystander. But right now, he was in the shower and she had to try to deal with things. 'It's, it's the dog ...' she stammered, 'It's dead.'

Chief Inspector Brooks was already in possession of this fact, because the Major had reported it only a few minutes ago.

'My husband is in the shower,' added the apprehensive Jillian, still looking at the floor and fidgeting with her hands.

'So, perhaps, madam, you could advise your husband that the police are here and are waiting for him?'

'Oh, yes ... yes ... of course. I'll go and tell him.'

An awkward silence ensued. Jillian hurried off to speak to her husband, whilst Arthur and Rosemary remained standing at the back of the room.

'If my memory serves me correctly, I have met you two before?' remarked the Chief Inspector.

'Yes, indeed you have. We are the two runners that first reported the ISIS flag incident.'

'Of course. And here you are again,' Brooks observed, with a slightly accusatory tone.

Rosemary and Arthur, between them, explained how they

were returning home after the power outage, and had found the disconsolate Major sitting on the side of the road soaked through, and how they had persuaded him to get into their car so they could return him to his unit.

'Are you taking notes, Constable? Brooks demanded. 'Give me the times, please. How long ago did you find the Major?'

'It must have been about fifteen minutes ago,' Rosemary replied.

'That would make it roughly 9.15pm. Write it down, Constable.'

The discourse was interrupted by the appearance of the Major and his wife, the former in a track suit and still vigorously rubbing his sparse covering of hair with a towel.

'Inspector, thank you for coming so quickly. I needed a hot shower after being out in the rain. Have you seen the dog?'

'No, Major. Perhaps you can show me?'

'Follow me,' ordered the Major, throwing his wet towel on the floor where his subservient wife dutifully retrieved it and hurried off to hang it up to dry.

The Major marched out with both Brooks and the constable in his wake. The rain had stopped at last and it was becoming a more pleasant, warm evening. They spent almost half an hour at the scene, the Inspector doing a thorough search and questioning the Major at length. Finally, the Chief Inspector advised the Major to come to the police station at 4.00pm tomorrow afternoon to sign a statement. Forensics, he advised, would arrive during the morning, and the back porch, where Timor still lay, was cordoned off with tape to make it an official crime scene.

The Chief Inspector and the constable left with the minimum of fuss, the constable carrying a plastic bag that contained the skewer and its sinister note still attached.

As soon as the police had departed, Arthur finally saw Rosemary safely home.

CHAPTER 29

Next morning, Arthur informed the manager, Robert Tinson, and Mike Fisher of the events of the previous evening. He did not go into detail and omitted to mention how he, and Rosemary, had found the Major sitting on the side of the road. The Major, Arthur reckoned, might not appreciate him disclosing how dramatically he had reacted to the loss of his precious dog, Timor. Mike wasted no time and called yet another meeting of the Residents' Committee for 1.00pm, to discuss the latest event, and how the committee might, once again, respond. All the committee members agreed to attend except Arthur who was unable to leave his heavy work commitments.

True to form, Betty and Gordon were first to arrive, bringing with them a tray containing a selection of meat and salad sandwiches, just in case anyone had not yet consumed lunch. Betty and her husband were convinced that the mood at such events was greatly enhanced by the presence of some gastronomic delights. They had now been officially installed as the volunteer caterers for Happy Hour gatherings in the village hall every Friday evening and their talents were already well known throughout Easytimes. The couple was a great asset and perhaps, even more remarkably, they were easy to get along with. By the time the other committee members arrived, they had plates, cups and saucers at the ready and the urn purring away quietly nearby. Gordon discretely left then, as he was not a member of the Residents' Committee.

Snoddy and Mary were next to rock up. Snoddy was grumbling about having to walk so far to the hall and then arriving too early. He would have preferred to drive and to have left much later. Mary, however, had insisted that they needed the exercise and, privately, had wanted to fetch up at the meeting early, just in case she could get to chat with her old heartthrob, Mike. Snoddy was still incapable of performing in the bedroom, despite continuing to slowly lose weight, whilst Mary occasionally succumbed to beautiful dreams in which she was being embraced by the strong, masculine arms of Mike Fisher. Snoddy's mood brightened, however, at the sight of two plates, full of delicious sandwiches, and he made a beeline for the nearer one. Mary, however, had anticipated this move, and was quick to hand Snoddy a plate with one small, lonely-looking salad sandwich, together with a curt warning, 'One sandwich only, Snoddy. I'll be watching.'

Claire Bury entered, wearing a rather more daring costume than usual. Her romance with Moses Lobrida had now been in progress for nigh three months, and she was gradually coming around to thinking that marriage might be a possibility after all. She was still terrified about the sex side of things, but was becoming fonder of the patient, kindly Moses. They were united in their religious beliefs, and she felt secure in the knowledge that he wouldn't try anything untoward, until they were properly joined in holy matrimony. The romance had already inspired her to purchase rather more colourful, stylish clothing, and she now even owned a pair of not very high, high heels. Her hair was neater, and she had taken to putting a little lipstick on whenever seeing Moses. She didn't like to admit it, but she found herself looking at her naked figure in the mirror after showering and wondering if Moses would approve. Interestingly, her new diet seemed to be making her slimmer and even more curvaceous.

Jock Nettleton was now obliged to use a walking stick because his arthritic leg was playing up so much but was in a festive mood as today was Anne's eightieth birthday. He had to explain to Claire and Betty that he was having a celebration that evening with family and a few close friends at which Anne was to receive the OBE (Over Bloody Eighty award). Both ladies were quick to congratulate her. Anne had had a special invitation to today's Board meeting.

The Major and Rosemary arrived at the same time, the Major looking somewhat haggard after the events of the previous evening. He nodded formally at the three members of the committee already assembled, then grabbed a plate, which he proceeded to fill with several of Betty's meat sandwiches.

'Bloody good sambos,' he remarked, to no one in particular, as he gobbled the first one.

'Betty very kindly made them for us,' remarked Claire.

'No doubt about you Betty. You can come around and cook my bloody tucker any time.' A comment the others thought rather unkind to poor little Jillian, who, everyone knew, slaved away tirelessly to keep the Major happy.

Rosemary, ever watchful of maintaining her slim figure, politely declined a sandwich, but headed for the urn to make a cup of green tea. Despite being involved in the drama of last night, she still managed to look fresh and relaxed. The Major eyed her over his sandwiches and mentally undressed her. A great pity, he thought, that this Arthur Stokes fellow was interested in this ravishing woman.

Last to appear, and offering his apologies, was the chairman himself, Mike Fisher. Without wasting any time, he asked everyone to be seated at the table, with the two trays of already depleted sandwiches acting as centrepieces.

'Thank you for attending again at such short notice. I have an apology from Arthur who cannot get away from important engagements at work. I have also invited Dr Anne Nettleton to join us today. Anne is not, of course, a member of the Residents' Committee, but she and Jock heard strange noises last night, so I thought it might be helpful if Anne also attended for the first part of this meeting when we share the sad events of last night. Lastly, I have taken the liberty of inviting the manager, Robert Tinson, and Chief Inspector Guy Brooks to join us as soon as the Inspector can get here. We need to all work together closely. I hope that's okay with you all?'

There were only murmurs of consent, so Mike continued. 'First up, on behalf of this committee, may I express our condolences to you Major, and to your good wife, for the ghastly event that occurred at your unit last night. We all know how fond you were of Timor and that this must have come as a horrid shock to you both. I'm sure you have the good wishes of everybody in the village.'

Everyone in the room was now looking at the Major, who felt obliged to respond. Swallowing down the remnants of his last sandwich, he cleared his throat, and looked directly at the chairman.

'Thank you, Mr Chairman, for those kind remarks. We are indeed gutted by the shocking murder of our dog by someone from ISIS. This is now the third malicious event in the village, but the police don't appear to be making any progress. I believe it's time to establish a vigilante corps within the village, and I'm putting forward my name as the commander, with the aim of forming said group immediately.'

The Major's forthright comments were met with stunned silence. His proposal to form a vigilante group was totally out of left field and unexpected. Mike was the first to recover.

'That's an interesting suggestion, Major. However, we can't rush into things like that. May I suggest that we first go over the events of last night to double check our facts before we try to come up with any possible actions?' This considered response met with everyone's approval except the Major.

'You don't want to bloody stuff around, checking facts etcetera, when something else could happen at any time. You have defenceless people in this village. What if ISIS targets a person next time? At least, if we have nightly patrols, we have a chance to catch these buggers.'

'Aye, that may be so,' Jock responded, 'but, in the first instance, it's the police who should be patrolling the village.'

'Fat chance of that happening,' declared the Major defiantly.

'Okay, I'm calling the meeting to order. First up, we should hear a detailed account of the events of last night from the Major, followed by Rosemary, who, along with Arthur, became involved, and finally from Jock and Anne. Major, would you mind ...'

At this juncture, Robert Tinson and Inspector Guy Brooks joined the group, with apologies for being late.

'Please, Major, would you give us your account of what happened?'

Grumpily, the Major outlined how he had heard a disturbance out the back of his unit, which had reminded him he had not taken Timor out for his evening walk. It was raining heavily, so he went to the loo, collected the leash, put on his raincoat, wellies and Akubra, unlocked the back door and then, to his horror, found Timor bleeding to death on the back porch with his throat slashed. The dog was still warm, so he knew it had just happened, and he ran out onto the road to see if he could see the perpetrator. He ran about the streets until he was exhausted but saw nothing. Whoever it was must have fled on foot because he didn't see, or hear, any cars. Tired and angry, he had sat down on the side of the road to get his breath back, and to think what to do next. Then Arthur and Rosemary had come along in their car and given him a lift home.

Rosemary then continued the part of the story that she and Arthur knew about, stressing how totally exhausted and distressed they had found the Major. Next, Mike asked Mary and Snoddy to add their comments.

Snoddy jumped in first. 'It was during an ad break that I got up and went out the back. It was pouring with rain, but I remembered I had forgotten to turn off the sprinkler on the back lawn. Not much point leaving it on in the rain,' he added sheepishly.

'He's always doing that,' chimed in Mary. 'He'd forget his head, if it wasn't screwed on,' she lamented.

'That's not fair,' retorted Snoddy, 'It was only the second time I'd left it on.'

'Oh, garbage Snoddy, what about last weekend ...'

Mike interrupted this flow of invective, 'Can either of you recall what time you heard something, and what it was you heard, please?'

'It was a dog yelping,' asserted Mary.

'And the time?' asked Mike.

'We were watching *24 Hours in Emergency* on SBS,' recalled Snoddy, 'I don't care much for the program myself, but Mary likes it, and it was her night to pick the telly programs. That geyser who had crashed his bike into the back of a bus was being checked over and it was touch and go whether he would survive without suffering serious brain damage.'

'No Snoddy, it was after that. Don't you remember? It was when they were trying to get that purple bead out of that little girl's ear. That's when you went out.'

'No, I went out during the ads. I didn't see that bit about the girl.'

'Yes, you did ...'

Mike intervened again. 'Can you agree on a rough time that you heard something?'

'The program started at 8.30 and we were about halfway through. So, I reckon it would have been about nine o'clock,' Snoddy suggested cautiously.

'A bit later I reckon,' responded Mary, looking pensive.

'Well, that agrees with my recollections,' the Major added.

'And what did you hear, Snoddy?'

'It was raining hard, but I'm sure I heard a dog give a frightened yelp and I could hear a scuffling sound.'

'May I ask a question, please?' It was Inspector Brooks.

'Of course,' Mike answered.

'How close is your backyard to the Major's backyard?'

'I could lob a stone easily into his place. Around twenty metres away probably.'

'You could perhaps when you were fit, Snoddy. No way you could do it these days,' snorted Mary.

'Thank you,' replied the Inspector, ignoring Mary's unpleasant remark. 'I will need to conduct more detailed interviews over the next couple of days with all who were involved. Please be sure to make yourselves available.'

Anne and Jock then recounted how they heard what they believed was a distressed dog when walking home. Between them all they were able to fix was the time of the dog's demise reasonably accurately.

Robert Tinson, once again, expressed his concerns that this latest event would have a serious detrimental effect on his marketing and the village's occupancy rates.

The Major's proposal, that a vigilante group be established, received no support at all. In fact, once the Major realised he had no support, it was touch and go whether he would even stay for the remainder of the meeting. He sulked until the end and refused to participate in any more discussions.

Finally, it was agreed that they must be totally open and transparent about the ugly death that had befallen the Major's dog. Claire, as secretary, agreed to type up, and distribute to every unit, a brief account of what had transpired, and to urge residents to keep a very close eye on their pets at all times.

Back home, Claire took an hour to get the wording of her short letter right and then sought Mike's approval. Later that afternoon, but well before dark, Claire did the rounds of the village ensuring that all the residents would find her letter in their letterboxes by the next day.

CHAPTER 30

After the meeting, Mike chatted around for a few minutes and then wound his way, thoughtfully, back to his unit. It was nearly three o'clock when he arrived home and Penny was just boiling the kettle. He flopped down on his favourite chair and requested a lemon and ginger tea. Bringing it over, Penny gave him a peck on the cheek, offered him a shortbread, and sat opposite. She thought her husband looked tired, or was it perhaps concern about the meeting he had just chaired?

'So, how did it go, darling?'

'It had its moments,' and he proceeded to explain what had happened, and who had said what to whom, in some detail. Penny liked this about her husband; he always had the time to tell her what was happening in his life. Now that her new kidney was firing on all cylinders, and dialysis was a thing of the past, she felt so much stronger and able to take an interest.

'They're an intriguing bunch,' mused Mike. 'I had to keep

them in order today. The Major, in particular, was hard to handle. He can't stand it when he doesn't get his own way.'

'Yes, I pity poor little Jillian. I reckon she gets treated like a servant, bossed about all day. Do you think he beats her up?'

'I don't know.'

'Perhaps not physically but I'm sure he bullies her. You can see how timid she is. At least she has been coming to the Ladies' Coffee mornings and seems to have become quite friendly with Claire,' Penny added.

'Have you noticed, by the way, how Claire seems much better groomed, happier and interested in her appearance since she moved into the village? She's doing a great job as secretary too.'

'Well, you know why? She's found a serious, male friend. A big tall African guy. I met him one day when he had come to take her out somewhere. Seemed a nice fellow. Apparently, they met at their church. Who knows, we might have the first Easytimes wedding coming up soon.'

'Not before the lovely Rosemary ties the knot with Arthur,' said Mike, reaching for a second shortbread.

'Do you think they are sleeping together?' asked Penny.

'Only in their dreams, I think. I had quite a long yarn with Arthur one afternoon, when he was out doing some gardening. He told me that they have both come from long and beautiful marriages where the spouse died, and that they want to keep their new relationship very special too. I may be wrong, but I suspect that means staying celibate.'

'They seem so well suited. I do hope something comes of it. They go out running together every morning and for dinner every Saturday night. Which reminds me ... when did you last take me out for dinner, Mike?

Taken aback by this question, Mike played for time. 'Um ...'

'Admit it, it was moons ago, Michael Fisher!'

'I can handle the dinner okay, it's the sexual demands that come après dinner that have me worried,' Mike jested.

'I'm surprised you can remember that far back,' countered Penny.

'One couple that doesn't have any action in that regard, I suspect, is the Snodgrasses,' claimed Mike, skilfully changing the topic. 'Those two can't agree on anything. They are constantly disagreeing over the pettiest things. I had to interrupt their squabbles again twice today.'

Penny laughed, 'It's a case of opposites attracting for them.'

'By the way, it was dear old Anne's eightieth birthday today. I'm going to propose that, in future, we have a special certificate and a little celebration in the village for anyone who hits eighty. It will be known as the OBE, or "Over Bloody Eighty" award.'

'Great idea.'

At this point there was a knock at the door. It was Claire coming around to ask Mike to look over the draft letter she had composed for distribution to all the residents. She politely declined the offer of a cup of tea and, with Mike's blessing, went on her way to photocopy 250 copies in the office.

* * *

Shortly afterwards, Mike rang Chief Inspector Brooks and asked for an appointment. The detective's secretary returned his call a moment or two later to inform him he could come down straight away. The station was only a ten-minute drive and the secretary took him into Brooks' office as soon as he arrived. Apparently, the Inspector was keen to have an "informal" chat.

'Ah, Mike, good to see you again. Grab a pew.'

Mike still hadn't worked the Chief Inspector out. Three ISIS incidents, but still no progress appeared to have been made. Why? Was the detective getting too old for the job, not particularly capable, or just unlucky, in that he had had no breakthrough yet? Brooks seemed to be thorough in his approach. Perhaps he lacked that spark of brilliance that the Sherlock Holmes and Poirots of this world enjoyed. The Inspector was a comfortable looking man, portly and pleasant, but surely more was needed?

'I'm glad you have called in Mike. Informal, off the record chats can be useful sometimes.' Mike wondered where this conversation was leading, but he gave the inspector a warm smile, and waited.

'Let me start by bringing you up to speed. Initially, we hypothesised that this criminal behaviour was the work of either young Muslim radicals, or we had an extremist working on the village's building sites. We did our checks, but nothing significant resulted. Interestingly, with the killing of this dog, I think we have virtually eliminated both these possibilities. The mosque youth have been away for several days on some kind of a retreat. All the "at risk" radicals that the Imam had identified were away in Melbourne. So, I think we can definitely eliminate that group. As you know, the construction work in the village is now almost completed. Very few tradies are about anymore; just the decorators and some landscape gardeners finishing off. I'll do another check on them, but I don't expect to find anything helpful.'

'Have the forensics come up with anything useful?' Mike inquired.

'Afraid not. There was nothing we could use from the pamphlets or the flag-raising episode. The very fact that we have found no clues tells us though, that the offender is well prepared, thoughtful, plans carefully and covers their tracks. Important items like the Australian flag and the weapon used on the dog have seemingly disappeared into thin air. This is no hot-headed young activist. The police psychologist believes we are dealing with someone working on their own, who is a clever operator.'

'What about the ISIS message left with the dog. Is that any help?'

'Forensics are still working on it. The language used, and the general appearance, is similar to the pamphlets, so it would seem realistic to believe it is the same offender.'

'And the skewer?'

'No help. Typical of any easily purchased skewer.'

'So, what's the theory now?'

The inspector stood up, stretched, and moved slowly over to hover by his window. The view from the window was hardly exhilarating, as the police station was built next door to a multi-storey car park. The inspector, however, needed a moment to consider his response.

'Well, if we eliminate the young radicals from the mosque, and the workers on the building site, who are we left with?'

'Everybody else, I suppose,' Mike responded.

'Potentially, yes. So, we need to look more closely for possible motives. Who would want to target the residents of a retirement village like Easytimes? Who would you suggest, Mike?'

Mike was rather taken aback. He had come to the police station to find out what, if anything, was happening. Now the Inspector was asking *him* questions! All along, Mike had believed that the offender must be an ISIS sympathiser, because the messages were about getting ISIS families returned to Australia. But perhaps this was a red herring? Perhaps the malefactor had another motive altogether? Could it be that the person was really opposed to the Easytimes village and all the residents who lived therein? It seemed a crazy idea; nevertheless, he passed it on to the inspector.

'Great minds think alike,' Brooks responded, much to Mike's surprise. 'I think you are on to something. Perhaps all this ISIS stuff is just a smokescreen? Is it not possible that there is somebody around who hates the Easytimes Retirement Village, and is doing their utmost to make it unattractive to the residents, and to any potential new residents? All this ISIS stuff might be a clever scare tactic that also puts everyone off the scent.'

Mike was intrigued. Perhaps the police were on to something after all? Whoever was behind these events had well and truly put the jitters up a lot of people, and must have done the owners of the village considerable financial damage in lost income.

'Perhaps ... perhaps then, we should be looking for

somebody, who for some reason, does not want the retirement village to be a success?'

'Exactly,' replied the inspector. 'So, who might have a grudge against this particular village, and why? Give me your ideas, Mike.' Again, the inspector seemed intent on hearing Mike's views.

'Well …' replied Mike, challenged once more to come up with ideas. 'Perhaps someone who lives locally did not want the bushland destroyed to make way for a big building project? A greenie possibly? I suggest someone goes back through recent Council papers to see who was opposed to the development from the outset. Another place to look is in the local rag. Articles and letters to the editor may reveal an ardent opponent.'

'Excellent thinking, Mike.' Inspector Brooks appeared genuinely impressed. 'Now, surprise, surprise, we have already pursued both your suggestions. My research officer has studied all the relevant Council papers going way back to the first proposal to develop the site over three years ago. Council, it appears, approved the development with ten votes in favour, no dissenters and just two abstentions. One of the two councillors who abstained has since died and, believe it or not, the other one has retired and is now living in Easytimes!'

'Well, that's a surprise. It's my turn to be impressed. What about letters to the paper then?'

'On the whole, the correspondence was in favour. Council conducted a proper Environmental Impact Study that didn't highlight any real problems. Even the local indigenous population raised no objections. Everything appears to have proceeded through Council surprisingly smoothly.'

'So, what you are saying is; it is unlikely there is anyone out there in the local community who is so embittered about the erection of Easytimes Retirement Village, that they would seek to undermine the initiative?'

'Precisely. I suppose it is still possible that we have missed someone who would like to do harm to the village, but I very much doubt it. If there is such a person, they have not overtly shown their displeasure and must be working on their own and secretly. Most unlikely, I would suggest.'

'So, where does this leave us?' inquired Mike.

'In a real quandary, I have to admit,' responded the inspector. 'At least, I hope I have convinced you, Mike, that we have been doing our homework. We badly need a breakthrough. I'm concerned that the crimes in the village are escalating in their severity. Who knows what is going to happen next?'

CHAPTER 31

It was early Sunday morning and Claire Bury was already up, showered and getting dressed. The forecast was for a hot day, with temperatures rising to the high thirties, little or no breeze and a warm night to follow. She took her new dress off its hanger and looked at it carefully again. Yes, it was appropriately summery, suitable for church, and she felt sure Moses would like it, as it was bright and colourful. Moses had the African flair for loud colours and Claire wondered what he must have thought of her when they first met, and she was dressed in her dour grey garments. What a difference going out with Moses had made to her dress sense. She would be the first to admit she still didn't wear "fashionable" clothing, but now what she wore had for the first time in decades become important to her. She wanted Moses to like how she dressed.

Today would be rather special. Moses had been asked for the first time to read the lessons in church. Delighted to be invited, Moses was, at the same time, quite petrified.

How would the congregation manage with his heavy, African accent? Would anyone understand him? He'd expressed these concerns to Claire, who had spent over two hours one evening, giving him a crash course in elocution, and had helped him with expression, pacing and projection. This morning, they had arranged to meet in the vestibule, half an hour before the service, to have one more final practice.

They sat together in church every Sunday nowadays. They never touched, except to shake hands, when the Minister asked members of the congregation to greet their fellow parishioners. Today Claire sensed how nervous Moses was as the service began. Normally he was a confident man, but today he was distinctly nervous. Instinctively, just before he left the pew to read the first lesson, she reached out and placed her hand on top of his much larger one and gave a gentle squeeze. He glanced at her, managed a slight smile, and then was up and heading for the lectern. Apart from stumbling on a couple of the trickier words, he did remarkably well, and returned to his seat, where he wiped the sweat off his brow, and reached for Claire's hand to give her a "thank you" squeeze. And so it was that they started to hold hands occasionally, but only within the safe, sacred walls of their church.

Claire and Moses had been going out now for four months. It was a comfortable relationship, but they were, Claire considered, just very good friends. She certainly didn't feel she was in love with this man, but then, she reflected, she had no benchmark against which to measure the intensity of her feelings. She had never been "in love" with anyone before, except perhaps the Lord. She did find herself thinking more about Moses. What was he doing? What did he think about certain environmental, social and political issues? What did he *really* think of her? Why did he want to marry *her*? Was it purely loneliness, or did he really have strong feelings for her? Claire didn't know what to think, so she had decided to just keep things going, on an even keel, and see what eventuated. The Lord, she knew, would guide them.

When the service was over, Claire and Moses stayed for a "cuppa" and chatted with colleagues from the congregation. The Minister made a point of congratulating Moses on the quality of his readings and asked whether he would be interested in being placed on the permanent roster of lesson readers, which would involve him reading the lessons every three months or so. Thrilled to be invited, Moses accepted readily. Claire had been a lesson reader for several years, so he felt doubly honoured to join the team.

Lunch was a quiet affair at a small cafe down on the waterfront. It was too hot for walking, so they were happy to linger over lunch and enjoy the air-conditioned comfort. They chatted happily about church matters and Claire updated Moses on the goings-on in Easytimes village. Moses, who still worked as a delivery man for Bunnings always had a couple of amusing stories to tell. They ordered ice-creams, and Claire was just scooping up the last of hers, when Moses extended his ample hand across the table, and placed it on hers, preventing her from enjoying this final mouthful.

'Claire, have you thought any more about marriage?'

Taken aback, Claire sat frozen, her hand still holding her spoon. Moses was leaning over, looking at her earnestly, waiting for her answer. When Claire finally marshalled some thoughts together, it came out all wrong.

'Oh no, Moses, certainly not ... I mean ... oh sorry ... I'll start again. I don't mean, certainly not ... what I mean to say is ... this is all far too quick for me. We have only known each other for a few months, and I'm not a youngster. I need much more time to think about everything. Marriage is an enormous decision, and I want to know it's going to work first.'

'Well, my dear, we are not getting any younger. I plan to keep working as long as I am physically able but heaving heavy boxes and stuff about at Bunnings is getting a bit much for me. When I retire, I want to be able to settle down and relax, but that's not going to be much fun on my own. I'm very much hoping you will be part of my retirement package?'

Claire was not sure she appreciated being referred to as part of Moses' "retirement package" but she happily excused his sometimes wrongly nuanced English.

'Moses, I'm very fond of you and you are a great friend to me. But I have remained a spinster all my life, and agreeing to share my life with somebody else at my age isn't an easy decision. We might enjoy going out together as friends once or twice a week but actually living together in the same house twenty-four/seven is a totally different scenario. You don't know enough about me yet, and I certainly don't know an awful lot about you.'

Moses flashed a disarming smile that displayed the whiteness of his teeth. 'Claire, I want a good Christian woman to spend the rest of my life with and I think *you* are that woman. Do you think you can let me know soon? I realise this is very different to when I fell madly in love with my first wife, in Ethiopia, and we got married as soon as our families could arrange things. How about I ask you again in the new year? That will give you another couple of months to think seriously about the idea. We are both patient, tolerant people and we can make this work, I know we can.'

'Okay Moses, I promise I will think very seriously about it.'

Claire finally consumed the last of her melted ice-cream and they paid the bill and left. Moses' car was like an oven, even though they had been lucky enough to have parked in the shade under a massive Norfolk pine. They cruised along the coast for a time, with the air conditioning full on, and then turned inland and headed back towards Easytimes.

They were driving along the road that ran parallel to the high brick wall surrounding Easytimes when they had a sudden blow-out of the front tyre on the passenger's side. Moses reacted with a string of angry words in his native tongue. *Expletives*, thought Claire, relieved that she couldn't speak his language and know what he had just said. They pulled over and Moses began the onerous task of changing the wheel in the fierce heat of the afternoon. Sparing a thought for Claire, he left the engine running, so she could continue to enjoy the air conditioning. Claire laid her head back and started to feel sleepy, while Moses, drenched in sweat, laboured on the offending wheel.

Claire glanced out of the window a couple of times to see how Moses was progressing and each time she did so, something on the ground a few metres away glinted brilliantly in the bright sun light. She wondered vaguely what it could be, a piece of glass perhaps, or a can? A few minutes later, Moses returned, sweaty and dirty, and not in a happy mood.

'Moses, you are wonderful for fixing that wheel and letting me stay here in the cool. Thanks so much. Could I ask one little favour please?'

'What's that?'

'There is something shiny over there, glinting in the sun. It has had me intrigued. Would you mind going to see what it is for me, please? You never know, it might be a diamond brooch, or something else equally exciting. Can you see where I'm looking?'

Moses had to lean over very close to Clair's face to see what it was she was looking at. For a fleeting moment Claire thought he was going to kiss her.

'Oh yes, I see what you are looking at. I'll check it out.'

Moses wandered over and discovered an object he was not expecting to find. Lying on the ground, at an angle, was a kitchen knife with a blade at least eight inches long. He picked it up and examined it. An ordinary looking kitchen knife with a black handle and a stainless-steel blade with the name of the manufacturer appearing at the top. The knife was sharp but dirty so he couldn't quite decipher the name of the manufacturer. The knife looked as though it had lain here, undetected, for some time. Why, he wondered, would someone throw out what appeared to be a perfectly serviceable kitchen implement that looked as though it came from a set of knives? Shrugging his shoulders, he threw it back down on the ground and returned to his car, to find Claire in an agitated state.

'What's up Claire?'

'Was that a kitchen knife, Moses?'

'Yes. Why?'

'I might be an alarmist, or have too vivid an imagination, but do you remember me telling you about the dog in the village that had its throat cut about a fortnight ago?'

'Yup.'

'Well, do you think that knife could be the murder weapon?'

'I suppose it could be. Who knows, anyone might have left it there.'

'People don't intentionally leave dangerous knives like that one lying about. It's very close to the village wall. Whoever killed the dog could easily have thrown that knife over the wall as they ran away. What do you think?'

'I suppose it's possible.' Moses replied, as he prepared to drive off.

'Moses, please go back and get that knife. I think we should take it down to the police station so they can examine it properly.'

'What, right now?'

'Yes, Moses, right now.' Realising Claire was adamant, Moses climbed back out into the heat and retrieved the knife. Returning again to his car, he passed the knife across to Claire who threw up her hands in horror. 'Don't give it to me. I don't want my fingerprints all over it. It's already got all your fingerprints on it. Put it on the floor at the back, please.'

This bossy, schoolteacher behaviour from Claire was something Moses had not witnessed before. Would Claire revert to this way of speaking if they married? He looked at her curiously.

'Come on Moses, get going. Do you know where the police station is?'

Ten minutes later they pulled into the car park at the station. Moses produced a large white handkerchief which he wrapped around the blade of the suspected weapon. Feeling rather conspicuous, he did his best to carry the knife against his side, with Claire walking beside him, helping to hide it from any prying eyes.

They were in luck, because the young policeman serving at the inquiry counter happened to be the one who had attended the demise of the dog, Timor, together with his boss, Chief Inspector Brooks. He thanked them most profusely, confirmed that the knife may indeed be what they were looking for, had them sign a statement, and requested their full contact details.

The whole procedure took almost half an hour, but they departed feeling they had done the right thing.

CHAPTER 32

The industrial sized kitchen in the Facilities Centre at Easytimes Retirement Village was splendidly appointed. No expense had been spared in establishing a kitchen designed to provide sterling service to the residents for many years. The gleaming work surfaces were easy to keep clean and the industrial dishwasher had proved a godsend for the men in the village allocated the task of "clean and shine" each week after Happy Hour. Generous cupboards, all well-labelled, meant that even the slowest residents on kitchen duty each week could find what they were after and store items away correctly afterwards. So pleasant was the kitchen environment, there was no shortage of volunteers to come and prepare the food, cook and serve and clean-up afterwards. The regular Friday Happy Hour, with its variety of tempting, two course, cooked meals was a great hit with residents.

Heading up the Happy Hour volunteers was the inspirational, and irrepressible, Betty Wise, whose fame as a chef had quickly been ensconced into the minds (and stomachs) of all her village customers. Betty, and her faithful husband, Gordon, were in paradise. Never before, during all their years as caterers, restaurateurs, chefs and bakers, had they enjoyed such a lavishly equipped kitchen. They took great delight in planning the Happy Hour menus weeks ahead, and releasing the information electronically, or in the village newspaper, appropriately named, *Nice and Easy*. The rosters were working well, most of the volunteer helpers in the kitchen had been satisfactorily trained to handle their tasks, and high standards of cleanliness and food safety had been firmly established. Betty and Gordon's superb people skills had guaranteed a happy, chatty, workforce every Friday.

One particular Friday morning, Betty and Gordon strode across to the kitchen in the Facilities Centre to check that the provisions for Happy Hour had been delivered. On the menu was roast lamb, served with seasonal vegetables, with a vegetarian choice of roasted aubergine and tomato curry. Dessert was the ever-popular sticky date pudding. They were pleased to find everything they had ordered had arrived and they spent five minutes checking quantity and quality. When satisfied that all was as it should be, Betty rang the four volunteers rostered on to prepare the vegetables to come and start their work. Whilst waiting for the volunteers to show up, she took out the cutting boards, bowls and knives and had them ready. She was annoyed to discover, however, that one knife from a set of six knives, was missing from its holder. Presumably, it had been misplaced. Betty went to the drawers, where the rogue knife might have been mistakenly placed, but had no success. The loss of any kitchen equipment was abhorrent to Betty's high professional standards, and a knife from a quality set of six, was particularly galling. She determined to raise the matter at the next meeting of the Residents' Committee.

* * *

Chief Inspector Brooks was in his office, enjoying his mid-morning coffee, with a single Tim Tam. He used to have two or three Tim Tam biscuits every morning, but his wife had taken a stand, and rationed him to one. Seated opposite him was an attractive young lady, Danielle, from the forensics department. He had noted her shapely legs, when she had entered his office a few minutes ago, now sadly hidden from view, because she was seated so close to his desk.

What a strange world we live in these days, mused Brooks. When he was a young man, you could compliment a woman on her looks by looking her up and down, giving her a smile and a wink, or even producing a wolf-whistle if she was walking by. Today, the women were still attractive, but if you dared to flirt, or even be seen to be admiring their features, you were likely to be up on a charge of sexual harassment, or accused of being "a dirty old man". For a man to compliment a young lady on her dress these days was simply out of the question; you would be considered to be making "an unwelcome and inappropriate pass".

Brooks licked his fingers to be sure he had not missed the last remnant of his Tim Tam and putting on his formal policeman's voice, opened the conversation.

'Thank you for calling in to see me, Danielle. I'm very

appreciative of the prompt work done by your forensics people. So, what's the news?'

Danielle produced a stapled report from her bag and placed it on his desk. Brooks was fascinated by Danielle's long green fingernails and wondered how she managed to do things like typing or the washing up. On closer scrutiny, he was surprised to see that one of Danielle's fingers boasted a yellow fingernail. Why, he wondered?

'Do you like them?' chirped Danielle, holding both hands up for him to see better.

'Oh yes, very nice.' replied Brooks, hoping he was not being rude.

'Green's my colour,' smiled Danielle, 'matches my eyes.'

Brooks risked all, and looked at Danielle's eyes, to verify this claim. Indeed, she was right.

'Now this forensics report is an interesting one,' said Danielle, abruptly moving from frivolous to serious and professional. 'We found small traces of blood on the knife, but alas, it is not human blood. Probably a cat or a dog.'

'Well, I'm actually pleased to hear that,' replied the Inspector. 'The last thing I wanted to hear was that it was human blood.'

'As for fingerprinting, nothing to go on there really. There are traces of many different people's digits on the handle, with the guy who brought the knife in predominating because his are the freshest.'

'Anything else that might be helpful?'

'Possibly ... we checked the knife itself. The manufacturer is a company called Laser Works, a British company that has been exporting to Australia for many years. This particular knife is one in a set of six knives. So, if you can find a set of Laser Works knives with one missing, you might be on to something. Our search revealed these particular knives have been in continuous production since 2015 in the UK, and that they were first sold down-under by David Jones in 2017. Still available today.'

Danielle passed the forensic report across to the Chief Inspector, folded her arms and sat waiting with a slight smile softening her face.

'Do you have any idea how long the knife had been lying out in the open?'

Danielle laughed and gave a rather cheeky reply. 'Inspector, we don't usually conduct carbon 14 dating assessments on inanimate objects.' The Inspector reddened a bit, realising that stupid questions deserve stupid answers.

'Well, thank you for your help Danielle, very efficient, and I hope, helpful sometime soon.'

'My pleasure, Inspector,' Danielle picked up her file and with a final smile, made her way to the door, displaying her pleasing figure to the Inspector once again.

* * *

The next monthly meeting of the Residents' Committee was the last meeting of the year. As it was only two weeks before Christmas, Betty and Gordon couldn't resist preparing some special Christmas treats, and two full plates of Christmas goodies welcomed the committee members as they arrived. The Residents' Committee now had three additional members, providing a total of twelve members. The manager, Robert Tinson, had also been invited to attend. The mood was jocular.

Mike delayed the start of the meeting until everyone had had a chance to informally meet the newcomers and fill their plates. Seeing it was Christmas, Mike had thought to bring in a couple dozen beers and a selection of soft drinks. He regretted having to break up the party to attend to village business, but eventually he called them to order.

They dispensed with the usual agenda items in record time. Mike was pleasantly surprised to sense the bonhomie in the room and wondered if he should perhaps provide beer at every meeting in future to hasten proceedings. Secretary Claire scribbled furiously to keep up with the pace of the meeting and soon they were through the agenda and on to "General Business".

Betty Wise was, perhaps, the quietest member of the committee and seldom had much to contribute verbally. She more than adequately made up for her reluctance to participate in discussions, however, by keeping the committee well fed and victualled. To be perfectly honest, Betty abhorred disagreements and arguments, and was firmly of the belief that if everyone was happily consuming good food, and imbibing sensibly, then most of the world's problems would disappear. Today, however, the members were surprised when Betty announced she had an item she wished to raise. Mike smiled at the favourite chef in the village and invited her to speak.

Clearly nervous, Betty looked directly at the Chair and declared, 'I think someone 'as pinched a knife from the kitchen. We 'ad a set of six and one 'as gone. I've searched the kitchen from top to toe, and it ain't there. We 'ad it a few weeks back 'cause I saw it with me own two eyes. We 'ad all six safely in their box. In all me days as a chef, I never lost nothing. I think we 'ave a thief in the village.' Betty's comments were met by respectful silence, until Mike found his tongue.

'Oh Betty, I'm very sorry to hear that. You don't think someone took it home by mistake and has forgotten to bring it back?'

'I doubt it. Last time we sent out the Friday 'appy 'our menus, I included a request for the knife to be returned if anyone had taken it 'ome by mistake. Nothing 'appened.'

Claire cleared her throat and looked up from the minutes she was compiling. 'Mike, may I comment please?'

'Of course, Claire.' Claire, usually busy with her secretarial duties, was the other member of the group who usually had little to offer. Mike was pleased to see these two getting more involved.

'Betty, Moses and I; he's a friend of mine from my church; were driving home last Sunday and we found a kitchen knife by the side of the road. It was quite by accident. We had a puncture and had to stop the car to change the wheel, and there it was, lying in the grass.'

'Where was this, Claire?'

'Along the side of the village wall, not far from the main gates.'

"Ave you still got it?' asked Betty.

'No, we haven't. We remembered the horrid story of the Major's dog, so we thought it best to hand the knife in at the police station.'

'Good heavens,' exclaimed the Major. 'It's possible this was the weapon used to kill my beloved dog, Timor. What have the police said about the knife?'

'Nothing to us,' replied Claire, 'But then, they are not likely to tell us anything, are they?'

There was general agreement with Claire's supposition and two or three separate conversations broke out simultaneously.

'Order please ...' called Mike. 'Betty, can you describe the missing knife, please?'

Betty was now quite enjoying making a spoken contribution to the group, after remaining virtually silent at every other meeting to date. 'Yes, I can. It's got a brown 'andle and the blade is about this long.' She held her hands out to reveal a length of around twenty centimetres.

'Do you know the manufacturer, Betty?'

'Yes, it was a Laser Works knife.'

'Claire, what about the knife you found?' Mike continued.

'Well, it had a name on it, but we couldn't read it. It was quite dirty. From memory, I think the handle was brown and it sounds about the same length as the one Betty has lost.'

Mike looked over at Robert Tinson. 'Robert, would you mind ringing Chief Inspector Brooks please, to let him know that a Laser Works knife is missing from the village's kitchen?'

'Happy to help.' Again, chatter broke out as the manager retired to the other end of the room to make the call. Several stood up to avail themselves of another item of Christmas fare, or to secure a second can of beer while there were still some remaining.

A few minutes later, Robert returned, and they quietened

to hear what he had to say. 'I got through to the Inspector. He was quite excited; he thinks we have a match.'

CHAPTER 33

Jock Nettleton left the Residents' Committee meeting after finishing his beer and relishing one more mince pie. His arthritis was playing up again, particularly in his knees, usually a sign of a change in the weather. He was glad he had driven down to the hall for the meeting, as walking back home up the slight hill would have been too painful. As he approached his unit, he was annoyed to see that his daughter, Jayne, had parked her car in the driveway again, preventing him from putting the car in the garage. Their daughter was, at times, a disappointment to them. She lacked their considerate ways and, although they had never stood in her way, or objected, they were saddened by her choice to lead a life as a lesbian. They had not yet met her lover, Madeleine. Sadly, neither of the women appeared interested in providing them with grandchildren.

Jock parked out on the road, smacked his lips together in anticipation of a decent wee drop of whisky (so much better than the beer Mike had brought to the meeting), and fumbled for his door key. Jayne, never a quiet one, was remonstrating in a loud voice to Anne about something or other. Bracing himself for an expected tirade from his daughter, about whatever it was that was bothering her, he pushed the door open, and entered without them hearing.

'She's a fucking bitch, Mum ... I know she is having an affair with a man ... but she won't admit it. Our sex life has gone to the dogs, and it's all because she opens her legs up for some idiot of a man.'

There was a slight cough from behind Jayne, and she and her mother wheeled around to find Jock quietly standing there.

'Oh, hi Dad. I was just telling Mum about my personal problems.'

'Yes, I heard Jayne. We are always interested in your personal problems, but perhaps you could use slightly less colourful language, dear?'

'Oh, come on Dad, everybody swears these days.'

'I still think there is a proper time and place, and speaking to your mother like that, is being disrespectful to her.'

'Sorry, Mum. My relationship with Madeleine is stuffed, Dad. Two months ago, we were planning to get married and now I can hardly bare to live in the same house as her. How would you feel if I come to live with you for a time? Just until I can get set up somewhere else?'

This was not the first time Jayne had had a major falling out with one of her various lovers and had asked to stay. Somehow her tiffs always got sorted out and she had never yet been obliged to come and live with them. Given a little time, this fracas would probably blow over too. Jayne was, quite simply too excitable.

Fortunately, Jayne shared a love of a decent whisky with her parents, and shortly they were sitting down together in the lounge in a rather more congenial mood. Jayne was given to hyperbole, but by the time she had downed her second whisky, she had become more amenable and happier to socialise.

'So, what's happening in the village, Mum? Any more dogs been butchered?'

'No dear, everything seems to have calmed down, thank heavens.'

'Something interesting came up at the Residents' Committee this afternoon,' remarked Jock.

'Oh goodo Dad, something bloodthirsty?'

'Well, not exactly, but intriguing nevertheless.' Jock then proceeded to report all that had transpired at the meeting with regard to Betty's missing knife.

'So, how does this help us find out who killed Timor?'

'Well, it shifts suspicion firmly from someone *outside* the village to someone who lives *in* the village. It seems more than likely that somebody in the village, who knew about the kitchen knives, stole one, killed the dog, and then threw the knife over the wall, where it was found by Claire and her boyfriend.'

'Well, that narrows it down,' Jayne laughed, sarcastically. 'How many live in the village? Four hundred people?'

'How did the Major react to the news?' asked Anne.

'Surprisingly calmly. Did you know, by the way, he's got another dog? You'll never guess what he's named it.'

'Cut-throat?' suggested Jayne.

The parents looked at their daughter, disapprovingly. 'The new dog is called Leste,' smiled Jock.

'What's that supposed to mean?' asked Jayne.

'The country where the Major last served is called, Timor Leste. It means, East Timor.'

'What's this Major like, Dad? I remember bumping into him briefly one evening, when he was here to sing with you.'

'Well, he's a strange cove. He's a bossy, imposing sort of fellow. Still thinks he's in the army and that everyone else is a lower rank than he is. He became quite angry when Mike was chosen to be chair of the Residents' Committee rather than him. He's not well liked, because of his superior attitude. In fact, some folk just can't stand the man.'

'So, there would be heaps of people happy to cut his dog's throat?' suggested Jayne.

'Yes, I suppose so,' Jock replied, 'but few would be so nasty as to carefully plan something like this and then carry it through. I guess many of us have had bad thoughts sometimes, but we don't carry them out.'

'So, come on Dad, who do you think did this? Is it the same person who hoisted the ISIS flag and circulated the ISIS pamphlets?'

'Sorry Jayne, I have no idea. This is what we pay the police for. Personally, I get along quite well with Charles, that's the Major's name by the way, because we perform together musically. He has a pleasant baritone voice and I accompany him on my violin. We have already done a couple of concerts together. Even difficult customers, like the Major, can be mellowed with a couple of whiskies, you know.'

*   *   *

Rosemary and Arthur were the last to leave the Residents' Committee meeting. They had chatted around but managed to resist most of the tempting Christmas treats that Betty had produced. They stayed back to clean up, put away the tables and chairs and sweep the floor. As they pulled the hall door shut behind them, they started talking about the knife and who could have possibly performed such a vicious act on the Major's dog, Timor.

'I think it would have to be someone who works in the kitchen for Happy Hour.' Rosemary surmised. 'They would know where the knives are kept and could easily sneak one out at the end of the evening.'

'You may be right,' Arthur agreed, 'but anyone living in the village can get into that kitchen. The room is not locked and nor are the cupboards.'

'What I don't understand,' continued Rosemary, 'is the connection to ISIS. That is a common theme across all three events. We should be looking for an ISIS sympathiser. Who, in the village, is an ISIS supporter, Arthur?'

'I have no idea. If you are an ISIS supporter you wouldn't go around broadcasting it, would you?'

As they turned the corner, they ran into Snoddy and his wife, Mary. They had both missed the meeting because Snoddy had an appointment with his cardiologist.

'Hello,' said Mary. 'Have you been at the meeting?'

'Yes, we have,' they replied as one.

'We heard about the missing knife,' said Snoddy, looking at them both, expectantly.

'Wow, news travels fast.' Rosemary responded.

'Who do you think it is?' asked Mary, keen to get any extra thoughts from two people who had been at the meeting.

'Sorry, Mary, we have no idea. Your guess is as good as ours,' shrugged Arthur.

'I reckon it's that Russian woman in number 209. Never liked the look of her. Shifty she is. She could be an ISIS supporter,' Mary asserted.

'Nah, it couldn't be her, Mary, she's riddled with arthritis. She couldn't hold a bulldog and cut its throat at the same time.' As usual, Snoddy was about to start arguing with his wife. 'My guess is, it's the Major, who's done it to his own dog,' claimed Snoddy, with a firm nod of his head.

'Well, if you don't mind my saying, I don't think it is helpful to throw people's names about as being possible suspects. How would you like it if someone was walking around the village saying they think Mary and Snoddy did this?' Rosemary put her point across forcefully, and Mary and Snoddy realised they were out of order. But Mary still couldn't help herself.

'Snoddy, the Major wouldn't kill his own dog. He really loved that bulldog.'

'He's got another one, you know,' replied Snoddy, 'I think it's called Testes.'

'I doubt it,' laughed Arthur. 'I think you will find the new puppy is called Leste.'

* * *

Arthur and Rosemary bade Snoddy and Mary farewell, and made their way slowly up the gentle slope, trying not to laugh out loud at Snoddy's unfortunate error.

'Actually, Snoddy did say one sensible thing,' Rosemary observed, 'He noted that the person would have to be quite fit and strong to be able to catch a bulldog, hold it still, and cut its throat.'

'True,' agreed Arthur. 'It would be almost like trying to shear a sheep. Perhaps we should go through everyone in the village and divide them into two groups; those strong enough to do the deed, and those too weak and feeble, who we can eliminate from any further scrutiny?'

Rosemary giggled, 'Be careful Arthur, I know which group you'd be in.'

'And you'd be in the same group as me,' Arthur fired back, with a grin.

They had reached Rosemary's unit, and she wanted to invite him in for an evening meal, but then realised it was his squash competition night, and he would have to put his skates on to get there in time.

Suddenly, and without warning, Arthur reached for her hands, and looked at her intensely.

'Rosemary, will you come out with me for dinner on Wednesday evening, please?'

'Why yes, of course, but why on a Wednesday? We always go out on Saturdays.'

'I know, but this one is special.'

'And do I have to come wearing something special, Arthur?'

'You always look special to me,' smiled Arthur, 'Smart casual will do fine.'

'Well ...' said Rosemary, with a playful smile, 'I'm looking forward to it already. Where are we going?'

'It's a secret.'

Arthur's heart was beating faster than usual, as he contemplated his plans for next Wednesday.

He surprised his squash opponent that evening by being in his best form for a very long time.

CHAPTER 34

It was a sultry afternoon with the temperature in the high thirties and a blustery northerly blowing dust and pollen about. A cool change was forecast to come through in the early hours of tomorrow morning and bring relief after a week of unpleasantly hot weather. The local bird life had quietened down and sought refuge in the shady trees and air conditioners were purring all over town. Small business owners remembered, with some nervousness, the lengthy blackouts Adelaide had experienced in recent years following intensely hot weather, with the accompanying loss of thousands of dollars' worth of frozen food stocks. The few pedestrians about hugged the shade or sheltered under assorted umbrellas. Roll on the cool change.

Two men sat, in relative comfort, in the office of Chief Inspector Brooks. The Inspector, with his weight problem, disliked the heat of summer and longed to be sipping a martini somewhere on the coast with a cool sea breeze playing about him. Some would think such a picture incomplete without a dazzling blonde for company, but Brooks was past worrying about the fairer sex. An azure pool was, however, essential for a cool dip, whenever required. His halcyon daydreaming was rudely and abruptly disturbed by someone speaking to him, and he opened his eyes to see which of the two invited men had spoiled his reverie. It was Robert Tinson, manager at Easytimes Retirement Village.

'So, how can we help you, Inspector?'

The simple answer to that question was for them to tell him who had been committing the minor crimes in the village. But, as the policeman in charge of this case, he knew only too well, it was for him to work this out. The problems in the village had been going on for months now and he was still fossicking about in the dark with no strong leads. The events at Easytimes were like an ulcer, eating away at him, festering and painful. He was due to retire in six months, and badly wanted to leave a clean slate for his successor.

Brooks cleared his throat and responded, 'I want to pick your brains. You two are probably the people most familiar with the residents in the village. I want to ask for your help in trying to establish a motive for the troublesome events at Easytimes. The more I think about it, the more I am convinced it is somebody in the village. Do you agree with my hypothesis?'

Mike Fisher, the second of his visitors, was first to reply. 'Makes sense to me, if you are sure that you have eliminated everyone from the building trade and the local mosque; then it's the next best bet.'

'Agreed,' added Robert.

Brooks continued, 'If anyone is being particularly targeted by the events in the village, it is the Major. Remember, it is the Major, who is in charge of the flag ceremonies in the village. He is the one who trains the volunteers to do all the hoisting and lowering. As a military man, any interference with the Australian flag, under which he has faithfully served all his working life, would seem like treason. Next, someone cuts his dog's throat. It would not be unreasonable to assume that the references to ISIS are additional cruel cuts. The Major may not have fought against ISIS personally but he would know plenty of servicemen who have, and possibly still are. I'm worried that the next event could even be an attempt on the Major's life. Does that make sense?'

Both Mike and Robert concurred with the Inspector's reasoning.

'So,' demanded Brooks, leaning across his desk, 'Give me some names. I want to make up a list of possible suspects. Give me names, and reasons, why they may be responsible.'

His request was met by silence as Robert and Mike cogitated. Mike was the first to respond.

'Look, the Major is not well-liked. He's overbearing, he's arrogant and he appears to look down on folk in the village. But this is more than disliking someone, this is hating them. I guess we are looking for someone in the village who may have a serious grudge, from way back in time, or who has come to loathe him since entering the village.'

'That makes sense to me,' Brooks replied, in an encouraging tone. 'What do you think, Robert?'

'Well, I had a couple of disagreements with the Major during the purchasing of his unit. I can't say I enjoy his company, but I certainly wouldn't want to harm him in anyway.'

'Quite a few of us have had a bit of a run in with the Major,' Mike followed up. 'Two or three times, as chair of the Residents' Committee, I have had to be forceful with him. He doesn't always abide by the norms expected with meeting procedures. I wish I was a General, and then I think he would respect me more.'

'Okay, keep it coming,' laughed Inspector Brooks, 'I only have you two on my list of suspects at the moment.'

'Have you done a character check on the Major? You know … what he did in the past … perhaps there is someone living in this village who has loathed him from way back and now has the chance to take revenge?' suggested Robert.

'I'm way ahead of you,' replied the detective. 'He has had a colourful past and trod on a lot of toes. As far as I can tell, if he had been better liked, he might have risen to a higher rank than Major.'

'So,' mused Mike, 'we are looking for someone who has developed a hatred of the Major during the short time we have lived in this village. The first residents moved in here only about eight or nine months ago.'

'Good point,' conceded Brooks.

'Perhaps we should be looking more closely at the guys who are in the Major's flag-bearing party or serve with the Major on the Residents' Committee?' posited Robert.

'I can't see anyone on the Residents' Committee going to

such extremes,' said Mike. 'If you like, I'll have a bit of a yarn with one of the guys I know in the flag group. He may know if any of the men there harbour a strong grudge. There are six of them altogether.'

'Yes, please do that,' affirmed the detective. 'At this stage then, you can't come up with a few names of people likely to have it in for the Major?'

Both men shook their heads.

*   *   *

Rosemary Tattersall sat in her favourite armchair on Wednesday evening in readiness for Arthur, who said he would pick her up around six o'clock. She always took considerable care with her appearance, whether it be on the beach, running early in the morning, or out with friends, but today she had been even more fastidious than usual, as she sensed tonight was going to be really special. She had always been conscious of looking her best. Even as a little girl she had wanted to look pretty and then her time at Roedean, an exclusive girls' boarding school near Brighton, had taught her to wear even a uniform smartly. Care of her appearance had been further reinforced when she joined BOAC as a stewardess. Back in those days, a bit of "glam" or sex appeal was well received, and she certainly had that.

She and Arthur had been "an item" for nine months now. It was over three years since the death of her first, and only husband, and now she definitely felt ready to move on. There was still the occasional spell of grieving for the wonderful experiences they had shared for so many years, but the excitement of this new relationship with Arthur was steadily becoming the dominant force in her life. She sensed that tonight would be so special because Arthur would propose marriage. The thought of what might be about to happen later in the evening made her nervous. She hoped it didn't show.

Arthur, on the other hand, had had a hectic day. As a social worker he could never predict how any workday might turn out. He had travelled to his consulting rooms thinking that his appointments would be plain sailing and he would be able to get home in good time to shower, catch his breath, and pick up the lovely Rosemary, on time for their special night. It was not to be. At ten to six he rang to say he was still driving home and it would be closer to seven before he would be at her unit. He apologised profusely and laid the blame on a potential suicide case that he had had to deal with at short notice. Rosemary, as always, was magnanimous, and did her best to put him at ease.

Rosemary now had another hour to fill. She switched on the TV to Channel 27 (ABC Classics) and was pleased to hear one of Mozart's piano concerti playing. She picked up the hefty book she was reading, Bryce Courtenay's, *Solomon's Song*, and settled down once more in her favourite chair. It was difficult to concentrate though, as emotionally she was unsettled and longing to be out with Arthur. Some time elapsed and she dozed off. Something disturbed her, however, and sitting up, she thought she could smell something burning. What could it be? It was summertime, so she had no heating appliances on. Perhaps something had shorted? Her smoke alarm had not been activated, meaning it must be something minor. Rosemary stood up and walked around her small unit, visiting every room, and sniffing to try to detect the source. Nothing, yet she could still smell something burning.

It was then that Rosemary realised the burning smell was coming from outside. Perhaps a bushfire had started in the woods behind the village? The residents were safe from bushfires within the village itself, as there were no trees left on the site and the land had been completely cleared. The only vegetation was the foot-high shrubs planted by management located in the small gardens surrounding each unit. The fire, Rosemary reasoned, would have to be somewhere outside the walls of Easytimes. Out of curiosity, she went to her main window and pulled back the curtains. What she saw was shocking!

The unit opposite hers was on fire. Flames were leaping from the windows and there was a frightening low roaring sound as the fire sucked in oxygen like a hungry uncontrolled beast. It took Rosemary less than a second to realise that the fire was at the home of the Major and his wife, Jillian. Where were they? Were they still in the building? There was no sign of life, so hopefully they were out somewhere. She ran to her front door and immediately felt a whoosh of hot air and sparks hit her as she stepped out. A few of the neighbours were already on the scene, holding hoses and doing their best to get close enough to douse the flames. Arthur appeared.

'Rosemary are you okay? I need to use your hose, please. The fire brigade has been called and are on their way.'

'Oh Arthur, how terrible. Where are the Major and his wife?'

'Out somewhere, thank God,' Arthur yelled back.

It was hopeless. Major and Mrs Rogers' unit was totally engulfed in flames and everyone was now directing their hoses onto the unit next door to prevent the fire spreading. As she watched, horrified, the fire brigade arrived and one of the crew ordered her and the other nearby neighbours to close and lock all their doors and windows and then scram. Arthur dragged her hose back and dropped it on the ground. 'It's up to the firies now. Are all your windows closed up?'

'I'll double check,' and Rosemary raced around her unit again. She always left a couple of bathroom windows open a little, but everything else was firmly shut. In a few seconds they were at the back door and left quickly, Rosemary, having the presence of mind to grab her handbag as they exited. Already the fire was almost under control, and the structural remnants of the roof, like a blackened ribcage, was visible between thick palls of black smoke still belching from inside. Most importantly, it was now clear that both their cars were missing; a huge relief, as it meant no loss of life.

They retired to Arthur's unit, talking excitedly about what they had just witnessed. 'I saw the fire as I arrived back in the village and rang for the fire brigade,' remarked Arthur, 'but someone else had rung before me. They got here quickly, though.'

'I can't believe the place went up so fast,' commented Rosemary. 'I wonder if anyone has contacted the Major and Jillian to give them the terrible news?'

'I'll ring the Major now.' Arthur reached the Major almost

immediately; he had been down at the RSL Club and was on his way home and sounded agitated. Apparently, Mike had already been in touch, and had reported that Jillian was presumed safe, since her car was missing.

'What about my bloody dog?' roared the Major, 'Has anybody seen Leste?'

'Sorry, Major, I don't know. I didn't see him anywhere.'

A string of expletives exploded from the Major's mobile. When he calmed down a little, Arthur asked him whether he and Jillian had anywhere to stay the night. 'No problem, mate. We'll stay at my daughter's place.'

Effectively, Arthur and Rosemary's special evening was now doomed. The events of the last hour had completely destroyed the feelings of heightened excitement and anticipation they had both felt.

The mood wasn't right. Arthur rang and cancelled.

CHAPTER 35

Most residential fires flare up and are extinguished in quick time; it is the cleaning up and investigation of the cause of the fire that takes the time. The Captain of the local fire brigade was immediately suspicious on arrival at the site. Within a couple of hours of dampening down the last smouldering embers, the Captain and Chief Inspector Brooks had agreed that the fire had been deliberately lit and they were dealing with the crime of arson. They completed their preliminary investigations by ten that night, cordoned the area off, declaring it a crime scene. The detective promised to return at eight-thirty next morning to complete his assessment and would be joined by an expert from the Fire Department. The escalation of criminal acts at Easytimes Retirement Village, that the detective had foretold, now confronted him.

It was a troubled night in Easytimes. Not even the deaf, or visually impaired, had escaped the horrors of the night, for the strong pungent smell of burnt materials had infiltrated every unit. Dawn saw a steady stream of residents emerge, to inspect the damage. The fit ones walked, the less fit hobbled on walking sticks, and the least mobile cruised there on their gophers. All were united in shock and there was much tut-tutting that such an awful thing could happen in *their* village.

Rumours were rife and surprisingly varied. Only two facts seemed to be accepted by the residents. The first was that the Major and Jillian's unit had been destroyed by a fire and the second, that the Major and his wife were safe. Outside of these two immutable facts, imaginations had blossomed to an extent, and range, that few would have thought a community of oldies could have envisaged.

One school of thought posited that there really was an ISIS supporter inside the village somewhere, and that he, or she, was out to torment and eventually kill the Major and his wife. According to this theory, the Major had served at some time in a theatre of war where he had been fighting ISIS. Clearly ISIS was now seeking retribution. How else could anyone explain the involvement of ISIS flags and threats in the three earlier episodes in the village?

Proponents of a second line of thinking argued that the Major was so unpopular amongst the village residents, that somebody in the village had determined that the Major must leave at all costs. This person, or persons, was carrying out a series of escalating "anti-Major events" that had become more and more serious in nature because the Major had, as yet, shown no intention of leaving. Now that his home had been destroyed, he and poor little Jillian, would finally be off, and the mysterious perpetrator would, presumably, be satisfied.

A third viewpoint was that it was the Major who had destroyed his own home. It was well known that the Major suffered from post-traumatic stress disorder (PTSD). Clearly, according to this group of rumour-mongers, he had become more unhinged than usual after the murder of his dog, Timor. Unable to cope, and mentally unstable, he must have decided to end it all. At the very last moment, having started the fire, he must have changed his mind and so jumped in his car and fled, just in time.

Yet another theory revolved around the belief that the village management were so sick of the problems surrounding the Major, and the subsequent damage being brought upon their business interests, that it was *they* who were behind the arson attack. Somebody even claimed to have seen the manager, Robert Tinson, prowling about near the unit that very evening and looking as though he was up to no good. It was suggested he had been ordered to carry out the crime by none other than the owner, the elusive Mr Crocombe.

Finally, there were the deniers. This small and radical break-away group claimed that no crime had been committed and that the police had got it all wrong. The fire, they argued, was the result of some unfortunate electrical failure and to declare the immediate area a crime scene was an overreaction. When the blaze was fully investigated, they argued it would be discovered that the fire was accidental.

Not surprisingly, with all these options being freely bandied about, the village rumour-mongers were having a field-day. Morning teas sprang up all over the village, and residents could be seen scurrying from one morning tea to another in a desperate bid to keep abreast of the latest thinking. A trained observer would have noted that some of the most enthusiastic residents managed to fit in two morning teas and then ended up at a third friend's place for lunch. By mid-afternoon, many of the good folk of Easytimes were exhausted by the excitement, and walked, limped or rode back to the peace and quiet of their units for a well-deserved, afternoon snooze.

* * *

There was no peace and quiet, however, for Chief Inspector Brooks, who had been obliged to set his alarm clock half an hour earlier than usual in order to be at Easytimes by 8.30am. On arrival at the burnt-out remnants of the Major and Jillian's home, he found Robert Tinson talking earnestly to a tall, slim young man, wearing a boilersuit and stout boots. Several villagers were already milling about and exchanging comments in hushed tones.

'Ah, Inspector, this is Jim Hardcastle, a specialist investigator into the causes and behaviour of fires.'

'Good morning, Jim,' greeted the detective, noting the rather academic appearance of the expert from the Fire Service. They shook hands. Jim sported a full black beard and a pair of horn-rimmed spectacles. He carried a clipboard tucked under his arm.

'A bit of a mess here, Inspector,' commented the young

man, looking down at the podgy detective. 'I'll probably only require an hour or two to come up with an assessment of what has happened here. Would you like me to drop into the station when I'm finished? You would probably appreciate a verbal report, before I complete a full written one later today?'

'Yes, that would be excellent, thank you, Jim. Is there anything I can do to assist you in your work here?'

'No thanks. If I need details about power outlets, smoke alarms and the like, I guess Robert here can fill me in?'

'Yes, of course,' responded the manager.

And with that, Robert accepted a lift back to his office with the Inspector.

'Robert, where did the Major and his wife spend the night? I will need to contact them to discuss this sad business. They are of course prime suspects.'

'Apparently they went to stay at the Major's daughter's place somewhere in Adelaide. I have a contact number for the daughter, and the Major's mobile as well.'

'Good, let me have them, please. Now, Robert, do you know anything about this dreadful business?'

'Only "hear-say" Inspector. Mike Fisher rang me about seven o'clock last night to put me in the picture. My main concern was for the Major and his wife, but they were both out at the time, so the cars were gone and the couple, presumably, are safe, although very shocked, I imagine.'

Pulling up outside Robert's office, the Inspector rang the Major's mobile.

'Major, this is Chief Inspector Brooks speaking.'

'Morning, Inspector.'

'First of all, I want to know if you and Mrs Rogers are okay, apart from the awful shock of last night's events?'

'Of course we're not bloody okay, Inspector. Some bastard burns your home down and then you ask if we're okay? How would you be?'

'I apologise, Major, I didn't put that very well. Now, your unit is the site of a criminal investigation and nobody, including you, and your wife, are allowed to enter the area until I say so. Is that understood?'

'Understood, Inspector. My wife got away, but what about my bloody dog, Leste? Has anyone found my dog?'

'Not as far as I know, Major. Now, because this is a full criminal investigation, you and your wife are not permitted to leave Adelaide and I want you both to come to the police station later today to hand in your passports. I have to confiscate these until further notice.'

'What the hell for, Inspector? Are you suggesting that I, or Jillian, deliberately burnt our home down? You have no chance of us handing you our passports. They were incinerated in the bloody fire!'

The detective realised he was not handling the situation at all well and mumbled another apology before trying to rectify the situation. 'Major, I am not suggesting anything untoward, however, as a matter of course, in cases of arson, the occupants of a home, or business, are automatically regarded as prime suspects, until cleared. Like it or not, you and Mrs Rogers are prime suspects, and I will need to interview you both at some length. I would like you both to report to the police station at three this afternoon.'

'Well, Inspector, I will be there, but I have no idea where Jillian is. I have been trying unsuccessfully to contact her since seven this morning. She is not answering her mobile. She knows that we were expected at my daughter's place last night, but she never showed up. I guess she has gone to stay with one of her own cronies somewhere.'

'Please do your best Major, to make contact with Mrs Rogers, and bring her to the interview. I hope to be in possession of more information with regard to the cause of the fire when I see you.'

'And hopefully somebody finds my bloody dog. See you later, Inspector,' and a grumpy Major abruptly rang off.

CHAPTER 36

On the morning after the fire, Mike and Penny Rogers were having breakfast, sitting in the early morning sun at the back of their unit. The native shrubs and bushes, planted by the village management, were doing well, but were still too small to provide any privacy from their neighbours. It would be another two or three years before the plants had matured enough to make their backyard more secluded. The pair was having their usual "healthy" breakfast of muesli, Weet-Bix and bran, covered in generous portions of fresh fruit and probiotic yoghurt. Penny's kidney transplant had settled down well and she continued to feel more vital and energetic each day.

Unsurprisingly, their main topic of conversation was the fire. As chair of the Residents' Committee, Mike was regarded, quite rightly, as the leader in the village. This position brought with it both positives and negatives. On the positive side was the willingness of most villagers to tell him everything about everything. Consequently, Mike had his finger on the pulse and little of any importance escaped him. On the negative side was all the crap he had to listen to. Many of the oldies were given to "waffling", others were wingers, and some, little more than tedious gossip merchants. Mike had developed an inbuilt filtering mechanism whereby he was able, most of the time, to pick up on the useful information and reject the rubbish. Penny joked, that he functioned just like a giant oversized kidney, filtering out the toxins but retaining the helpful nutrients.

Part of the role of the chairperson was to demonstrate leadership by holding meetings for villagers, whenever necessary, to keep the residents informed. Failure to maintain such lines of communication left a vacuum into which the rumour-mongers injected all sorts of fake news. Mike was more than aware that the rumour-mongers were currently having a feast with regard to the dramatic fire the previous evening. He knew he needed to take the initiative and call an Easytimes Retirement Village residents' meeting. However, prior to doing so, he wanted to meet with his Residents' Committee to seek their advice. Before he poured his second cup of coffee he had decided, with Penny's blessing, to have the Residents' Committee around for another lunch meeting and to call a whole village meeting sometime tomorrow at a time recommended by his committee members.

Penny offered to provide some dessert and the irrepressible Betty Wise promised to unfreeze a pavlova. Everyone was asked to bring along their own sandwiches, or whatever, and to arrive around midday. Mike would have an urn on the ready for those who wanted tea or coffee. Robert Tinson was also invited but said he could only spare time for the actual meeting itself.

Mike was delighted when everyone on the committee arrived, except the Major. By shortly after midday, they had all assembled on his back porch to discuss the recent events. Mike began by asking the manager, Robert Tinson, to update them.

'Thank you, Mike, for inviting me. I'm not sure that I can add much that is new, but I can tell you what Inspector Brooks imparted to me about half an hour ago. Firstly, it is now confirmed that this *is* a case of arson and that the fire was started by someone pouring petrol around the entire unit. The burnt-out petrol container has been retrieved. Sadly, the body of the Major's newest dog, Leste, was also found in the ruins. Both the Major and Jillian are now wanted for questioning and the Inspector will be seeing them at 3.00pm this afternoon. Strangely, Jillian has disappeared. Nobody knows where she is, despite all her usual haunts having been checked out. She never turned up at the place she was invited to stay at last night. Where she slept remains a mystery. The police are now worried for her safety.'

'So they didn't leave the village together?' inquired Jock.

'No. They own two cars. The Major shows up on the front gate monitoring system as having left the village on his own at thirty-six minutes past six. Nine minutes later, Jillian is recorded exiting alone through the same gates in her white Toyota Yaris. We know that the Major was headed for the RSL Club, a place he frequents perhaps once a week. Jillian's planned destination is not known.'

'Do we know precisely when the fire broke out?' asked Rosemary.

'Not exactly. An electric clock was found in the bedroom that had stopped at six-fifty, which is when the fire must have destroyed it, or the electricity ceased to function.'

'Um ... that's only five minutes after Jillian went through the village gates. It would have taken her a minute or two to get out of her garage and drive down to the gates, so she either left a few minutes before the fire started or ...' observed Arthur.

Everyone assembled was now following along the same line of logic. Was Jillian the arsonist? The evidence appeared to point to her, but she was such a meek, timid little soul. Surely she would not have the guts to do such a terrible thing? Quietly spoken, almost shy, it didn't fit anyone's perception of her character. Nobody suggested out loud that the arsonist was Jillian, but that thought now rested uneasily in everyone's mind. It was common knowledge that the Major treated his wife disgracefully, and presumably had been doing so for many years. Could it be that Jillian had finally snapped and decided she had had enough?

It was Rosemary who finally broke the silence and began the conversation that members of the committee needed to have.

'Look, I'm no psychologist but I think there is a pattern here. Whoever is behind all these crimes, has been gradually escalating events over several months now, and the criminal acts appear to be targeting the Major, but placing the blame on ISIS. There is intensive planning and careful execution behind each crime. Think about it for a moment; the pamphlets, the flag incident, and the murder of the Major's dog, were all linked to ISIS. But why? Is it possible, this whole ISIS thing is some sort of a red herring to confuse us all? Until last night's horrendous fire, we have all been suspecting someone from ISIS, or at least an ISIS sympathiser. Perhaps that's a smoke screen? Perhaps we are dealing with a very clever person whose main motivation is to attack the Major and Jillian. If I'm right, then the police should be looking for somebody who hates Major and Mrs Rogers so much, they are prepared to try and kill them by setting their unit on fire when they are home.'

'That sounds logical, Rosemary. What we don't know though, is whether the person who is doing all this has a hatred of only the Major, or whether the person has a grudge against both of them,' added Betty.

'My reading of all this, is that the Major is the prime target and that poor meek Jillian is just caught up in it all because she just happens to be married to the man,' commented Jock.

'Sorry, but I can't agree with you, Jock,' interjected Mary. 'If anyone has the motivation to hurt the Major, it would have to be Jillian. Living with that man for all her married life must be unbearable. Jillian never says anything against her husband, she just bottles it all up. Eventually, a person can't take any more, and they break down, or does something about it. I think Jillian has endured domestic violence for umpteen years and when she moved into this village decided she could stand it no longer. The fact that she has now strangely disappeared adds weight to my argument.' Mary looked around the group for support.

The members of the Residents' Committee appeared to be divided on the issue. Arthur spoke up next.

'It's still possible that the perpetrator of all these crimes is someone unknown to us all. We still can't rule out someone living outside the village. Perhaps there is someone from the Major's military past who is intent on revenge? Sadly, the Major is very adept at upsetting people. You only have to see how unpopular he has become in this village in less than a year to see that. Quite possibly the Major has made a number of enemies across his army postings here in Australia and overseas.'

Claire chipped in next. 'I may know Jillian better than anyone else on this committee. We have been getting together for a coffee, nearly always at my place or downtown, on a weekly basis for months now.'

'So, how have you found her, Claire?' asked Arthur.

'Well, she is a bit of an enigma really. I feel really sorry for her, which is why I have made it my business, as a Christian woman, to befriend her and perhaps help her in some way.' Claire looked around, and seeing the interested faces listening, felt encouraged to continue.

'The first thing, I would say, is that Jillian is clever. As the wife of an army officer, who has been based in many parts of the world, she often had time on her hands, so she enrolled in university distance education courses. It is not easy studying at home on your own, but she has chalked up no less than three university degrees over the years. So, she may come across as shy and timid, but she is actually very knowledgeable, and extremely widely read. Jillian could probably engage with anyone in the village on an intellectual level.'

'That's interesting,' commented Mike, 'Anything else you can tell us, Claire?'

'Sometimes when we met, I could see that Jillian was really uptight. She would arrive tense and wouldn't look me in the eyes. She never opened up and explained what her problems were, even though I tried to get her to confide in me. I think its problems at home with her relationship with Charles. I have never seen any signs of physical abuse, so I put it down to verbal, or emotional, abuse. It sounds awful, I know, but I get the feeling that he constantly belittles her and this affects her self-esteem. I did my best to build her up again during our get-togethers.'

'Thanks Claire. Arthur, you are a social worker. What do you make of all this?' queried Mike.

'Well, I have never worked with Jillian in a professional capacity, however, what you are describing Claire, is indeed typical of a dysfunctional relationship where one person is totally dominant and the other becomes subservient. This is acutely unhealthy, and if it goes on long enough, will often lead to serious consequences.'

'What sort of consequences, Arthur?' Jock asked.

'Well, every case is different, so it is impossible to predict precisely what may happen, unless I'm involved with the family professionally. Even then, I sometimes can't make significant progress, and it all ends in grief.'

'I think what we are asking, Arthur,' Rosemary added, 'Could this highly dysfunctional relationship have led to Jillian carrying out these acts of aggression against her husband?'

All eyes were now fixed on Arthur's, anxious to hear his professional opinion.

'Again, I must stress, that I have *not* been professionally involved in this case, and it is perhaps unfair of me to even try to make a valid comment. However, based on numerous cases I have had experience with over many years, I would have to agree that such a dysfunctional relationship will eventually break down, unless the couple seek counselling.'

'And what sort of "break down" is likely?' persisted Rosemary.

'By far the most common outcome is separation or divorce. Occasionally, there are more violent outcomes. These may be suicides or violence against the perpetrator.'

'So, it is not out of the question then that Jillian may have resorted to violence to end the impossible situation she found herself trapped in?' asked Mike.

There was a moment's silence as everyone awaited Arthur's response.

'Yes, it is possible,' Arthur agreed.

* * *

Chief Inspector Guy Brooks had endured a frantic day. The arson attack at Easytimes Retirement Village yesterday had made it onto the ABC and commercial news outlets and he had been hounded, relentlessly, by journalists, despite giving an official press statement at noon. It had long been his intention to quietly wind down his workload as retirement approached, now only a few short weeks away. At the age of sixty-six he had reached that time in his life when he longed to leave work and start to enjoy all the activities largely denied him as a serving policeman. High up on his wish-list was travel. His wife, Irene, had for several months now, been exploring likely trips online and the piles of travel brochures in the lounge room were mounting up. Instead of having the time to devote to planning future world trips with Irene, he was being overwhelmed with the workload emanating from this tiresome retirement village.

ISIS pamphlets, and the removal of the Australian flag incident, he had been able to manage easily enough, even the murder of the Major's dog, though more demanding on his time, had been handled without too much fuss. But arson! Arson was a serious crime and this case had attracted national interest. Instead of a smooth quiet slide into a well-deserved retirement, Brooks found himself back in the public eye, the chief investigator of a major crime.

The Inspector's stomach was grumbling, a reminder that he hadn't eaten since breakfast, and it was nearly three o'clock, the time he had set aside for a lengthy interrogation of Major Charles Rogers and his wife, Jillian. Both had been instructed to appear at the police station and were regarded as "persons of interest". The Inspector rang through to his secretary and requested she bring him a strong black coffee and two meat pies with plenty of tomato sauce from the canteen and as quickly as possible. His secretary hesitated, 'Inspector, Major Rogers is already here. Shall I ask him to wait until you have eaten?'

'Oh, bugger. Excuse my French. Has Mrs Rogers arrived?

'No, sir'

'Good, that gives me the perfect excuse to delay the

meeting until I have had my pies. Would you also call Senior Constable June Scott, please? I want her present for the interviews. I briefed her earlier.'

'Certainly, sir.'

The Inspector heaved his large, and somewhat cumbersome frame, out of his comfortable executive chair and moved across to his filing system where he retrieved an ever-expanding file entitled, "Easytimes Retirement Village". He had barely resumed his seat when there was another knock at the door.

'Come in.'

The door opened to reveal the smiling face of Senior Constable June Scott.

'Come on in June and grab a seat.'

'Thank you, sir.'

June was a cheerful, dependable policewoman who you could trust. She was in her early forties, and, despite her happy disposition, had never married. The Chief Inspector had raised this with June, quietly, at last year's Christmas party after everyone had had a few, but she dismissed his well-meant inquiry quite happily by saying it was a case of never finding the right person. Now she looked after her elderly mother and relished every opportunity she had to be with her nephews and nieces. After the press conference at noon, the Inspector had briefed the Senior Constable thoroughly on the events leading up to the arson attack.

'June, I'd like you present please, for the formal interview to be conducted with Major Charles Rogers, and his wife, Jillian. You know the background, and I value your opinion.

I'm dying of hunger and have two pies coming up from the canteen. We are scheduled to be in the interview room two in ten minutes. That okay?'

'No problem, sir. I'll see you there in ten.'

As June left, the Inspector's pies and coffee arrived. Eating two hot meat pies, without pressure to finish them quickly, could be a hazardous activity, but to stuff them in with only a few minutes available could be catastrophic. The Chief Inspector was relieved that he was eating privately, behind closed doors, as he made an awful mess of it. As always happened in a hurry, the pies would turn up piping hot, and the roof of the Inspector's mouth was scolded. The stupid little sauce containers exploded in the wrong direction and the pastry was far too flaky and quickly littered his desk. Worse still, the canteen must've been on some kind of cost-saving strategy, for they had supplied only one small paper serviette. Surely, the Inspector mused, two pies merited two serviettes? He licked his fingers vigorously, grabbed the waste-paper basket and shovelled most of the detritus on his desk in the general direction of the bin. Tucking the Easytimes file under his armpit, he grabbed the remnants of his coffee and hurried off down to interview room two.

The Inspector arrived a moment later still feeling pressured, to find Senior Constable June Scott waiting inside and a grumpy looking Major Rogers seated outside. It was already five minutes past three. Shuffling in, he closed the door behind him and inquired whether June was ready to start.

'Did you enjoy your pies, Inspector?'

'Yes, thank you.'

June produced a tissue from somewhere and walked over to the Inspector where she proceeded to wipe a prominent tomato sauce stain off the front of his shirt.

'Umm … I was in a bit of a hurry.'

'So I see, Inspector.'

'Shall we get started? Please ask the Major to come in.'

Major Rogers presented as a tall, good-looking man, straight backed and athletic looking. A thin moustache greyed his upper lip, whilst well-shaped, tidy, white hair, afforded him a rather distinguished appearance. He wore what looked like a regimental tie, a tweed jacket, cavalry twill trousers and well-polished brown brogue shoes. Looking the seated policeman in the eye, he nodded, 'Inspector …'

The Inspector held the army man's gaze and invited him to be seated.

'Inspector, my lawyer will be here shortly. I want him present throughout these proceedings.'

'No problem there, Major. Let me introduce my colleague, Senior Constable June Scott.'

June Scott smiled pleasantly, and in return, received a curt nod.

'Okay, let's get started,' announced the Inspector.

'Nothing happens until my lawyer is present, thank you, Inspector,' countered the Major.

There was an awkward silence, blissfully interrupted by a knock at the door.

'Come in please.'

The door opened to reveal a tubby gentleman, with a full

white beard and moustache, a ruddy face, typical of a frequent drinker, and a stern, unfriendly manner.

'Good afternoon, Inspector. I am here at the request of my client, Major Rogers. My name is Jeremy Shoebridge, and I'm from the law firm, Shoebridge, Cromwell and Shoebridge.'

'Welcome, sir. Please take a seat. We are ready to begin.'

Shoebridge took his time. He removed his jacket, placed it on the back of the vacant chair, sat down, and produced a small pocket-sized writing pad, a pen and a watch that he placed carefully in position in front of him. This done, he looked up at the Inspector and gave an affirming nod.

The recording gear was activated with the usual declaration of the time and date of the interview, together with those present noted. Special mention was made of the fact that Mrs Jillian Rogers had failed to obey the police order to attend.

'Major Rogers, may I start by commiserating with you, on the loss of the unit you and your wife have been occupying for almost a year? As you know, the destruction of your home has now been proven, without doubt, to have been the work of an arsonist. It is my job to apprehend the arsonist and any accomplices. In cases of arson, it is standard police procedure to interview the occupants first. I'm sure you understand that in many cases, it is the owners of a building who are found to be the criminals, usually illegally seeking insurance pay-outs.'

'I hope, Inspector, that you are not in any way insinuating that my client would do such a thing?' interjected Shoebridge.

The Inspector ignored this comment and pressed on.

'Major Rogers, we appreciate you being here, as requested;

however, your wife was also expected. Are you able to enlighten us, as to why she is not present?'

'No, Inspector, I cannot. I have not seen my wife since before the fire, nor have I heard from her. I sent her a text and tried to contact her several times on her mobile to tell her that she is very welcome to stay with me and my daughter in North Adelaide. Sad to say, she has not bothered to reply to any of my communications.'

'Where then, Major, did she spend the night?'

'I have no idea. My daughter rang the friends and family my wife knows well, to try and trace her, but to no avail.'

'Well, Major, she is *your* wife. You must know her better than anyone? Where would you suggest she has gone?'

'Sorry, Inspector. I have no idea.'

'Has she ever disappeared before?'

'No,'

'As soon as this interview is over, I will issue a warrant for her arrest. I also have the full details of the car she was last seen driving just a few minutes after the fire broke out.'

'Inspector, you should withdraw that statement. Once again, by implication, you are suggesting that Mrs Rogers may be involved in this crime.'

'Mr Shoebridge, I am issuing an arrest warrant because Mrs Rogers has failed to attend a police inquiry.'

The lawyer realised he was out of order and made no comment.

'Let's change tack, Major. Can you think of anyone in the village, or during your long military career, who might wish to attack you in this way? Do you have any known enemies?'

'Inspector, the very essence of my career as an army officer was to order people to do things. When you are in command of men and women in the armed forces you give the orders. The recipients don't always like these orders, and sometimes may become resentful. I am not, however, aware of anyone who has been so offended by my orders that they would seek some sort of revenge.'

'Thank you Major. I want now to turn to a more delicate matter. How would you describe the relationship you have with your wife?'

'Objection, Inspector. Domestic affairs have nothing to do with this case.'

'On the contrary, Mr Shoebridge, I have every reason to believe that the relationship between the Major and his wife is central to solving this matter. Several witnesses have told me this from the Easytimes Retirement Village, including the manager and the chair of the Residents' Committee. To refuse this line of interrogation could jeopardise a just and fair result.' The Inspector glared defiantly at the lawyer, who once again remained silent.

'So, Major, your comments, please?'

'I don't see why my relationship with my wife is anyone's business. We have been married for nearly forty years. Surely that tells you something?'

'Major, you know as well as I do, that many marriages continue for thirty, forty or even longer years, but the people in these long-standing marriages are not necessarily always happy. Would you describe your marriage as being a happy one?'

'Yes.'

'Do you think your wife would agree with you?'

'Yes.'

Realising that this interview was leading nowhere, the Inspector abruptly brought it to a conclusion.

'Major Rogers, I am not satisfied with the way this investigation is proceeding. Therefore, you, and your wife, remain prime suspects and are not at liberty to leave the city. You must report here at this police station three times a week on Mondays, Wednesdays and Fridays until further notice. In the meantime, the police will do everything possible to find your wife. I hope you will be fully cooperative and inform us immediately if you hear anything from her. She will now also be placed on the "Missing Persons" register. Do you have any questions?'

'No questions, Inspector.'

'Interview terminated at 3.35pm.'

Without further comment, the lawyer and his client left the room, leaving the Inspector and Senior Constable June Scott to conduct a brief review.

'What do you think, June?'

'I don't think we learnt much from that, sir. It's more important than ever that we find Jillian Rogers. I think she is the key to solving this crime.'

CHAPTER 37

'Here you are.' Claire Bury handed a glass of white wine to Moses Lobrida as he sat comfortably sprawled across a wooden garden seat on her back porch. Is this what married life will be all about, she pondered? Sitting about, relaxing, with wine and entrees before the evening meal? Until she had met Moses, she had rarely partaken of a wine in the evenings, it just didn't seem right when you lived on your own. She rather enjoyed "unwinding" as Moses called it. Somehow, sitting outside on a beautiful barmy evening, with enjoyable company, a glass of vino and some nibbles, combined to create a thoroughly pleasant ambience. Perhaps marriage to Moses would be a good thing after all?

Claire parked herself on the spare seat and leant back, allowing the last of the sun's rays to fall across her. She pulled her sunnies down and closed her eyes. Her relationship with Moses had steadily matured as she had become more accustomed to his ways. Only a few weeks back, she would never have been able to chill out like this in his presence. Now, it seemed almost natural and even comforting. She could handle this; in fact, she found she was starting to really look forward to their quiet evenings together. Her only concern was how she could handle the sex stuff that Moses had told her in no uncertain terms, was an integral part of married life.

A few weeks ago, Claire had driven to a shopping centre, about ten kilometres away, and visited the bookshop there. She was terrified of meeting someone she knew if she had gone to her local bookshop, because she was looking for a book about sex. She was staggered to discover such an extensive selection of books on the topic and felt deeply embarrassed as she started thumbing through a few of the publications. A couple of young teenage girls were there too, making comments such as, 'Oh my God, look at this,' 'Heh, how would you like to do this?' 'That looks gross!' Neither of the girls appeared to notice Claire, who was blushing and feeling deeply ashamed. Unable to stay close to this array of sex manuals for another moment, Clair grabbed three or four of the smaller books closest to her and hurried off to some vacant chairs well away from the offensive collection. Positioning herself as far as possible from the prying eyes of other bookshop customers, she hid the books under her shopping bag, and when no one seemed to be looking, pulled out the first one.

The book was called, "Starting Your Sex Life" and was aimed at the young teenage market. Claire thumbed through, stopping from time to time, to look closer. She skipped over the first few chapters that explored the differences between males and females but was fascinated by parts two and three that dealt with mysterious topics such as foreplay, arousal, sexual positions, fetishes, orgasms and sexual preferences. Gobsmacked by the extent of material that was almost totally foreign to her, she decided, there and then, that this book would do nicely as an introduction. Placing the other books back on the shelves, where the two teenage girls were still gawping and giggling, she hurried over to the girl at the cash register, with the book clutched firmly against her stomach in case anybody saw the title.

Claire reached the counter, just ahead of two men, who fell into line directly behind her.

'Hello,' the young female cashier greeted her cheerfully.

'Hello,' Claire replied, blushing.

'Are you buying that book?'

'Yes, please.'

The cashier placed the book on the counter for all to see, as if it was a book of recipes or motorbikes or something else equally mundane. Claire avoided looking the cashier in the eye, and just mumbled, unconvincingly, 'It's … it's for my granddaughter.'

'Yeah, there's some good stuff in there. We sell lots of those. She'll be an expert in no time.'

Heartened by the fact the book was apparently popular, Claire felt she had done well, paid with her visa card and left the shop with a deep sigh of relief.

A smile played across Claire's face as she now recalled her visit to that bookshop. To say that she had devoured the book, was no exaggeration. Within a couple of days, she had read it through, from cover to cover. The joint authors, a married,

Christian couple, would you believe, had portrayed sex and sexuality as a God-given blessing, something to be deeply respected, revered, and never abused. She had not expected this spin on an act she had sometimes regarded as dirty and sordid. Instead she was uplifted, and, although still fearful of her total lack of experience, she believed that Moses could gently lead her into the joys of a satisfying and beautiful sexual relationship. Being a believer in destiny, she thanked the Lord for guiding her to the best book on the shelves of that bookshop.

She opened her eyes and gazed across at Moses, who was sleeping peacefully, and felt a stirring of desire for the very first time in her sheltered life. He must have sensed her looking at him for he suddenly woke up.

'Claire, what's the latest on the fire at the Rogers' place?'

Over the next five minutes or so, Moses sat quietly, sipping his wine, as he listened to Claire recount all she knew. After a moment's contemplation, Moses, glancing across at the women he hoped to marry, asked, 'Do you think Jillian is behind this string of crimes?'

'I really don't know Moses. I probably have spent more time with Jillian than anyone else in this village, apart from her husband, but she remains an enigma.'

'A what?'

'An enigma. It means somebody who is puzzling, inexplicable, a riddle.' Occasionally Claire forgot that English was Moses' third language.

'It seems strange, that since the fire, she has just vanished,' added Moses.

'I know. I'm really worried about her. I just hope she hasn't committed suicide.'

'Why would she do that?'

'Well, think about it. She was constantly being verbally and psychologically abused by her husband, which made her life a misery. That, in itself, would be enough for some women to contemplate suicide. And then, if she has been the perpetrator of all these crimes, she has all that guilt to try to deal with, on top of her own tragic life. If she is found guilty of this series of crimes, she will have to serve years in jail. Not much to look forward to, is it?'

'But is there any proof?'

'Only what they call "circumstantial".'

And there the conversation ended. A cool breeze had come up, so they retired indoors and enjoyed the hot Fijian curry Claire had been warming up in the microwave.

* * *

A few units away, another romantic couple was sharing an evening meal. Tripping off to restaurants every Saturday night, delightful as it was, had become rather too expensive for Rosemary and Arthur. Now they took it in turns to cook on Saturday evenings and only went out for a restaurant meal if there was a special excuse, such as a birthday. Tonight, it was Arthur's turn to provide the gastronomic delights.

Inevitably, the conversation focused on the doings in the village. Arthur was stirring the beef stroganoff and trying to keep an eye on the steaming vegetables at the same time.

There was nothing worse than overcooked, soggy vegetables. He poured himself another glass of red wine, offered to fill up Rosemary's glass, and then asked her who she thought had burnt down the Rogers' unit.

'Who knows? Nobody saw it happen, so I don't know how they will ever find out. Of course, Jillian has to be the main suspect. Now that she has, apparently, disappeared, it makes it seem even more likely that she is the culprit. What do you think, Arthur?'

'Yes, I would have to agree. I'm wondering though if the Major was involved in some way?'

'Why would he be? What motivation would he have had to burn down his own home?'

'I think he may be of unsound mind sometimes,' reasoned Arthur. 'Everybody knows he suffers from PTSD. Perhaps he completely lost it and went berserk?'

'He can certainly get very depressed as we saw that night when we found him sitting out in the rain after his dog was slaughtered. But this must have been a pre-meditated act. People don't normally keep containers of petrol, or whatever it was, around the house, ready to burn the place down.

'Well, they do if they have to mow the grass.'

'Yes, but there is no grass to mow here. The gardeners do it for us.'

'True.'

'Where do you think Jillian has gone?'

Arthur was busy serving up, and being a mere male, couldn't do two things at once. He brought over the beef stroganoff on their plates with the vegetables in two separate dishes so they could help themselves. Four vegetables were on offer; buttered broad beans, mashed sweet potato, spinach and carrots in some kind of creamy cheese sauce. Once they had taken what they wanted, and Rosemary had congratulated Arthur on his efforts, he responded to the question.

'God knows, where she's gone. Apparently they have checked with all her friends and family and nobody has seen her. I'm sure the police are searching for her little white Toyota Yaris. Trouble is, there are an awful lot of white Yaris's about.'

'You don't think she has committed suicide?'

'I hope not.'

'Is there anything, Arthur, we can do to help to find her?'

'I don't think so.'

Rosemary and Arthur, like everyone else in the village, were at a loss to know what more they could do. Everything now was in the hands of the police. To date, the police had failed to solve any of the crimes committed within the walls of Easytimes Retirement Village during the first year of its existence. Distressingly, the residents didn't hold out much hope that things were going to improve.

CHAPTER 38

Chief Inspector Guy Brooks had not slept well. The string of unsolved criminal events at Easytimes was playing on his mind and had kept him awake. He had been so restless last night that his wife had finally told him to go and sleep in the spare bedroom. Tired and irritable, he had sought out clean sheets and pillowcases in the wee small hours of the morning to make up the spare bed. It was no wonder he arrived at work in a seriously grumpy mood.

Senior Constable June Scott sat on the other side of her boss's desk and realised she could be in for a torrid time, unless she could somehow calm the Inspector. There was no helpful news to give him with regard to the search for Jillian Rogers and a final examination of the burnt-out ruins of the unit had been unproductive. There was no trace of Jillian's laptop amongst the embers, so she must have taken it with her. Had they found the laptop, the experts in IT would probably have been able to retrieve any ISIS notes that she may have generated. The Senior Constable resolved to try to be extra patient and understanding. In her view, the quicker the Chief Inspector retired, the better it would be for all concerned.

'Can I get you another coffee, Chief?'

'If I drink anymore, I'll wet my pants.' The Inspector snorted. 'June, we must find this woman urgently; she can't have just disappeared into thin air. Are you sure that we are pursuing every possible line of inquiry?'

'Yes, sir.'

'Then, why haven't we found her yet?'

'We just have to be patient, sir. I'm sure there will be a sighting of her, or the car, soon.'

'I have run out of bloody patience, June. What did you find out about Jillian Rogers when you ran the police profile?'

'Some interesting stuff, sir. According to her husband, Jillian was, many years ago, in the army, serving as a junior officer. That's where they first met. Apparently, Jillian excelled in the army, and had a reputation for being one of the toughest women, at a time when women were only, reluctantly, being admitted into the armed forces. She had wanted to join the commandos but was refused because of her gender. She remained in the army until children came along and retired on a full army pension at the age of thirty-five, with the rank of Captain. During her army career she completed many tough courses in bush survival, mapping, endurance, even jungle warfare.'

'So … the meek and mild woman, that the villagers all reported her to be, has a hardened core that nobody knew about, except the Major, of course. In fact, with her military background, she would be more than capable of looking after herself out in the bush. All her training was thirty years ago but that is a skill set she won't ever forget. She might not be nearly as fit as when she was a young army officer, but we now know that underneath the quiet, timid persona is a really tough cookie. Interesting ...'

'According to the villagers who knew Jillian, she had been endlessly abused by the Major, which explained her down-trodden, sad appearance. Constant, psychological abuse eventually would break down even the strongest woman. It seems feasible that finally she could stand it no longer and has been fighting back.'

'This extra information about Jillian's past possibly helps to explain the brutal murder of the Major's dog. Until now, I could not imagine a timid woman going out and catching that dog, physically holding it down, and then being able to slit its throat with a knife. However, now we know about Jillian's army background, it becomes more plausible.'

'Agreed, sir. The thing I still don't understand though, is the connection with ISIS. The first three incidents all featured messages attributed to ISIS. Why? We have found no evidence to support the notion that ISIS sympathisers were behind these three events. So, what's going on? Is it possible that Jillian is a covert ISIS supporter?'

The Chief Inspector dwelt on this idea for a moment or two before replying. This had already been a valuable conversation with his Senior Constable and he felt his despondent mood lifting. Throwing ideas about like this was always useful.

'Are you suggesting, June, that Jillian is a terrorist?'

'No, sir, not at all. Terrorists are indiscriminate in their killings and attacks and design their shocking crimes to do as much damage as possible. The events at Easytimes are not indiscriminate, they are all aimed at the Major.'

'The first one wasn't. Remember, the pamphlet drop, supposedly from ISIS, was distributed around the village to everyone living there at the time. It's hard to see how that was directed specifically at the Major.'

'Yes, you have a good point there, Inspector. I can't explain that.'

'June, I have another appointment in five minutes, so we will have to curtail this conversation. Be sure to get in touch if anything new comes in.'

* * *

The Inspector's phone rang several times during the afternoon with frustratingly little additional information that might help in the search for Jillian Rogers. Just before 4.00pm however, Senior Constable June Scott rang to advise that an elderly couple had just arrived at the station and wanted to speak with him. They were from Easytimes Retirement Village and their names were Dr Anne Nettleton, and her husband, Jock Nettleton.

'Show them in please June. Can you stay as well?'

'No problem, sir.'

A few minutes later, there was a knock on his door, and two slightly breathless elderly folk shuffled in, followed by Senior Constable June Scott. Inspector Brooks welcomed them, invited them to sit and asked whether they would like tea or coffee. They both declined the offer and started to settle themselves into the two chairs available. June Scott ducked out and brought in an extra chair.

The Inspector offered, what he hoped, was an inviting, warm smile to his elderly visitors, placed his arms on his desk, and waited.

'We were not sure whether we should bother you, Inspector, but Anne here felt that every bit of information could be helpful, so here we are.'

'Thank you for taking the trouble,' assured the policeman, with another smile.

Jock continued. 'Major Rogers is a bit of a loner. He can't stand small talk and finds it difficult talking to folk in the village. However, I discovered he has a very passable baritone voice, and, as I'm a musician, by profession, I suggested we get together musically to provide some entertainment for the people in Easytimes.'

'That sounds very commendable,' commented the Inspector.

'Nobody can offer anything with a shred of musical quality without some solid practice, Inspector, so we got into a routine of practising every week. 8.00pm Tuesdays was our time and the Major would always come around to our place.

'I always saw to it that they had some nice refreshments,' Anne chimed in. 'At the end of their practice, they might have a couple of beers too,' she confided. 'I made sure we were well stocked.' She gave the Inspector a knowing smile.

Inspector Brooks was beginning to wonder whether this

meeting was going to be productive in any way. He was anxious not to be late home tonight, as he had tickets for a show.

'Did you ever go to the Major's place for a practice?' inquired the Senior Constable.

'No, never,' Jock replied.

'That doesn't seem very fair?' suggested the detective.

'It was a bit strange, we thought,' agreed Anne.

'Anyway, we were never invited back to their place. It didn't really worry us,' added Jock. 'We were quite happy to entertain at our unit.'

Jock paused and seemed hesitant about how to continue the conversation. Eventually he gathered his thoughts together and went on. 'One night, Inspector, Charles and I had a few extra drinks. We had been singing some of my favourite Scottish ditties, so I cracked open a Chivas Regal.' Jock was clearly rather embarrassed, but went on. 'We both got a wee bit tiddly, Inspector.'

'It has been known to happen,' the Inspector smiled, encouragingly.

'I went to bed,' Anne interrupted, 'and left the men to it.'

'Very wise, I'm sure,' laughed June Scott.

'Well … Charles started to open up, the whisky really made him speak freely. We talked for a couple of hours, at least, about everything and anything. I think it was therapy for the Major. I can't possibly repeat some of the stuff he told me because he could get into trouble, even though it happened many moons ago. But one thing kept coming through in his drunken ramblings that I felt I should tell you Inspector.'

'I'm all ears,' smiled the Inspector.

'Charles, the Major, has an obsessive hatred of ISIS, and everything remotely to do with ISIS. It kept coming up in his inebriated wanderings. Quite out of the blue, he would return to the same topic and rant and rave about the organisation.'

'That's most interesting, Mr Nettleton. Please go on,' urged the Inspector.

'Apparently he never fought against ISIS, but nevertheless, he detests the organisation and its abhorrent tactics. Clearly it haunts him and his hatred is fanatical,' added Jock.

'Thank you, Mr Nettleton. May I ask how you see this assisting our inquiries?'

It was Anne's turn to join the conversation. 'It was my idea to come and tell you this Inspector. It seems abundantly clear to me, that whoever is behind this campaign to destroy the Major and his wife, is well aware of his intense feelings about ISIS. The easiest way to really upset the Major is to identify ISIS as the perpetrators of these various crimes.'

'It makes a lot of sense,' commented the Senior Constable.

'If, what you surmise, is correct, Mr and Mrs Nettleton, we need to be looking for a person, or persons, who are fully aware of the Major's extreme sensitivity to ISIS. Who do you think knows this weakness?'

Once again, Anne took the initiative. 'Sadly, I'd have to suggest that Jillian would know it best of all. It would be almost impossible to be married to someone, and not know that he, or she, harboured such a fanatical hatred. Quite likely, the Major would have had nightmares and yell out things.'

'That makes sense,' the Senior Constable remarked.

'Can you think of anyone else who would know?' the Inspector inquired.

'Perhaps other close family members, or his doctor, or a psychiatrist?' suggested Jock.

'Okay, thank you very much, Doctor and Mr Nettleton. I'm so pleased you decided to come and talk to us. It helps us to complete another part of this sorry puzzle. Now, we will follow up on the people you suggest who were possibly aware of the Major's obsessive behaviour.' The Inspector stood and extended his hand for a warm handshake.

Anne and Jock returned to their small unit feeling they had done the right thing.

* * *

Senior Constable June Scott was assigned the task of chasing up other people who may have been aware of the Major's ISIS obsession, and might also have been in a position to commit the crimes. It was not an easy assignment. The Major was most reluctant to give her the names of his close family members, his doctor and the psychologist he visited on a regular basis. Perhaps understandably, he failed to see the necessity.

It transpired that the Major had only three close relatives, his two children and an elderly sister. The sister was in a nursing home with advanced dementia, and his son, Ronald, was working on an oil rig in the North Sea. The Major's daughter, with whom he was currently staying, was living in North Adelaide with her husband and two young children.

She was permanently confined to a wheelchair following a car accident a few years ago, so was deemed physically incapable of committing the crimes in the village.

The female psychologist refused point blank to speak about her patient, claiming that to do so would be a betrayal of professional trust. She confirmed only that the Major was a regular client and was being treated for PTSD. Doctor Hawthorn, the general practitioner, had only been the Major's doctor since he moved into the village about a year ago, and claimed he knew nothing of significance about the mental health of his new patient.

This research took the Senior Constable the best part of two days; at the end of which, she reported to her boss that, as far as it was possible to ascertain, Jillian alone was aware of the Major's ISIS obsession. This finding supported the theory that only Jillian, knowing of her husband's intense revulsion of all things connected with ISIS, was likely to have orchestrated the series of ISIS inspired events, targeting the Major.

The Chief Inspector reflected on the dire situation he was facing; the Major, with his obsessive hatred of ISIS, and the Major's wife, with her obsessive hatred of her husband. A ghastly thought began slowly to crystallise in his mind. The four events at Easytimes had escalated each time in severity. Torching the unit was, so far, the most extreme; it had been potentially life threatening.

If Jillian was behind all four events, what might she attempt next?

CHAPTER 39

The village's Happy Hour was in full swing. The main course (roast of the day) was being dispensed to around 150 chatty old-timers, who queued up, table by table, to collect their servings. A range of alcoholic and non-alcoholic drinks were being provided at the bar and a warm buzz of comfortable chatter enveloped the hall. Usually, Happy Hour was for the residents only, but tonight, as an experiment, residents, who so wished, could invite one "outsider" to join the festivities. Claire had seized this opportunity, and invited her beau, Moses, to attend. It saved her cooking a meal for her man tonight.

'Snowballs and landing strips,' Moses whispered into her ear.

'What on earth are you talking about, Moses?' asked Claire.

A smiling Moses explained how, looking around the room, he had noticed many of the elderly ladies had dense fluffed-up white hair (the snowballs) and most of the men were either bald, or rapidly going that way (the landing strips).

'That's not very nice, Moses,' scolded Claire, good naturedly.

'But it's true.'

Claire glanced at the top of Moses' head, where a thick crop of greying hair sat neatly, defying the trend in the room. 'You're just lucky,' she giggled.

'What are you two lovebirds whispering about?' inquired Anne Nettleton from across the table.

'I was just joking with Moses about his full head of hair,' responded Clair.

Jock overheard Clair's reply, and ran his hand over his own bald pate, cleared his throat, and looking pointedly at Moses with a twinkle in his eye, announced, 'If you're bald at the front of your head, you're a thinker; if you're bald at the back, you're virile. If you're bald right through, you only think you're virile!' Jock's joke was met with much laughter by those at table eight.

Table eight consisted entirely of members of the Residents' Committee and their partners: Mike and Penny Fisher, Rosemary and Arthur, Snoddy and Mary, Anne and Jock Nettleton and even Betty and Gordon Wise, who had been given a rare night off from their catering duties. With the exception of Rosemary, Claire and Moses, the diners at table eight would be hard put to deny membership of the "snowball and landing strip" brigade.

Suddenly, the energetic clanging of a bell rang out across the hall, the room hushed and chairperson Mike stood up with a hand-held microphone to his mouth, 'Ladies and Gentlemen, your attention please.' The last of the deafer residents finally got the message, when shushed by others sitting nearby, and near silence finally descended on the gathering.

'Ladies and Gentlemen, I have been harangued by a constant barrage of questions about what is happening in the village. So, please bear with me for a moment or two, and I can update you all.'

The expectant hush that followed was punctuated by a few calls from the more vociferous of the men present, 'Good on yer Mike,' 'Let's 'ave it then,' and 'Give us the gory details.'

'Today, the burnt-out remains of the Major and Mrs Rogers' unit was bulldozed and the rubble removed. The manager has advised me that a new unit will be built there later in the year. The news about the Major and Mrs Rogers is not good, however. The Major has had a mental breakdown and has been admitted today to the Margaret Tobin Centre at Flinders Medical Centre. Mrs Rogers, and her car, are both still missing. She never turned up at the Major's daughter's place where she had been offered accommodation. Mrs Rogers has now been formally listed as "a missing person". Sadly, she remains the prime suspect for the arson attack. That's all I can tell you. Any questions?'

Pete Johnson, the village smart-arse, true to form, jumped to his feet with alacrity. A groan rippled around the diners, but Pete was not so easily distracted.

'Mr Chairman, I have a question.'

'Go ahead, Pete.'

'Is it true that the quiet, demure, shy, Jillian Rogers, once served in the Australian army, where she applied to enter the commandoes, but was refused on account of her gender?'

'Yes, Pete, I believe that is correct.'

'So, Mr Chairman, might we conclude from that, that Mrs Rogers is quite capable of serious crimes, such as arson?' Another murmur of low voices encompassed the villagers before Mike's voice cut through again.

'Pete, it's easy to think that way, but we must be careful not to make unfounded assumptions without strong supporting evidence. At the moment, I am advised that there is no proof that Jillian has committed any crimes, so she remains innocent. I would ask you all to keep an open mind please.'

Mary looked dotingly up at Mike, her lifetime hero, and sighed. *Why couldn't her Snoddy display such high-minded ideals?*

Mike waited a moment, but no more questions were forthcoming.

'Thank you everyone. Enjoy the beautiful meal and the rest of the evening.'

Soon it was table eight's turn to queue up for their main course.

* * *

Rosemary and Arthur left Happy Hour promptly after desserts, because they had important matters to discuss and walked slowly back to Arthur's unit. It was a clear, starry night and a romantic gibbous moon hovered over the village, lighting their way. They held hands.

Only last Saturday, Arthur had finally summoned up the courage to ask Rosemary to marry him. The second time round, he had found, was just as nerve-racking as when he had proposed to Sophia, his first wife, over forty years ago. There was no gallant kneeling down stuff this time though; he had simply taken Rosemary to their favourite restaurant, where he had booked a table in a secluded corner. He had engineered affairs a little beforehand; he had called in to speak with the restaurant owner to ensure Rosemary's favourite dishes and wines would be available on Saturday evening. The owner, well briefed, had treated them like royalty.

For several weeks prior, Rosemary had been expecting Arthur to "pop the question" but every time they were out together, she came home disappointed. She had started to wonder if there was something wrong. Why was Arthur hesitating? She knew she loved and passionately wanted this man months ago, having deliberately adopted the traditional female role of waiting to be asked for her hand in marriage. Perhaps Arthur was expecting a role reversal, and *she* should take the initiative and ask the question? When she had had moments of weakness, she had even considered seducing Arthur. She was more than aware of her powerful feminine charms, but desperately wanted to save these until they were legally man and wife. This way, marriage would be so much more beautiful and fulfilling. Finally, last Saturday, it had happened; Arthur had presented her with an adorable engagement ring, and she had been on a high ever since.

Tonight, they had left early to explore possible honeymoon options. They spent the evening online, hunting for interesting package deals. The plan was to lock in their honeymoon dates first, and then set the date for their wedding. They wanted the wedding to be a quiet affair, with only close family and friends present, nothing too elaborate. They had yet to decide whether to invite the members of the Residents' Committee. Arthur had already approached his boss, who had agreed to grant him three weeks leave whenever they made their travel bookings. Nobody in the village had been told of their engagement yet, although everybody seemed to anticipate it was going to happen. Rosemary only wore her engagement ring when she and Arthur were alone.

By the end of the evening, Arthur and Rosemary had agreed that a South Pacific cruise sailing aboard a luxury, five-star, Silversea liner, was the way to go. Silversea cruises were top of the range, and they would want for nothing. Some serious pampering was called for. They successfully narrowed the options down to one of two cruises and decided that they would have to visit a travel agent to help them make the final decision. Sometime in July or August, Adelaide's wintery months, looked most promising for their honeymoon.

*   *   *

Rosemary and Arthur's romantic thoughts were not the only ones this evening. Claire had invited Moses back for a nightcap. She had stressed that the victuals on offer would be only tea, coffee or milo, and Moses had not objected. They had both enjoyed a glass of wine at Happy Hour. Clair was not averse to alcohol in moderation but had no time for people who over-indulged and created trouble. Moses shared her views.

'So what did you think of all the snowballs and landing strips at Happy Hour, Moses?'

Moses had lowered his long body into one of Claire's easy chairs and was watching her, as she fussed around, organising supper in the kitchen. 'Everyone seemed very friendly, but I was surprised at how slowly everybody moved about. It's as though someone had switched everything in the hall to slow motion.'

Claire laughed. 'Are you saying, Moses, that you wouldn't want to live in a retirement village?' A seemingly innocent question, but an important one, in view of their developing relationship.

'No, I don't think so. Remember, this is the first time that I have been at a function with 150 retirees. It's a bit of a shock. Most of them are flabby, and obviously don't exercise enough, and I'm sure that if you pack nearly 400 retired people into a retirement village together, they all start to feel older and then to act old. I wonder if they age faster in here because they are spending so much time discussing their various ailments, aches and pains? I couldn't help over-hearing several conversations as I queued up for my tucker. "How are those corns coming on, Mavis?" "My back's killing me, would you be able to collect my desserts for me, please?" "Doris, dear, I have found a place where I can get my incontinence pads much cheaper."'

'Oh, come on Moses, you're exaggerating! We are not all like that.'

'I know. My argument still stands though. Back home in Africa, this concept of having retirement villages is non-existent. We live more naturally, several generations sharing one home. There is Mum and Dad and a pile of kids, also in the house are the grandparents and even great grandparents, if they are still alive. Everyone mucks in and the oldies stay young because they are surrounded by the nippers. You would never think of breaking up the family unit by removing the grandparents to a retirement village and, God forbid, dumping the really old and frail into nursing homes to rot and die.'

Claire placed a large mug of hot chocolate next to Moses and a plate with a serviette. She passed him a decorative plate on which she had arranged a tempting array of sweets and biscuits. 'You know, Moses, fifty years ago we were the same here in Australia. There were no retirement villages and the oldies stayed at home with their family and, probably, even died there.'

'So, why has it changed?'

Claire eyed off a chocolate Jaffa biscuit, but sadly concluded that if she was to continue to lose weight, she must resist. Moses, however, was happy to oblige. She had long ago noted how much extra food he required.

'It's hard to say,' responded Claire. 'We are all so busy these days, and the pace of life seems to have increased, so I reckon we are generally less caring. We don't seem to have the time available to look after our oldies anymore. Perhaps we have become more selfish as we get time-poor? Parents are so flat-out these days, they want the oldies to be "on call" to come and babysit, do the shopping, clean the house, pick up the kids from school, or whatever.'

'I'm not sure Western society is going in the right direction,' Moses opined.

'Moses, if we ever do get married ...'

'It's not an "if" it's a "when",' Moses interrupted.

Claire blushed, ignoring Moses' correction, and went on to ask her question. 'If ... we get married, will you live here with me in the retirement village, or will you expect me to move out?'

'I'm happy either way, Claire. It's not where you live that's important, it's who you live with.'

Claire smiled. As she sat, looking at Moses, some of the more graphic pictures and diagrams she had been looking at in her book suddenly popped up in her mind. For a brief moment she imagined the two of them naked and locked together in one of the extraordinary intercourse positions she had been reading about. A tangle of black and white legs moving rhythmically together. Was this really going to happen to her? She felt excited at the prospect but then quickly dismissed the whole idea. She had not yet made up her mind to marry this tall dark man, and to even think of having sex with him was surely sinful.

'Would you like another cup of hot chocolate, Moses?'

<h1 style="text-align:center">CHAPTER 40</h1>

The meticulous plans of Jillian Rogers were finally coming to fruition. Ever since her husband had declared nearly eighteen months ago that they were going to sell up and move into a newly constructed retirement village called Easytimes, she had been skilfully executing various schemes. Now, her revengeful work accomplished, it was time to disappear.

She leant forward and turned the hot tap on again, then stirred the welcome warm water to surround her body deliciously. With a contented sigh, she relaxed against the back of the bathtub then had another generous sip from her glass of wine. As she lay there, she reflected on the life she had at long last escaped.

It was just over forty years ago that she had been accepted into the Royal Military College, Sandhurst, to train to become an army officer in the British Army. After three years, she graduated as a second lieutenant along with some two hundred others. The course had been physically and mentally demanding and the attrition rate high, particularly amongst the female recruits.

In those days, a blind eye was shown towards "bastardisation". The practice was seen to be an essential part of the student "sub-culture". Provided students were not badly injured, certain highly unpleasant activities were regarded as being merely part of the initiation process. The commanding officers at Sandhurst had all endured the same kinds of experiences when they were neophytes and consequently happily argued that bastardisation never did them any harm, so there was no need to ban it.

Bastardisation, quite simply, had to be endured, and most students survived. When these surviving students reached their third and final year at Sandhurst, it became their turn to inflict the same demeaning practices on the next batch of new recruits. It was essential to keep these traditions going.

Female students were also exposed to other more alarming degradations in the form of sexual harassment. Rape was not uncommon. The topic of rape remained strictly taboo, however, and when it occurred, a veil of silence descended, and everyone denied any knowledge of the events. A number of the more enlightened new female students were able to avoid most of the unwelcome overtures from male students by deliberately pairing off very early with a strong second- or third-year male student. If you were known to have a boyfriend who would look out for you, you were far less likely to be harassed. And so it was that Jillian had willingly attached herself to a tall, good-looking, athletic third-year officer cadet by the name of Charles Rogers. Charles was not to be messed with, for he was the heavyweight boxing champion at Sandhurst. Jillian had selected well, and consequently never had any serious problems with sexual harassment. Except, of course, that Charles Rogers saw it as his unassailable right to have his way with her. In return for his protection, he expected exclusive sexual favours.

Jillian knew the score before she began her officer's training at Sandhurst. Fortunately, she quickly became fond of Charles and also found him great fun. She happily accepted the deal. She provided, and enjoyed, her sexual encounters with him and in turn benefitted enormously from Charles' knowledge of the Sandhurst program. He was a source of much valuable information about the assignments she could expect, the textbooks required and the eccentricities of various lecturers. In addition, he introduced her to the best pubs where the students wassailed and advised her about which were the best elective courses to take. Sleeping with Charles was a small price to pay for all the advantages that Jillian acquired from the liaison. She was, however, particularly careful not to fall pregnant.

Marriage was not on her agenda. After Charles graduated, and was posted to an army barracks close to Sandhurst, they maintained their relationship. Everybody at Sandhurst knew that, in effect, Jillian remained Charles' property. It suited Jillian to stay with Charles until she was safely through her Sandhurst program. She suspected though, that Charles might not be playing fair with her and was having other liaisons from time to time. This did not worry her too much, because she always intended to completely break off the relationship once she graduated, so she would be free to search for her special partner in life.

A few weeks before Jillian was due to graduate, she was shocked to discover that despite taking all precautions, she was pregnant. Quite how this had happened remained a mystery. She had only slept with Charles, so there was no doubt about the paternity. An expectant unmarried female officer was not acceptable in the British Army forty years ago. Unless she married Charles, she would lose her commission and her three years of intensive Sandhurst training would be wasted. So it was a case of marry Charles Rogers, or sacrifice her career. Her time at Sandhurst had convinced her that she was ideally suited to life as an army officer and she was determined to realise her ambitions.

As it turned out, Charles had considered marrying Jillian but had never got around to actually proposing. A major reason for his reluctance to "pop the question" was that he was having too good a time sleeping around. Taking Jillian as his wife would require him to behave and remain faithful to her. He would have to forego all his other sexual dalliances and start to lead a "respectable" life. However, when Jillian confronted Charles with the knowledge that he was going to be a father, and what the implications were for her, he came to his senses and did the decent thing.

Their circumstances were not a good foundation for a long and happy marriage. They wed hastily, with the inevitable whispers from all who knew them, and the child was born exactly seven months after the marriage ceremony. For a year or two, Charles contained himself, but once their second child was conceived, began to misbehave again. At first he was discrete, and Jillian, with two little ones to care for, was more than fully occupied, and remained blissfully unaware. By the time they had reached their fifth wedding anniversary, however, she had become suspicious. Of course, Charles denied everything, but eventually the truth was revealed. Jillian stayed with Charles only because she was desperate to resume her career as a serving officer. She reasoned she could ignore Charles' unfaithfulness if it would save her career.

There are many unhappy marriages. Nevertheless, some couples choose to stay together for a complex plethora of reasons. And so it was with Jillian and Charles. Staying married was best for their young children; they wanted to avoid all the scandal; Charles was a Catholic; divorce was not well-regarded by the powers that be in the British army and would affect both their chances of promotion.

Once the children were at school, Jillian resumed her commission and served for ten years, reaching the rank of Captain. Tragically, she was forced into early retirement at the age of thirty-five as a result of a heart condition. From thereon, she could only manage work that was not too physically demanding, or mentally stressful, and picked up casual jobs such as teaching English to migrants and refugees as she traipsed around the world with Charles to his various postings. She remained a devoted and loving mother and was the glue that held the family together. In 1996, Charles transferred to the Australian army under a lucrative arrangement.

As Charles slowly went up through the ranks, he became increasingly aggressive and domineering. Often, he would verbally abuse Jillian and the children and at times beat the youngsters. Jillian did everything she could to protect them from his rages. It was a great relief to her when both children were old enough to leave home, shortly before Charles was posted to East Timor in 1999. It was while stationed in Dili, the capital, that he was badly wounded and evacuated to Darwin for a long and painful recovery period. Eventually he was invalided out of the army, and they retired to Adelaide, where they bought a house in seaside Glenelg. Charles was later diagnosed with PTSD, a condition that made him even more difficult to live with.

Over the years, Jillian developed her own coping mechanisms to deal with the irrational and unpredictable behaviour her husband displayed. With expert medical advice and support, Charles improved somewhat, and they settled into a bearable life together with simple daily routines in their pleasant, rambling house in Glenelg. Jillian's great joy was her garden, where she spent countless happy hours landscaping, planting and nurturing Australian natives. Out the back, she had space for a few orchard trees and a chook house. Escaping into her garden was not only therapeutic, but the steady outside exercise was also kind to her heart condition. Despite Charles' PTSD, Jillian loved her house, her garden and the Glenelg area. On a couple of occasions, her garden was even accepted by the ABC as an annual Open Garden exhibit. All proceeds went to support folk suffering from PTSD.

For some reason, Charles got it into his head that he wanted to sell up and move into a retirement village. At first, Jillian thought he was just going through one of his irrational periods where he didn't think sensibly, and the whole idea of moving would dissipate, in the same way that some of Charles' other hair-brain notions had come and gone. Give it time, Jillian reasoned, and it will blow over, and be archived like several other of his wilder ideas.

She was wrong.

Charles was quick to sense Jillian's resistance to moving. The more she tried to ignore his wishes, the more ardent he became about making the shift. Like a person on the autistic spectrum, he had absolutely no comprehension of the pain and grief he would be inflicting on Jillian, if she was forced to surrender her much loved garden. Her life revolved around her little bit of paradise and to deprive her of this joy was tantamount to destroying her soul. Charles was determined to have his way, as always. He would fly into a rage every time he believed Jillian was obfuscating, and his health began to deteriorate. Jillian thought long and hard whether to finally leave Charles, but either way, she would not be able to retain her beloved garden. Effectively, Charles' selfishness would ruin what little happiness she still enjoyed. As she reluctantly accepted that her life in Glenelg was over, she resolved, in turn, to ruin Charles' life at Easytimes.

Jillian was not usually given to vindictiveness. She had endured Charles' unfaithfulness, his mistreatment of the children, his selfishness, and had stood by him after his wounding in East Timor and subsequent PTSD. After nearly forty years of enduring Charles' abusive behaviour, she could stand it no longer. Revenge would be sweet.

*   *   *

The embittered Jillian never let on to anyone that she was bent on revenge. She worked hard to make the move into Easytimes as painless as possible and exercised great patience in stabilising Charles through his difficult transition. Accustomed to a highly regimented life to assist in his management of PTSD, the whole process of selling the home in Glenelg and re-establishing in a unit, only about a third of the size of their Glenelg home, was hugely challenging to the ex-army officer. But with Jillian's tireless help, they survived.

After a few months at Easytimes, when Charles had become more settled, Jillian started to exact her revenge. She was well aware that Charles had a deep-seated hatred of ISIS ideology and those that practised this particularly evil doctrine. Hearing about ISIS atrocities on the ABC News or reading of their hateful slaughter of innocent people around the globe, incensed him. If she could conjure up some means, whereby Charles felt he was being targeted by ISIS or ISIS sympathisers, she could exact the most pain.

Jillian's first revengeful act was low key, but easily handled. Using her own laptop, she concocted a short leaflet message, supposedly from an ISIS member, or sympathiser. With only sixty units in the new village occupied at the time, it was easy to duck out after dark one evening and pop them into everyone's letterbox. Quite often she took the dog, Timor, out for an evening walk, so her actions didn't arise any suspicions with Charles. The result was amazing. The village people were predictably upset, and totally fooled by her covert leaflet drop, but Charles ranted and raged against ISIS for days.

There and then, he wanted to bring the ISIS perpetrator, or perpetrators, to justice.

Emboldened by her first successful attempt to infuriate her husband, Jillian began to explore how she might repeat the process. Charles had been made responsible for the daily raising and lowering of the Australian flag and had set up a small group of volunteers to undertake this task. He relished the opportunity to train them up and to oversee correct routines were observed. All Jillian needed, for step two, was to order, and pay for, an ISIS flag over the internet. As an ex-army officer, she knew precisely what had to be done to first lower, and then raise, a flag. One morning, with the ISIS flag safely stowed in a shopping bag, she slipped out, just after the Australian flag had been masted, and Charles was out exercising Timor, and made the swap successfully, in just under five minutes. Nobody was about. She brought the Australian flag back with her, correctly furled, and hid it neatly amongst her clothing.

Jillian was amazed at the furore that erupted after the flag swap. This deed had really tapped a raw nerve and everyone was furious. The police came buzzing around like flies, and Charles, incensed by this act of treason, proposed the immediate setting up of a vigilante group. His proposal was not, however, supported, much to his further annoyance. Again Charles ranted and raged for days. Jillian expressed great sympathy but was secretly enjoying every minute. Her first two ISIS-inspired actions had been directed at everyone in the village, although Jillian realised that Charles would probably take it to heart more deeply than anyone else. Now it was time to start to focus more specifically on Charles, not at the village in general, but against the Major as he was known by all in the retirement village.

Stage three was far more daring, and Jillian needed to wait until a suitable evening before she made her move. Slaughtering Timor, Charles's beloved bulldog, would only be possible under the cover of darkness and if she could procure a sharp long-bladed knife. Finding the knife was easy. One night, when she was on "clean and shine" following Happy Hour, she smuggled out one of the almost brand new, and alarmingly sharp knives, from a set in the kitchen. It probably wouldn't even be missed. She put aside a meat skewer and printed out a note on her laptop, supposedly from ISIS, and waited patiently for the right evening to strike.

The perfect evening came within the week. A fierce storm rolled in one night with heavy rain, thunder and lightning. It was ideal for the thuggery she had planned and the whole episode took barely a couple of minutes. While Charles was washing up, she donned her raincoat and boots, grabbed the knife, skewer and the ISIS message and left, unseen, through the backdoor. Timor was delighted to see her, for he hated storms. She gave him a cuddle and slit his throat. It was not as silent as she had hoped and the dog gave a loud yelp before he expired. Momentarily panicked by the dog's noise, she ran out onto the road and hurled the knife over the village wall. As quickly as possible, she plunged the skewer, with its gruesome message, into the dog's flank, whipped off her wet clothes, hid them, and re-entered the unit as if nothing had ever happened. Charles was still complaining about the amount of washing-up they had generated that evening.

Jillian thought long and hard about the final step in her revenge tactics. Murder was out of the question. Malicious she might be, although in her view, deservedly so, however, she drew the line at the taking of a life. Her vengeance would culminate in the destruction of the miserable little apartment Charles had forced her to live in. Afterwards, she would escape to somewhere beautiful to live out the rest of her life. The arson part of the plot was easy. Each week, she purchased a two-litre container of lawnmower fluid, always from a different service station, so as not to arouse suspicions, until she had six full containers stashed away. When she was ready, all she needed to do was wait for Charles to go off to his golf club, or the RSL, and place the six containers strategically around the inside of their unit. Igniting the first container would start a chain reaction. She would have her car safely parked outside beforehand, ready for a fast getaway. Her only regret was that she wouldn't be able to stay and watch the fiery event.

The tricky part was deciding how to make good her escape and where to go. Over the years, she had maintained contact with three of her closest colleagues at the Royal Military Academy, Sandhurst. They had exchanged visits since she had emigrated to Australia, and she knew she would be most welcome to stay with each of them for at least a month or two. Jillian planned to "disappear" somewhere in the UK. It was well known that every year, thousands of illegal migrants from Europe and Africa were smuggled into the United Kingdom and stayed on. If *they* could manage it, surely she could! She had the added advantages of being born and bred English, knowing the country, being well-educated, resourceful and in moderately good health.

Jillian's greatest challenge was getting to London and through passport control before the South Australian police suspected her of being the arsonist and took the necessary steps to prevent her leaving the country. If she was en route to London, Interpol would be waiting for her in London if requested by the South Australian police. Meticulous planning was therefore required.

Being a creature of habit, Charles always spent Thursday evenings at his Golf Club or the RSL, usually leaving shortly after six-thirty. This was the only evening in the week he could be guaranteed to be out. Jillian figured, if she was packed and ready to leave the unit immediately after Charles left, she could set fire to the unit, drive to the airport to catch the eight-thirty flight to Perth arriving just in time to connect with the non-stop Perth to Gatwick flight leaving the same evening at 10.00pm. It was tight, but possible. If everything went to plan, twenty hours after leaving her unit at Easytimes, she would land at Gatwick. Jillian planned to abandon her car in the Adelaide Airport carpark; it would most likely be a day or two before the car was found there and impounded.

Feeling reasonably confident her plan would succeed, she went ahead and made her bookings for next Thursday.

CHAPTER 41

'More pavlova anybody?' called Betty, with her server poised at the ready. Snoddy immediately glanced across at Mary, who was in deep conversation with Anne, and decided he could risk it. He moved across the room, with surprising alacrity for such a large man, and had just reached Betty with his empty plate held out expectantly in front of him, when there was a loud and angry bellow from his dearly beloved.

'No, Snoddy, no! Don't you dare!'

Betty's nourishment philosophy was beautifully simple. If somebody wanted to eat something, then let them eat it. She looked across at Mary, smiled innocently, and teased, 'Just a teeny, weeny bit more, Mary?' It worked. Mary glared at Snoddy as if to condemn him for life but refrained from saying anything more. With a sly wink, Betty dished out a second helping for Snoddy that was anything but "teeny weeny" and Snoddy did his utmost to keep his more than generous portion hidden from Mary's accusing eyes.

The Residents' Committee had finished its monthly meeting nearly half an hour ago and the members were sitting about enjoying being splendidly hosted by Betty and Gordon in their apartment. Everyone was present, including the Major, who had been especially invited to join the meeting, despite the fact he did not live in a unit in the village currently, which possibly disqualified him. Inviting the Major to attend was meant as a kindly act, but to be perfectly honest, everyone was longing to hear the latest "goss". It was almost three weeks now since the fateful night of the fire, and all were hungry to hear if there had been any further developments.

'Any news yet, Major?' initiated Mike, in a voice loud enough that everyone heard him, and instantly paid attention.

The Major put down his plate, realising he was required to provide a response, as a way of repaying his hosts.

'Not much,' he replied, simply.

'Any news of Jillian then?'

'The British police think she is still in hiding somewhere in the UK. As you know, she managed to get into Gatwick before our plodding old detective, Inspector Guy Brooks, got around to alerting Interpol. Brooks was disgracefully slow to act. Jillian managed to travel halfway around the world before the authorities were even alerted.'

'Does she have family or friends she can stay with over there?' inquired Arthur.

'Possibly,' the Major replied. 'I know she has a couple of grown-up nieces and nephews somewhere in the country, but I don't know whether she was still in touch with them.'

'What about friends?' probed Rosemary. 'I think you both

migrated here only twenty years ago, so you must still have some contacts there?'

'We do, but the address book, with all our contact details, was either taken by Jillian, or destroyed in the fire. The police have asked me two or three times for the names and addresses of people we know in the UK, but I can't remember more than a few names. I certainly can't remember any of their addresses.'

Claire piped up next, 'Has Jillian tried to get in touch with you, Major?'

The Major shook his head and looked glum.

'So what happens now?' queried Rosemary.

'Well, there's a warrant out for Jillian's arrest and the matter now rests with Interpol and Scotland Yard. She is accused of all four of the incidents that occurred here in Easytimes as well as evading police. Along the way, she has also cleaned out a couple of our joint bank accounts, so she has enough money to last at least six months if she lives frugally.'

'When do you expect to be able to return to the village, Major?'

'I move back in a couple of months, hopefully. Apparently a lady in unit 202 died suddenly about a month ago and they are letting me move in there on a temporary basis. They are about to start erecting a new unit where ours was, before it was destroyed.'

'Has your insurance company paid up?' asked Jock.

'The building itself was insured by Easytimes, so that was not my concern, but all our household gear was covered by my own home insurance policy. They have paid up reasonably generously.'

'So, what are you planning to do until you move in, Major?' Snoddy inquired.

'I'm expecting to be cleared for travel any day now and to get my new passport delivered very soon. I plan to travel to the UK.'

'Are you going over to find Jillian?' asked Claire, looking somewhat concerned.

'No, certainly not. She left me, not the other way around, so I have no desire to seek her out in the UK. I still have some army colleagues over there, and I hope to attend some of the Prom Concerts whilst there too.'

'What will you do if you bump into her?' questioned Mary.

'That's hardly likely, Mary. There are 65 million people in the UK and she's in hiding, remember.'

There was a feeling amongst most of the committee members that the Major had possibly had enough of being interrogated; they switched back to talking amongst themselves about more mundane matters.

* * *

It was a pleasant enough Bed and Breakfast facility located at 34 The Royal Crescent in the Georgian city of Bath, set in the heart of the west country. Jillian had a soft spot for this architecturally stunning place because she had lived very near here for a time as a young girl.

The Royal Crescent, built by Wood, and completed in 1765, had survived the second world war reasonably unscathed and was a superb example of the use of Doric,

Ionic and Corinthian style columns. Built to impress, it remained a major attraction for tourists, which unnerved Jillian somewhat, as there seemed to be innumerable coaches disgorging thousands of tourists there every day. The tourists never stayed longer than five to ten minutes, photographing and taking the inevitable selfies, because their next stop was lunch or afternoon tea down at the famous Pump Room. Nevertheless, all these people wandering about was unsettling for someone who wished to remain as incognito as possible.

Jillian had travelled down to Bath aboard a Greyhound coach the same day she had arrived at Gatwick. Her plan was to remain at this bed and breakfast place for a few days and then move in with one of the three army colleagues she had known ever since her days at Sandhurst. These arrangements were now in place and tomorrow she would journey down to Rottingdean, a small town on the Sussex coast, where she would be the guest of retired major, Angela Campbell, and her husband, Ralph. Jillian and Angela had been bosom friends whilst at Sandhurst and had continued to enjoy each other's company whenever possible ever since. Jillian had explained she and Charles were going through a nasty divorce, and she needed a complete break from all the angst and unhappiness. Angela was delighted to have Jillian stay as long as she wished.

The next day, Jillian awoke to find the sun streaming through her bedroom window. She dressed, packed her meagre belongings, enjoyed a full English breakfast and paid the landlady, who very kindly dropped her off at the railway station on her way to do some shopping. Her train pulled into London's Paddington Station at 11.57 precisely, the time her timetable had stated. She had twenty minutes to grab a Subway six-inch salad roll, before boarding another train bound for Brighton. Arriving shortly after 4.00pm she was relieved to find Angela and Ralph waiting for her on the platform. Within the hour, they pulled into the driveway of the Campbell's house, overlooking the sea, and were soon enjoying drinks on the balcony. Jillian felt far more secure staying with friends in a private home and away from the maddening crowds of tourists endlessly invading Bath.

A lazy month went by. Ralph was still working as an accountant and Angela was more than happy to show Jillian around the South Downs and the delightful villages nestled in the valleys. They visited the Brighton Pavilion, the famous Brighton Lanes and several stately homes. They usually managed to find a decent pub for lunch and then wound their way back home in time to cook tea. Jillian, no slouch as far as cooking was concerned, took it in turns with Angela to prepare the evening's repast. This idyllic life could not, however, go on forever, and after a month both women had had enough. Angela wanted to return to her hobbies and Jillian felt she had already overstayed her welcome. It was time to move on.

Contacting her second friend in England was easy, and it was arranged that she would make the trip to Clewer Manor, a suburb of Windsor, on Friday. Angela offered to drive her there, a journey of perhaps three hours, and stay for lunch before setting off home again. Everything, mused Jillian, was going so well, although she appreciated that she couldn't go on sponging off her friends for ever. She needed to come up with a long-term plan because in a few months' time her money would be drying up. Being a wanted woman was hardly an enviable position to be in, if she needed to look for work.

* * *

They arrived in Clever Manor well in time for lunch and drove straight to the home of Martha Middleton. Martha was delighted to welcome them and had a magnificent salad laid out in readiness. The three ex-Sandhurst friends settled down for a boozy afternoon with more than ample white wine, although Angela limited herself to two glasses, conscious of the fact she was driving home later.

Martha Middleton was an interesting character. Tall and athletic, she had shone at all sports at Sandhurst and become something of a cult figure. She was strikingly good looking in a handsome sort of way, with her hair kept short and controlled, and positively glowed with fitness. Her height allowed her to look down on all the women at Sandhurst and most of the men too. She cut a fine figure, particularly when in military uniform. Jillian possibly would not have befriended Martha at Sandhurst; had she not been obliged to share a room with her. At first, they merely tolerated each other, but as the months went by, the relationship warmed. Martha never protested if Charles came to visit Jillian at night, thereby breaking the strict rules banning visits to the rooms of members of the opposite sex. Jillian never had to reciprocate, however, since Martha showed little or no interest in any of the men at Sandhurst.

Martha Middleton had graduated at the same time as Jillian and was immediately posted to Cyprus. Her military career was short but distinguished. After ten years she resigned her commission and landed a job straightaway as the manageress of a London hotel. Once again, she excelled and was soon snapped up by a larger hotel offering a more generous salary. It was at this second hotel that she finally decided to no longer hide the fact that she was a lesbian. She had many liaisons whilst a hotelier but always handled them professionally. At the age of sixty she retired, and bought an attractive cottage in Clewer Manor, where she lived with her faithful partner for several years. About a year before Jillian came to stay, the devoted partner died suddenly from surgery to remove an ovarian cyst that went horribly wrong. Martha had recovered sufficiently to now be on the lookout for a new lesbian partner and was quietly wondering whether her old friend, Jillian, might be interested.

The wine flowed freely and the three colleagues enjoyed reminiscing about their days at Sandhurst and recounting stories about their service in the British Army. Around four o'clock, Angela announced that she must leave, if she was to avoid driving home after dark, and with fond farewells, climbed into her car and headed off. Martha and Jillian remained to finish off the last bottle together and became more and more inebriated. Martha seriously contemplated making sexual advances towards Jillian who was looking more and more desirable and less inhibited by the minute. She restrained her urges, however, fearing that to move too quickly might frighten Jillian off altogether. Jillian, on the other hand, was well aware of Martha's sexual preferences. The thought of having a sexual relationship with another woman had never appealed to her, and she certainly didn't intend to start now that she was in her mid-sixties.

The days following their boozy afternoon were uneasy ones. Jillian sensed that Martha was watching her carefully, and on a couple of occasions had come into her bedroom on some flimsy pretext. She would sit on the side of Jillian's bed and call her "darling" or some other term of endearment. They never touched and Jillian was careful to keep her hands and breasts well hidden under the bed clothes. She knew it was only a matter of time before Martha would make her move.

One evening they were both in the warm kitchen preparing tea together when Martha made her move. Jillian was stirring the browning onions when she felt Martha come up behind her and slide her hands forward to fondle her breasts. Jillian reacted sharply. Spinning around, she glared at Martha and raised the wooden stirrer threateningly. Martha was a foot taller, but Jillian was livid.

'Don't you ever touch me like that again!'

'Oh, I'm so sorry Jillian. You looked so attractive standing there. I thought you might like to have some closer company.'

'No, I'm not interested Martha. It's nothing personal, but I find same-sex relationships repulsive.'

'Okay, forget it ever happened. Those onions are starting to burn.'

The damage, however, was done. The situation in the cottage became virtually unbearable and Jillian knew she must move on as soon as possible. That night, she rang her third and last friend to ask whether she could come and stay. Her friend was most welcoming, but had a frantically busy weekend coming up, so asked Jillian to wait a couple of days and then she would have the time to drive over on Monday and pick her up. Jillian, very reluctantly, had to accept the situation and to find ways to spend the next couple of days avoiding any close contact with Martha.

CHAPTER 42

Sunday morning looked promising weather-wise. Jillian awoke from a restless sleep and heard a chorus of thrushes and blackbirds welcoming the day below her window. She dressed quickly and crept down to the bathroom at the end of the passageway doing her best not to awaken Martha. She had taken to locking her bedroom door now and never wore her nightie to visit the bathroom in case it provoked unwelcome attention from Martha. Jillian had become quite terrified that Martha might try and use her superior height and strength to rape her. She had had enough of that kind of behaviour from Charles and couldn't face it again. There was no sign of Martha, so Jillian gently negotiated the twisty staircase, avoiding the creaky floorboards as much as possible, and entered the kitchen. Quickly, she crushed up four Weet Bix, added milk and poured herself a fruit-juice. She didn't want to risk boiling the kettle in case the sound woke Martha. So far, so good.

Still no sign of Martha. Perhaps she was out on one of

her early morning runs? Her hasty breakfast finished, Jillian retraced her steps, cleaned her teeth and grabbed her coat, waterbottle and hat and was out through the front door still without encountering Martha. Jillian had a plan for the morning that would keep her well away from Martha until sometime after lunch. At the end of the street was the start of an eight-mile walking circuit, which professed to have clear markers along the whole trail. It was recommended that walkers allow at least three hours to complete the walk. Jillian noted it was a few minutes after nine o'clock when she started her hike. If she was back by midday, she would have lunch at the cute little café she had noticed near the start of the walk where a simple fare of pies, pasties, sandwiches and ice-creams were on offer. After lunch, she would catch the local bus into Windsor and take in a movie. The day was well planned, with total avoidance of Martha its main aim.

It was mid-autumn and the deciduous trees had jettisoned most of their leaves. The ground was a thick carpet of damp decaying matter mostly from the beeches and massive oak trees. Acorns crunched under her feet as she penetrated farther and farther into the woods. The occasional squirrel scurried along a branch carrying nuts to store for winter. It was, she noted, surprisingly quiet and peaceful and the track appeared almost deserted. The only folk she encountered were a middle-aged couple out walking their two Labradors. They stopped momentarily to exchange niceties.

* * *

Janet Clarke, Jillian's third English friend, had left home shortly after nine o'clock on Monday and planned to be at Martha's place by lunchtime to pick up Jillian. With any luck, Martha would invite her to stay for lunch. Janet had had a crazy busy weekend. Her florist shop had been flat out all Saturday which, with one of her staff ringing in sick, had meant no let up all day. There had been two weddings in the vicinity and Janet had been contracted to supply the floral decorations at both events. She closed the business at five o'clock, rushed home to shower and get ready to go to her Book Club at 7.00pm. Sunday had been no easier. She spent the morning helping at her Rotary Club's BBQ and the afternoon visiting her elderly parents residing at two separate nursing homes several miles apart. Janet finally scrambled home a bit after five to cook tea for the family she had hardly seen all weekend.

Today would be a rest day. A leisurely drive down to Clewer Manor, lunch with Martha and Jillian, and then a relaxed drive home with Jillian for company. Jillian had mentioned her break-up from Charles, so she imagined she may wish to unload on her at some stage. Coincidentally, Janet and her husband had been planning their first trip "down under" next year and she desperately wanted to sound Jillian out about places to visit, what to do and what to avoid. Perhaps they would be able to stay a few nights with Jillian in Adelaide? All in all, Janet was looking forward to a pleasant, restful day.

Driving through Eton and Windsor was as hectic as ever. The traffic seemed worse than usual and the place was teeming with noisy camera-clicking tourists who milled across the roads outside Windsor Castle as if they owned the place. The crowds would, of course, reduce somewhat as the colder weather arrived, but as yet there was no sign of that happening. Janet drove on and pulled up at Martha's cottage about half an hour later than she had planned, pulling in behind a police car. Grabbing the beautiful bunch of flowers she had made up for Martha early that morning, when she had popped into her florist business, she approached the weather-beaten wooden door of the cottage and rang the doorbell.

There was no answer, so she rang again. This time the door was opened by a young policewoman, who looked sharply at Janet, holding her gorgeous large bunch of flowers at the ready. Without a trace of warmth, the constable demanded, 'Are you Mrs Janet Clarke?'

Taken aback, and with her face showing obvious concern, Janet managed to bleat out, 'Yes, that's me. Is there something wrong?'

'Could be,' the young woman remarked, somewhat mysteriously. 'Please come in. We were expecting you.'

Like many old English cottages, the entrance was cramped and Janet had to carefully manoeuvre herself, together with her floral gift, in order to enter. Once indoors, she was surprised to find a worried looking Martha sitting on the edge of her settee, with two husky policemen sitting opposite her. Martha, it seemed, was being interrogated.

A stout policeman with a ruddy complexion and a bulbous nose was speaking.

'Let me get this straight. This friend of yours, a Mrs Jillian

Rogers from Adelaide, Australia, has been staying with you for a few days and behaving quite normally. Yesterday, at about eight in the morning, you heard her leave the cottage. You were still in bed, but awake. Mrs Rogers never told you where she was going and has not contacted you since leaving. Her things are still upstairs in her bedroom, including her passport, which indicates she was definitely coming back.'

'That's correct, Officer,' Martha responded.

'When she failed to turn up for tea last night you began to worry, but knowing Mrs Rogers is an ex-army officer, you felt certain she could handle herself if she had got into difficulties. However, when Mrs Rogers was still missing this morning, you felt the matter should be reported to the police. We received your call a little over thirty minutes ago. Do I have my facts correct?'

'Yes, you do,' Martha replied.

'And who's this?' the tubby policeman inquired, turning stiffly to look at Janet, half hidden behind her oversized bunch of flowers.

'My name is Janet Clarke, officer, and I've just arrived from Glen Parva, near Leicester.'

'And with a bunch of flowers big enough to sink a ship,' chortled the second, slimmer policeman, with a smirk on his face.

His smart-arse comment went unheeded. The young policewoman suggested to Janet that she place the flowers in the kitchen and come and join the group. Janet did as she was bid and returned to hear the stout policeman speaking again.

'Mrs Middleton ...'

'It's "Ms" not "Mrs",' interrupted Martha, with a sharp edge to her voice.

'I'm sorry, Ms Middleton.' The policeman cleared his throat and started again.

'In situations like this, it is helpful, before we start searching, to have a clear profile of the person we are looking for. Where do you think she may have gone, and why? What are Mrs Rogers' interests? Is she in a relationship with anyone? Was anything worrying her? All that sort of thing.'

The next ten minutes or so was spent trying to paint a picture of Jillian, with Martha contributing nearly all the detail. Janet was only able to assist with a couple of minor interjections, for it was years since she had last seen Jillian. Eventually, the ruddy faced policeman stopped scribbling in his little notebook, looked up at Martha, and announced, 'It's time for action. I'm going to call my boss and request we begin a Grade B search.'

'What does that mean?' asked Martha.

'It means, Ms Middleton, that we call out the volunteers to work alongside any police we have available to search the suburb of Clewer Manor, within a radius of approximately five miles of the Town Hall. Before I do that, however, I want you to describe what Mrs Rogers looks like, what she was wearing, anything you think she might have been carrying, and, if you have one, give me a photograph.'

Another ten minutes was taken up with descriptions and finding a couple of photos that Martha had on her phone. They checked Jillian's belongings upstairs, and it was noted that her small backpack and water bottle were missing.

Unfortunately, she had left her mobile phone in the bedroom. Had she taken this, it would have been possible to locate her. Contact was then made with the Chief Inspector, who, after satisfying himself that a Grade B search was justified, gave the order to proceed.

With Windsor Great Park close by, a Grade B search was not uncommon. Using social media, an impressive number of local volunteers descended on the small Clewer Manor Police Station in readiness for a briefing at 2.00pm. Most of the volunteers were ramblers, or retirees, and came appropriately dressed for the weather which had turned cold and wet. So many volunteers had turned up, the sergeant in charge of the operation was obliged to address the assembled crowd in the police car park. Not surprisingly, Martha and Janet were present. Martha wore gumboots, a long raincoat and a slouch hat. Janet, who had not anticipated being involved in such an activity when she left home that morning, had borrowed some old gear from Martha that was at least three sizes too large.

The sergeant, holding a microphone, called for quiet. Martha and Janet noted that it was the same stout policeman who had interrogated them that morning.

'Ladies and Gentlemen, thank you for turning out in such large numbers in this lousy weather. Clewer Manor has a proud record for conducting searches like this. For those who don't know me, I'm Sergeant George Millman and I have conducted half a dozen searches like this one over the last five years. Today we are looking for an Australian woman, although she was born in England. Aged 62. She was here visiting a friend and left for an unknown destination at around 8.00am yesterday. She does not have a car. She is slimly built, and I have photos of her here. Please come and have a good look at these photos before you set out. Her name is Mrs Jillian Rogers. Her husband, Major Charles Rogers, we believe, is still in Australia and we will be trying to contact him this afternoon. As far as we can tell, Mrs Rogers was wearing flat black walking shoes, jeans and a blue jumper over a white blouse, but this may not be correct. Mrs Rogers has a slight Aussie accent and is friendly and sociable. We are not aware of any mental illness, although she has recently separated from her husband of many years. Any questions?'

A crusty old man with a shooting stick called out, 'How do we know she is still around here? For all we know, she could have jumped on a bus, or a coach, or even caught a train somewhere?'

'Good question. I'm afraid we just don't know. You may be right. However, when looking for a missing person, policy dictates that we thoroughly search the local area first. This is what we are doing today. Any other questions?'

A plump lady, at the front of the crowd, with a lively spaniel in her arms, wanted to know whether Mrs Rogers knew anyone else in Clewer Manor or Windsor. Sergeant Millman referred the question on to Martha who informed the crowd that Mrs Rogers had only been staying with her for a few days, and, as far as she knew, had not formed any friendships with anybody else in town.

There were no more questions, so Sergeant Millman concluded the briefing by checking that each new volunteer was assigned to one of the eight groups that regularly conducted searches. He then double checked with the leaders of the eight groups that they would be phoning in regularly, at the set times, to the police station where the search was being coordinated by the sergeant and his staff. Martha and Janet quietly attached themselves to the Green Group that they heard covered some of the forest trails in and around Clewer Manor. They felt this would be more interesting than traipsing about the streets and shops. The rain was easing as they padded off with ten others in search of their mutual friend.

CHAPTER 43

Easytimes was abuzz. Mike Fisher had announced at the beginning of Friday evening's Happy Hour that he had two special announcements to make before the night was over. He asked the 144 residents present to please stay after the meal so they could all celebrate the good news together.

Speculation was rife. Members of the Residents' Committee and their partners were sitting together, as usual, at the same table, enjoying each other's company. Snoddy was holding court at one end of the long table, trying to convince those near him that one of the special announcements concerned approval for a massive solar panel system to be placed across the roof of the village's indoor swimming pool, thereby saving tens of thousands of dollars in electricity costs every year. Jock was not so sure. He had heard rumours that the village management had definite plans to extend the size of the village and build a further thirty units. There was ample space for this to happen around the village and some scrub clearing was already occurring to the north. One of the more controversial rumours circulating around the dining hall was that a sporting VIP, and his wife, had decided to take up residence in the village, and would be moving in soon. But who was it? Most South Australians are fanatical about AFL (Australian Football League) so the sporting experts in the room were speculating which of their past heroes would now be in their sixties or seventies and at the right age to join them.

Betty and Gordon Wise were back in control of the kitchen and all that happened therein. Tonight's meal was a village favourite; fish and chips served with mushy peas (a South Australian specialty), green beans and buttered carrots. Desserts were strawberries and cream served with a small pavlova. The bar was doing a steady trade, and everyone was in a festive mood. Respecting Mike's call to stay for the two announcements, almost everyone had remained. Finally, Mike rose and moved towards the microphone.

'Good evening again everyone. May I have your attention, please?'

There was so much racket in the hall that Mike had to reiterate his request for quiet twice. Eventually, the room hushed and only a couple of hearing aids were still giving off their piercing sounds as their owners struggled to bring them under control. Even this evening's volunteers, charged with taking out the last of the dessert plates and condiments, stopped pushing their trollies to listen.

'Thank you for staying back as requested. I think you will be pleased you did. Easytimes has been open for business for fifteen months now and we have almost every one of the

250 units occupied. Despite a few unfortunate incidents with leaflets, flags, pets and even one case of arson, we remain a happy and vibrant bunch of people. Life at Easytimes is great and you are the people who make it so.'

'Hey, spare us all the bullshit Mike, and get on with it!' called a guy sitting with a few mates and holding his mug of beer aloft.

This rather uncouth interruption caused a stir amongst some of the residents. Several were moved to tell the gentleman, in no uncertain terms, where he might like to go. He had, however, a few supporters as well.

'Good on yer, Gus.'

'That's right Gus, old boy, keep 'em honest.'

Sensing that the majority of the room was still wanting him to continue, Mike cleared his throat and returned to the little speech he had prepared.

'One of the most satisfying aspects of life in Easytimes is the way that people have united together to start so many social groups. At last count, we had almost forty groups functioning, ranging from line dancing to bushwalking, from IT to film reviewing. Undoubtedly, the formation of such a varied smorgasbord of activities is contributing enormously to the quality of life here in the village.'

This last statement was altogether too much for Gus, who had clearly drunk to excess. This time he rose to his wobbly feet and rudely called out.

'Oh, piss off Mike. You're full of crap. You ain't got nothing to tell us, so why don't you bloody well sit down?'

Gus's three or four mates, realising that he had well and

truly overstepped the mark this time, quickly surrounded him and started to escort him towards the door. Gus waved his arms about protesting, like some kind of an octopus, as he was ushered, unceremoniously, to the exit. He let out a string of expletives as he disappeared from view. There was a collective sigh of relief as the door swung shut behind Gus and his colleagues. Drunkenness in the village was rare, and many of those present felt embarrassed to have had to witness this unfortunate event. Mike, however, appeared unfazed , and happily resumed his soliloquy.

'During the last year, or so, we have had a number of "firsts". Our first Christmas, our first AGM, our first ANZAC Day service, sadly the first death of a resident when dear Agnes Oldfield left us last month. Tonight I want to announce another "first". It is a very special "first" because it involves four people who, today, are announcing the first marriage engagements to happen in our village.'

Mike's announcement was welcomed by a joyful round of applause, a few wolf calls and much chatter as the residents posited who these four people were. Many felt they knew, but all were anxious to hear Mike confirm the two matches. Mike was still waiting patiently with his microphone for the hubbub to die down. At last he had his chance.

'In a moment, I will tell you who the happy pairs are and introduce them to you. What is even more exciting though, is that both pairs have agreed to hold a joint wedding ceremony here at Easytimes, a week before both couples tie the knot. And everybody in the village is invited to come to the joint ceremony. How good is that?'

Another round of wild applause prevented Mike continuing. Gradually the noise subsided and he called again for quiet.

'Let me now introduce these couples to you. Perhaps they might like to stand when called, so we can all see them? The first couple are Claire Bury from unit 44, and her husband to be, Moses Lobrida from outside the village.'

Mike called their names out, as if he was the MC at a variety concert, calling the names of the next elite entertainers. The tall frame of Moses shot up immediately followed more slowly by a rather shy, blushing Claire. They turned, holding hands, to face their audience and received a huge ovation. As Claire and Moses resumed their seats, he leant across and gave her a little peck.

'And now to our second pair of love-birds. This is a couple probably noticed about the village a lot. Yes, you guessed it: Rosemary Tattersall and Arthur Stokes.'

Another roar of applause filled the hall as the pair stood up holding hands and waving to everyone with their free hands. Then, to much whistling and calling out, they kissed and sat down again.

Mike was almost in tears. He struggled to control the emotion in his voice, as he wrapped things up for the evening.

'So, ladies and gentlemen, the big night is next Friday. There will be no Happy Hour. Instead there will be a huge BBQ, complete with salads, to be served in and around this hall. The bar will open at 5.00pm and we will start serving food at 6.00pm. We will have our very own village band playing led by the irrepressible Jock Nettleton, and those that wish may dance the night away after we have cleared up. Wear your party clothes and bring five bucks per person to help cover the cost of the meat. And … bring some dessert to share! Last of all, please thank our wonderful chefs, Betty and Gordon Wise, and their great team, for tonight's meal. Good night everyone.'

*   *   *

It was another hour before the star couples of the evening could leave the hall. They were smothered with good wishes, congratulatory comments and even endured some ribald cracks from a few of the men. Finally, after 10.00pm they escaped back to their units.

Claire and Moses walked back to unit 44 laughing about some of the best comments of the evening. They were to be married Sunday week at their own church and their minister would be conducting the service. The few relatives from Claire's side of the family had been more than surprised to receive an invitation to Auntie Claire's wedding, for she had many years ago been assigned to the "spinster-for-life club". Moses, on the other hand, had possibly a hundred relatives, most of whom lived back in Ethiopia and could never afford to make the trip. He dearly wished for his ninety-year-old mother to attend but she was in poor health. At least his two children, now residing in Australia, would be there. The honeymoon was to be a two-week cruise on the River Rhine, paid for by Claire, as she was, by far, the better off. On their return they would squeeze into unit 44, putting most of

Moses' furniture into storage to be sold later, or donated to the Salvation Army.

Arthur and Rosemary had very different plans. They were to be wed in the Adelaide Botanical Gardens by a registrar with the reception at the National Wine Centre a short walking distance away. Both had many relatives attending and a surprising number of friends too. They had tried to keep the occasion low key, but the more they tried, the bigger the event became. At last count, there were over ninety guests. The honeymoon was to be a four-week Pacific affair with stays at resorts in Fiji, Samoa, Tonga and the Cook Islands. On their return they would live in Rosemary's unit and relinquish Arthur's.

The Residents' Committee were planning a special celebratory evening for the two couples on Wednesday next week.

CHAPTER 44

In charge of the Green Group was a female scout master. This seemed incongruous, but Shirley Masters assured Martha and Janet that they didn't have "mistresses" running the scouts. She was, she asserted categorically, a scout master. Shirley was a no-nonsense lady, broad in the beam, with a pleasant well-tanned face, displaying impressive crow's feet radiating from her eyes. She was a confident, homely soul, certainly knowledgeable about the innumerable tracks that criss-crossed the rural countryside around Clewer Manor. Shirley had lost count of the number of times she had led search parties during the last ten years. At a guess, it may have been eight or nine times, usually looking for a small, lost child. Adults, she claimed, seldom landed in trouble, unless drunk or drugged. Twice, she had been called out to help bring back an injured walker.

Shirley produced a well-worn geological survey map of the district, showing the walks, trails and bridle paths. Turning to Martha, she inquired whether Mrs Rogers was a keen walker and asked Martha to pinpoint exactly where she lived. Walks within easy reach of Martha's home were the obvious ones to check first. This done, Shirley selected the two walks close to Martha's that seemed the most likely places for Jillian to have ventured. Next, Shirley briefed her group.

'There are twelve of us. We need to follow strict walking rules as near as possible. That means, as leader, I will be in the front. Nobody is to pass me. Is that clear? Fred, you are an experienced walker, and have been with me several times before, so you will be the backmarker. Fred's job is to make sure we don't lose any of this group and so he will always be at the back. If anyone has had enough, or needs to leave, please check with me first. We will stop every hour or so to have a rest. I assume you all have brought adequate water and snacks?'

Martha and Janet had forgotten about water and snacks and had to confess. The others in the group had plenty, so assured them they could share. Shirley continued with her briefing.

'If someone becomes disoriented, they are likely to wander off the track, so it is important that we keep searching on either side of the trail. The men in the group will be responsible for scanning to the left and the women to the right. Look out for signs too; a piece of clothing, or footprints. My job is to look ahead, to ring the base on the hour to report our progress and get the Green Group back safely. This first walk is an eight-mile loop walk with signage along the way and quite popular with locals. Please avoid any idle chit-chat along the way. This is not a social stroll through the woods. We may be able to save someone's life if we stay focused on the task at hand. Any questions?'

There were murmurs amongst the group, but no questions.

'The walk will take about three hours and basically goes through gently undulating wooded country and along the edge of a few fields. Anybody wish to pull out?'

There was silence.

'Okay, it's time to go.'

Shirley dug in her walking poles and set off, expertly crossing a style and entered the woods. The members of the Green Group obediently fell into single file behind her. Martha and Janet took up their places in the middle of the line. The trail was, indeed, well-marked, with easily spotted, four-foot high, wooden posts located on the left-hand side of the track. The path curved its way into the woods passing a mixture of oaks, chestnuts, poplars, beech and pines. A thick carpet of damp leaves covered the ground exuding the pungent smell of rotting vegetation. Fallen branches presented hazards in some places, and a couple of times rabbit burrows threatened the unwary. Blackberry bushes had surrendered their fruit, but the brambles still reached out and snagged careless walkers. They met a cross-country runner wearing a sweat band who seemed peeved when he had to run around such a large group.

After an hour, Shirley called a halt, as promised, told everyone to take a five-minute rest, and pulled out her mobile to call base. Sergeant Millman advised that, as yet, none of the other groups had sighted Mrs Rogers or received any useful information. Speculation was rising that Mrs Rogers had left the district altogether, using some form of public transport. Martha and Janet thought otherwise. They were sure she would not have left the district without her passport.

The Green Group trudged on for another hour or so meeting nobody except a farmer doing some fencing with his son along the side of the trail. They traversed a couple of fields and then entered another wooded area where Shirley again called a halt. They had been maintaining a good pace for a search party, and she expected another hour's walking would see them back at the start again. Base had one very interesting piece of information for Shirley when she rang in this time. A couple, who yesterday had been walking the same trail the Green Group was currently on, claimed they had met a woman walking on her own around ten o'clock that morning. They had exchanged pleasantries, and the couple thought they detected an Australian accent. They had described a woman in her sixties wearing jeans, no walking poles with plimsolls. Martha was excited to hear this, for it surely sounded like Jillian. The couple claimed to have met her near where two men were fixing a fence.

Assuming this information from base was accurate, a woman, fitting the description of Jillian, had been spoken to somewhere near where the two men were still working today, and was seen heading the same way the Green Group was travelling. Shirley decided to split the Green Group into two. She would lead a group of four back to the two men and question them about what they had seen yesterday. Meanwhile, Fred would take charge of the rest of the group and conduct a more thorough search of the last two or three miles of the trail. Fred would then wait at the end of the walk for Shirley and her three companions to catch up. Martha and Janet opted to stay with Fred.

Fred was an instantly likeable human being and naturally instilled confidence. He now took the lead and they set off once again into the woods. It was a peaceful place, with the rays of the sun shining through the trees and the sound of bees going about their business. Butterflies fluttered about but there was little sound, apart from the tread of the eight walkers. This was a particularly damp part of the woods and mosses and lichens were well established on the trees. Mistletoe hung from some of the higher branches. It was difficult to imagine a more beautiful place.

Suddenly, Fred raised his right arm, indicating the party should stop. A few yards to his left he had caught sight of a plimsoll, half hidden amongst the leaf litter. He turned to speak to the group.

'Folks, I've just spotted a plimsoll over there in amongst the leaves, and I remember the couple said that the woman they met along this track was wearing plimsolls. Can you see what I'm looking at?'

Within a moment or two everyone confirmed they could see the shoe and a ghastly sense of foreboding crept over the party. The tranquil beauty of the location now assumed a sinister, cold, eerie feel. Imaginations ran wild. Nobody was game to say anything, until Fred broke the silence.

'I don't want to sound alarmist, but I don't like finding what looks like a newish plimsoll lying here on its own. I think we have to prepare ourselves for what may be a bad outcome. I very much hope I'm wrong. We need to search this area carefully. If we find anything more, we will contact the police. So, I'm calling for those of you who wish to help me search to now come forward. If you prefer to remain here on the footpath, that is absolutely fine.'

Nobody opted out.

'Please form a long line with arms outstretched, so you can touch the person's hands next to you. That's the way. Now, we will start walking very slowly in a line down this slight slope until I ask you to stop. Be very careful as you go, because we are off the path, and there are lots of rocks, branches and rabbit burrows to trip you up. If you see anything suspicious, stop and yell out. If this happens, we all stay in our positions in the line and you leave it to me to come and have a look at what has been found. Nobody is to touch the plimsoll as this may become part of a crime scene. Is that clear?'

His request was met by grunts and nods.

Slowly and cautiously, the line moved forward. They reached the plimsoll and went on.

Martha and Janet both saw it at the same time. A leg was sticking out from a low bush behind a tree. The leg was shoeless and displayed faded blue jeans.

'Over here!'

The line stopped. Fred scrambled over to where Martha and Janet stood, frozen. Both had served in theatres of war but this was somehow ghastlier than a war casualty. Violence in peacetime was totally abhorrent. Fred took one look and using his walking pole to gently push back a couple of the lower branches revealed a semi-naked female body.

'Is this her?'

Martha and Janet nodded.

'Thank you everybody. Please move quietly back to the footpath and wait there while I call the police, and then Shirley.'

* * *

Shirley and her three colleagues had made fast progress back along the trail until they came to the field where the two men had almost completed their fencing. Shirley wasted no time.

'Excuse me gentlemen. I'm leading a party of searchers, looking for a missing woman we think came along this track yesterday, around ten o'clock. Do you remember seeing a woman walking on her own, aged in her sixties and going this way?' Shirley pointed out the direction.

The two men stopped what they were doing and stood behind their new fence. The older man answered. 'Aye, we did. Would have been a bit afore ten, because we knocked off for a smoko at ten.'

Shirley and her colleagues couldn't help noticing that the younger man appeared to be most uncomfortable. He had reddened and avoided looking at them, preferring instead to lean on his shovel and look at the ground.

'Do you remember what she looked like, or what she was wearing?'

'What you reckon, Rod?'

The younger man shrugged his shoulders and continued to find the ground at his feet enthralling.

'I dunno,' replied the older man. 'She wasn't young and had a funny way of talking. That's all I remember.'

'Do you remember her coming back along the track?' Shirley persisted.

'Nah,' the older man responded.

'And how about you?' Shirley asked, pointedly approaching closer to the younger man. 'Do you remember seeing her return?'

'He wouldn't bloody know,' replied the older man. 'He buggered off for a couple of hours after smoko. Wasn't back 'ere till lunch at midday, lazy bugger.'

'Okay, thanks for your help, guys. Have a good day.'

The four walkers returned to the track and retraced their steps. They joked about how embarrassed the younger man had been, especially when it was revealed that he had scarpered off for a couple of hours during the middle of the day.

Shirley's phone rang, and she stopped to take the call. It was Fred, reporting what they had discovered. Fred believed the person they had found was indeed Mrs Rogers, and that she had been raped and murdered. The joking about the young man disappearing for a couple of hours, shortly after seeing the woman pass by, suddenly took on a more menacing tone.

Sergeant Millman was shocked to receive the news from Fred. He gathered his wits together quickly though, and asked Fred exactly where he was along the trail and if he would kindly request his group to stay near the body, until he could get a team of investigators to the location. He stressed, most emphatically, the importance of not touching anything. It was now a crime scene. He remembered to thank Fred and his team for their efforts. Next, he ordered his second-in command to call in the other teams, still out searching, whilst he called out the detectives and forensics to urgently attend the murder site.

Things moved quickly. Two homicide squad detectives, three uniformed police, a doctor and a forensics expert were on the scene within half an hour. Fred and Shirley were interviewed briefly with the detectives showing a high level of interest in the meeting that Shirley had had with the two men working on the fence. Shirley was directed to come to the police station at six o'clock for further questioning. The area was cordoned off, and a more rigorous search commenced.

There was no doubt that this was a vicious rape/murder case. The victim had been crudely bludgeoned to death, suffering horrific wounds about the head. Nearby, a large blood-stained branch was found. It appeared to be the work of a maniac or some kind of sexual deviant. Two hours after arriving, the investigative team were almost finished with their work when, to their horror, a second body was discovered.

The second body was that of a man, probably in his mid-sixties. He too had been bludgeoned to death with savage blows about the head. The investigative team worked on into the night and were relieved not to find any more victims.

The two men fencing farther back along the track immediately became the prime suspects. The younger of the two, who had appeared so embarrassed when questioned by Shirley, admitted he had left the fencing job for two hours during the middle of the day. The police noted he would have easily had enough time to follow Jillian along the track, attack her and get back to his fencing. Possibly the murdered man had stumbled across the crime actually being perpetrated, had tried to intervene, and then paid with his own life.

The young man asserted, strenuously, that during his smoko he had gone straight down to the Swan and Cygnet Pub, about five minutes' walk away, where he had watched the England versus Spain football match on television. His story was collaborated by around a dozen other young men who were also watching the game at the same pub and had shared a beer with him. Suspicion then turned to the older fencer. However, when the police interviewed him, it was discovered that he had suffered a badly clubbed foot since birth. He could get along unaided, but only slowly. It would have been physically impossible for him to have travelled along the track, committed the murders and returned within two hours.

Forensics were soon able to shed some further light on the double murder. It became clear that Jillian had first been raped and then murdered by the mysterious man who was also found murdered at the site. The man's semen was evidence enough. Having committed this shocking rape and murder, the man in turn, was attacked. Someone else must have witnessed the rape/murder and decided to take the law into their own hands.

The police never identified who the second murderer was. However, a couple of days after the ghastly events perpetrated in this beautiful spot deep in the English woods, the identity of the man found murdered there became known.

His name was Major Charles Rogers.

EPILOGUE

It was a week before the horrific murders, in those tranquil English woods, became known to the residents of Easytimes. Naturally, the news came as a shock, but not many were deeply saddened. Jillian was not well known in the village as she had lived quietly under the yoke of her husband's domination. It was Claire who missed Jillian most, since she had gone out of her way to try to help and understand her.

The Major, on the other hand, was known by almost everyone in the village, yet was liked by few. His arrogant, military manner hardly endeared him to anyone. The members of the Residents' Committee and the flag-raising party had learnt to tolerate Charles, but there was little genuine affection. Jock Nettleton, who had accompanied the Major at musical events, had come closer to knowing him, as a person, than anyone else.

For a time, there was speculation around the village as to who had murdered the Major. But once it was established that nobody from Easytimes had been visiting the United Kingdom at the time, interest waned rapidly. It was Penny who remarked wistfully one evening that two more "firsts" for Easytimes had recently occurred; the first Easytimes' resident to be murdered and the first murderer from Easytimes Retirement Village. The story of Charles and Jillian Rogers became part of the Easytimes' folklore and no new residents were ever spared the gory details. After all, very few retirement villages could claim their very own murders and murderers. Thankfully, the murders had been committed on the other side of the world. No ghosts had yet appeared in the village!

Robert Tinson, the manager, was particularly put out by the unfortunate events in the United Kingdom. He had already dealt with costly and time-devouring administration work organising for a new unit to be erected to replace the one destroyed in the fire. This had involved lengthy legal and insurance issues, and then he had had to find another unit for the Major to occupy. As soon as the Major moved into his second unit, he showed his gratitude by going off to England and getting himself murdered, leaving Robert with yet another load of extra work. Even more serious for Robert though, was the bad publicity that once again dogged the village of Easytimes. The journalists at the local paper loved a juicy murder or two and feasted off the spoils for days. Fortunately, few residents died, or moved elsewhere, for a year or two, so that Robert didn't have to try and find new tenants very often. Inevitably, potential new residents had heard about the events in the village and overseas, and always managed to mention it, perhaps in the hope that a discount might be in the offing. Despite these worries, Robert stayed on as the manager for a further fifteen years and was sadly missed when he retired.

Mike Fisher, chair of the Residents' Committee, continued to serve the village, in that capacity, for another four years, and was instrumental in seeing a number of improvements in the village, and establishing an excellent working relationship with Robert Tinson. His wife, Penny, enjoyed much better health with her new kidney, and started a successful environmental club within the village. Together they enjoyed many holidays overseas. The average life of a transplanted kidney is fifteen years and Penny intended to go way past the average.

Snoddy continued to wrestle with his restrictive diet until it became a part of him. Slowly, he also began to exercise more, until eventually he even became one of the regular early morning walkers. This combination of better eating and sensible exercise produced a new, more vital, and leaner Snoddy. The unwelcome predictions about his sex life made by his dietician many months before, proved correct. As a result of the new Snoddy though, a satisfying sexual life resumed, and all those who knew them remarked on how much happier he and Mary seemed. The never-ending bickering between the pair disappeared almost entirely and they presented as a happy couple once again.

Betty and Gordon Wise, the superb village foodies, became an institution. Every Friday evening for ten years, except when away on holidays, they supervised the menus, the ordering of food, its preparation, cooking, presentation and serving for Happy Hours. The meals became so popular that bookings would fill up within an hour or two of opening, and it was even suggested that a second Happy Hour be introduced for Thursday nights. Much as Betty and Gordon enjoyed Friday evenings, they drew the line at doing it all twice a week. After ten years it started to become a drag. They were ageing and it was time for younger folk to take over. Betty still had small, more intimate parties, where she could thrill her guests with culinary delights.

Anne and Jock Nettleton enjoyed another year at Easytimes. Although Jock had lost his musical partner, he continued to entertain the villagers at appropriate occasions. Sadly, he died suddenly of a heart attack two years after entering Easytimes, leaving Anne distraught after nearly sixty happy years together. What nobody expected, however, was the arrival of Jayne, the daughter. Apparently, she had run out of lesbian partners, and unhappy relationships, and decided to throw her lot in with her mother. For a time, this arrangement didn't look promising, but patience on Anne's part eventually made it workable. Jayne is still trying hard to curb her language, although the neighbours report the air still going blue, occasionally.

Chief Inspector Guy Brooks was severely reprimanded for his failure to stop Jillian Rogers leaving the country after her arson attack. At the time, Guy was only four months from retirement, so no further action was taken. Guy and his wife had been thinking of moving into Easytimes after his retirement, but the embarrassment about his poor policing in the village precluded this move. The Brooks' moved to another retirement village instead, where Guy resumed his interest in fishing.

Claire and Moses were married, as planned, in their local church. The weather was perfect and that night they flew to Dubai, en route to Amsterdam, where they spent their first night together in a posh motel. Claire was acutely embarrassed about the whole business of sex and had no idea what to do. When the time came the books she had read didn't help. She managed to get into her nightie in the motel bathroom without Moses seeing her, and then left the bathroom silently, in the hope that Moses had fallen asleep. She was shocked to find him sitting up in bed naked and waiting. She was too uptight to be responsive and found the whole thing confronting. She was even more surprised to find that Moses wanted intercourse almost every second night. Gradually, as she got used to his attentions, it didn't seem too bad. A few months later she found she looked forward to their sexual encounters and was actually enjoying them. By the year's end she was even initiating intimacy. Most importantly, however, the bond between them deepened and their marriage developed into a happy, rewarding partnership.

The marriage of Arthur and Rosemary was a quiet, but joyful occasion, and the Pacific honeymoon that followed a great success. On their return, Arthur sold most of his furniture and moved into Rosemary's unit. When Mike resigned from being chair of the Residents' Committee, Rosemary took over and served the village well for four years. Arthur served as her secretary. Both maintained their keen interest in staying fit well into their eighties and were an inspiration to all the other residents.

Life at Easytimes Retirement village today stays much the same. Residents still gather around their mailboxes for a natter, most of the clubs and activities prosper, and Happy Hours are always well attended. Despite Robert Tinson's best efforts, there are usually a few units available for new residents to occupy. You might like to think of moving in?

www.ingramcontent.com/pod-product-compliance
Lightning Source LLC
Chambersburg PA
CBHW060729190726
48285CB00001B/129